WHERE'S WAARI?

Witi Ihimaera was the first Maori writer to publish a short story collection (*Pounamu Pounamu*, 1972) and a novel (*Tangi*, 1973), and has followed those with a further six novels, four short story collections, and numerous works of non-fiction. He has edited several previous anthologies of Maori writing, including *Growing Up Maori* and the five-volume *Te Ao Marama*. A former career diplomat, he teaches English and creative writing at the University of Auckland.

WHERE'S WAARI?

A History of
the Maori through
the Short Story

Edited by
Witi Ihimaera

REED

Published by Reed Books, a division of Reed Publishing (NZ) Ltd,
39 Rawene Rd, Birkenhead, Auckland (www.reed.co.nz).
Associated companies, branches and representatives throughout the world.

ISBN 0 7900 0735 5

Designed and typeset by Graeme Leather

First published 2000

Printed in New Zealand

Contents

Introduction

THE title of this anthology comes from a game introduced to me by one of my neighbour's young daughters. She showed me a book called *Where's Wally?* The book was filled with crowd scenes and, in each crowd — at the beach, at a rugby game, at a busy city intersection — you had to find Wally, a gawky young man wearing a beanie and striped scarf. Sometimes Wally was easy to locate. Other times I had difficulty and suspected that Wally wasn't there at all. Whatever, the fun was in the search and — 'There's Wally!' — the discovery.

In compiling this anthology, the fun has also been in the search. In this case, the search has been for 'Waari' — the Maori as he or she has been seen in the eyes of the beholder, be they Pakeha, Maori or (Henry Lawson) Australian. The process of following the sightings of Waari has taken me down into the dusty archives of our literary past. From a whole swag of stories I've selected a sample which I think best represents the ways in which Maori identity has been constructed by our writers.

What has prompted this book? Perhaps these words by my colleague, Alex Calder provide the best explanation: 'I have assumed that the joint entanglement of Maori and European in colonialism has been the most salient context for the stories we tell about ourselves.' The words come from Alex's marvellous *The Writing of New Zealand* (Reed, 1993), which traces the history of non-fiction texts in New Zealand. I have assumed the same joint entanglement, but I have traced it through the New Zealand short story. And why the short story? First, because it is the most pervasive and enduring New Zealand prose form. Second, just about all our major writers have, at one time or another, written short fiction.

Alex's book is subtitled *Inventions and Identities*. In many respects, this could also be the subtitle of this anthology. The earliest stories in this collection amount to our birth records. Indeed, until New Zealand was 'created' by being written about or defined by art, 'New Zealand' didn't exist and nor did Waari. Aotearoa existed in Maori oral tradition, of course, but its pre-European inhabitants defined themselves by tribe rather than race. The Maori was an introduced, written concept; the first to write about Waari were Pakeha.

Thus *Where's Waari?* begins with representations of Maori from some of the earliest New Zealand writers, like Alfred A. Grace, Blanche Baughan and Katherine Mansfield. Several of these writers produced a number of stories about Maori. In Mansfield's case, 'How Pearl Button Was Kidnapped' was her only essay into a recognisably Maori story with recognisably Maori characters. (Interestingly, when the story was first published in England, the English reading public thought the little girl had been kidnapped by Gypsies.)

Looking back on New Zealand's literary history, it has been fascinating to find who our writers saw, what they saw, and how they wrote when they created Maori characters. There's the Maori as savage; the inevitable Maori princess (Will Lawson's 'The Slave's Reward'); the Maori as happy-go-lucky; the Maori woman as object of fantasy or image of fantasy (as in the forgotten 'Hinemoa' of Annie Wright); the Maori as urban warrior. Indeed, stories about Maori have presented writers both Maori and Pakeha with a problematic task: to articulate how we are to the other. But what *we* as readers see in the stories is also problematic, and depends on the personal and cultural backgrounds we bring to reading.

For instance, I first read Douglas Stewart's 'The Whare' in 1958 when I was a student at Te Karaka District High School. Some of my friends still remember how I was so outraged about the perspective of the story — I saw it as demonising Maori — that I threw it out of the window and got caned by the headmaster, Jack Allen. However, my reading of the story is not the only reading. Will you read it the same way as I did, I wonder, or will you see more redeeming characteristics in it?

Maori perspectives were not represented in fiction until 1966, when J.C. Sturm became the first Maori writer to be anthologised. Until then, Pakeha writers had had the field to themselves. We are fortunate indeed that some of New Zealand's best writers — Robin Hyde, Roderick Finlayson, Frank Sargeson, Maurice Duggan, Janet Frame, Noel Hilliard and Maurice Shadbolt — have provided classic stories involving Maori characters which have become part of our literary consciousness. Sometimes Maori are well-rounded characters, sometimes not. For some Maori readers, Maurice Duggan's Fanny Hohepa is a mere object of fantasy, more imaginative than real, but for just as many Pakeha readers she nevertheless also embodies an escape from puritanical Pakeha life. Maori found more reality in Noel Hilliard's Girl from Kaeo, who still packs as much punch today as she did in the 1970s. Yet Hilliard is the object of less academic attention than Duggan.

The advent of Maori writers brought new perspectives on Waari. J.C. Sturm marked out the path and a new generation of writers followed: Arapera Blank, Patricia Grace, Bruce Stewart, Keri Hulme, Witi Ihimaera and Ngahuia Te Awekotuku. In most cases, the Maori came in from the margins of Pakeha stories to the centre of their own Maori stories. Arapera Blank's 'One Two Three Four Five' is a classic among the literature, a beautifully told story of young Maori entering the New Zealand education system. 'Broken Arse,' by Bruce Stewart, provides a harrowing insight into life for Maori and Pakeha within the New Zealand prison system. Patricia Grace's 'Ngati Kangaru' re-positions the Maori story from rural idyll to urban Maori politics in a satire about repossession of land.

Subsequently, younger Maori writers like Briar Grace-Smith and Phil Kawana have continued the process of telling it how young Maori see it. Together with Pakeha writers like Bill Payne, they confirm that the story of Waari is as problematic and as fascinating as ever.

At least we should count ourselves lucky that the writers in *Where's Waari?* actually *saw* the Maori, unlike Rudyard Kipling who visited and wrote a story called 'Our Lady of Wairakei' — and instead of a Maori 'lady' in the thermal pool what do we get? Some kind of Tennysonian fairy more Celtic in origin.

A final word: this is not entirely a personal selection. In making it I have been guided by what previous anthologists have chosen. In other words, most of the stories in *Where's Waari?* have attained iconic status. They are the ones considered by editors like Dan Davin, C.K. Stead and Vincent O'Sullivan best to reflect the Maori and the relationships between Maori and Pakeha. Do they bear scrutiny? I want you to make up your own minds about how rightly — or wrongly — writers have perceived and continue to perceive Maori. Punctuation and editorial style have been standardised in this edition, but most spelling, and the use of italics or macrons for Maori words, remain as in the originals.

Here, then, are 28 stories — 28 scenes if you like — covering the Maori in the New Zealand short story from the beginning of our history. I considered many ways of putting them together — alphabetically by surname, by theme, and so on — and in the end assembled them in order of each author's date of birth. Together they form a collection which tells some of the story of Waari, but not all of the story. Waari is somewhere in them. Correction. Waari is in *some* of them. In others, the character looks like Waari and has Waari's name — but is it Waari? Is Waari more real for being written about by Maori? And where is Waari going from here?

You be the judge.

Witi Ihimaera
July 2000

Te Wiria's Potatoes

Alfred A. Grace

VILLIERS was on good terms with the dispossessed lords of the soil. He had a sort of romantic regard for them. He considered they were an ill-treated, down-trodden race; he used to tell his *pakeha* friends so; and when men met him in Auckland they would ask him how his protégés the Ngati-Ata were getting on. Of course he spoke the Maori lingo. He doctored the members of his pet tribe when they fell ill; bought their *kumara* at exorbitant prices; helped them in their land transactions with the grasping *pakeha*; gave them the use of his outhouses for sleeping in, and of his paddocks for their horses.

So far the Ngati-Ata had done nothing for Villiers in return, beyond warning him of the approach of pack-horses from the interior; bony, pinch-bellied pack-horses were the bane of his life and a menace to his clover-paddocks.

Villiers lived in an old *pa* close to the sea. Its earthen walls stood twenty feet high, and were surrounded by a ditch fifteen feet deep. The whole earthwork was overgrown with maidenhair fern and lycopodium, in token of the return of peace. In the middle of the *pa*, commanding a view of the sea, Villiers had built his house, and his farm stretched its rich acres all round.

He had grown a phenomenal crop of potatoes, but the question was, who would dig them up? He himself was turning sixty; his sons had gone to the Thames to dig gold; all the able-bodied men of the district had caught the gold-fever, too; worn-out old-soldier Saunders and one-armed constabulary-man Murphy were the only men left.

Villiers stood on the *pa* bank and pondered. The bay stretched glittering before him; a gentle breeze stirred the trees in the orchard below and rippled the surface of the sea. Of a sudden, two big canoes came in sight round the nearest point, and made for the shore in front of the house. Villiers anticipated a day spent in *korero* and eating.

Two score Maoris came straggling up from the beach through the gap in the *pa* bank, and stood in picturesque groups on Villiers' veranda.

'We come from Tohitapu, our chief,' said the spokesman of the party, a huge fellow of sixteen stone. 'Tohitapu loves the *pakeha* people, but most of all he loves Te Wiria, his great friend. Tohitapu has stored up in his heart all the good things Te Wiria has done for the Maoris, especially for the Ngati-Ata *hapu*. Nothing can ever make Tohitapu forget the kindness Te Wiria has shown him and his *kainga*. Therefore Tohi' has said to us: "What can we do to show Te Wiria our thanks? How can we return this great *rangatira's* services? How can we preserve the regard of our *pakeha* friend for a long time? I will tell you. Te Wiria has a fine crop of potatoes, just ready for digging — Hakiri has seen them, and so has Titoré. But how will Te Wiria dig up his crop at this time, when all the *pakeha* have gone to the goldfields and men are scarce? Now, you men of Ngati-Ata, I will tell you what you must do. You must take the largest canoes you have, the biggest of all, and go over to Te Wiria, and dig up his *riwai* crop for him. Then we shall show that the Maori people love Te Wiria, and there will be great friendship between him and us." '

Villiers replied almost with tears. He was overjoyed to know that the Ngati-Ata had his welfare so near their hearts. He had tried to show that he looked on them as friends: they had come to prove that they were such indeed. They were good men; they thought of the needs of others. They deserved to enjoy plenty all their lives. Might they never lack *kumara* and potatoes, pigs and tobacco. As for his *riwai* crop, it was a good crop and ready for digging, as they had guessed. He would be glad to accept their generous offer. He considered Hakiri and Titoré and Haneke and the rest of them had shown a very proper spirit in coming over to help him just in the nick of time. It was what he might have expected of such generous fellows.

Forks and spades were taken down to the potato-field. The Maoris, men and women, began to dig for all they were worth.

Towards mid-day Villiers' women-folk took down to the workers large quantities of pork and a huge iron cauldron. The Maori women, with many smiles, fixed up a cooking-place, and soon the *kohua* was sizzling over a bright fire. The pork was boiled with potatoes and thistles in the same pot. The Maoris gathered round, squatted on the ground, dipped their fingers in the stew, and ate till they were full. Then they stretched themselves. They praised Te Wiria, his house, his horses, his pork, his potatoes. And Villiers' little son, who had watched them eat, coveted their feeding capacities.

In the evening the work was finished; fifty sacks of potatoes stood piled in Villiers' sheds. With many flattering speeches, and laughter, and chattering, the Maoris got into their canoes, and disappeared round the cape.

Villiers went to sleep with a light heart that night — his endeavours to maintain friendly relations with the Ngati-Ata were not in vain. But at one o'clock his big kangaroo-hound began to bark with all its might, and tugged furiously at the bullock-chain that held it. The dog often barked at night — usually at wild-cats or the moon. Villiers put his head out of the window, but could see nothing; so he went to bed again. But the dog barked on for hours.

Next morning Villiers went to the sheds to feast his eyes on his wealth of potatoes. He opened the door of shed No. 1 — it was empty. He went to No. 2 — there, also, not a sack was to be seen. His potatoes were gone.

Villiers did not go for the police — there were no police to fetch. He saddled his horse, and rode over to Tohitapu's *pa*.

Tohi' met him with all the dignity of the true *rangatira*, and his mouth full of pork — Villiers had arrived there at dinner-time. The *pakeha* quickly told his story. Tohi' listened with the deepest respect. Villiers pointed to some sacks, marked with a great red V, hanging on a fence near by. Tohitapu acknowledged that it was strange that they should be there — marked with a V, too. Beyond a doubt, some of his fellows were arrant rogues; he would see to it. Villiers pointed to a newly-dug *rua*, almost under his horse's feet. Tohitapu acknowledged that it had been dug recently. Villiers remarked that it was full of potatoes. Tohi' relinquished his hold on Villiers' rein, and called his people to him.

'You Ngati-Ata are a bad people,' he said. 'You always were a greedy, thieving set of men! I have long felt ashamed of you. Te Wiria here is my *pakeha*; he has long been my friend, and the friend of the Ngati-Ata. So you men there, Hakiri, Titoré, and Haneke, when you hear that Te Wiria has got a fine *riwai* crop, you go to him and say that I, Tohitapu, told you to dig it up. Te Wiria is a guileless man — he let you do the work. You store the *riwai* in Te Wiria's sheds. You are a low-bred set of men, *taurekareka*, all of you. You have no shame; you forget that the *pakeha* thinks stealing is a sin; you forget that the *pakeha* people put thieves into gaol and make them *heréheré* — prisoners. So you go and take Te Wiria's *riwai* crop; you steal it in the night — you dare not go in the day. You are great cowards, you Ngati-Ata! And you bring the potatoes to the *kainga*, and say to yourselves: "It is well: we shall have plenty of food for the winter." *He ware te iwi nei!* You are a wicked, lazy lot of people; you are a set of cowards and thieves; you are an ungrateful tribe; you have disgraced me in the eyes of my *pakeha*, Te Wiria. I am ashamed to be your chief. Get out of my sight, every one of you!'

And Tohitapu strode through the spell-bound Ngati-Ata, and resumed his interrupted meal, his meal of pork and baked potatoes — Te Wiria's potatoes.

Villiers sat on his horse, wondering whether Tohitapu was a great actor or a great liar. He rode home wondering. He wondered till the potatoes had long rested in the capacious stomachs of the Ngati-Ata. He is wondering to this day.

A Daughter of Maoriland

A sketch of poor-class Maoris

—

Henry Lawson

THE new native school-teacher, who was green, soft, and poetical, and had a literary ambition, called her August, and fondly hoped to build a romance on her character. She was down in the school registers as Sarah Moses, Maori, sixteen years and three months. She looked twenty; but this was nothing, insomuch as the mother of the youngest child in the school — a dear little half-caste lady of two or three summers — had not herself the vaguest idea of the child's age, nor anybody else's, nor of ages in the abstract. The church register was lost some six years before, when Granny, who was a hundred, if a day, was supposed to be about twenty-five. The teacher had to guess the ages of all the new pupils.

August was apparently the oldest in the school — a big, ungainly, awkward girl, with a heavy negro type of Maori countenance, and about as much animation, mentally or physically, as a cow. She was given to brooding; in fact, she brooded all the time. She brooded all day over her school work, but did it fairly well. How the previous teachers had taught her all she knew was a mystery to the new one. There had been a tragedy in August's family when she was a child, and the affair seemed to have cast a gloom over the lives of the entire family, for the lowering

17

brooding cloud was on all their faces. August would take to the bush when things went wrong at home, and climb a tree and brood till she was found and coaxed home. Things, according to pah-gossip, had gone wrong with her from the date of the tragedy, when she, a bright little girl, was taken — a homeless orphan — to live with her sister, and, afterwards, with an aunt-by-marriage. They treated her, 'twas said, with a brutality which must have been greatly exaggerated by pah-gossip, seeing that unkindness of this description is, according to all the best authorities, altogether foreign to Maori nature.

Pah-gossip — which is less reliable than the ordinary washer-woman kind, because of a deeper and more vicious ignorance — had it that one time when August was punished by a teacher (or beaten by her sister or aunty-by-marriage) she took to the bush for three days, at the expiration of which time she was found on the ground in an exhausted condition. She was evidently a true Maori or savage, and this was one of the reasons why the teacher with the literary ambition took an interest in her. She had a print of a portrait of a man in soldier's uniform, taken from a copy of the *Illustrated London News*, pasted over the fire-place in the whare where she lived, and neatly bordered by vandyked strips of silvered tea-paper. She had pasted it in the place of honour, or as near as she could get to it. The place of honour was sacred to framed representations of the Nativity and Catholic subjects, half-modelled, half-pictured. The print was a portrait of the last Tsar of Russia, of all the men in the world; and August was reported to have said that she loved that man. His father had been murdered, so had her mother. This was one of the reasons why the teacher with the literary ambition thought he could get a romance out of her.

After the first week she hung round the new schoolmistress, dog-like — with 'dog-like affection', thought the teacher. She came down often during the holidays, and hung about the veranda and back door for an hour or so; then, by and by, she'd be gone. Her brooding seemed less aggressive on such occasions. The teacher reckoned that she had something on her mind, and wanted to open her heart to 'the wife', but was too ignorant or too shy, poor girl; and he reckoned, from this theory of Maori character, that it might take her weeks, or months, to come to the point. One day, after a great deal of encouragement, she explained that she felt 'so awfully lonely, Mrs Lorrens'. All the other girls were away, and she wished it was school-time.

She was happy and cheerful again, in her brooding way, in the playground. There was something sadly ludicrous about her great, ungainly figure slopping round above the children at play. The schoolmistress took her into the parlour, gave her tea and cake, and was kind to her; and she took it all with broody cheerfulness.

One Sunday morning she came down to the cottage and sat on the edge of the veranda, looking as wretchedly miserable as a girl could. She was in rags — at least, she had a rag of a dress on — and was barefooted and bareheaded. She said that her aunt had turned her out, and she was going to walk down the coast to Whale Bay to her grandmother — a long day's ride. The teacher was troubled, because he was undecided what to do. He had to be careful to avoid any unpleasantness arising out of Maori cliquism. As the teacher he couldn't let her go in the state she was in; from the depths of his greenness he trusted her, from the depths of his softness he pitied her; his poetic nature was fiercely indignant on account of the poor girl's wrongs, and the wife spoke for her. Then he thought of his unwritten romance, and regarded August in the light of copy, and that settled it. While he talked the matter over with his wife, August 'hid in the dark of her hair', awaiting her doom. The teacher put his hat on, walked up to the pah, and saw her aunt. She denied that she had turned August out, but the teacher believed the girl. He explained his position, in words simplified for Maori comprehension, and the aunt and relations said they understood, and that he was 'perfectly right, Mr Lorrens'. They were very respectful. The teacher said that if August would not return home, he was willing to let her stay at the cottage until such time as her uncle, who was absent, returned, and he (the teacher) could talk the matter over with him. The relations thought that that was the very best thing that could be done, and thanked him. The aunt, two sisters, and as many of the others, including the children, as were within sight or hail at the time — most of them could not by any possible means have had the slightest connection with the business in hand — accompanied the teacher to the cottage. August took to the flax directly she caught sight of her relations, and was with difficulty induced to return. There was a lot of talk in Maori, during which the girl and her aunt shuffled and swung round at the back of each other, and each talked over her shoulder, and laughed foolishly and awkwardly once or twice; but in the end the girl was sullenly determined not to return home, so it was decided that she should stay. The schoolmistress made tea.

August brightened from the first day. She was a different girl altogether. 'I never saw such a change in a girl,' said the young schoolmistress, and one or two others. 'I always thought she was a good girl if taken the right way; all she wanted was a change and kind treatment.' But the stolid old Maori chairman of the school committee only shrugged his shoulders and said (when the schoolmistress, woman-like, pressed him for an opinion to agree with her own), 'You can look at it two ways, Mrs Lorrens.' Which, by the way, was about the only expression of opinion that the teacher was ever able to get out of him on any subject.

August worked and behaved well. She was wonderfully quick in picking up English ways and housework. True, she was awkward and not over cleanly in some things, but her mistress had patience with her. Who wouldn't have? She 'couldn't do enough' for her benefactress; she hung on her words and sat at her footstool of evenings in a way that gladdened the teacher's sentimental nature; she couldn't bear to see him help his wife with a hat-pin or button — August must do it. She insisted on doing her mistress's hair every night. In short, she tried in every way to show her gratitude. The teacher and his wife smiled brightly at each other behind her back, and thought how cheerful the house was since she came, and wondered what they'd do without her. It was a settled thing that they should take her back to the city with them, and have a faithful and grateful retainer all their lives, and a sort of Aunt Chloe for their children, when they had any. The teacher got yards of copy out of her for his 'Maori Sketches and Characters', worked joyously at his romance, and felt great already, and was happy. She had a bed made up temporarily (until the teacher could get a spring mattress for her from town) on the floor in the dining-room, and when she'd made her bed she'd squat on it in front of the fire and sing Maori songs in a soft voice. She'd sing the teacher and his wife, in the next room, to sleep. Then she'd get up and have a feed, but they never heard her.

Her manners at the table (for she was treated 'like one of ourselves' in the broadest sense of the term) were surprisingly good, considering that the adults of her people were decidedly cow-like in white society, and scoffed sea-eggs, shell-fish, and mutton-birds at home with a gallop which was not edifying. Her appetite, it was true, was painful at times to the poetic side of the teacher's nature; but he supposed that she'd been half-starved at home, poor girl, and would get over it. Anyway, the copy he'd get out of her would repay him for this and other expenses a hundredfold. Moreover, begging and borrowing had ceased with her advent, and the teacher set this down to her influence.

The first jar came when she was sent on horseback to the town for groceries, and didn't get back till late the next day. She explained that some of her relations got hold of her and made her stay, and wanted her to go into public-houses with them, but she wouldn't. She said that *she* wanted to come home. But why didn't she? The teacher let it pass, and hoped she'd gain strength of character by and by. He had waited up late the night before with her supper on the hob; and he and his wife had been anxious for fear something had happened to the poor girl who was under their care. He had walked to the treacherous river-ford several times during the evening, and waited there for her. So perhaps he was tired, and that was why he didn't write next night.

The sugar-bag, the onion-basket, the potato-bag and the tea-chest began to go down alarmingly, and an occasional pound of candles, a pigeon, a mutton-bird (plucked and ready for Sunday's cooking), and other little trifles went also. August couldn't understand it, and the teacher believed her, for falsehood and deceit are foreign to the simple natures of the modern Maoris. There were no cats; but no score of ordinary cats could have given colour to the cat theory, had it been raised in this case. The breath of August advertised onions more than once, but no human stomach could have accounted for the quantity. She surely could not have eaten the other things raw — and she had no opportunities for private cooking, as far as the teacher and his wife could see. The other Maoris were out of the question; they were all strictly honest.

Thefts and annoyances of the above description were credited to the swaggies who infested the roads, and had a very bad name down that way; so the teacher loaded his gun, and told August to rouse him at once if she heard a sound in the night. She said she would; but a heavy-weight swaggie could have come in and sat on her and had a smoke without waking her.

She couldn't be trusted to go a message. She'd take from three to six hours, and come back with an excuse that sounded genuine from its very simplicity. Another sister of hers lay ill in an isolated hut, alone and uncared for, except by the teacher's wife, and occasionally by a poor pah outcast, who had negro blood in her veins, and a love for a white loafer. God help her! All of which sounds strange, considering that Maoris are very kind to each other. The schoolmistress sent August one night to stay with the sick Maori woman and help her as she could, and gave her strict instructions to come to the cottage first thing in the morning, and tell her how the sick woman was. August turned up at lunch-time next day. The teacher gave her her first lecture, and said plainly that he wasn't to be taken for a fool; then he stepped aside to get cool, and when he returned the girl was sobbing as if her heart would break, and the wife comforting her. She had been up all night, poor girl, and was thoroughly worn out. Somehow the teacher didn't feel uncomfortable about it. He went down to the whare. August had not touched a dish-cloth or broom. She had slept, as she always did, like a pig, all night, while her sister lay and tossed in agony; in the morning she ate everything there was to eat in the house (which, it seemed, was the Maori way of showing sympathy in sickness and trouble), after which she brooded by the fire till the children, running out of school, announced the teacher's lunch hour.

August braced up again for a little while. The master thought of the trouble they had with Ayacanora in *Westward Ho*, and was comforted and tackled his romance again. Then the schoolmistress fell sick and things went wrong. The groceries went down faster than ever, and the house got very dirty, and began to have a native smell about it. August grew fat, and lazy, and dirty, and less reliable on washing-days, or when there was anything special to do in the house. 'The savage blood is strong,' thought the teacher, 'and she is beginning to long for her own people and free unconventional life.' One morning — on washing-day, too, as it happened — she called out, before the teacher and his wife were up, that the Maoris who supplied them with milk were away, and she had promised to go up and milk the cow and bring the milk down. The teacher gave her permission. One of the scholars usually brought the milk early. Lunch-time came and no August, no milk — strangest of all, only half the school children. The teacher put on his hat, and went up to the pah once more. He found August squatted in the midst of a circle of relations. She was entertaining them with one of a series of idealistic sketches of the teacher's domestic life, in which she showed a very vivid imagination, and exhibited an unaccountable savage sort of pessimism. Her intervals of absence had been occupied in this way from the first. The astounding slanders she had circulated concerning the teacher's private life came back, bit by bit, to his ears for a year afterwards, and her character sketches of previous teachers, and her own relations — for she spared nobody — would have earned a white woman a long and well-merited term of imprisonment for criminal libel. She had cunningly, by straightforward and unscrupulous lying, prejudiced the principal mother and boss woman of the pah against the teacher and his wife; as a natural result of which the old lady, who, like the rest, was very ignorant and ungrateful, turned nasty and kept the children from school. The teacher lost his temper, so the children were rounded up and hurried down to school immediately; with them came August and her aunt, with alleged explanations and excuses, and a shell-fish. The aunt and sisters said they'd have nothing to do with August. They didn't want her and wouldn't have her. The teacher said that, under those circumstances, she'd better go and drown herself; so she went home with them.

The whole business had been a plot by her nearest relations. They got rid of the trouble and expense of keeping her, and the bother of borrowing in person, whenever in need of trifles in the grocery line. Borrowing recommenced with her dismissal; but the teacher put a full stop to it, as far as he was concerned. Then August, egged on by her aunt, sent a blackguardly letter to the teacher's wife; the sick sister, by the way, who had been nursed and supplied with food by her all along, was in it, and said she was glad August sent the letter, and it served the schoolmistress right. The teacher went up to the pah once more; an hour later, August in person, accompanied, as usual, by a relation or two, delivered at the cottage an abject apology in writing, the composition of which would have discouraged the most enthusiastic advocate of higher education for the lower classes.

Then various petty annoyances were tried. The teacher is firmly convinced that certain animal-like sounds round the house at night were due to August's trying to find out whether his wife was as likely to be haunted as the Maoris were. He didn't dream of such a thing at the time, for he did not believe that one of them had the pluck to venture out after dark. But savage superstition must give way to savage hate. The girl's last 'try-on' was to come down to the school fence, and ostentatiously sharpen a table-knife on the wires, while she scowled murderously in the direction of the schoolmistress, who was hanging out her washing. August looked, in her dark, bushy, Maori hair, a thoroughly wild savage. Her father had murdered her mother under particularly brutal circumstances, and the daughter took after her father.

The teacher called to her and said: 'Now, look here, my lady, the best thing you can do is to drop that nonsense at once' (she had dropped the knife in the ferns behind her), 'for we're the wrong sort of people to try it on with. Now you get out of this and tell your aunt — she's sneaking there in the flax — what I tell you, and that she'd better clear out of this quick, or I'll have a policeman out and take the whole gang into town in an hour. Now be off, and shut that gate behind you, carefully, and fasten it.' She did, and went.

The worst of it was that the August romance copy was useless. Her lies were even less reliable and picturesque than the common Jones's Alley hag lie. Then the teacher thought of the soft fool he'd been, and that made him wild. He looked like a fool, and was one to a great extent, but it wasn't good policy to take him for one.

Strange to say, he and others had reason to believe that August respected him, and liked him rather than otherwise; but she hated his wife, who had been kind to her, as only a savage can hate. The younger pupils told the teacher, cheerfully and confidently, that August said she'd cut Mrs Lorrens's throat the first chance she got. Next week the aunt sent down to ask if the teacher could sell her a bar of soap, and sent the same old shilling; he was tired of seeing it stuck out in front of him, so he took it, put it in his pocket, and sent the soap. This must have discouraged them, for the borrowing industry petered out. He saw the aunt later on, and she told him, cheerfully, that August was going to live with a half-caste in a certain house in town.

Poor August! For she was only a tool after all. Her 'romance' was briefly as follows: She went, per off-hand Maori arrangement, as 'housekeeper' in the hut of a labourer at a neighbouring sawmill. She stayed three months, for a wonder; at the expiration of which time she put on her hat and explained that she was tired of stopping there, and was going home. He said, 'All right, Sarah, wait a while and I'll take you home.' At the door of her aunt's house he said, 'Well, good-bye, Sarah,' and she said, in her brooding way, 'Good-bye, Jim.' And that was all.

As the last apparent result of August's mischief-making, her brother or someone one evening rode up to the cottage, drunk and inclined to bluster. He was accompanied by a friend, also drunk, who came to see the fun, and was ready to use his influence on the winning side. The teacher went inside, brought out his gun, and slipped two cartridges in. 'I've had enough of this,' he said. 'Now then, be off, you insolent blackguards, or I'll shoot you like rabbits. Go!' and he snapped his jaw and the breech of his gun together. As they rode off, the old local hawk happened to soar close over a dead lamb in the fern at the corner of the garden, and the teacher, who had been 'laying' for him a long time, let fly both barrels at him, without thinking. When he turned, there was only a cloud of dust down the track.

The teacher taught that school for three years thereafter, without a hitch. But he went no more on universal brotherhood lines. And, for years after he had gone, his name was spoken of with great respect by the Maoris.

Pipi on the Prowl

—

Blanche Baughan

IPI was very happy. To an indifferent observer, it is true, the little mummy-like old Maori woman, bundled about with a curious muddle of rag-bag jackets and petticoats, and hobbling along the high-road on crippled bare brown feet, might have presented a spectacle more forlorn than otherwise. But then, what does the indifferent observer ever really see? That grotesque and pitiful exterior was nothing but an exterior; and it covered an escaping captive: it clothed incarnate Mirth. For Miria had gone to town, and Pipi, one whole long afternoon, was free!

She chuckled as she thought of Miria — Miria the decorous, Miria the *pakeha* coachman's wife, Miria, who wore tan shoes. Miria did not like her grandmother to go roaming at her own sweet will along the roads; she did not even like her to smoke; what she did like was to have her squatted safe at the *whare* door, holding on to little Hana, whose kicking really began to be painful, and looking out that little Himi did not get hold of the axe and chop himself to bits. She had left her like that half an hour ago; probably she imagined her to be still like that — submissive, stationed, and oh, how lack-lustre, how dull! Well, Pipi might perhaps be a little *porangi* (crazy) at times, but she was never anything like so *porangi* as that. How lucky that Ropata's wife was a trustworthy crony! How fortunate that the babies could neither of them speak! Pipi smiled, and showed her perfect teeth; she took out, from deep recesses of her

26

raiment, her treasured pipe, and stuck it in her mouth. *E! Ka pai te paipa!* — a good thing, the pipe! There was no *topeka* (tobacco) in it, to be sure; but who could say whence *topeka* might not come, this golden afternoon? To those newly at liberty all the world belongs. And, like stolen waters, stolen sport is sweet. No urchin who, having safely conveyed himself away at last out of earshot of mother or teacher, bounds breathless to the beloved creek where 'bullies' wait the hook, knows more of the mingled raptures of lawlessness and expectation than this old great-grandmother Pipi did, out upon the high-road, out upon the hunt!

Although it was midwinter, the afternoon was warm — there is never really cold weather upon that sheltered northern coast. The road ran right round the head of the league-long harbour, and showed a splendid view; for the tide was in; every cove and inlet was full, and the sinuous, satin-blue sheen of the water reflected with the utmost fidelity every one of the little long, low spits, emerald-turfed and darkly crowned with trees, that fringed, as with a succession of piers, the left-hand shore; while the low, orange-coloured cliffs of the fern-flats opposite burned in the brilliant sun like buttresses of gold. But what was a view to Pipi? Her rheumy old brown eyes sought but the one spot, where, far down the glittering water-way, and close to the short, straight sapphire line that parted the purple Heads and meant the open sea, the glass of the township windows sent sparkles to the sun. The township — seven miles away, and Miria not there yet! *Ka pai!* Pipi was ready for whatever fish Tangaroa might kindly send her on dry land, but meanwhile freedom, simple freedom, mere lack of supervision, was in itself enough; and happily, happily she trudged along, nodding, smiling, and sucking vigorously at her empty pipe.

Before very long she came to the river — the sinister-looking river, black and sluggish, that drains the valley-head. In the swamp on the other side of the long white bridge, dark *manuka*-bushes with crooked stems and shaggy boles, like a company of uncanny crones under a spell, stood knee-deep in thick ooze; some withered *raupo* desolately lined the bank above. Even on that bright day, this was a dismal place, and the *raupo*, with its spindly shanks and discoloured leaves fluttering about them, looked lamentably like poor Pipi. *Poor* Pipi, indeed? Dismal place?

Huh! what does a fool know?

With brightened eyes, with uncouth gestures of delighted haste, out across the bridge scurried Pipi, slithered down into the swamp, clutched with eager claws at a muddy lump upon the margin, and emitted a deep low grunt of joy. Old snags, quite black with decay, lay rotting round her, and the stagnant water gave forth a most unpleasant smell. But what is foulness when glory beckons through it? Squatting in the slime, her tags and trails the raiment dabbling in and out of the black water, Pipi washed and scraped, scraped and washed, and finally lifted up and out into the sunshine with a grin of delight, a great golden pumpkin, richly streaked with green. The glint of its rind had caught her eye from the other side of the bridge. Evidently it had fallen from some passing cart, and rolled down into the swamp. It was big; it was heavy; it was sound. The goodness of this pumpkin! the triumph of this find! Pipi untied one of her most extra garments, tied the treasure securely in it, slung the bundle on her back as though it had been a baby, and went on.

From the river, the road runs straight uphill, through a cutting between high banks of fern and gorse, with a crumbly crest of *papa* clay boldly yellow on the full blue sky. The road is of yellow *papa* also, and un-metalled, and rather heavy. Pipi grunted a good deal as she toiled up it; and about halfway up stood still to get her breath, for the pumpkin, precious as it was, lay like lead upon her frail old shoulders. Why! at the very top of the bank, glaring in the sunshine against the yellow *papa*, what was that? A white paper only, with nothing in it — or a white paper parcel? Steep as the bank was, go she must, of course, and see; and up, pumpkin and all, she climbed. Aha! Something inside. What? . . . Bread; and, inside the bread? Jam; thick, sweet, deep-red jam, very thick, very sweet, *very* good!

Next to tobacco, Pipi loved sweet things. She did not expend much pity upon the school-child that, heedlessly running along the top edge of the bank that morning, had lost its lunch and spent a hungry dinner-hour; neither did the somewhat travelled appearance of the sandwich trouble her. She scrambled down again on to the firmer footing of the road, and there she stood, and licked and licked at the jam. Miria's face, if she had caught her at it! Oho, that face! — the very fancy of its sourness made the tit-bit sweeter. The bread itself she threw away. Her stomach was not hungry, Miria saw to that; but her imagination was, and that was why this chance-come, wayside dainty had a relish that no good, dull dinner in the *whare* ever had. Sport was good to-day. First that pumpkin, now this jam! *Ka pai* the catch! What next?

She resumed her journey up-hill, but had no sooner reached the top than she suddenly squatted down on the bank by the roadside, as if at a word of command, with next to no breath left in her lungs, but hope once more lively in her heart — for here, surely, advancing to meet her, was the Next — a tall young *pakeha* woman, with a basket on her arm. Only a woman. That was a pity, for there was less chance of *topeka*; still, what had that kit got in it?

Pipi knew all about strategical advantages by instinct. She sat still and waited on her hill-top as her forefathers had sat still on theirs, and waited for the prey. Soon it came; a little breathless, and with footsteps slackening naturally as they neared the brow, just as Pipi had foreseen. Yes, she would do, this *pakeha*, this pigeon; she would pay to be plucked. She was nicely dark and stout; she smiled to herself as she walked; and such good clothes upon the back denoted certainly a comfortable supply of *hikapeni* (sixpences) in the pocket.

'*Tenakoe! Tenakoe!*' (greeting!) cried Pipi, skipping up from her bank with a splendid assumption of agility, as the stranger came alongside; and extending her hand, expanding her smile, and wagging her wily old head, as if this strange young *pakeha* were her very dearest friend in all the world. And the bait took! The *pakeha*, too, stretched forth her hand, she, also, smiled. A catch, a catch to Pipi the fisher! Let us, though, find out first how much she knows, this fish . . . Not to speak the Maori tongue means not to read the Maori mind, so:

'*E hoa!*' says Pipi leisurely, '*E haere ana koe i whaea?*'

Good! it is all right. The *pakeha* stands still, laughs, and says, 'Oh, please say it in English!'

She is ignorant, she is affable, she is not in a hurry. She will do, this nice young *pakeha*! Pipi translates.

'Where you goin'?'

'I am going — oh, just along this road for a bit,' says the girl vaguely.

Pipi considers. 'Along the road,' in the stranger's present direction, means back towards home for Pipi; it would surely be a pity to turn back so soon? A fish on the line, however, is worth two in the water; also, after the feast is eaten, cannot the empty basket be thrown away? In other words, as soon as ever it suits her, cannot she pretend to be tired and let the stranger go on alone? Of course she can! So Pipi says, 'Me, too,' and, turning her back, for the time being, upon the enticement of the open road ahead, goes shambling back, hoppity-hop, down the hill again, at the side of her prey. She shambles slowly, too, by way of a further test, and, see, the girl instinctively adapts her pace. Excellent! Oh, the pleasantness, the complaisance, of this interesting young friend! Pipi takes hold of her sleeve, and strokes it.

'Ah, the good coat,' she cries, with an admiration that she does not need to assume. 'He keep you warm, my word! My coat, see how thin!' and she holds out for inspection a corner of her topmost covering, an old blouse of faded pinkish print, phenomenally spotted with purple roses. It is true that she has the misfortune to hold out also, quite by mistake, a little bit of the layer next beneath, which happens to be a thick tweed coat; but this she drops immediately, without an instant's delay, and it is well known that *pakehas* have as a rule only pebbles in their eye-sockets — they see nothing; while their ears, on the other hand, are as *kokota*-shells, to hold whatever you please to put in. 'I cold, plenty, plenty,' says Pipi accordingly, with a very well-feigned shiver. 'How much he cost, your good, warm coat?'

'Why, I don't quite know,' replies the *pakeha*. 'You see, it was a present; somebody gave it me.'

'Ah, nobody give poor Pipi,' sighs Pipi, very naughtily. Is it a good thing or not, that two of the Colonel's old flannel shirts, Mrs Cameron's knitted petticoat, and Miria's thickest dress, all of them upon her person at that moment, have no tongues? 'Nobody give *kai* (food) even. What you got in your big kit?' she asks coaxingly. '*Plenty* big kit!'

'Ah, nothing at all. Only air. It's just cramful of emptiness,' says the girl, sadly shaking her head. 'What you got on your back in the bundle there? Plenty big bundle!'

It is useless, of course, to deny the existence of so plain a fact as that pumpkin. Why had not Pipi had the wit to hide it in the fern?

'On'y punkin,' she says, with a singular grimace, expressive at first of the contemptibility of all the pumpkin tribe, then changing instantly to a radiant recognition of their priceless worth, for her mind has been

Stung with the splendour of a sudden thought.

'He *fine* punkin, big, *big* punkin,' she cries, and then, munificently, 'You give me coat, I give you this big, big punkin!' She exhibits her treasure as one astounded at her own generosity.

The *pakeha*, however, seems astounded at it, too.

'Why!' says she, 'my coat is worth at least three thousand pumpkins.'

Perhaps it is? Pipi tries to imagine three thousand pumpkins lying spread before her, with a view to assessing their value; but, not unnaturally, fails. Ah well! Bold bargaining is one weapon, but tactful yielding is another.

'*E!* You give me *hikapeni*, then, I give you punkin.' She concedes, with an air of reckless kindness, and a hope of sixpence-worth of *topeka* to be purchased presently on the sly from Wirimu, the gardener.

'But I don't care much for pumpkins,' says the stupid *pakeha*. 'And I haven't any *hikapeni*,' she adds. The stingy thing! A fish? Why, the creature is nothing at all but an empty cockle-shell not worth the digging. And Pipi is just thinking that she shall soon feel too tired to walk a single step farther, when, suddenly producing a small, sweetly-familiar-looking packet from her coat, 'You like cigarettes?' inquires the *pakeha*.

'*Ai! Homai te hikarete! Ka pai te hikarete!* (Yes! Give me a cigarette! I do like cigarettes),' cries Pipi, enraptured, and the *pakeha* holds out the packet. Alas! there are only two cigarettes left in it, and manners will permit of Pipi's taking only one. This is very trying. 'You smoke?' she asks innocently. The girl denies it, of course, as Pipi knew she would: these *pakeha* women always do, and Miria, their slavish advocate and copyist, declares they speak the truth. Vain words; for, in the hotel at Rotorua, has not Pipi seen the very best attired of them at it? Moreover, why should this girl trouble to carry cigarettes if she does not smoke, herself? Plenty stupid, these *pakeha* women! Plenty good, however, their cigarettes, and greed (oh Miria!) overcoming manner, '*E!* you not smoke;

you give me other *hikaret'*, then,' she says boldly.

This miserable *pakeha*, however, proves to be as a pig, that, full of feed, yet stands with both feet in the trough — she only shakes her head, laughs sillily, and mutters some foolish remark about keeping the other for somebody else she might meet. Ah, well, never mind; Pipi has at least the one, and she would like to smoke it at once and make sure of it, but 'No right!' she says plaintively — she means 'no light'; she has no matches, and no more, it appears, has the *pakeha*. Boiled-headed slave! How, without matches, can she expect anybody to smoke her cigarettes?

'Perhaps this man has some,' suggests the *pakeha*, pointing to the solitary driver of a wagon coming down the hill behind them. She explains the predicament, and the man, with a good-natured smile, pours out half a boxful into Pipi's upstretched palms, and drives on. Ah, and perhaps he had *topeka* with him, too, real, good, dark, strong *topeka* in a stick; and, had Pipi only been wise enough to wait for him, and let this miserable person go by, she might by now, perhaps, have been having a real smoke. As for this *hikarete*, by the smell of it, Hana, aged thirteen months, could smoke it with impunity. No coat, no *kai*, no *hikapeni*, one *hikarete* of hay — Huh! the unprofitableness of this *pakeha*!

'You go on!' says Pipi, with an authoritative gesture. They have got as far as the bridge, and she squats down by her swamp. All that long hill to toil up again, too!

But behold, the black-hearted one at her side says, actually, 'Oh, I'm in no particular hurry. I think I'll sit down a bit, too,' and does so. Now, who that has found the *riwai* (potato) rotten wants to look at the rind?

Worse and worse — who can grow melons in mid-air, drink water without a mouth, or strike a match without something to strike it on? . . . What now? Here is the *pakeha*, in reply to this reproach, sticking out her thick leather boot right into Pipi's hand — an insult? She would kick the *hikaret'* out of it? Not so, for her eyes are soft . . . Swift as a weather-cock, round whirl Pipi's mobile wits.

'*E hoa!*' she cries with glee. 'You give me the *hu* (shoe)? Poor Pipi no *hu*, see! I think *kapai*, you give me the *hu*.'

But the *pakeha* only shakes her head vigorously and laughs out loud.

Is she *porangi* quite? No, not quite, it seems, for, taking a match from Pipi's hand, she strikes it on the clumsy sole, and lo! a flame bursts out. Pipi can light her *hikaret'* now, and does so, coolly using the *pakeha's* skirt the while, as a breakwind, for she may as well get out of her all the little good she can. And now, how to get rid of this disappointment, this addled egg, this little, little cockle with the big thick shell? Aha, Pipi knows. She will do what she has done so often with the prying Mrs Colonel Cameron — she will suddenly forget all her English, and hear and speak nothing but Maori any more. That will soon scrape off this *piri-piri* (burr). What shall she start by saying? Anything will do; and accordingly she mechanically asks again in Maori her first question, the question she asks every one. 'You are going, where?' But, O calamity! This time, the *pakeha*, the ignorant one, not only understands, but answers — and in the same tongue — and to alarming purpose!

'*E haere ana ahau ki a Huria* (I am going to Judaea),' she says. And Judaea is the name of Pipi's own *kainga!*

'*Ki a Huria!* and you know to speak the Maori!' she exclaims, started into consternation.

'Only a very little as yet,' replies the girl. 'But Miria is teaching me.'

'Miria! which Miria?' cries Pipi, in an agony of foreboding.

'Why, Miria Piripi, Colonel Cameron's coachman's wife — *your* Miria, isn't she?' says this monster, with a sudden smile. 'She has told me about you, often.'

The truant who should suddenly see his captured 'bully' pull the hook out of its jaws in order to plunge it in his own, might very well feel as Pipi felt at this frightful moment. True enough, she had often heard Miria speak of the *pakeha* lady who came to visit Mrs Cameron and was 'always so interested in the natives'; and with the greatest care she had always kept out of her way, for Pipi had her pride — she resented being made into a show. And now — !

'Yes, and I have often seen you, too, though you may not have seen me,' pursued the relentless *pakeha*. 'You, and little Hana and Himi. Where are Hana and Himi now? I shall be sure to tell Miria I've met you,' she finished brightly.

Alas, alas for Pipi's sport! The fish had caught the fisher, and with a vengeance. She collected her scattering wits, and met the *pakeha's* eye with a stony stare, for she came of a princely race; but cold, too, as a stone, lay the heart within her breast.

The heart of the *pakeha*, however, had also its peculiarities. For all she was a *pakeha*, clad in a fine coat, wearing boots, and carrying cigarettes about with her only by way of Maori mouth-openers: for all this, her heart was the heart of a fellow-vagabond. It understood. She *had* heard Miria, and Mrs Cameron too, talk of Pipi; but with a result of which those superior speakers were not conscious. How often she had silently sympathised with the poor old free-lance kept so straitly to the beaten track of respectability; how often she had wished for a peep at Pipi *au naturel*! And now she had got it; and she meant to get it again. She could not help a little mischievous enjoyment of the confusion so heroically concealed, but she took quick steps to relieve it.

'Well, I must go on,' she said briskly, rising as she spoke. 'Take the other cigarette, Pipi, and here's a shilling for some *topeka*. E noho koe (good-bye)! Oh, and, Pipi, don't let's tell Miria yet that we've met, shall we? It will be so nice for her to introduce us properly some day, you know!'

Pipi was game. '*Haere ra*' (good-bye) was all she answered, unemotionally. But she could not help one gleam of joy shooting out of her deep old eyes, and Lucy Willett saw it, and went on with a kindly laughter in her own.

That night, when she had rolled herself up in her blanket, and lain down on the *whare* floor (she disdained the foppishness of beds), Pipi glowed all through with satisfaction. Miria, on coming home, had found her seated, patient, pipeless, before the fire, Hana and Himi one upon each knee, both intact, both peacefully asleep; and had been so pleased with this model picture, as well as with the size of Pipi's pumpkin, that she had indulged her grandmother with schnapper for supper. And Pipi had found that pumpkin; she had harvested red jam from a fern-bank; she had had one cigarette to smoke, and with another had been able to encourage Ropata's wife to future friendly offices. More than that, she had had time for one blessed pipeful of real Derby, richly odorous, and in her most intimate garment of all could feel now, as she lay, safely knotted up, the rest of a whole stick. Nor was even that all. By some extraordinary good management that she herself did not quite understand, she had eluded the hook as it dangled at her very lips while yet she had secured the bait; and she had an instinctive, shrewd suspicion that, in cleverly causing the eye of the pakeha to wink at guilt, she had made sure of more patronage in the future. Who could tell? Perhaps, some fine day, that good thick coat, even, might find its way to Pipi's back. *Taihoa* (just wait)! Meanwhile, what a good day's sport!

The Slave's Reward
—

Will Lawson

T AIRUA, the slave girl, stood on the heights of Kapiti gazing out over the sea. It was an hour before dawn and the waters lay calm and leaden between the island and the mainland of New Zealand. Beyond Otaki and Paekakariki the mountains loomed against a sky filled with stars. The land lay dark, save away to the northward, where a glare lit the night.

Another woman as well as Tairua was watching this light. She was tall and straight, and her face was much tattooed in delicate designs, showing her noble birth. In her arms she carried her son, who was also the son of Te Waharoa, chief of the Kapiti tribe. Parekohu was the name of this princess, meaning 'plume of mist,' and she was lovelier than that synonym suggested.

'Te Rauparaha is victorious once more,' Parekohu said. 'He sets the world ablaze when he conquers. Our warriors will be slain. None will come back to Kapiti. Only Te Rauparaha will come after Te Waharoa is dead.'

'Courage, lady,' Tairua said softly. 'The fight is not yet ended. We may have good news soon.'

'No,' Parekohu insisted, fear in her eyes, not for herself, but for her son, who would one day be chief. 'There is only one thing to do, to save the child. And what can we do when all the canoes have gone? Even if we had a patiki, what would it avail? There will be warriors everywhere.'

The slave girl spoke.

'There will be none in the sea,' she said.

Tairua, too, was of noble birth, but she had been taken as a slave from Arapawa Island in Cook Strait before she was old enough to be tattooed with royal emblems.

'We must swim to Arapawa,' she went on calmly.

'To Arapawa?' Parekohu turned to look across the sea, where in the distance, as a dim shadow, very far away, the peaks of the South Island made misty outlines. 'How can we do that? It is too far.'

Tairua spoke proudly:

'Are you not an ariki-taniwha?' she said, 'and will not the sea-gods, the atuas, help you?'

'But the child?' the mother said anxiously.

'We will carry him on our backs,' Tairua said. 'I too am an ariki-taniwha, though now a slave. The gods will guard me too. We can carry food and clothing in a small bag. It is far to swim, yet better to go than to wait here till Te Rauparaha comes with his warriors to violate and slay.'

'Aie,' Parekohu answered sadly, for her heart was heavy with grief. 'Waharoa will be slain. We must save the young chief. Let us go.'

As they turned to descend the bush path to the pah a sweet-tongued tui, most melodious of birds, whistled a song, startlingly clear in the still darkness. It was answered by a fainter call, yet very sweet.

'Hark!' said Tairua. 'The birds know that the light will come, so they whistle. So for us the light will shine again. The kori-makos are waking for their morning song.'

From all parts of the island now were coming sweet, small notes of song, each one too faint to be heard far away. The bell-birds, little song-sters, were preparing to greet the dawn in a chorus which is still the most marvellous bird-music in the world of birds.

'I will take the boy,' Tairua said when they reached the beach.

'No, I will take him,' Parekohu said. 'You take the bag with some food of the tawa and fern roots and berries, and some dry clothing to put on when we reach Arapawa. These you can carry on your head.'

At the mention of Arapawa and their arrival there Tairua's heart stood still, then beat madly.

'Arapawa,' she said softly under her breath.

The other women and the old men and boys in the kainga were stirring. They came from their beds, astonished to see their chieftainess preparing to depart. When they saw the glare which now filled the skies as the flax swamps which Te Rauparaha had set fire to blazed amain, fear came into their eyes.

'Where do you go without a canoe?' one woman asked.

'To Arapawa, to save the child,' Parekohu said. 'When Te Rauparaha comes he will find him gone. We will swim to Arapawa, the gods will aid us.'

'How do you know?' the woman asked. She ran to a flax bush and pulled out the rito-harakeke, the inner stalk of the plant. It came intact; if it had broken it would have been a bad omen. Crying her joy, she ran back to Parekohu and told her the omens were good.

'So, even if we perish, it is better than to await Te Rauparaha's vengeance,' Parekohu said. 'Farewell, my people. Te Waharoa will be dead, but his son will return to Kapiti when Te Rauparaha has been killed, too.'

Quietly in the growing dawn, with the song of the kori-makos now loud, like the ringing of millions of small silver bells, chiming in their ears, the two women entered the water. Soon they were swimming steadily away from the island, using the slow breast-stroke with which Maori women could go a long way and stay afloat for as much as twelve hours.

Side by side they swam, with the child happy on his mother's back and crowing as the sea gurgled past his sides.

'To Mana first,' Tairua said, indicating the low, flat-topped island lying off Porirua, the harbour where whaler and other ships called for water and spars and flax.

Mana Island lay ten miles ahead of the swimmers, across waters now growing pink with the coming dawn-lights. To their eyes, low in the sea, Mana seemed far away. But Tairua spoke cheerfully.

'Already the gods help us,' she said. 'It is the beginning of Tainui, the Great Tide, which surges through Raukawa, between the two mainlands. See, it helps us in its flow to the south.'

Parekohu saw that she spoke truly. They were being carried by the tide towards Mana and Cook Strait. A school of kahawai — sea mullet — flashed past as if in flight.

'Repeat a karakia, O chieftainess,' Tairua said. 'Te Arawa the shark will be pursuing the fish, and will pass near. It is more fitting for you to say it than I.'

Parekohu, 'Plume of the Mist,' looked at her faithful maid, her lovely dark eyes shining.

'No, you do so,' she said. 'You of Arapawa are of the sea. It is better that you should pray to the sea atuas.'

Tairua, smiling till her handsome face was radiant, began to recite in a soft sing-song these words:

'O mothers who wave your hands to the southern clouds,
Lift up your voice, weep loudly for the parent dead.
The god has left his cave and gone far, far away.
O, my protecting power, my shade from heat of heaven,
Protect us in the sea.'

'Te Arawa passes by,' Parekohu said presently as a grey shape dashed past in chase of the kahawai.

Tairua did not answer her. She was beginning a new chant, a love-song to her people:

'O gentle western breezes,
So softly blowing o'er the sea,
Across Tawake's distant peak,
Ye bring me fond thoughts of love
For one who's far away,
For him to whom I am betrothed
While yet but a little one.
O, would that I could go with him
Across the swelling sea
To see some island of our own. . . .'

Parekohu said: 'It is happier for you. You are swimming homewards. But I leave my heart behind me in the vales of Kapiti.'

'Nay. All is not grief with you,' Tairua said. 'You have a son who is a chief.'

Steadily they swam, exerting themselves as little as possible. Tupoupou the porpoise and his brothers came to play around them, an omen of good import, though the dashing, splashing creatures frightened the child.

Next came Pakake the humpback whale with his wives, four in all, to blow vapour from their heads and dive deeper than anything else alive could dive, save Paraoa the great sperm whale. Tairua was happy, for all the atuas were helping them; even Ratahui the killer came, cheeky and bold-eyed, to watch them and roll about lazily, he who can dart from sky to sky across the sea at amazing speed.

Now Parekohu began to chant:

'Let quiet be over all
That Mana may in sunshine pass the stream
Of River Pakihi and Marouri's rippling tide. . . .'

The crying of the child interrupted her. She stroked him with her hand as she swam and calmed him.

Before noon they stepped ashore on Mana, lonely isle looking out at Arapawa across the Sea of Raukawa, and rested on its shingle beach. Far away they could see Kapiti, ten miles at least, with clouds shining above it and the sunshine on its slopes. So keenly did the sight affect Parekohu, she wept into her hands, while her child lay on a patch of soft sand and Tairua found shellfish — pipis and pauas — and brought fresh water in a paua shell.

Tairua's eyes were on Arapawa, so near now, less than twelve miles across the strait behind Te Whatu — the rocks which to-day are called The Brothers, where a lighthouse flashes. Arapawa was a pleasant sight to Tairua, who had not seen it since she had been captured by a war

party, when all her kin were killed, and taken to Kapiti, and none had
come to seek her, princess though she was.

In the late afternoon, when Parekohu had ceased her weeping and had
rested awhile and fed her baby, they started off once more, two women
and a baby in a wide rolling sea, but as brave as ever — one spurred on
with the hope of saving her son, and the other with joy of going home.
The red sun sank into the sea, making the Broad Path of Tane for the
souls of the dead to travel over to the great Meeting-House in the West
— so do the Maoris still believe.

The fingers of night stretched out over the waters, the hands of
darkness came down on the sea, shutting out all light save that of the
stars. In the dark sea the women swam, making for the faint loom of land
of Arapawa, till they were in the strait itself close to The Rocks. But
Tainui, the Great Tide, was not helping them now. It was flowing full
from the eastward and meeting the west wind, so that the sea was
choppy and spray filled their eyes; moreover, often they had to turn their
mouths aside from the waves to breathe fully.

The child was crying, hungry again. In desperation, and fearing that
they all would be lost in the deep waters and that she would never reach
Arapawa, Tairua cried aloud to the sea-god which lives by Nga-whatu
and helps voyagers in peril:

'Come, O Pane-iraira, Great Speckled Head,
Whose back is hallowed for sheltering,
Come to the aid of woman and child,
Let thy shadow calm the seas and bring us peace.'

Fearful that she might not have said the karakia correctly, Tairua
asked Parekohu to say it too. Though she was on the verge of collapse
with weariness and the weight of the child, which she would not let
Tairua carry, Parekohu repeated the words.

'Now he must come,' said Tairua confidently. 'Never was karakia said
so sweetly and truly.'

It was not long after this that Parekohu cried:

'See, he comes! Great Speckled Head, he comes!'

Tairua, peering into the darkness ahead, saw a great bulk rolling in the sea. Eagerly she swam, faster than Parekohu, joy giving her strength. In a short space she swam in the lee of a great dead whale drifting with wind and tide, having broken away from boats which were towing it to Te Awaite whaling station on Arapawa Island, or perhaps the harpooner had been clumsy and his line had broken, releasing the whale, which had since died of the harpoon wound.

Around the whale were sharks and killers, snatching morsels out of the whale's mouth and throat or tearing strips of blubber from its sides. They took no notice of the swimmers when they sought a handhold on the whale.

Suddenly Tairua's hands touched a rope and she clung to it, calling to Parekohu to come. The rope was fast to the harpoon in the whale's back. Tairua scrambled to the high back of the great creature and then lowered the rope again, telling Parekohu to tie it round herself and Tairua would pull her up. After a struggle this was done. A killer, coming up from underwater to eat more titbits, gave her an accidental lift which helped her, and she and the child sat with Tairua on the whale. It was cold and wet and dark, but Tairua was happy, for she was near Arapawa, towards which the whale must drift, when they could go ashore.

'There are no kori-makos making their song,' Parekohu said sadly when the dawn began to break. 'Soon we shall be hearing the voices of Te Reinga.' She referred to the songs of another world.

'Nay. The gods have been good to us,' Tairua cried. 'We are almost at Arapawa. When the day comes my people must see us and come in their canoes.'

'How will they regard us, me and my son?' Parekohu asked.

'You are my friends. All will be well,' Tairua said. She was almost delirious with joy. But the sea has strange ways of helping those who fall into its power. When the sun rose it shone on the sails of the brig *Belinda*, sailing from Sydney to Wellington, and just entering the strait. Towards the dead whale she steered, no doubt those on board wishing to have a closer view. Tairua had taken from her bag not only the remainder of their food, but the woven mats that were used as skirts. They were wet, but she and Parekohu put them on, hiding some of their nakedness.

The coming of the brig frightened them, for such ships had rude men on board.

Far away they heard a voice, the shout of the lookout man, but they could not catch his words. He was saying:

'There's two women on that whale, sir.'

Orders came from the quarterdeck. The brig came round into the wind, her mainyard was backed to heave her to, and a boat was lowered. Over the waters it came towards the frightened women. It ran alongside the whale, and the coxswain shouted:

'Ahoy there! Can you come down?'

The women stared and talked together in Maori. Before they could move, a young seaman swarmed up the rope and stood smiling before them. He saw that Parekohu was a chieftainess, for he had been in ships to New Zealand before.

'Tene koe,' he said.

They smiled and answered 'E koe'; but he could say little more in Maori. However, by signs he asked them to get into the boat, and they went with him, he helping them down, for he was like a monkey on a rope. The men in the boat were astounded to see a baby.

'Jonah ain't in it with this lot,' a gnarled old salt said.

They rowed swiftly back to the brig, whose captain, Henry Todd, a Welshman, had keen ideas of values. He was experienced in New Zealand trade. To him Parekohu and Tairua were taken, Parekohu shrinking yet proud, and Tairua composed with the composure of despair. She saw her visions of getting home to Arapawa fading, for this ship would go to some other place.

Captain Todd spoke to Parekohu in Maori, telling her not to be afraid and he would take her home. She told him then of the happening at Kapiti and of Te Rauparaha's victorious advance. The women were shy about going into his cabin, but once there they forgot their fears and took some wine and biscuits.

Soon the brig was heading for Kapiti and the captain was telling the mate the story of Parekohu and Tairua.

'Swum from Kapiti they did, mister,' he said, 'to get away from that murderer Te Rauparaha, who's raising hell with guns sold him by some scallywag seamen. I'll see what can be done to stop his game, at any rate as far as Kapiti is concerned. They're friends of mine there; I buy flax from them. Good people. Look after these two, mister — no funny business.'

'Aye, aye, sir,' the mate grunted, and went to get his anchors ready. On the afterdeck Tairua stood staring at Arapawa, now fading into the spray.

With an armed brig lying off, Te Rauparaha did not dare to cross to Kapiti, but passed on towards the south to sail in his canoes across the strait to the Wairau. Te Waharoa came home alive, though badly wounded, and with him came two score of warriors whom he had led with others now dead in a vain effort to stop the onward march of Te Rauparaha. On Kapiti there was happiness for all but Tairua.

On the beach at sunset she sat, looking over the sea towards Arapawa and singing softly through her tears. Nobody heard and nobody cared, for she was a slave.

> 'O gentle western breezes
> So softly blowing o'er the sea,
> Across Tawake's distant peak
> Ye bring to me fond thoughts of love
> For one who's far away. . . .'

Her grief grew wilder. She cried aloud to the gods of the sea to help her, and went into the waves to swim once more to Mana and on to Arapawa. Perhaps the sea-gods helped her, perhaps the tides carried her on their breasts lovingly. But there is no story to tell us.

How Pearl Button Was Kidnapped

Katherine Mansfield

—

P EARL Button swung on the little gate in front of the House of Boxes. It was the early afternoon of a sunshiny day with little winds playing hide-and-seek in it. They blew Pearl Button's pinafore frill into her mouth, and they blew the street dust all over the House of Boxes. Pearl watched it — like a cloud — like when mother peppered her fish and the top of the pepper-pot came off. She swung on the little gate, all alone, and she sang a small song. Two big women came walking down the street. One was dressed in red and the other was dressed in yellow and green. They had pink handkerchiefs over their heads, and both of them carried a big flax basket of ferns. They had no shoes and stockings on, and they came walking along, slowly, because they were so fat, and talking to each other and always smiling. Pearl stopped swinging, and when they saw her they stopped walking. They looked and looked at her and then they talked to each other, waving their arms and clapping their hands together. Pearl began to laugh.

The two women came up to her, keeping close to the hedge and looking in a frightened way towards the House of Boxes.

'Hallo, little girl!' said one.

Pearl said, 'Hallo!'

'You all alone by yourself?'

Pearl nodded.

'Where's your mother?'

'In the kitching, ironing-because-it's-Tuesday.'

The women smiled at her and Pearl smiled back. 'Oh,' she said, 'haven't you got very white teeth indeed! Do it again.'

The dark women laughed, and again they talked to each other with funny words and wavings of the hands. 'What's you name?' they asked her.

'Pearl Button.'

'You coming with us, Pearl Button? We got beautiful things to show you,' whispered one of the women. So Pearl got down from the gate and she slipped out into the road. And she walked between the two dark women down the windy road, taking little running steps to keep up, and wondering what they had in their House of Boxes.

They walked a long way. 'You tired?' asked one of the women, bending down to Pearl. Pearl shook her head. They walked much further. 'You not tired?' asked the other woman. And Pearl shook her head again, but tears shook from her eyes at the same time as her lips trembled. One of the women gave over her flax basket of ferns and caught Pearl Button up in her arms, and walked with Pearl Button's head against her shoulder and her dusty little legs dangling. She was softer than a bed and she had a nice smell — a smell that made you bury your head and breathe and breathe it. . . .

They set Pearl Button down in a log room full of other people the same colour as they were — and all these people came close to her and looked at her, nodding and laughing and throwing up their eyes. The woman who had carried Pearl took off her hair ribbon and shook her curls loose. There was a cry from the other women, and they crowded close and some of them ran a finger through Pearl's yellow curls, very gently, and one of them, a young one, lifted all Pearl's hair and kissed the back of her little white neck. Pearl felt shy but happy at the same time. There were some men on the floor, smoking, with rugs and feather mats round their shoulders. One of them made a funny face at her and he pulled a great big peach out of his pocket and set it on the floor, and flicked it with his finger as though it were a marble. It rolled right over to her. Pearl picked it up. 'Please can I eat it?' she asked. At that they all laughed and clapped their hands, and the man with the funny face made another at her and pulled a pear out of his pocket and sent it bobbling over the floor. Pearl laughed. The women sat on the floor and Pearl sat down too. The floor was very dusty. She carefully pulled up her pinafore and dress and sat on her petticoat as she had been taught to sit in dusty places, and she ate the fruit, the juice running all down her front.

'Oh!' she said in a very frightened voice to one of the women, 'I've spilt all the juice!'

'That doesn't matter at all,' said the woman patting her cheek. A man came into the room with a long whip in his hand. He shouted something. They all got up, shouting, laughing, wrapping themselves up in rugs and blankets and feather mats. Pearl was carried again, this time into a great cart, and she sat on the lap of one of her women with the driver beside her. It was a green cart with a red pony and a black pony. It went very fast out of the town. The driver stood up and waved the whip round his head. Pearl peered over the shoulder of the woman. Other carts were behind like a procession. She waved at them. Then the country came. First fields of short grass with sheep on them and little bushes of white flowers and pink briar rose baskets — then big trees on both sides of the road — and nothing to be seen except big trees. Pearl tried to look through them but it was quite dark. Birds were singing. She nestled closer in the big lap. The woman was warm as a cat, and she moved up and down when she breathed, just like purring. Pearl played with a green ornament round her neck, and the woman took the little hand and kissed each of her fingers and then turned it over and kissed the dimples. Pearl had never been happy like this before. On the top of a big hill they stopped. The driving man turned to Pearl and said, 'Look, look!' and pointed with his whip.

And down at the bottom of the hill was something perfectly different — a great big piece of blue water was creeping over the land. She screamed and clutched at the big woman. 'What is it, what is it?'

'Why,' said the woman, 'it's the sea.'

'Will it hurt us — is it coming?'

'Ai-e, no, it doesn't come to us. It's very beautiful. You look again.'

Pearl looked. 'You're sure it can't come,' she said.

'Ai-e, no. It stays in this place,' said the big woman. Waves with white tops came leaping over the blue. Pearl watched them break on a long piece of land covered with garden-path shells. They drove round a corner.

There were some little houses down close to the sea, with wood fences round them and gardens inside. They comforted her. Pink and red and blue washing hung over the fences, and as they came near more people came out, and five yellow dogs with long thin tails. All the people were fat and laughing, with little naked babies holding on to them or rolling about in the gardens like puppies. Pearl was lifted down and taken into a tiny house with only one room and a veranda. There was a girl there with two pieces of black hair down to her feet. She was setting the dinner on the floor. 'It *is* a funny place,' said Pearl, watching the pretty girl while the women unbuttoned her little drawers for her. She was very hungry. She ate meat and vegetables and fruit and the woman gave her milk out of a green cup. And it was quite silent except for the sea outside and the laughs of the two women watching her. 'Haven't you got any Houses of Boxes?' she said. 'Don't you all live in a row? Don't the men go to offices? Aren't there any nasty things?'

They took off her shoes and stockings, her pinafore and dress. She walked about in her petticoat and then she walked outside with the grass pushing between her toes. The two women came out with different sorts of baskets. They took her hands. Over a little paddock, through a fence, and then on warm sand with brown grass in it they went down to the sea. Pearl held back when the sand grew wet, but the women coaxed, 'Nothing to hurt, very beautiful. You come.' They dug in the sand and found some shells which they threw into the baskets. The sand was wet as mud pies. Pearl forgot her fright and began digging too. She got hot and wet, and suddenly her feet broke a little line of foam. 'Oo, oo!' she shrieked, dabbling with her feet. 'Lovely, lovely!' She paddled in the shallow water. It was warm. She made a cup of her hands and caught some of it. But it stopped being blue in her hands. She was so excited that she rushed over to her woman and flung her little thin arms round the woman's neck, hugging her, kissing. . . .

Suddenly the girl gave a frightful scream. The woman raised herself and Pearl slipped down on the sand and looked towards the land. Little men in blue coats — little blue men came running, running towards her with shouts and whistlings — a crowd of little blue men to carry her back to the House of Boxes.

White Man's Burden

—

Frank Sargeson

I T was a long road, that road up North, but I'd been told I'd find a pub there. I did. You may know the sort of pub. It sometimes has a notice up, FREE BEER HERE TOMORROW.

I found I knew the barman and I felt bucked when I saw him. When you're on the road and you see someone you know you feel that way. You can't explain it. I asked him how he was, and he said that he was a ball of muscle. I said it was a hole of a place. Oh boy, but it's a quiet dump, he said. All Dagoes. Do I have some long serves!

We talked and he pumped some air into a benzine lamp and it fizzed and lit up bright enough to blind you. Then I couldn't see out the window but I didn't mind that. The mudflats had looked too fat and juicy, and the hills had looked starved. Why, coming along the road I'd watched a cocky ploughing, and he was turning up yellow clay. If you ask me there's a hell of a lot too much of this land of hope and plenty like that.

I asked Bill if there weren't any *pakehas* and he said there were a few. I can't describe what they're like, he said, except they wouldn't wake up if . . . It was a good crack, but there's a law against putting such things in print.

We heard a car pull up and Bill said it would be only his third or fourth serve that day.

They came in, about six Maoris. They were the fleshy sort, their trousers held up by leather belts that finished with only about half an inch

50

of leather to spare. They asked for hard stuff. They asked me to have some too, and I did. They asked Bill what about him, but he said no. He told me he was keeping strictly off the hops. If you once went on the bust in a place like this it was good-bye McGinnis, he said.

A lot more Maoris came in and a few white chaps. Gosh, Bill was right. They were rough, rougher than the Maoris. Bill said that one of the Maoris wrote the best hand he'd ever seen. I noticed he spoke nicely too. He told me that at one time he was going to be a parson. They all started on hard stuff and went on to beer later. There wasn't a radio, but Bill put an H.M.V. portable on the counter and a pile of records, and they took turns in putting the records on. Puddin' Head Jones was popular, then someone wanted Clara Butt to sing Daddy, but Bill couldn't find the record so for a joke he put on Gipsy Smith singing one of those Blood and Fire hymns.

Talk, there was plenty of talk. You may know the sort of talk. And plenty of cigarettes too. They were all chain smokers. Sometimes they crooned with a crooner and did fox-trots.

Then a woman looked in the door. She gave me a nod. Then she caught Bill's eye and I caught her giving me another nod — a reverse one. Bill winked. He said that I was O.K. When the woman went I asked Bill how he knew I was O.K.

Well, you are, aren't you?

I suppose I am, I said.

A man's got to think first of his living.

I told him that was true enough, but a man had the feeling it was the devil's gospel all the same.

There was a young Maori who came and talked to me. He told me he made money ploughing for whoever would give him any ploughing to do. Then he'd go to town and blow his money in, usually at the races. He told me it made him sick to look at a race. When he'd put his money on he went and stood behind the tote. He liked the talkies too, he said. Joan Crawford was the best actress. If it showed her in bed you always got a better kick out of seeing her in bed than you did out of seeing anyone else in bed. Well, I told him that so far as I was concerned Joan Crawford was just a gangster's girl. Then he asked me if I had a sweetheart. He said he had a sweetheart. She lived in town, a *pakeha* girl. She was very good and very young, he said, but too dear.

While Bill went and had his supper the woman came and looked after the bar. She was a titian blonde and the lipstick she was using didn't match. She told me the Maoris were good customers, and when they'd spent all their money they didn't want you to let them go on drinking on credit like the Europeans do. And another thing, they *did* have a sense of refinement. Why, some evenings when a few *pakehas* she could name were down it wasn't safe for her to put her head outside the front door.

Before Bill came back about half a dozen Maoris had shouted her, and each time she had less than half a glass beer and the other half she put in out of a bottle that didn't have a label. Bill told me afterwards that it was squash. Oh, she was keen enough on the hops he said, but she was like that. Never missed a chance of making a bit.

I slept out in a shed that night but it was hard to get to sleep because the row in the bar came across the yard. At any rate I had Maoris on the brain. You see I was brought up in the South and never saw many Maoris. But I've seen the press photos of the Arawas turning out for Lord what's his name, and the pictures in the Art Gallery. And once I read a couple of books by a man called Elsdon Best.

Gosh, there's a great day coming for Abyssinia when civilisation gets properly going there.

The Totara Tree

Roderick Finlayson

P EOPLE came running from all directions wanting to know what all the fuss was about. 'Oho! it's crazy old Taranga perching like a crow in her tree because the Pakeha boss wants his men to cut it down,' Panapa explained, enjoying the joke hugely.

'What you say, cut it down? Cut the totara down?' echoed Uncle Tuna, anger and amazement wrinkling yet more his old wrinkled face. 'Cut Taranga down first!' he exclaimed. 'Every one knows that totara is Taranga's birth tree.'

Uncle Tuna was so old he claimed to remember the day Taranga's father had planted the young tree when the child was born. Nearly one hundred years ago, Uncle Tuna said. But many people doubted that he was quite as old as that. He always boasted so.

'Well it looks like they'll have to cut down both Taranga *and* her tree,' chuckled Panapa to the disgust of Uncle Tuna who disapproved of joking about matters of tapu.

'Can't the Pakeha bear the sight of one single tree without reaching for his axe?' Uncle Tuna demanded angrily. 'However this tree is tapu,' he added with an air of finality, 'so let the Pakeha go cut down his own weeds.' Uncle Tuna hated the Pakehas.

'Ae, why do they want to cut down Taranga's tree?' a puzzled woman asked.

'It's the wires,' Panapa explained loftily. 'The tree's right in the way of the new power wires they're taking up the valley. Ten thousand volts, ehoa! That's power, I tell you! A touch of that to her tail would soon make old Taranga spring out of her tree, ehoa,' Panapa added with impish delight and a sly dig in the ribs for old Uncle Tuna. The old man simply spat his contempt and stumped away.

'Oho!' gurgled Panapa, 'now just look at the big Pakeha boss down below dancing and cursing at mad old Taranga up the tree; and she doesn't know a single word and cares nothing at all!'

And indeed Taranga just sat up there smoking her pipe of evil-smelling torori. Now she turned her head away and spat slowly and deliberately on the ground. Then she fixed her old half-closed eyes on the horizon again. Aue! how those red-faced Pakehas down below there jabbered and shouted! Well, no matter.

Meanwhile a big crowd had collected near the shanty where Taranga lived with her grandson, in front of which grew Taranga's totara tree right on the narrow road that divided the straggling little hillside settlement from the river. Men lounged against old sheds and hung over sagging fences; women squatted in open doorways or strolled along the road with babies in shawls on their backs. The bolder children even came right up and made marks in the dust on the Inspector's big car with their grubby little fingers. The driver had to say to them: 'Hey, there, you! Keep away from the car.' And they hung their heads and pouted their lips and looked shyly at him with great sombre eyes.

But a minute later the kiddies were jigging with delight behind the Inspector's back. How splendid to see such a show — all the big Pakehas from town turned out to fight mad old Taranga perching in a tree! But she was a witch all right — like her father the tohunga. Maybe she'd just flap her black shawl like wings and give a cackle and turn into a bird and fly away. Or maybe she'd curse the Pakehas, and they'd all wither up like dry sticks before their eyes! Uncle Tuna said she could do even worse than that. However, the older children didn't believe that old witch stuff.

Now as long as the old woman sat unconcernedly smoking up the tree, and the Pakehas down below argued and appealed to her as unsuccessfully as appealing to Fate, the crowd thoroughly enjoyed the joke. But when the Inspector at last lost his temper and shouted to his men to pull the old woman down by force, the humour of the gathering changed. The women in the doorways shouted shrilly. One of them said, 'Go away, Pakeha, and bully city folk! We Maoris don't yet insult trees or old women!' The men on the fences began grumbling sullenly, and the younger fellows started to lounge over toward the Pakehas. Taranga's grandson, Taikehu, who had been chopping wood, had a big axe in his hand. Taranga may be mad but after all it was her birth tree. You couldn't just come along and cut down a tree like that. Ae, you could laugh your fill at the old woman perched among the branches like an old black crow, but it wasn't for a Pakeha to come talking about pulling her down and destroying her tree. That smart man had better look out.

The Inspector evidently thought so too. He made a sign to dismiss the linesmen who were waiting with ladders and axes and ropes and saws to cut the tree down. Then he got into his big car, tight-lipped with rage. 'Hey, look out there, you kids!' the driver shouted. And away went the Pakehas amid a stench of burnt benzine, leaving Taranga so far victorious.

'They'll be back tomorrow with the police all right and drag old Taranga down by a leg,' said Panapa gloatingly. 'She'll have no chance with the police. But by korry! I'll laugh to see the first policeman to sample her claws.'

'Oho, they'll be back with soljers,' chanted the kiddies in great excitement. 'They'll come with machine guns and go r-r-r-r- at old Taranga, but she'll just swallow the bullets!'

'Shut up, you kids,' Panapa commanded.

But somehow the excitement of the besieging of Taranga in her tree had spread like wildfire through the usually sleepy little settlement. The young bloods talked about preparing a hot welcome for the Pakehas tomorrow. Uncle Tuna encouraged them. A pretty state of affairs, he said, if a tapu tree could be desecrated by mere busybodies. The young men of his day knew better how to deal with such affairs. He remembered well how he himself had once tomahawked a Pakeha who broke the tapu of a burial ground. If people had listened to him long ago all the Pakehas would have been put in their place, under the deep sea — shark food! said Uncle Tuna ferociously. But the people were weary of Uncle Tuna's many exploits, and they didn't stop to listen. Even the youngsters nowadays merely remarked: 'oh, yeah,' when the old man harangued them.

Yet already the men were dancing half-humorous hakas around the totara tree. A fat woman with rolling eyes and a long tongue encouraged them. Everyone roared with laughter when she tripped in her long red skirts and fell bouncingly in the road. It was taken for granted now that they would make a night of it. Work was forgotten, and everyone gathered about Taranga's place. Taranga still waited quietly in the tree.

Panapa disappeared as night drew near but he soon returned with a barrel of home-brew on a sledge to enliven the occasion. That soon warmed things up, and the fun became fast and more furious. They gathered dry scrub and made bonfires to light the scene. They told Taranga not to leave her look-out, and they sent up baskets of food and drink to her; but she wouldn't touch bite nor sup. She alone of all the crowd was now calm and dignified. The men were dancing mad hakas armed with axes, knives and old taiahas. Someone kept firing a shot-gun till the cartridges gave out. Panapa's barrel of home-brew was getting low too, and Panapa just sat there propped against it and laughed and laughed; men and women alike boasted what they'd do with the Pakehas tomorrow. Old Uncle Tuna was disgusted with the whole business though. That was no way to fight the Pakeha, he said; that was the Pakeha's own ruination. He stood up by the meeting-house and harangued the mob, but no one listened to him.

The children were screeching with delight and racing around the bonfires like brown demons. They were throwing fire-sticks about here there and everywhere. So it's no wonder the scrub caught fire, and Taikehu's house beside the tree was ablaze before anybody noticed it. Heaven help us, but there was confusion then! Taikehu rushed in to try to save his best clothes. But he only got out with his old overcoat and a broken gramophone before the flames roared up through the roof. Some men started beating out the scrub with their axes and sticks. Others ran to the river for water. Uncle Tuna capered about urging the men to save the totara tree from the flames. Fancy wasting his breath preaching against the Pakeha, he cried. Trust this senseless generation of Maoris to work their own destruction, he sneered.

It seemed poor old Taranga was forgotten for the moment. Till a woman yelled at Taikehu, 'What you doing there with your old rags, you fool? Look alive and get the old woman out of the tree.' Then she ran to the tree and called, 'Eh there, Taranga, don't be mad. Come down quick, old mother!'

But Taranga made no move.

Between the woman and Taikehu and some others, they got Taranga down. She looked to be still lost in meditation. But she was quite dead.

'Aue! she must have been dead a *long* time — she's quite cold and stiff,' Taikehu exclaimed. 'So it couldn't be the fright of the fire that killed her.'

'Fright!' jeered Uncle Tuna. 'I tell you, pothead, a woman who loaded rifles for me under the cannon shells of the Pakeha isn't likely to die of fright at a rubbish fire.' He cast a despising glance at the smoking ruins of Taikehu's shanty. 'No! but I tell you what she died of,' Uncle Tuna exclaimed. 'Taranga was just sick to death of you and your Pakeha ways. Sick to death!' The old man spat on the ground and turned his back on Taikehu and Panapa and their companions.

Meanwhile the wind had changed, and the men had beaten out the scrub fire, and the totara tree was saved. The fire and the old woman's strange death and Uncle Tuna's harsh words had sobered everybody by now, and the mood of the gathering changed from its former frenzy to melancholy and a kind of superstitious awe. Already some women had started to wail at the meeting-house where Taranga had been carried. Arrangements would have to be made for the tangi.

'Come here, Taikehu,' Uncle Tuna commanded. 'I have to show you where you must bury Taranga.'

Well, the Inspector had the grace to keep away while the tangi was on. Or rather Sergeant O'Connor, the chief of the local police and a good friend of Taranga's people, advised the Inspector not to meddle till it was over. 'A tangi or a wake, sure it's just as sad and holy,' he said. 'Now I advise you, don't interfere till they've finished.'

But when the Inspector did go out to the settlement afterwards — well! Panapa gloatingly told the story in the pub in town later. 'O boy,' he said; 'you should have heard what plurry Mr. Inspector called Sergeant

O'Connor when he found out they'd buried the old woman right under the roots of the plurry tree! I think O'Connor like the joke though. When the Inspector finish cursing, O'Connor say to him, "Sure the situation's still unchanged then. Taranga's still in her tree." '

Well, the power lines were delayed more than ever, and in time this strange state of affairs was even mentioned in the Houses of Parliament, and the Maori members declared the Maoris' utter refusal to permit the desecration of burial places, and the Pakeha members all applauded these fine orations. So the Power Board was brought to the pass at last of having to build a special concrete foundation for the poles in the river bed so that the wires could be carried clear of Taranga's tree.

'Oho!' Panapa chuckles, telling the story to strangers who stop to look at the tomb beneath the totara on the roadside. 'Taranga dead protects her tree much better than Taranga alive. Py korry she cost the Pakeha thousands *and* thousands of pounds I guess!'

The Little Bridge
—

Robin Hyde

TE Kawhaia put down his copy of the new history of the Maori wars and said with a dry smile, 'This is excellent; so fairly told.'

'Why shouldn't we tell things fairly?' I demanded, having reason to suspect Te Kawhaia's dry smile.

For Te Kawhaia is the last of the seriously anti-English chiefs. He speaks beautiful mellow English, is a hundred years old, some say, and can be a very excellent host. His face is like the bark of a tree, for its brown skin and its tiny wrinkles and lines, and his eyes are black, with that peculiar ruby light behind them which startles white people. Do not take him for a fermenter of petty wars, a quarreller with health inspectors and school teachers. He is against the English as a man may be against earthquakes and original sin, without hope of remedy. But the old lost battle-cries are remembered in his heart.

'The most curious and subtle thing about the English,' said Te Kawhaia, 'is their friendliness to the people they have just conquered, or propose to conquer.

'See, now. An English resident lives among head-hunters in some strange, swampy archipelago which you'd think of no use, even to an Englishman. Perhaps he's killed. In any case, that place sows the seeds of death in his body. But if, by the power of the law and a revolver, he proves to the natives that head-hunting must be done in a strictly private way, he at once writes a book, saying what magnificent fellows his savages are, and how, though in days of dark ignorance they had an amiable little weakness for heads, they shuddered at the bare idea the moment someone taught them better.

'And the British trusted their sepoys an hour before the rising — and an hour after the rising was over — and look! All through this quaint book there are stories of Maori gallantry, Maori wit, Maori friendship to the British. Long paragraphs about the stalwart citizens the Maoris will make when properly trained — all very true, but it's an odd point of view for a conqueror.

'I don't believe, though, that it's stupid. It's subtle. You say to your natives, "Every day and in every way you are getting better and better," and the poor devils do. You don't say, "I saw a horde of painted demons shaking greenstone merés in their hands and stamping the earth with their feet. They struck terror of old and foreign things into my heart." You say, "I saw a splendid, courteous, knightly fighter." '

'But, Te Kawhaia, whatever your battle songs and battle-axes may have been, there was genuine friendship between Maori and Britisher from the start.'

'Ah, yes,' admitted Te Kawhaia. 'There was friendship, as you say, between our tribes and the men of the ships that came out of the rising moon. But I disapproved of it. In those days, one had power to make one's disapproval rather forcible.

'There was a woman in my village — her name in your language would be "Twilight Star" — who had friendship with a pakeha. The circumstances were peculiar. A small ship — it came from Sydney, I believe — touched against our coast. We, as you know, were the people of the sacred mountain. For two days we feasted them well and consulted the spirit of the mountain, intended on the third day to kill and eat them. But, warned by the white man's atua, they set sail in the darkness of the second night, our village losing besides a dozen maidens who had gone aboard the ship to entertain them and in the hope of getting many beautiful gifts.

'In a little while it became known that the atua of the white man's ship had stayed behind and haunted the village, more particularly the whare of Twilight Star, who dwelt with her mother, a woman both deaf and blind. The atua, said a woman who had seen him, was very splendid, tall and wearing a black shirt, torn open from a throat white and strong as marble. None saw him, but by night, but I am told he had the build of a warrior.

'In the end I saw him myself, entering the whare of Twilight Star. Creeping close, I pressed my face against the walls of dry tea-tree, and through a crevice saw enough to convince me that this atua was no spirit at all, but a man with hair like fine gold, and straight, laughing lips, who lay with his head in Twilight Star's lap. And the old woman, deaf and blind, knew nothing of this, but sat against the small red fire, singing and crooning songs that had charmed many in the days of her youth.

'My men, two of them, waited for the white man on the next night, and stood at his side as he came out of the whare with his blue eyes sleepy and full of content. A torch shone upon him, and at that signal he died quickly, with only one cry, which brought Twilight Star to the door of her house, the red flax flowers which he had brought her tangled in her hair. She stood there, that woman, tall and straight as a young kauri-tree, and watched me, eyes burning with a hatred I could understand. Perhaps she thought she, too, would die, and with bare feet follow this man to his reinga, but I had quarrel only with the whites. So we left her there in the moonlight, standing with silent lips, and the white man had no sign of mourning, but that strange and ancient chant of that blind woman who sat by the fire.

'When the rata was red along the hills, and all the forest of the sacred mountain filled with the damp, rotting scents of autumn, a child was born to Twilight Star. And as she lay on the floor of the whare she whispered the name, "David, David!"

'So that name the child was given, though since I have heard that she did wrong, for in the white man's tongue this is the name of a man and a king. And the child was only a girl.

'It was not long before Twilight Star, with all her dark, damp hair loose about her, smiled and, closing her eyes, lay still. So the child David was laid in the arms of the old blind woman, who, feeling its body with her withered hands, rose up, and in a strange voice cried words of prophecy. The child, said she, would bend the pride of a chief, and, feeling again the warmth and softness of the babe, the days of her motherhood came back to her and great tears ran down her face.

'She only of the tribe did not know that the child was the daughter of an enemy race. If I had so chosen, the babe would have been no more than a slave, if indeed the tohunga had not offered her as a sacrifice to the tall gods that dwelt in the mountains. But she was little and white as a flower, or as the fairy people themselves, and from the day when first she laughed, showing no fear of her father's slayer, I loved her at once, as I loved her mother.

'So if there were a queen in the tribe it was she, and my men brought her presents of greenstone and mako, shark's teeth, and white feathers for a cloak. The old tohunga taught her, at my will, learning more suitable for a priestess than for a lowly-born child; and queen in truth she might have been, for I, who had once thought to make the mother my wife, waited now for the daughter.

'There were strange times for our race: treaties and new cities of wood that sprang up by the blue, lonely seas, beggary for the chiefs that had been old and proud, war first — but that is no part of the story — and then a kind of peace, so precarious that in no town could one walk without seeing the uniform of soldiers.

'Yes, now there was friendship between white men and brown; and how, that great atua of yours may know, but some of the chiefs, coming to learn the wisdom of the pakeha that they might use it as a sword against him, were captured themselves by this wisdom, this bright, childish sword. They looked with new eyes and saw a Maori race who would grow rich in playing with the white man's toys, and who would have a share in a wider empire than this green narrow land; who would be safe in peace and terrible in war.

'Safety. Yes, I think that was their chief desire, for none trusted his neighbour and each believed that if he turned to the white man his lands would be protected, and perhaps added to by those of the defiant.

'And while this went on (and I gave feasts to the scarlet uniforms) a movement grew up from the heart of the Maori race. It was our last hope, and the music of it had whispered in our reeds. "Hear!" it said. "Fear one another no more! You have a common danger.

' "Fight one another no more! There is one enemy. Strike no more for your little seats of chieftainship! Raise up one throne, from which the whole of the Maori world may be governed and directed.

' "Make you a king's head, to give life to the Maori body." In the Waikato there was first talk of a king, but here it was never at home. In the heart of the Urewera — that part which now you call the King Country — there the fortresses were built at last, fortresses hollowed in carved wood, and canoes sped down the river on king's business, and even from the south, from the island of greenstone, came the old men who could remember the day when the first pakeha came, and how he died. Under our sacred mountain I still lived, I and all my people, for they worship this tall, snow-capped splendour, calling it their Father. But we were in constant touch with the king's party, and day and night the canoes waited, ready to take us to these last fortresses. I entertained many of your soldiers — yes, and did not let the tohunga, as he wished, put too much bitter tutu in their wine. From these, as from the traders, I had many guns and much ammunition. They were simple young men, as tall as the spears of warriors, and with the blue eyes of the children of the sea. I hated them, but quietly, until one day David spoke to me in the English tongue. She was a child still, David, with hair pale gold, as the noon sunshine, and the dark eyes of her mother set in a pointed face. No maiden of the tribe could sing with a sweeter voice or dance more quickly than she danced with her naked feet; and she danced now, a dance as little and graceful as the shadows, and sang a laughing song of the English fields.

'I said to her, "Who is your teacher, maiden?" And she replied: "A guest of yours, Te Kawhaia. A young soldier, one of the redcoats; and he wears high black boots and walks so — with a sword clanking at one side, and cannot dance, and stumbles over our speech!"

'But her laughing eyes grew soft and very pensive. "He is very fair, Te Kawhaia."

'Red were the pohutukawas, red as if a sudden flame had leapt among their branches, red the honey-filled cups of the drooping flax flowers. The last snows melted on the head of our father mountain, and the mists walked there in the evenings like tender spirits. But to my people I said, "The canoes go. We leave our mountain for ever, until at last this country shall be truly our own." And in a dim blue twilight, under hanging branches, the canoes gathered on the river. There was weeping and the waiata of farewell. An old woman, she who held the child David in her arms, gave herself as sacrifice that the atuas might bless our journey.

'But I walked through the empty village, I and six of my warriors, and put torches to the walls of the whares, till the flames blazed up like long red hair. It was a warning to the country and to the white man that all he would ever take of the Maori world would be ashes.

'In the bottom of my canoe, her wrists bound with flax, lay the girl David, flax flowers in her hair and dress that perhaps a young soldier had plucked for her on some happy walk through the forest. She was exhausted, for she had struggled against the warriors, and her eyes were closed, making her face like the face of a beautiful weary child.

'I had been gentle enough with her at first, asking her what fortune her mother had of the white race, but she whispered. "Murderer!" for all that I had spared her young soldier, whom I might easily enough have trapped on the forest road.

'Moonrise and moonset we saw along the river; and leaving the canoes, we came at last into the paths that led to the mountains, where all things had been made ready. We lived there, not in any pah, but in the caves of the living stone, which even our tohunga feared for the devils that inhabited them.

'Even today, this country is left alone. You say it is because the soil is too poor for your sad little farms to thrust their roots into it. But that is not all. It is a haunted land — haunted by the spirit of a brown man who speaks none but the ancient tongue, and makes old music on the flutes that are no longer fashioned by the carver. It is haunted by the youth of such men as myself, pakeha, and by the memories of the old men who watched the first of you die. None might come into my fortress from before, except by a little swinging bridge of brushwood, lashed with flax, that might very easily be broken down before an advancing enemy. And we dwelt here until the little girl David grew as pale as a fading flower, and the hearts of the tribe sickened for fear of the devils and for memory of the light on their own mountain. But men of many tribes sent their greeting to me, and in the evening, in the great caverns, the tohunga would tell of the ancient glories and deeds of the people, until they shook the earth in their war-dance.

'It was after one of those assemblies, pakeha, that I went to my own place, which was a deep narrow cavern hollowed in the rocks, and heard a breathing in the darkness. Then, as I stood listening, something cold and round pressed against my shoulder, and, in the hard English which I so fortunately understood, a voice said, "Don't move or you're dead." I kept quite still and asked very civilly if I might call for lights.

'"Call for what you like!" said the savage voice, and at my command the yellow torches were brought.

'It was really a very pretty situation. There, with his back against the wall, stood my young soldier, his scarlet coat grey and tattered, his feet absolutely bare and, I should say, cut to pieces by the rocks, his face old and lined. I admired him very much. How he had tracked us God knows. A red flower here from David's hair, I suppose, a white feather there from her cloak; or, more likely, some English-glamoured tribe had helped him.

'The main point was that a spear thrown at him would transfix myself. And if I moved he would certainly shoot, for the blue boyish eyes held hatred and death.

'"Where's David?" he asked. I nodded to one at the door, and the girl was brought in.

'"Not hurt, David?" whispered that strange, hoarse voice; and the girl shook her head.

'"Te Kawhaia," said the young man steadily, "I know you to be a devil, and a man of your word. Swear to me that David and I can go untouched by you or any of your tribe and I'll keep the secret of your fort. I'm a deserter, anyhow, liable to be shot on sight. We'll go away and live peaceably — but if you don't, I'll get you now and try to shoot the girl afterwards."

'"You must give me time to think," I replied, staring over his head at the dark-eyed tohunga. And presently those eyes smiled. The tohunga slipped away.

'David came and stood beside the boy. Somehow, in spite of her fair skin I saw her mother in her eyes. They knew well enough that Te Kawhaia was not beaten. Yet Te Kawhaia stood helpless before his tribe. As the old woman had foretold, she had bent the pride of the chief.

'Presently I saw that the tohunga had returned.

'I spoke then. "You are free to go," I said. "No man will lay hands upon you."

'The young man bowed gravely.

' "David," I said, "will you not stay with your mother's people?" But she shook her head — I have always thought that she knew, but she shook her head.

'They went out into the darkness, and the people parted gently to let them through. Then I nodded to the sighing women; they began to chant a farewell. It was very weird and sad, echoing through that savage torchlit place. The young man had his arm round David's waist, and she looked back and smiled as they stepped out on the little bridge. Then, at the third step, the bridge parted, for the tohunga had cut the flax lashings, and Te Kawhaia's word was saved, and also his pride.

'But the love of Te Kawhaia was lost. Aye! The women of those days! They had lustrous eyes and singing voices, and they come no more.

'The young men whose war-dance shook the earth, they also are gone. You have only the ashes of our world, pakeha.'

The Whare

—

Douglas Stewart

T was six months since those fleas had tasted anything but Maori. They leaped at a white skin like a shoal of herrings at a loaf of bread. They came from the dust under the raupo mats and they were there in millions. Every ten minutes or so, when the irritation became unendurable, you could roll up your trousers and scrape them off like sand or bid-a-bid seeds. But attacking them was a waste of time, and unless a particularly savage pang forced you into action, you just sat and let yourself be devoured.

The old chief and his wife, with their hard, leathery skins, hardly seemed to notice them. Sometimes when the woman saw that I was in trouble she would say, 'Ah! You got te flea, eh?' and she would promise to boil a kerosene tin of water, shift the mats and scald the brutes to death. 'T'ose flea! We boil 'em, t'at te way to fix 'em!' If the chief on some rare occasion, sitting by the open fire in the whare at night, felt a pinprick through his hide, he said 'Flea! Bitem!' in a tone of pleased discovery. He took a pride in his fleas. Their presence cheered him, their habits interested him, and their prowess delighted him. They were his *lares et penates*, or the flocks and herds of a patriarch.

Maybe I exaggerate the importance of the fleas. In the long run, for there were processes of the mind more powerful than those ridiculous irritations of the flesh, I should probably have come to the same decision without their prompting. But I don't want memory, always a romantic, to sentimentalize them out of existence. They did force a decision.

I drifted into the Maori settlement with the greatest simplicity. I was trudging along the road in the sunny midday, heading north, when a tall native, riding bareback on an old grey mare, came cantering up the road behind me. He stopped short beside me, the mare grunting with relief and indignation, and said, 'You've got a heavy swag, Jack. Carry it for you?'

The morning seemed sunnier after that. It was good to be able to walk freely. The road wound along a ridge from which the ragged country, broken into gullies and patchworked with leaden tea-tree and an occasional acre of ploughed land or yellowish grass, fell with the slow sweep of a glacier into the shallow harbour of Kaipara. The water, so far away, had lost its quick sparkle and become some new element more like metal, a sheet of silvery tinfoil among the gigantic hills. It was hard desolate country, but it couldn't depress you when the sun was shining on the red clay cuttings and the mare's hooves were clip-clopping on the stones, and you had nothing to do but walk along the road and look at things.

The Maori, who seemed to be about thirty-five years old, was slim and sombre. He spoke little, and appeared to be turning something over in his mind. At last he said, 'My father will give you some lunch.'

I said 'Good!' and then wished I hadn't, for the monosyllable might have sounded like pidgin-English, and his own was perfect. He had probably been to one of the Maori colleges and then, as most of his people do, come back to the pa.

We plodded on until we caught sight of a tumble-down whare standing among the rushes of an upland swamp on a plateau above the harbour. 'That's my place,' said the horseman. 'You can sleep there if you like, have a rest for a day or two. I don't live there now. It's pretty rough,' he added.

He wasn't very enthusiastic. Afterwards I found out that various swaggies in the past had abused the hospitality of the little tribe, and I came to the conclusion that the young Maori resented it and that, although the tradition of welcome to the stranger was too strong for him to break, maybe his children would rebel against it.

The whare, like all deserted homes, was dirty and forlorn. The broken iron bedstead, the torn mats, the cooking-pot lying on its side in the dust, the rain-sodden, long-dead ashes, the cobwebs and the rat-droppings — they were the apparatus of ghosts. Behind the building was the Maori's inevitable totem — a broken-down limousine, rusting in the grass. The Maori dropped my swag and we went back to the road and up to the settlement on the hill-side.

Half a dozen Maoris, squatting on the grass outside one of the whares, stared at us in good-humoured curiosity. They were all eating and drinking. One of the young fellows said something in Maori to a squat, dumpy girl, and she laughed. They went on eating.

The Maori took me to the whare door and introduced me to his father and mother, chief and chieftainess of the settlement. The woman, bent and skinny and weather-beaten like a twist of a withered grass, smiled a welcome. From her beaked nose her face fell away in a landslide of wrinkles to a toothless mouth, achieving some dignity again in a firm, tattooed chin. The old man had the stamp of aristocracy both in manners and features. His hair and moustache were grey, his brown eyes clear, his cheeks smooth. But for his colouring and his thick lower lip he could have passed for a European.

'Eh, Jack,' he said, 'you come a long way?'

'From Taranaki,' I told him.

'Eh, Tara-naki,' he drawled in soft amazement, as if I had come from the moon. His geography was vague. He had been to Auckland, though. He and the old woman had stayed with relations in the city — probably at that squalid settlement by the blue harbour — for several months, and then come back to the kumara patch and the whare. I imagined them labouring along Queen Street, staring in wonder and delight at the shops and the traffic. It would be like a visit to a foreign country.

The woman came out of the darkness of the whare with a mug of tea and a place piled with pipis and something which looked like green string and which I was told was boiled watercress.

'You like te pipi?'

'Kapai!'

'Kapai!' She laughed. There was no fear of insulting her by using pidgin-English. Her pakeha vocabulary was small, and you had to speak simply and slowly to make her understand. She treated the barrier of tongues as a joke laughing with pleasure when she could comprehend and with amusement when she couldn't. Her conversation was full of expressive 'what-you-callums'.

Some sort of council-of-war, which I sensed concerned me, went on while I was negotiating the shellfish and the boiled watercress (which tasted like barbed wire), and when it was over the young Maori went off on the mare and the old man said, 'You stay wit' me, eh, Jack? T'at other place no good. You stay here wit' me. The missus make you a bed in te wharepuni.'

That was better. The deserted whare would have given you the horrors. Only I had yet to meet the fleas.

That first night, sitting around the fire with the two old Maoris, I found everything, even the fleas, strange and exhilarating. It was an open fire built on the dust in a sort of alcove at one end of the whare, and the smoke, guided by the corrugated-iron walls of the alcove, found an uncertain track to a hole in the roof. Strips of shark meat and bunches of reddish corncobs hung on the walls, drying in the heat and collecting the savour of smoke and smuts. The firelight danced across the room, colouring the far wall and giving a touch of mystery to the Maoris' sleeping-place — a continuation of the main room, screened by a wall of mats. The narrow entrance and the black interior made it look like a cave. The room where we sat was full of moving shadows, with highlights glowing on the bare table and the wooden form beside it, and gleaming on a shelf of chipped crockery. Near the fire stood a kerosene tin of pipis. A big enamel teapot rested at the edge of the embers and an iron kettle swung over the flames.

We drank many cups of tea, ate pipis and smoked. The teapot, steaming by the fire day after day, was never emptied. When the black juice ran low, the old man would throw in a handful of tea-leaves and pour in boiling water.

The woman, washing dishes, mixing a damper or peeling kumaras, was always busy in a leisurely mechanical way. Sometimes, in a cracked voice, she sang a fragment of a Maori song. I asked her to sing the cradle song 'Hine e Hine' for me, and she was pleased, and sang the sweet air through. But she sang very badly. I talked to her about bird-voiced Ana Hato at Rotorua. She made a show of interest, but it was only her politeness. She wanted to peel the kumaras and sing to herself in her cracked voice and not to talk. I remembered the grey Tuwehirangi at Manutahi, reputed to be one hundred and fifteen years old, who would simply walk away when a white man talked to her. She wasn't interested. The old Maori women like to gossip with each other.

The old man, brightening at the mention of Rotorua, told me he had a cousin there. It was a peg to hang a conversation on, but the conversation wouldn't follow. There was no common ground on which we could meet, and, worse, no common background where the pakeha's way of thought could have commerce with the Maori's. Instead of asking him about the ancient legends of his race, I fell back on the fleas. We had them in common, anyhow.

When it came to supper-time, he said, 'You rest tomorrow, Jack. You done up. You don't do anyt'ing tomorrow and t'en we see. Maybe you stay wit' us for a while.'

He'd already begun to say that word 'Jack' in a different tone. At first, especially with the young Maori, it was the familiar, faintly contemptuous nickname that would be fastened on a stray dog and a swaggie alike, and I had been inclined to resent it. Now it had become my name, not my nickname.

He led me over to the meeting-house, a long, low, gusty barn of a building where the old woman, by piling mats on an iron bedstead, had made me a sleeping-place. A cloud of sparrows stormed from the rafters, chirping in alarm. When the old man had gone, I lifted one of the mats and saw that here, too, the livestock abounded. There was nothing to be done about it; I lay down on the mats. Rats began to squeak and rustle and thump about the floor, and cautiously in twos and threes the sparrows came back.

Tired, and feeling security in the roof and the bed despite the rats and sparrows, I slept that night.

The next night was harder. I felt a bit foolish and out of place to be living with the Maoris, and lay awake thinking things over. My bloodthirsty bed-fellows made sleep impossible. In the early hours of the morning I put on an overcoat and sat out on the hill-side, looking at the harbour and waiting for daylight. The landscape had the dramatic, electric stillness of night, as if the hills as well as the sweet-scented moonlit tea-tree, stretching for miles, had awakened into some secret life quite different from their torpor in the daylight. The harbour, too, was brighter by moonlight than sunlight, a wash of pure silver around the dark bases of the ranges. A faint rushing sound might have been air dragging across the valleys, or the waves breaking on the coast, a long way off. I thought of Auckland asleep, and the two old Maoris asleep on the mats in the cubby-hole at the end of their whare, so remote from the city, lapped in this tranquillity, as self-sufficient as the fallow deer on the ridges beyond Wanganui or the wild drake and his mate that nested on the cliff above the Waingongora at home.

I had loafed all day. The old man disappeared and came back in the evening and gave me a tin of tobacco he had bought for me at the store. I didn't want to take it, but couldn't refuse for fear of offending him. In the whare at night, breaking one of his long silences, he told me about the white woman — God knows who she was, and how poverty-stricken or how mad she was to be tramping the lonely road through the tea-tree — who had stayed at the pa all through the spring, and about a white man who had stayed for six months and then slipped away in the night, stealing their blankets and an axe.

'He need 'em, or else he wouldn't take 'em,' the Maori woman said.

'Aye, t'at orright,' the old man agreed. 'If he want 'em he can have 'em. He can come back again if he want to, t'at one.'

I began to understand something of Maori hospitality and of their outlook on life, simple but realistic, tolerant but not sentimental. It arose partly from the fact that understanding was easier than anger. They were happy and didn't want their happiness to be disturbed by the feeling that they had been let down.

It became obvious that they were expecting me to stay for a long time. They were hinting at that by telling me about the others. I had a notion they liked having a pet white man about the place. It satisfied their religious instincts in a way as well as their good nature. You were at once a homeless dog to be comforted, a fabulous animal to wonder at, and a god to be propitiated. Owning you enhanced the chief's prestige in the pa, and gave the old couple something different to do, something different to talk about.

There was no effort of adjustment needed to settle into the life. You ate and slept and scratched and from time to time said something, not so much for its meaning but as a token of friendship. You said something to the old woman, or she said something to you, in the comradely way you'd talk to a dog you were fond of. The response was the same — a tail wagged in the mind.

On the second day I helped the tribe to store the kumaras for the winter. They gave me a black stallion to ride — not, unfortunately, a great proud snorting beast with a fiery eye and a flowing mane, but a typical product of Maori horse-breeding, a dusty, ragged, somnambulistic runt — and I made repeated trips from the whare to the field across the road where the women were digging the earthy red-purple sweet-potatoes. Taking their time about it, grubbing in the earth with their hands, they'd fill a sack and lift it up to me while I sat on the stallion. They cracked jokes to each other in Maori and laughed a lot.

The men had a pit dug at the back of the whare, lined with fern leaves. They tipped the kumaras into the pit and, when there was a fair-sized mound, laid more fern leaves around the sides and on top, then covered the pile with clay. It was easy work, very pleasant in the light May sunshine. The men smoked and lazed between trips. Nobody hurried. The little stallion was the only one tired enough to feel relieved when I brought the last load home in the dark and sent him off into the tea-tree with a smack on the rump.

Both the Maoris were sympathetic about the fleas that night. They would 'get te boiling water and kill 'em all for sure' one day — tomorrow. It wouldn't be long till the frosts came, and they weren't so bad then.

The futile promises were a bit irritating; the fleas were maddening. I'd get up and stamp about the room for relief, then sit down beside the old man and stare at the fire again. When the fleas had drunk their fill and were sleeping it off, there was something curiously attractive about the whare, especially one night when it rained and the big drops fell hissing into the fire. You thought of those miles of lonely wet hills, and it was good to be indoors. We sat for hours, it seemed, without talking, listening to the rain hammering on the iron roof. It drove us closer together, wove us into a primitive human companionship — three against the storm. I imagined the old couple sitting together by the fire year after year, and saw myself with them, staring at the flames interminably, not talking and not thinking, sunk in a dark tide of physical sympathy, with somewhere in the chasms of the mind a vague sadness. There was a touch of night-mare about the vision and afterwards it haunted me.

That wet night the woman, grinning, asked me, 'You got a girl, eh? You sad. You got a girl somewhere, a long way away? You leave te girl behind and forget her now?'

'Yes,' I told her. 'I've got a girl. She's a long way away.'

'Maybe you get te Maori girl, eh? How you like te Maori wife?'

Then she told me there was to be a dance at the meeting-house on the Saturday. 'You meet te nice girl at te dance. Plenty wahine!'

When I was alone with the rats and the sparrows, with the feeble light of the candle emphasizing the cavernous gloom of the wharepuni, I began to see that the woman had been testing me out. The old man that day had bought me another tin of tobacco and broached a great scheme whereby we were going to earn twelve pounds between us cutting rushes for a pakeha farmer down the road. Before the job started, we were to go down to the harbour and get in a store of pipis from the mud-flats. He was including me in all his plans as a matter of course. I had come to stay.

'You not want to go, eh? You stay here as long as you like. You stay wit' us. You not want to go away.'

I didn't work the next day. I felt restless and went for a walk along the road. A farmer — perhaps the one for whom we were to cut the rushes — saw me leaning over a bridge and had a yarn. He said if I registered on the unemployed he'd give me a job, with five bob a week added to the Government subsidy. I told him I'd think it over.

I was thinking everything over, and thinking with a queer urgency, almost panic, in the whare that night.

'Tomorrow we get te pipi.'

'We cut te rushes, contrac' for a fortnight; make twelve poun'.'

'Plenty nice Maori girl come on Saturday.'

'You not want to go away.'

Well, it would be interesting getting the pipis. I'd often watched the Maoris wading in shallow waters and reaching into the blue mud for the shell-fish, and it would be good to help them. I wouldn't mind rush-cutting, either. That would be something new and it ought to be pleasant as scything the ragwort at Whangamomona. As for a Maori girl, the ukuleles and steel guitars and the rattle-trap piano all going like mad and the young bucks shouting the choruses — the way I'd often seen them — good!

Or would it be? Wouldn't you be isolated, mooching about on your own between dances, a stranger at the party? Maybe they'd be a bit antagonistic; certainly they'd be curious. Even if they gave you a good time and you joined in the singing, you'd be acting a part. You wouldn't belong.

'How you like te Maori wife, eh, Jack?'

I looked at the old couple nodding by the fire, the light on their dark faces. What did I really know about them? What went on in those secretive Maori minds? They weren't animals. They had their own thoughts, based on a conception of life beyond my understanding. What possible communion could there be between the white man and the native? The memory of that deep, mindless sympathy when we sat quietly by the fire on the wet night was uncannily disturbing, horrible. The friendly little whare was a prison.

'T'at flea! Tomorrow I kill te lot of 'em.'

When I went to bed they bit like devils. It was going to be a long, restless night. I thought of the Maoris' incredible kindliness. What lovable people they were! But I saw how their generosity was binding me to them. 'Tomorrow we get te pipis.' 'Next week we cut te rushes.' Next month, next year ——

After a while I climbed out of bed and wrote a note.

Thank you for being so good to me. I hope I can repay you some day. I'm sorry to go away like this without saying good-bye. I hope you'll understand; it's just that I have to be moving on. Don't think I'm not grateful.

JACK.

Feeling as guilty as if I'd been the swaggie who stole the blankets, I packed my swag and crept out of the whare. There was a full moon, and the old mysterious enchantment in the vast hills and the tea-tree. Along the ridge above the glitter of the harbour, the road was white. I could have shouted for joy at the way it ran over the rise and disappeared into the country I'd never seen.

I walked hard all night, half expecting to see the young Maori come galloping after me on the indignant grey mare and force me to go back to the pa for fear of hurting his feelings.

Hinemoa

—

Annie Wright

S HE was a child of the wilds, born when nature was in the making, and absorbing all her instincts from the primitive. As a babe she crept under the tree ferns, screamed to the music of the tuis, slept and awoke to their voices, and knew no other playmates but the wild creatures of the bush. Offspring of a white man and a primitive woman, she was endowed with a fairer skin than the mother who clasped her to her fond breast — she who crooned lullabies in the twilight, washed, clothed and fed her daughter in her own simplicity, scattered the blossoms of a loving spirit, and asked for nothing in return.

In this atmosphere Hinemoa grew up. Her father viewed her with somewhat mixed feelings. What, he asked in his reflective moments, was his duty towards her? This winsome little bundle of humanity, this puzzling mixture of happiness and pathos, with those melting, liquid-brown eyes that faced him so steadfast and enquiring — somewhere, he supposed, she would find her niche in the scheme of things.

Meanwhile matters could rest where they were. The mother taught her the little that she knew and left nature to do the rest. In the clearing amid the bush where they had built the semblance of a house, called in native language a whare, her father — a rolling stone in search of adventure — had come, breaking away from the ties of his original home. Fate chanced to throw him in with a party of romantic beings to whose dusky beauty he fell a willing and irresponsible victim, and one who soon found himself in bondage. For facts became history with the birth of a little daughter, and a new strand was added to the web of fate.

Conscience, in the shape of memories of his own mother, kept the white man uneasy in idle moments. What would she and all the rest of his relatives think of the position? Possibly they would throw up their hands in amazement as the truth burst upon them. Then after a welter of criticism, good and bad, they would decide among themselves that it was only what might be expected, and in this case the rolling stone had gathered his moss and must now sleep on it.

Hinemoa among the sheep and cows that they had slowly acquired grew into a being of rare beauty. In the nearby stream she paddled, bathed and gazed at her reflection in the still waters. Nourished chiefly on milk, nature's berries and the delightful viands of the virgin bush, she blossomed like the pohutukawa. Hers was a rosy red complexion surrounded by a framework of black hair. Hers was the mind unspotted by association with evil things.

Often in the twilight or the lotus pageantry of moonlight she would ramble among the tree-ferns singing little melodies that her mother sang, or some old ballad that on rare occasions she caught her father singing. Often she would amalgamate the two forms of speech, gaining a quaint effect from her efforts.

Finally the time came when she must have some kind of schooling. To her mother it did not matter whether her daughter had a white girl's education, but her father knew that the future would demand some compensation for her unexpected mixture of ideas. So to school she went; and here began another link in the silver and gold chain. Which link would survive the strain that life would put upon it? Would she remain a replica of her mother's race or ascend to the so-called heights of her father's? A keen inquiring intelligence and delightful innocence made her path through school days an easy one. Not too much was demanded of her — short hours she had and pleasant school companions that made her absorb her lessons quickly. Language, for which she had a natural talent, spread its poetical mantle around her. The golden solitude of her life expressed itself at last in little sonnets to the birds, the trees, the bush and the amazing beauty of everything. An animal's pain caused her agony; she would attend its wants and soothe it in its misery.

Ted Maloony, cruising about the world in a more or less haphazard fashion, secure in the knowledge that with his bank account he could command what he wished, left his friends in the cities and set out to explore the bush.

Hinemoa, fresh from her spring bath, and pure and sweet as the morning blossoms, danced unknowingly into his path. Steeped in the sublimity of beauty, with all his senses keyed to their highest pitch, Ted Maloony stood spellbound at the picture before him. From the bush there crept over him a web of finest gossamer, invisible, intangible. Was it the spirit of her ancestors forging a link that would never be broken?

Raising his cap, he enquired, when he had recovered his mental balance, where the path went to.

'My home. Come, see, I will show you.'

Hinemoa, singing softly, led him through the bush:

> 'The sunrise of the merry day,
> The deep nooks where the spirits play,
> The silver stream, the shining fish,
> that dance and sparkle as I wish,
> The tiny wood house and the fire,
> the springtime of the heart's desire;
> Where the soft wood nymphs spend their time
> In lofty Kauris, or in cares sublime,
> Come, gentle stranger, come with me
> to haunts of love, and mystery.'

Astounded at the sweetness of it all he followed as in a dream.

The interior of the whare struck him as a complexity of ideas. Only the bare primitive needs of life were in evidence.

A simple table, chairs, stools, crockery. Another little room containing beds and boxes with a miscellaneous collection of native mats, bush baskets, the work of the leisure hours of Hinemoa and her mother in the neighbouring bush.

The mother was preparing a simple meal. Did the soft evening breezes whisper to her to prepare for an important event in their lives? Certainly the meal was somewhat unusual — chicken cooked in her own delicious fashion with vegetables surrounding it, sweet thick cream and native fruit.

The introduction was of the simplest: 'Mother, a gentleman!' With characteristic grace she ushered him to a seat. Here was the innate courtesy born before the event of civilised education.

With the father's return from the day's labour, Ted Maloony comprehended the situation. They accepted him as a desired change in the even tenor of their lives. Seeing that he was without visible means of support, they asked him to stop awhile until he wearied and desire took him further. Had they known his thoughts, they would have realized that nothing would have induced him to move on at that moment from the magnet Hinemoa and her attendant hand-maidens, the bush and its denizens.

Weeks passed in an enchantment of beauty. Ted revelled in the free life, spent the hours in a succession of spirited excursions, bringing back birds, rabbits and wonderful specimens of natural history, ringing the music of human voices down the glades and listening to the returning echoes, teaching the amazed Hinemoa new songs, new thoughts, new ideas, new ideals.

Occasionally he described the land far away, from whence he had come; and meanwhile in a certain old world home in England anxiety arose that no news had been heard from their master. What had become of him? What was he doing?

At that moment, Ted Maloony was leaning against a giant kauri tree, his deep, baritone echoing through the bush, and Hinemoa musing in her room listened from pure joy:

> 'I found my love as a lily white,
> A beacon star on a moonlight night;
> A diamond clasped from the deepest mine,
> A living spring of the choicest wine.
> The world were darkness but for thee

My lovelight through eternity.
O Hinemoa, sweet or sad,
My calmness; when the world is mad
Thy chains enfold me to the end,
My wild-rose blossom, sweetheart, friend.'

She knew now that it was she herself who kept him from wandering away. Thrilled, she did not notice the rustle among the pungas, and listened only to the silver stream of love which stirred the depths of her primitive soul.

'Why, Ted, at last we have found you! And, by jove, what an amazing improvement? But why did you not return to the stated meeting-place?'

Over Maloony's face for a moment dismay and disgust were apparent. Why couldn't his friends have forgotten him, or at any rate left him in peace. With a shock he realized things were happening in another corner of the earth which he could hardly indefinitely neglect. What should he do? Should he say good-bye temporarily to this gorgeous existence and to Hinemoa? To think of such a thing caused him a spasm of grief.

Calling his friends into the nearby bush, he explained the situation, pointing out the beauty that had captivated him and arranging to meet them at a certain port.

With the best of intentions and resolutions, Ted Maloony faded out of Hinemoa's life. The parting was a repression of emotion on her part. Not daring to express herself, she apparently accepted it as an inevitable fact, and kept her thoughts hidden till she could commune in solitude. He, after a loving farewell, sang her his good-bye song, teaching her the words and the music to be ever remembered:

'I will come back to thee, dear love,
Return as the soft clouds up above,
Live as the sweet things in the wild;
Smile when thou smilest, dearest child,
Call; when thou callest I will hear;
Fear; when thou fearest I will fear;
Rest; and when resting I will sleep.

Wavelets will carry thee over the deep;
Thoughts that our parted days are o'er,
Clasp you in spirit for evermore.'

And the souls of Hinemoa's ancestors, the silent and unassailable watchers, asked one another: 'Will he keep his promise and in what way?'

Often in the remote recesses of the bush Hinemoa would practise the parting song, living in the spirit of the fond words, till her voice assumed a pathos that only sadness can define. Hinemoa from that time grew into womanhood as the loveliest rosebud slowly unfolds its petals to the sun, and matured to the knowledge of the divine passion. And all this time Ted Maloony reluctantly drew nearer the land of his ancestors and further away from the inspiration that for him encircled the universe.

Hinemoa's mother, seeing her varying moods, suggested a visit to the colony of Good Sisters who lived some distance away. Knowing something of her history and noting her beauty, gift of poetry and song, they persuaded her to stay awhile and take some lessons in music and languages which they would gladly teach her. And now began for Hinemoa a riot of the good things that her soul had felt the need of. Yet not forgotten was the bush, the beauty of her surroundings or her loved one. But asking nothing and expecting nothing till it came, she moved about amid the saintly atmosphere of the Sisters' dwelling. This was the moulding pot for a delightful personality. This was the testing refinement of the gold and silver chain. Great ideals slowly arose in her mind. Hers should be the unspotted love without blemish; thoughts of evil she banished. Ted was the actual goal of her existence. To be what he would have her to be, to be skilled in the refinements of life as she observed them, was the acme of her aspirations.

A prolonged stay from an estate such as that to which Ted Maloony had just returned, finds large arrears in business. His friends gave him little time for thoughtful reflection. They were struck by his appearance, noting the evidence of some subtle beauty of development. Speculation ran rife as to the reasons, and then faded away. He could not pick up the old thread of his life again, for in his busiest moments like the tinkle of sweet bells would come the voice of Hinemoa and with it a picture of the bush, the glades, the Whare, and the spots they loved to ramble through.

Several years went by for Ted Maloony and Hinemoa. She developed a glorious voice, and with love as the incentive speedily passed from one stage of development to another in her art. Artists, recognising her talent, were quick to assist her, and a Grand Opera Company secured her for a leading part.

The chrysalis of the sweet bush emerged as the magnificent butterfly. 'Dona Rosalie,' with her wonderful personality, at once, arresting and pathetic, amazed and enchanted audiences in the great cities through which she toured. The roles she enacted, the lovely contralto songs she sang, the unusual love scenes, stirred her hearers to the depths. She was a great new star in the firmament. Who she was, her history, her nationality, were a closed book which no one might reopen. Lost was all touch with the land of her birth. Her mother, she knew, had joined the great majority. Her father, still wandering, neither knowing nor caring about her, was yet convinced that she would keep her face to the sunshine. Her lover she awaited. Often at the end of renewed encores, she would finish her programme with his song, 'I will come back to thee dear love.' The amazing pathos left her audience quiet and subdued. No one had heard it before; nor could they buy the music or the words. Only memory served to keep it alive.

Lovers she had — passionate lovers — but they could not move her. Life was beautiful and interesting, but incomplete. Often, after an exciting evening, in the quiet solitude of her room, she would feel with intensity, a sense of some power that was encircling, guiding, uplifting her.

'Clasp you in spirit for evermore.'

Remembrance of that farewell scene was the guiding star which would eventually bring their parted ways together.

Ted Maloony, after a long period of routine work, finally decided to escape the blandishments of his friends. Many were the speculations as to why he did not get married. With everything that his heart could desire apparently, the position became more complex among his feminine circle who combined to cast a halo of beauty around his existence. As a host he was jolly, generous and attentive, but there it ended.

Cool and dispassionate he appeared to be until he sang some of his old songs, and then the full force of his vitality became apparent, and his whole nature called out for Hinemoa. Did she know? Most assuredly repercussions carried their message of his love and yearning to her, leaving her tender and content and making her certain that time would bring the sweet fulfilment of her dreams.

When Ted Maloony finally broke away from his ties and set out to find Hinemoa, he thought his task would be a fairly easy one. At the old enchanted spot he arrived at last. But time had wrought many changes there. The bush of yesterday had become a farm of some importance, cleared and built upon, with only here and there, in the valleys, traces of the springtime of his love. Nor could he find Hinemoa or her family. The farmer had brought the land cheaply and had promptly desecrated it by setting fire to the part he wanted to farm. A great weariness fell over the spirit of Ted Maloony. Why had he not returned at once and rescued Hinemoa from her fate? However, if need be, he would search the world for her.

It was a sad journey for Ted Maloony from that moment. Money could not buy him his pearl of great price. All he could do was hunt about and pick up some thread that might lead him to success. But in what direction should he look? Maybe she was still hidden away in some quiet corner that was like her first home. Thus it came about that he spent some months in the solitude of the bushland. But to recapture the spirit of it without Hinemoa beside him was impossible. Each rustle among the pungas and long grasses reminded him only of her absence. Each bird call was only a tantalizing mockery. Apparently life or death had swallowed her up, and only her spirit remained with him. Finally he decided to return by slow stages to his own interests and begin the carving out of his future.

If he had but known, a swift ship was carrying her at that very moment back to her own land. And had she but known his real name or anything about him, her course might have been easier; but the spiritual union was awaiting its own time to materialize.

Her operatic career finally took her to London, the city of cities — London, where, to lose oneself is easier than in the bush, but never so enchanting an experience. Here Dona Rosalie was billed to appear in Grand Opera and here she remained for some months.

Ted Maloony returned to his own estate and started life in real earnest. His interest in farming, sport, politics and mankind generally made him an important asset to the community. He did not hesitate to answer calls on his time, charity or estate. To be a country gentleman in the highest sense of the word was his ambition and achievement.

'But why,' asked his neighbours, 'doesn't he marry?' It was a matter they could not hope to solve, but fate, with her silken web, was fast drawing the matter to a conclusion, and London at last attracted him into that net.

Certainly it was a jolly party that sat in a box at the very theatre that billed Dona Rosalie that evening. Her reputation as a singer and actress had been the talk of the town.

Wildly interested, Ted watched the play unfold, watching the singers that preceded the star, finally watched the entrance of Dona Rosalie herself and felt his heart rapidly beating at the remembrance of some other form divine at the back of his mind. With his expression drawn and set, his thoughts a garden of happy memories, knowing it was she, yet hardly daring to believe his eyes, he cried, 'Hinemoa, Hinemoa!' And Dona Rosalie caught his voice and looked towards the place from whence it came. It was her last encore, and hoping and believing that her lover was there, she sang his farewell song.

'I will come back to thee, dear love.'

The effect was electrical. As a man possessed, Ted arose and passed out to the stage door, while inside, the audience applauded with tears in their eyes. They did not know of the re-union of two fond hearts, of the silent intensity of the recognition, of the caress that has no beginning or end. All they knew was that Dona Rosalie's substitute was to complete the performance.

But they did know, in due time, that Dona Rosalie, the great singer, and the Hon. Edward Maloony were married in the beautiful old church that had been his family's for centuries.

And time, which has no regard for anybody, brought a wonderful fulfilment of life; and Hinemoa sings to her children and lover-husband the song of her happy wooing on those wonderful evenings in the bush of her childhood.

'I will come back to thee, dear love. . . .' Perhaps spirits among the kauris heard the message. They knew that the gold and silver chain had stood the test and was welded together for ever.

Along Rideout Road That Summer

Maurice Duggan

J'D walked the length of Rideout Road the night before, following the noise of the river in the darkness, tumbling over ruts and stones, my progress, if you'd call it that, challenged by farmers' dogs and observed by the faintly luminous eyes of wandering stock, steers, cows, stud-bulls or milk-white unicorns or, better, a full quartet of apocalyptic horses browsing the marge. In time and darkness I found Puti Hohepa's farmhouse and lugged my fibre suitcase up to the verandah, after nearly breaking my leg in a cattlestop. A journey fruitful of one decision — to flog a torch from somewhere. And of course I didn't. And now my feet hurt; but it was daylight and, from memory, I'd say I was almost happy. Almost. Fortunately I am endowed both by nature and later conditioning with a highly developed sense of the absurd; knowing that you can imagine the pleasure I took in this abrupt translation from shop-counter to tractor seat, from town pavements to back-country farm, with all those miles of river-bottom darkness to mark the transition. In fact, and unfortunately there have to be some facts, even fictional ones, I'd removed myself a mere dozen miles from the parental home. In darkness, as I've said, and with a certain stealth. I didn't consult dad about it, and, needless to say, I didn't tell mum. The moment wasn't propitious; dad was

87

asleep with the *Financial Gazette* threatening to suffocate him and mum was off somewhere moving, as she often did, that this meeting make public its whole-hearted support for the introduction of flogging and public castration for all sex offenders and hanging, drawing and quartering, for almost everyone else, and as for delinquents (my boy!). . . . Well, put yourself in my shoes, there's no need to go on. Yes, almost happy, though my feet were so tender I winced every time I tripped the clutch.

Almost happy, shouting Kubla Khan, a bookish lad, from the seat of the clattering old Ferguson tractor, doing a steady five miles an hour in a cloud of seagulls, getting to the bit about the damsel with the dulcimer and looking up to see the reputedly wild Hohepa girl perched on the gate, feet hooked in the bars, ribbons fluttering from her ukulele. A perfect moment of recognition, daring rider, in spite of the belch of carbon monoxide from the tin-can exhaust up front on the bonnet. Don't, however, misunderstand me: I'd not have you think we are here embarked on the trashy clamour of boy meeting girl. No, the problem, you are to understand, was one of connection. How connect the dulcimer with the ukulele, if you follow. For a boy of my bents this problem of how to cope with the shock of the recognition of a certain discrepancy between the real and the written was rather like watching mum with a shoehorn wedging nines into sevens and suffering merry hell. I'm not blaming old STC for everything, of course. After all, some other imports went wild too; and I've spent too long at the handle of a mattock, a critical function, not to know that. The stench of the exhaust, that's to say, held no redolence of that old hophead's pipe. Let us then be clear and don't for a moment, gentlemen, imagine that I venture the gross unfairness, the patent absurdity, the rank injustice (your turn) of blaming him for spoiling the pasture or fouling the native air. It's just that there was this problem in my mind, this profound, cultural problem affecting dramatically the very nature of my inheritance, nines into sevens in this lovely smiling land. His was the genius as his was the expression which the vast educational brouhaha invited me to praise and emulate, tranquillisers ingested in maturity, the voice of the ring-dove, look up though your feet be in the clay. And read on.

Of course I understood immediately that these were not matters I was destined to debate with Fanny Hohepa. Frankly, I could see that she didn't give a damn; it was part of her attraction. She thought I was singing. She smiled and waved, I waved and smiled, turned, ploughed back through gull-white and coffee loam and fell into a train of thought not entirely free of Fanny and her instrument, pausing to wonder, now and then, what might be the symptoms, the early symptoms, of carbon monoxide poisoning. Drowsiness? Check. Dilation of the pupils? Can't check. Extra cutaneous sensation? My feet. Trembling hands? Vibrato. Down and back, down and back, turning again, Dick and his Ferguson, Fanny from her perch seeming to gather about her the background of green paternal acres, fold on fold. I bore down upon her in all the eager erubescence of youth, with my hair slicked back. She trembled, wavered, fragmented and re-formed in the pungent vapour through which I viewed her. (Oh, for an open-air job, eh mate?) She plucked, very picture in jeans and summer shirt of youth and suspicion, and seemed to sing. I couldn't of course hear a note. Behind me the dog-leg furrows and the bright ploughshares. Certainly she looked at her ease and, even through the gassed-up atmosphere between us, too deliciously substantial to be creature down on a visit from Mount Abora. I was glad I'd combed my hair. Back, down and back. Considering the size of the paddock this could have gone on for a week. I promptly admitted to myself that her present position, disposition or posture, involving as it did some provocative tautness of cloth, suited me right down to the ground. I mean to hell with the idea of having her stand knee-deep in the thistle thwanging her dulcimer and plaintively chirruping about a pipedream mountain. In fact she was natively engaged in expressing the most profound distillations of her local experience, the gleanings of a life lived in rich contact with a richly understood and native environment: A Slow Boat To China, if memory serves. While I, racked and shaken, composed words for the plaque which would one day stand her to commemorate our deep rapport: *Here played the black lady her dulcimer. Here wept she full miseries. Here rode the knight Fergus' son to her deliverance. Here put he about her ebon and naked shoulders his courtly garment of leather, black, full curiously emblazoned — Hell's Angel.*

When she looked as though my looking were about to make her leave I stopped the machine and pulled out the old tobacco and rolled a smoke, holding the steering wheel in my teeth, though on a good day I could roll with one hand, twist and lick, draw, shoot the head off a pin at a mile and a half, spin, blow down the barrel before you could say:

Gooday. How are yuh?

All right.

I'm Buster O'Leary.

I'm Fanny Hohepa.

Yair, I know.

It's hot.

It's hot right enough.

You can have a swim when you're through.

Mightn't be a bad idea at that.

Over there by the trees.

Yair, I seen it. Like, why don't you join me, eh?

I might.

Go on, you'd love it.

I might.

Goodoh then, see yuh.

A genuine crumpy conversation if ever I heard one, darkly reflective of the Socratic method, rich with echoes of the Kantian imperative, its universal mate, summoning sharply to the minds of each the history of the first trystings of all immortal lovers, the tragic and tangled tale, indeed, of all star-crossed moonings, mum and dad, mister and missus unotoo and all. Enough? I should bloody well hope so.

Of course nothing came of it. Romantic love was surely the invention of a wedded onanist with seven kids. And I don't mean dad. Nothing? Really and truly nothing? Well, I treasure the under-statement; though why I should take such pleasure in maligning the ploughing summer white on loam, river flats, the frivolous ribbons and all the strumming, why I don't know. Xanadu and the jazzy furrows, the wall-eyed bitch packing the cows through the yardgate, the smell of river water . . . Why go on? So few variations to an old, old story. No. But on the jolting tractor I received that extra jolt I mentioned and am actually now making rather too much of, gentlemen: relate Fanny Hohepa and her uke to that mountain thrush singing her black mountain blues.

But of course now, in our decent years, we know such clay questions long broken open or we wouldn't be here, old and somewhat sour, wading up to our battered thighs (forgive me, madam) at the confluence of the great waters, paddling in perfect confidence in the double debouchment of universal river and regional stream, the shallow fast fan of water spreading over the delta, Abyssinia come to Egypt in the rain . . . ah, my country! I speak of cultural problems, in riddles and literary puddles, perform this act of divination with my own entrails: Fanny's dark delta; the nubile and Nubian sheila with her portable piano anticipating the transistor-set; all gathered into single demesne, O'Leary's orchard. Even this wooden bowl, plucked from the flood, lost from the hand of some anonymous herdsman as he stopped to cup a drink at the river's source. Ah, Buster. Ah, Buster. Buster. Ah, darling. Darling! Love. You recognise it? Could you strum to that? Suppose you gag a little at the sugar coating, it's the same old fundamental toffee, underneath.

No mere cheap cyn . . . sm intended. She took me down to her darkling avid as any college girl for the fruits and sweets of my flowering talents, taking me as I wasn't but might hope one day to be, honest, simple and broke to the wide. The half-baked verbosity and the conceit she must have ignored, or how else could she have borne me? It pains me, gentlemen, to confess that she was too good for me by far. Far. Anything so spontaneous and natural could be guaranteed to be beyond me: granted, I mean, my impeccable upbringing under the white-hot lash of respectability, take that, security, take that, hypocrisy, take that, cant, take that where, does it seem curious?, mum did all the beating flushed pink in ecstasy and righteousness, and that and that and THAT. Darling! How then could I deem Fanny's conduct proper when I carried such weals and scars, top-marks in the lesson on the wickedness of following the heart. Fortunately such a question would not have occurred to Fanny: she was remarkably free from queries of any kind. She would walk past the Home Furnishing Emporium without a glance.

She is too good for you.

It was said clearly enough, offered without threat and as just comment, while I was bent double stripping old Daisy or Pride of the Plains or Rose of Sharon after the cups came off. I stopped what I was doing, looked sideways until I could see the tops of his gumboots, gazed on Marathon, and then turned back, dried off all four tits and let the cow out into the race where, taking the legrope with her, she squittered off wild in the eyes.

She is too good for you.

So I looked at him and he looked back. I lost that game of stare-you-down, too. He walked off. Not a warning, not even a reproach, just something it was as well I should know if I was to have the responsibility of acting in full knowledge — and who the hell wants that? And two stalls down Fanny spanked a cow out through the flaps and looked at me, and giggled. The summer thickened and blazed.

The first response on the part of my parents was silence; which can only be thought of as response in a very general sense. I could say, indeed I will say, stony silence; after all they were my parents. But I knew the silence wouldn't last long. I was an only child (darling, you never guessed?) and that load of woodchopping, lawnmowing, hedgeclipping, dishwashing, carwashing, errandrunning, gardenchoring and the rest of it was going to hit them like a folding mortgage pretty soon. I'd like to have been there, to have seen the lank grass grown beyond window height and the uncut hedges shutting out the sun: perpetual night and perpetual mould on Rose Street West. After a few weeks the notes and letters began. The whole gamut, gentlemen, from sweet and sickly to downright abusive. Mostly in mum's masculine hand. A unique set of documents reeking of blood and tripes. I treasured every word, reading between the lines the record of an undying, all-sacrificing love, weeping tears for the idyllic childhood they could not in grief venture to touch upon, the care lavished, the love squandered upon me. The darlings. Of course I didn't reply.

I didn't even wave when they drove past Fanny and me as we were breasting out of the scrub back on to the main road, dishevelled and, yes, almost happy in the daze of summer and Sunday afternoon. I didn't wave. I grinned as brazenly as I could manage with a jaw full of hard boiled egg and took Fanny's arm, brazen, her shirt only casually resumed, while they went by like burnished doom.

Fanny's reaction to all this? An expression of indifference, a down-curving of that bright and wilful mouth, a flirt of her head. So much fuss over so many fossilised ideas, if I may so translate her expression which was, in fact, gentlemen, somewhat more direct and not in any sense exhibiting what mum would have called a due respect for elders and betters. Pouf! Not contempt, no; not disagreement; simply an impatience with what she, Fanny, deemed the irrelevance of so many many words for so light and tumbling a matter. And, for the season at least, I shared the mood, her demon lover in glossy brilliantine.

But as the days ran down the showdown came nearer and finally the stage was set. Low-keyed and sombre notes in the sunlight the four of us variously disposed on the unpainted Hohepa verandah, Hohepa and O'Leary, the male seniors, and Hohepa and O'Leary, junior represent-atives, male seventeen, female ready to swear, you understand, that she was sixteen, turning.

Upon the statement that Fanny was too good for me my pappy didn't comment. No one asked him to: no one faced him with the opinion. Wise reticence, mere oversight or a sense of the shrieking irrelevance of such a statement, I don't know. Maori girls, Maori farms, Maori housing: you'd only to hear my father put tongue to any or all of that to know where he stood, solid for intolerance, mac, but solid. Of course, gentle-men, it was phrased differently on his lips, gradual absorption, hmm, perhaps, after, say, a phase of disinfecting. A pillar of our decent, law-abiding community, masonic in his methodism, brother, total abstainer, rotarian and non-smoker, addicted to long volleys of handball, I mean pocket billiards cue and all. Mere nervousness, of course, a subconscious habit. Mum would cough and glance down and dad would spring to attention hands behind his back. Such moments of tender rapport are sweet to return to, memories any child might treasure. Then he'd forget again. Straight, mate, there were days, especially Sundays, when mum would be hacking away like an advanced case of t.b. Well, you can picture it, there on the verandah. With the finely turned Fanny under his morose eye, you know how it is, hemline hiked and this and that visible from odd angles, he made a straight break of two hundred without one miscue, Daddy! I came in for a couple of remand home stares myself, bread and water and solitary and take that writ on his eyeballs in back-hand black while his mouth served out its lying old hohums and there's no reason why matters shouldn't be resolved amicably, etc, black hanging-cap snug over his tonsure and tongue moistening his droopy lip, ready, set, drop. And Puti Hohepa leaving him to it. A dignified dark prince on his ruined acres, old man Hohepa, gravely attending to dad's mumbled slush, winning hands down just by being there and saying nothing, nothing, while Fanny with her fatal incapacity for standing upright unsupported for more than fifteen seconds, we all had a disease of the spine that year, pouted at me as though it were all my fault over the back of the chair (sic). All my fault being just the pater's monologue, the remarkably imprecise grip of his subject with consequent proliferation of the bromides so typical of all his ilk of elk, all the diversely identical representatives of decency, caution and the colour bar. Of course daddy didn't there and then refer to race, colour creed or uno who. Indeed he firmly believed he believed, if I may recapitulate, gentle-men, that this blessed land was free from such taint, a unique social experiment, two races living happily side by side, respecting each other's etc. and etc. As a banker he knew the value of discretion, though what was home if not a place to hang up your reticence along with your hat and get stuck into all the hate that was inside you, in the name of justice? Daddy Hohepa said nothing, expressed nothing, may even have been unconscious of the great destinies being played out on his sunlit verandah, or of what fundamental principles of democracy and the freedom of the individual were being here so brilliantly exercised; may have been, in fact, indifferent to daddy's free granting tautologies now, of the need for circumspection in all matters of national moment, all such questions as what shall be done for our dark brothers and sisters, outside the jails? I hope so. After a few minutes Hohepa rangatira trod the boards thought-fully and with the slowness of a winter bather lowered himself into a pool of sunlight on the wide steps, there to lift his face broad and grave in full dominion of his inheritance and even, perhaps, so little did his expression reveal of his inward reflection, full consciousness of his dispossessions.

What, you may ask, was my daddy saying? Somewhere among the circumlocutions, these habits are catching among the words and sentiments designed to express his grave ponderings on the state of the nation and so elicit from his auditors (not me, I wasn't listening) admission, tacit though it may be, of his tutored opinion, there was centred the suggestion that old man Hohepa and daughter were holding me against my will, ensnaring me with flesh and farm. He had difficulty in getting it out in plain words; some lingering cowardice, perhaps. Which was why daddy Hohepa missed it, perhaps. Or did the view command all his attention?

Rideout Mountain far and purple in the afternoon sun; the jersey cows beginning to move, intermittent and indirect, towards the shed; the dog jangling its chain as it scratched; Fanny falling in slow movement across the end of the old cane lounge chair to lie, an interesting composition of curves and angles, with the air of a junior and rural odalisque. Me? I stood straight, of course, rigid, thumbs along the seams of my jeans, hair at the regulation distance two inches above the right eye, heels together and bare feet at ten to two, or ten past ten, belly flat and chest inflated, chin in, heart out. I mean, can you see me, mac? Dad's grave-suit so richly absorbed the sun that he was forced to retreat into the shadows where his crafty jailer's look was decently camouflaged, blending white with purple blotched with silver wall. Not a bad heart, surely?

As his audience we each displayed differing emotions. Fanny, boredom that visibly bordered on sleep: Puti Hohepa, an inattention expressed in his long examination of the natural scene: Buster O'Leary, a sense of complete bewilderment over what it was the old man thought he could achieve by his harangue and, further, a failure to grasp the relevance of it all for the Hohepas. My reaction, let me say, was mixed with irritation at certain of father's habits. (Described.) With his pockets filled with small change he sounded like the original gypsy orchestra, cymbals and all. I actually tried mum's old trick of the glance and the cough. No luck. And he went on talking, at me now, going so wide of the mark, for example, as to mention some inconceivable, undocumented and undemonstrated condition, some truly monstrous condition, called your-mother's-love. Plain evidence of his distress, I took it to be, this obscenity uttered in mixed company. I turned my head the better to hear, when it came, the squelchy explosion of his heart. And I rolled a smoke and threw Fanny the packet. It landed neatly on her stomach. She sat up and made herself a smoke then crossed to her old man and, perching beside him in the brilliant pool of light, fire of skin and gleam of hair bronze and blue-black, neatly extracted from his pocket his battered flint lighter. She snorted smoke and passed the leaf to her old man.

Some things, gentlemen, still amaze. To my dying day I have treasured that scene and all its rich implications. In a situation so pregnant of difficulties, in the midst of a debate so fraught with undertones, an exchange (quiet there, at the back) so bitterly fulsome on the one hand and so reserved on the other. I ask you to take special note of this observance of the ritual of the makings, remembering, for the fullest savouring of the nuance, my father's abstention. As those brown fingers moved on the white cylinder, or cone, I was moved almost, to tears, almost, by this companionable and wordless recognition of our common human frailty, father and dark child in silent communion and I too, in some manner not to be explained because inexplicable, sharing their hearts. I mean the insanity, pal. Puti Hohepa and his lass in sunlight on the steps, smoking together, untroubled, natural and patient; and me and daddy glaring at each other in the shades like a couple of evangelists at cross pitch. Love, thy silver coatings and castings. And thy neighbours! So I went and sat by Fanny and put an arm through hers.

The sun gathered me up, warmed and consoled; the bitter view assumed deeper purples and darker rose; a long way off a shield flashed, the sun striking silver from a water trough. At that moment I didn't care what mad armies marched in my father's voice nor what the clarion was he was trying so strenuously to sound. I didn't care that the fire in his heart was fed by such rank fuel, skeezing envy, malice, revenge, hate and parental power. I sat and smoked and was warm; and the girl's calm flank was against me, her arm through mine. Nothing was so natural as to turn through the little distance between us and kiss her smoky mouth. Ah yes, I could feel, I confess, through my shoulder blades as it were and the back of my head, the crazed rapacity and outrage of my daddy's Irish stare, the blackness and the cold glitter of knives. (Father!) While Puti Hohepa sat on as though turned to glowing stone by the golden light, faced outward to the violet mystery of the natural hour, monumentally content and still.

You will have seen it, known it, guessed that there was between this wild, loamy daughter and me, sunburnt scion of an ignorant, insensitive, puritan and therefore prurient, Irishman (I can't stop) no more than a summer's dalliance, a season's thoughtless sweetness, a boy and a girl and the makings.

In your wisdom, gentlemen, you will doubtless have sensed that something is lacking in this lullaby, some element missing for the articulation of this ranting tale. Right. The key to daddy's impassioned outburst, no less. Not lost in this verbose review, but so far unstated. Point is he'd come to seek his little son (someone must have been dying because he'd never have come for the opposite reason) and, not being one to baulk at closed doors and drawn shades, wait for it, he'd walked straight in on what he'd always somewhat feverishly imagined and hoped he feared. Fanny took it calmly: I was, naturally, more agitated. Both of us ballocky in the umber light, of course. Still, even though he stayed only long enough to let his eyes adjust and his straining mind take in this historic disposition of flesh, those mantis angles in which for all our horror we must posit our conceivings, it wasn't the greeting he'd expected. It wasn't quite the same, either, between Fanny and me, after he'd backed out, somewhat huffily, on to the verandah. Ah, filthy beasts! He must have been roaring some such expression as that inside his head because his eyeballs were rattling, the very picture of a broken doll, and his face was liver-coloured. I felt sorry for him, for a second, easing backward from the love-starred couch and the moving lovers with his heel hooked through the loop of Fanny's bra, kicking it free like a football hero punting for touch, his dream of reconciliation in ruins.

It wasn't the same. Some rhythms are slow to re-form. And once the old man actually made the sanctuary of the verandah he just had to bawl his loudest for old man Hohepa, Mr Ho-he-pa, Mr Ho-he-pa. It got us into our clothes anyway, Fanny giggling and getting a sneezing fit at the same time, bending forward into the hoof-marked brassiere and blasting off every ten seconds like a burst air hose until I quite lost count on the one-for-sorrow two-for-joy scale and crammed myself sulkily into my jocks.

Meantime dad's labouring to explain certain natural facts and common occurrences to Puti Hohepa, just as though he'd made an original discovery; as perhaps he had considering what he probably thought of as natural. Puti Hohepa listened, I thought that ominous, then silently deprecated, in a single slow movement of his hand, the wholly inappropriate expression of shock and rage, all the sizzle of my daddy's oratory.

Thus the tableau. We did the only possible thing, ignored him and let him run down, get it off his chest, come to his five battered senses, if he had so many, and get his breath. Brother, how he spilled darkness and sin upon that floor, wilting collar and boiling eyes, the sweat running from his face and, Fanny, shameless, languorous and drowsy, provoking him to further flights. She was young, gentlemen: I have not concealed it. She was too young to have had time to accumulate the history he ascribed to her. She was too tender to endure for long the muscular lash of his tongue and the rake of his eyes. She went over to her dad, as heretofore described, and when my sweet sire, orator general to the dying afternoon, had made his pitch about matters observed and inferences drawn, I went to join her. I sat with my back to him. All our backs were to him, including his own. He emptied himself of wrath and for a moment, a wild and wonderful moment, I thought he was going to join us, bathers in the pool of sun. But no.

Silence. Light lovely and fannygold over the pasture; shreds of mist by the river deepening to rose. My father's hard leather soles rattled harshly on the bare boards like rim-shots. The mad figure of him went black as bug out over the lawn, out over the loamy furrows where the tongue of ploughed field invaded the home paddock, all my doing, spurning in his violence anything less than this direct and abrupt charge towards the

98

waiting car. Fanny's hand touched my arm again and for a moment I was caught in a passion of sympathy for him, something as solid as grief and love, an impossible pairing of devotion and despair. The landscape flooded with sadness as I watched the scuttling, black, ignominious figure hurdling the fresh earth, the waving arms, seemingly scattering broadcast the white and shying gulls, his head bobbing on his shoulders, as he narrowed into distance.

I wished, gentlemen, with a fervour foreign to my young life, that it had been in company other than that of Puti Hohepa and his brat that we had made our necessary parting. I wished we had been alone. I did not want to see him diminished, made ridiculous and pathetic among strangers, while I so brashly joined the mockers. (Were they mocking?) Impossible notions; for what was there to offer and how could he receive? Nothing. I stroked Fanny's arm. Old man Hohepa got up and unchained the dog and went off to get the cows in. He didn't speak; maybe the chocolate old bastard was dumb, eh? In a minute I would have to go down and start the engine and put the separator together. I stayed to stare at Fanny, thinking of undone things in a naughty world. She giggled, thinking, for all I know, of the same, or of nothing. Love, thy sunny trystings and nocturnal daggers. For the first time I admitted my irritation at that girlish, hic-coughing, tenor giggle. But we touched, held, got up and with our arms linked went down the long paddock through the infestation of buttercup, our feet bruising stalk and flower. Suddenly all I wanted and at whatever price was to be able, sometime, somewhere, to make it up to my primitive, violent, ignorant and crazy old man. And I knew I never would. Ah, what a bloody fool. And then the next thing I wanted, a thing far more feasible, was to be back in that room with its shade and smell of hay-dust and warm flesh, taking up the classic story just where we'd been so rudely forced to discontinue it. Old man Hohepa was bellowing at the dog; the cows rocked up through the paddock gate and into the yard: the air smelled of night. I stopped; and holding Fanny's arm suggested we might run back. Her eyes went wide: she giggled and broke away and I stood there and watched her flying down the paddock, bare feet and a flouncing skirt, her hair shaken loose.

Next afternoon I finished ploughing the river paddock, the nature of Puti Hohepa's husbandry as much a mystery as ever, and ran the old Ferguson into the lean-to shelter behind the cow shed. It was far too late for ploughing: the upper paddocks were hard and dry. But Puti hoped to get a crop of late lettuce off the river flat; just in time, no doubt, for the glutted market, brown rot, wilt and total failure of the heart. He'd have to harrow it first, too; and on his own. Anyway, none of my worry. I walked into the shed. Fanny and her daddy were deep in conversation. She was leaning against the flank of a cow, a picture of rustic grace, a rural study of charmed solemnity. Christ knows what they were saying to each other. For one thing they were speaking in their own language: for another I couldn't hear anything, even that, above the blather and splatter of the bloody cows and the racket of the single cylinder diesel, brand-name Onan out of Edinburgh so help me. They looked up. I grabbed a stool and got on with it, head down to the bore of it all. I'd have preferred to be up on the tractor, poisoning myself straight out, bellowing this and that and the other looney thing to the cynical gulls. Ah, my mountain princess of the golden chords, something was changing. I stripped on, sullenly: I hoped it was me.

We were silent through dinner: we were always silent, through all meals. It made a change from home where all hell lay between soup and sweet, everyone taking advantage of the twenty minutes of enforced attend-ance to shoot the bile, bicker and accuse, rant and wrangle through the grey disgusting mutton and the two veg. Fanny never chattered much and less than ever in the presence of her pappy: giggled maybe but never said much. Then out of the blue father Hohepa opened up. Buster, you should make peace with your father. I considered it. I tried to touch Fanny's foot under the table and I considered it. A boy shouldn't hate his father: a boy should respect his father. I thought about that too. Then I asked should fathers hate their sons; but I knew the answer. Puti Hohepa didn't say anything, just sat blowing into his tea, looking at his reputedly wild daughter who might have been a beauty for all I could tell, content to be delivered of the truth and so fulfilled. You should do this: a boy shouldn't do that — tune into that, mac. And me thinking proscription and prescription differently ordered in this farm world of crummy acres. I mean I thought I'd left all that crap behind the night I stumbled along Rideout Road following, maybe, the river Alph. I thought old man Hohepa, having been silent for so long, would know better than to pull, of a sudden, all those generalisations with which for seventeen years I'd been beaten dizzy — but not so dizzy as not to be able to look back of the billboards and see the stack of rotting bibles. Gentlemen, I was, even noticeably, subdued. Puti Hohepa clearly didn't intend to add anything more just then. I was too tired to make him an answer. I think I was too tired even for hate; and what better indication of the extent of my exhaustion than that? It had been a long summer; how long I was only beginning to discover. It was cold in the kitchen. Puti Hohepa got up. From the doorway, huge and merging into the night, he spoke again: You must make up your own mind. He went away, leaving behind him the vibration of a gentle sagacity, tolerance, a sense of duty (mine, as usual) pondered over and pronounced upon. The bastard. You must make up your own mind. And for the first time you did that mum had hysterics and dad popped his gut. About what? Made up my mind about what? My black daddy? Fanny? Myself? Life? A country career and agricultural hell? Death? Money? Fornication? (I'd always liked that.) What the hell was he trying to say? What doing but abdicating the soiled throne at the first challenge? Did he think fathers shouldn't hate their sons, or could help it, or would if they could? Am I clear? No matter. He didn't have one of the four he'd sired at home so what the hell sort of story was he trying to peddle? Father with the soft centre. You should, you shouldn't, make up your own mind. Mac, my head was going round. But it was brilliant, I conceded, when I'd given it a bit of thought. My livid daddy himself would have applauded the perfect ambiguity. What a bunch: they keep a dog on a chain for years and years and then let it free on some purely personal impulse and when it goes wild and chases its tail round and round, pissing here and sniffing there in an ecstasy of liberty, a freedom for which it has been denied all training, they shoot it down because it won't come running when they hold up the leash and whistle. (I didn't think you'd go that way, son.) Well, my own green liberty didn't look like so much at that moment; for the first time I got an inkling that life was going to be simply a matter of out of one jail and into another. Oh, they had a lot in common, her dad and mine. I sat there, mildly stupefied, drinking my tea. Then I looked up at Fanny; or, rather, down on Fanny. I've never known such a collapsible sheila in my life. She was stretched on the kitchen couch, every vertebra having turned to juice in the last minute and a half. I thought maybe she'd have the answer, some comment to offer on the state of disunion. Hell. I was the very last person to let my brew go cold while I pondered the nuance of the incomprehensible, picked at the dubious unsubtlety of thought of a man thirty years my senior who had never, until then, said more than ten words to me. She is too good for you: only six words after all and soon forgotten. Better, yes, if he'd stayed mum, leaving me to deduce from his silence whatever I could, Abora Mountain and the milk of paradise, consent in things natural and a willingness to let simple matters take their simple course.

I was wrong: Fanny offered no interpretation of her father's thought. Exegesis to his cryptic utterance was the one thing she couldn't supply. She lay with her feet up on the end of the couch, brown thighs charmingly bared, mouth open and eyes closed in balmy sleep, displaying in this posture various things but mainly her large unconcern not only for this tragedy of filial responsibility and the parental role but, too, for the diurnal problem of the numerous kitchen articles, pots, pans, plates, the lot. I gazed on her, frowning on her bloom of sleep, the slow inhalation and exhalation accompanied by a gentle flare of nostril, and considered the strength and weakness of our attachment. Helpmeet she was not, thus to leave her lover to his dark ponderings and the chores.

Puti Hohepa sat on the verandah in the dark, hacking over his bowl of shag. One by one, over my second cup of tea, I assessed my feelings, balanced all my futures in the palm of my hand. I crossed to Fanny, crouched beside her, kissed her. I felt embarrassed and, gentlemen, foolish. Her eyes opened wide; then they shut and she turned over.

The dishes engaged my attention not at all, except to remind me, here we go, of my father in apron and rubber gloves at the sink, pearl-diving while mum was off somewhere at a lynching. Poor bastard. Mum

102

had the natural squeeze for the world; they should have changed places. (It's for your own good! Ah, the joyous peal of that as the razor strop came whistling down like tartar's blade.) I joined daddy Hohepa on the verandah. For a moment we shared the crescent moon and the smell of earth damp under dew, Rideout Mountain massed to the west.

I've finished the river paddock.

Yes.

The tractor's going to need a de-coke before long.

Yes.

I guess that about cuts it out.

Yes.

I may as well shoot through.

Buster, is Fanny pregnant?

I don't know. She hasn't said anything to me so I suppose she can't be.

You are going home?

No. Not home. There's work down south. I'd like to have a look down there.

There's work going here if you want it. But you have made up your mind?

I suppose I may as well shoot through.

Yes.

After milking tomorrow if that's okay with you.

Yes.

He hacked on over his pipe. Yes, yes, yes, yes, yes is Fanny pregnant? What if I'd said yes? I didn't know one way or the other. I only hoped, and left the rest to her. Maybe he'd ask her; and what if she said yes? What then, eh Buster? Maybe I should have said why don't you ask her. A demonstrative, volatile, loquacious old person: a tangible symbol of impartiality, reason unclouded by emotion, his eyes frank in the murk of night and his pipe going bright, dim, bright as he calmly considered the lovely flank of the moon. I was hoping she wasn't, after all. Hoping; it gets to be a habit, a bad habit that does you no good, stunts your growth, sends you insane and makes you, demonstrably, blind. Hope, for Fanny Hohepa.

Later, along the riverbank, Fanny and I groped, gentlemen, for the lost rapport and the parking sign. We were separated by just a little more than an arm's reach. I made note then of the natural scene. Dark water, certainly; dark lush grass underfoot; dark girl; the drifting smell of loam in the night: grant me again as much. Then, by one of those fortuitous accidents not infrequent in our national prosings, our hands met, held, fell away. Darkness. My feet stumbling by the river and my heart going like a tango. Blood pulsed upon blood, undenied and unyoked, as we busied ourselves tenderly at our ancient greetings and farewells. And in the end, beginning my sentence with a happy conjunction, I held her indistinct, dark head. We stayed so for a minute, together and parting as always, with me tumbling down upon her the mute dilemma my mind then pretended to resolve and she offering no restraint, no argument better than the dark oblivion of her face.

Unrecorded the words between us: there can't have been more than six, anyway it was our fated number. None referred to my departure or to the future or to maculate conceptions. Yet her last touch spoke volumes. (Unsubsidised, gentlemen, without dedication or preamble.) River-damp softened her hair: her skin smelled of soap: Pan pricking forward to drink at the stream, crushing fennel, exquisitely stooping, bending. . . .

And, later again, silent, groping, we ascended in sequence to the paternal porch.

Buster?

Yair?

Goodnight, Buster.

'Night, Fanny. Be seein' yuh.

. . . .

Fourteen minute specks of radioactive phosphorus brightened by weak starlight pricked out the hour: one.

In the end I left old STC in the tractor tool box along with the spanner that wouldn't fit any nut I'd ever tried it on and the grease gun without grease and the last letter from mum, hot as radium. I didn't wait for milking. I was packed and gone at the first trembling of light. It was cold along the river-bottom, cold and still. Eels rose to feed: the water was like pewter; old pewter. I felt sick, abandoned, full of self-pity. Everything washed through me, the light, the cold, a sense of what lay behind me and might not lie before, a feeling of exhaustion when I thought of home, a feeling of despair when I thought of Fanny still curled in sleep. Dark. She hadn't giggled: so what? I changed my fibre suitcase to the other hand and trudged along Rideout Road. The light increased; quail with tufted crests crossed the road: I began to feel better. I sat on the suitcase and rolled a smoke. Then the sun caught a high scarp of Rideout Mountain and began to finger down slow and gold. I was so full of relief, suddenly, that I grabbed my bag and ran. Impetuous. I was lucky not to break my ankle. White gulls, loam flesh, dark water, damsel and dome; where would it take you? Where was there to go, anyway? It just didn't matter; that was the point. I stopped worrying that minute and sat by the cream stand out on the main road. After a while a truck stopped to my thumb and I got in. If I'd waited for the cream truck I'd have had to face old brownstone Hohepa and I wasn't very eager for that. I'd had a fill of piety, of various brands. And I was paid up to date.

I looked back. Rideout Mountain and the peak of ochre red roof, Maori red. That's all it was. I wondered what Fanny and her pappy might be saying at this moment, across the clothes-hanger rumps of cows. The rush of relief went through me again. I looked at the gloomy bastard driving: he had a cigarette stuck to his lip like a growth. I felt almost happy. Almost. I might have hugged him as he drove his hearse through the tail-end of summer.

The Lagoon

Janet Frame

AT low tide the water is sucked back into the harbour and there is no lagoon, only a stretch of dirty grey sand shaded with dark pools of sea water where you may find a baby octopus if you are lucky, or the spotted orange old house of a crab or the drowned wreckage of a child's toy boat. There is a bridge over the lagoon where you may look down into the little pools and see your image tangled up with sea water and rushes and bits of cloud. And sometimes at night there is an underwater moon, dim and secret.

All this my grandmother told me, my Picton grandmother who could cut supple-jack and find kidney fern and make a track through the thickest part of the bush. When my grandmother died all the Maoris at the Pa came to her funeral, for she was a friend of the Maoris, and her mother had been a Maori princess, very beautiful they said, with fierce ways of loving and hating.

See the lagoon, my grandmother would say. The dirty lagoon, full of drifting wood and seaweed and crabs' claws. It is dirty and sandy and smelly in summer. I remember we used to skim round white stones over the water, and catch tiddlers in the little creek near by, and make sand castles on the edge. This is my castle, we said, you be Father I'll be Mother and we'll live here and catch crabs and tiddlers for ever.

I liked my grandmother to talk about the lagoon. And when we went for a holiday to Picton where Grandma lived I used to say, Grandma, tell me a story. About the Maori Pa. About the old man who lived down the Sounds and had a goat and a cow for friends. About the lagoon. And my grandmother would tell me stories of the Sounds and the Pa and herself when she was young. Being a girl and going out to work in the rich people's houses. But the lagoon never had a proper story, or if it had a proper story my grandmother never told me.

See the water, she would say. Full of seaweed and crabs' claws. But I knew that wasn't the real story and I didn't find out the real story till I was grown up and Grandma had died and most of the old Maoris were gone from the Pa, and the old man and the cow and the goat were forgotten.

I went for a holiday in Picton. It was a long journey by train and I was glad at the end of it to see the green and blue town that I remembered from childhood, though it was smaller of course and the trees had shrunk and the hills were tiny.

I stayed with an aunt and uncle. I went for launch rides round the harbour and I went for picnics with summery people in floral frocks and sun hats, and kids in print frocks, or khaki shorts if they were boys, especially if they were boys with fathers in the army. We took baskets with fruit and sandwiches, not tomato, for tomato goes damp though some like it damp, and threepences in the pocket for ice-creams. There were races for the kiddies and some for the men and women, and afterwards a man walked round the grounds throwing lollies in the air. They were great days out picnicking in the Sounds with the Maoris singing and playing their ukuleles, but they didn't sing the real Maori songs, they sang You are my sunshine and South of the Border. And then it got dark and the couples came back from the trees and the launches were got ready and everybody went back singing, with the babies crying because they were tired and sunburnt and bitten by sandflies. Sandflies are the devil, everybody said, but they were great days, they were great days for the kiddies.

Perhaps I liked the new Picton, I don't know. If there were things I hadn't noticed before there were also things gone that I thought would be there for ever. The two gum trees that I called the two ladies were gone, or if they were there I couldn't find them, and the track over the

Domain Hill wasn't there. We used to climb up and watch the steamer coming in from the straits. And there was gorse mixed up with the bush, and the bush itself didn't hold the same fear, even with its secret terrible drippings and rustlings that go on for ever.

There were more people in the town too. The Main Trunk Line brings more tourists, my aunt said. There were people everywhere, lying on the beach being burned or browned by the sun and sea, people whizzing round the harbour in motor-boats like the pop-pop boats we used to whizz round in the bath on Christmas morning. People surf-riding, playing tennis, fishing in the Straits, practising in skiffs for the Regatta. People.

But my grandmother wasn't there to show me everything and tell me stories. And the lagoon was dirtier than ever. See the lagoon, said my aunt. Full of drifting wood and seaweed and crabs' claws. We could see the lagoon from the kitchen window. We were looking at photographs that day, what silly clothes people wore in those days. There was Grandma sitting on the verandah with her knitting, and there was my great-grandmother, the Maori princess with her big brown eyes, and her lace dress on that her husband bought her, handmade lace, said my aunt, he loved her till he met that woman from Nelson, men are crazy sometimes, but I suppose women are crazier.

— Is there a story? I said. I was a child again. Grandma, tell me about . . .

My aunt smiled. She guesses things sometimes.

— The sort of story they put in *Truth*, she said. On the morning of the tragedy witness saw defendant etc. etc. Your great-grandmother was a murderess. She drowned her husband, pushed him in the lagoon. I suppose the tide was high, I don't know. They would call it 'The Woman From Nelson', she mused. They would have photos. But then nobody knew, only the family. Everybody thought he had had one over the eight and didn't know where he was going.

My aunt drew aside the curtain and peered out. She reminded me of the women in films who turn to the window in an emotional moment, but the moment wasn't emotional, nor was my aunt.

— It's an interesting story, she said. I prefer Dostoevsky to *Truth*.

The water was brown and shining and to the right lay the dark shadow of Domain Hill. There were kids playing on the edge, Christopher Robins with sand between the toes, sailing toy warships and paddling with bare feet in the pools.

— Grandmother never told me, I said.

Again my aunt smiled. The reason (she quoted) one talks furthest from the heart is the fear that it may be hurt.

And then my aunt dropped the curtain across the window and turned to the photographs again.

Was it my aunt speaking or was it my grandmother or my great-grandmother who loved a white lace dress?

At low tide there is no lagoon. Only a stretch of dirty grey sand. I remember we used to skim thin white stones over the water and catch tiddlers in the little creek near by and make sand castles. This is my castle, we said, you be Father I'll be Mother and we'll live here and catch crabs and tiddlers for ever . . .

For All the Saints

J.C. Sturm

I HADN'T been working long at the hospital before I noticed Alice. She was the kind of person who stands out right away in any crowd, even in an institution where everyone has to wear a nondescript uniform. At first I thought it was her Maori blood — she was at least halfcaste — but there were several other Maoris on the staff and a few Rarotongan girls too, so that colour didn't really make much difference unless someone started a fight, and then the important thing was not the kind of person you were but what side you belonged to. But to get back to Alice. If it wasn't colour, I decided, it certainly wasn't glamour either that made her so notable, far from it, though some might have thought her handsome in a dignified statuesque kind of way. She was a tall heavily built woman round about the thirty mark, though it was hard to guess her age, with smooth black hair drawn tightly back into a bun and a smooth pale olive skin that never showed the slightest trace of make-up. Over the usual blue smock we all had to wear, she wore a long shapeless gown, always spotlessly white and just showing her lisle stockings and black button-up shoes. From what I could make out, her work was like her uniform, scrupulously clean and neat and done quietly and methodically without any fuss or bother, in spite of the first cook who would have hustled an elephant. She was the kind of woman boss who is happiest cracking a stock-whip. But even after I had noted these details about Alice and the deliberate way she moved about the kitchen, seldom smiling and never joining in the back-chat with the porters, I still wasn't satisfied. I felt there was something else I couldn't recognise or understand because I had never met it before, some indefinable quality that made her quite different from the rest of us.

I was a servery maid in the nurses' dining-room, and my chores often took me across the corridor to the main kitchen where Alice worked. I made overtures whenever I got the chance, offering to help lift things I knew she could manage quite easily by herself, smiling and nodding and generally getting in her way. Nice day, I'd say, or going to be hot again, but never a word back did I get. Sometimes she'd respond with a grunt or smile or scowl, but most times she would just walk away, or worse still, wait silently for me to move on. This went on for several days, but Alice wouldn't be hurried. She had her own way of making introductions.

One morning I went as usual to collect several big enamel milk jugs from the freezer outside the kitchen door — this was my first job every day — and I was just reaching for a jug when *clump* the heavy door slammed shut behind me. I put the jug down very carefully. *Keep still*, someone shouted inside me, as every muscle in my body threatened to batter me against the four inches of door, *don't move, keep still*. I waited till the shouting had stopped, and then I very gingerly approached the barrier and tapped on it timidly like a guilty child outside the headmaster's office. 'Are you there?' squeaked a voice I didn't recognise, as though it were using a telephone for the first time. 'It's me here, can you hear me?' I waited several lifetimes for the answer that didn't come, then turned away slowly like the lion on the films. Jugs, I thought dully, looking at a wall of them, nice useful harmless things jugs. But at that the whole shelf began to slant and sway drunkenly. I'm at a party, dozens of people around me, talking and laughing and singing and shouting and dancing and stomping to hot boogie woogie. I strained my ears to catch the sound. Drip went a drop of icy water on the concrete in front of me. Now we're all sitting on the floor round a blazing orange fire, eating steaming savs and drinking hot hot coffee and playing a quiet sort of guessing game. I concentrated on a large wooden box against the far wall. How many pounds of boxes to a butter no, no, how many pounds of — the door swung open slowly behind me, and I crawled back to life and warmth and sanity. Alice was propped up against the kitchen door, tears rolling down her face, and shaking so much with laughter I thought her head would fall off.

'Good joke?' she gasped, while I tried to force my knees to keep me upright, 'Funny, eh?' And she gave my shoulder a thump that sent me sprawling into the kitchen like a new-born lamb. From now on, I told myself afterwards, rubbing salt into my wounds, you're going to mind your own darn business. But the next morning when I came on duty, the milk jugs were waiting in the servery. Alice had been to the freezer before me.

After this, Alice and I got on like a house on fire, and it wasn't long before the rest of the staff saw what was happening and started giving me advice. It might have been because they didn't like Alice, or because I was a new chum and as green as they come and they thought I needed protecting, but whatever the reason, several of them took me aside and told me Alice was a woman with bad blood, a treacherous character with the worst temper on God's earth, and the kind of friend who would turn nasty over nothing at all. Soon after, I found out what they really meant and why Alice was the terror of the kitchen.

It had been a particularly trying day, with the thermometer climbing to ninety degrees by mid-morning and staying there, and everybody got so irritable they didn't dare look each other in the eye. I was the last to finish in the servery and thought I'd pop into the kitchen and say goodbye to Alice before I went home. The huge cavern of a place was nearly empty and uncannily quiet. The cooking coppers round the walls had boiled all their strength away, the big steamers that stood higher than a man had hissed their life into the air around them, and the last tide of heat was ebbing slowly from the islands of ovens in the middle of the floor. Alice was alone with her back towards me, mopping the red tiles with long swinging movements, never going over the same place twice, and never missing an inch. As I watched her from the doorway, the little man who worked in the pot-room slipped through a side door and cat-stepped it daintily with exaggeration over the part Alice had just washed.

She leaned on the mop and looked at his dirty footmarks with an expressionless face. A minute later he was back again, singing in a weak nasal voice through the top of his head.

'Ah'm a leedool on the lornlee, a leedl on the lornlee sahd.' He brushed against Alice and blundered into her bucket so that the soapy water slopped over the sides. 'So sorree,' he backed away, but he was too late. Alice had him firmly by the coat-collar, lifted him off his clever feet, and shook him up and down as I would shake a duster. As she threw him half the length of the kitchen through the door into the yard, I crept down the corridor, remembering the freezer and feeling that thump on the shoulder again.

But the next day I found out something much more important about Alice than the quality of her temper. She came and asked me if I would write a letter for her. I was a bit surprised and wanted to know why she didn't do it herself. She couldn't. She had never learned to read or write. At first I was incredulous, then as the full significance of the fact sank in, I was horrified. Words like progress civilisation higher standards and free secular compulsory, sprang to their feet in protest.

'Why, Alice, why?'

'My mother was not well when I was a little baby so she gave me to my Auntie who took me way way out in the country and the two of us lived there on Auntie's farm. My Auntie was a very good woman, very kind to me, but she could not read or write and school was too far away so I never learned. I just stayed at home with Auntie and fixed the farm. But one day when I grew big Auntie said to me, we've got no more money Alice, you must go away and work and get some money and bring it back to fix the farm. So I did. And now I am writing to Auntie to say I am getting the money fast and will come back very soon.' I tried to guess Alice's age once more, decided on thirty again, and reckoned that 'Auntie' might have been about twenty when Alice was 'given' to her. That made her at least fifty now — getting a bit old for fixing farms.

'You read and write, Jacko?' That was the name she liked to call me.

'Oh yes, I read and write.'

'You pretty clever, eh Jacko?' she asked wistfully. 'You better show me how.'

113

And so, every afternoon for the next two or three weeks, I tried. The two of us were working the same broken shift from 6.30 a.m. to 6.30 p.m. with an hour for lunch and three hours off in the afternoon. We started with writing, but I had to give up, I just couldn't take it. It was far worse than working in the pot-room. Alice would grip the pencil as though it were a prison bar and strain and sweat and grunt and poke out her tongue, and I'd sit beside Alice and strain and sweat and grunt and poke out my tongue. I rummaged around the book shops down town and eventually found an easy learn-to-read little book, strictly unorthodox, and not crammed with highly coloured pictures of English villages and stiles and shepherds in smocks and meadows with ponds and oak trees and sheep with the wrong kinds of faces and blue-bells at the edge of the wood. Our book was illustrated in red, white and black, and the few words on each page were put in little boxes, and you jiggled them round so that each box had a slightly different meaning though the words were nearly the same. I would say — first box: look! here is a dog; the dog's name is Rover. And Alice would repeat it after me slowly, pointing at the right box and looking intently at the words in the picture, and then she would roar with laughter and slap the book and very often me too. It was fun for both of us at the beginning and Alice went ahead like nobody's business, but towards the middle of the book the boxes got bigger and the pictures fewer and the game became hard work. One morning I noticed Alice was looking pale and very glum. Her work in the kitchen was as good as usual but she dragged her feet listlessly and kept her eyes down even when I spoke to her. In the end I asked her what was the matter. At first I thought she wasn't going to answer, and then she burst out —

'That damn dog, Rover! All night I try to remember what he did when he jumped over the gate, but it was no good, I couldn't think. All night I try to remember and I got no sleep and now I'm tired Jacko, tired tired.' And to my dismay the immobility of her face broke for the first time, wrinkled up like a child's and a tear slipped down her cheek.

'Look, Alice,' I said, feeling smaller and more helpless than I'd ever felt before, 'you don't want to worry about a silly old dog or a book or reading or anything,' and I steered her into the corridor where the sharp kitchen clowns couldn't see her crying. 'Look, it's a lovely day. Let's have a holiday this afternoon. Let's pretend it's someone's birthday and have a good time. Oh damn, we can't, it's Sunday. What can we do, Alice?' I waited while she shrugged with her voice.

'You do something for me, Jacko? You take me to church tonight, eh?'

She was waiting for me after work. I took one look at her, closed my eyes, and opened them again carefully. She was looking happier and more excited than I had ever seen her, the despair and tiredness of the morning had quite gone, but so had the neat uniform. She was wearing a long pale pink garment that looked suspiciously like a nightgown, and round her neck she had tied a skinny mangy length of fur that even a manx cat wouldn't have looked at twice. But it was the hat that took my breath away. I had only seen such a hat in old photos or magazines about Edwardian England. It was a cream leghorn with a wide flopping brim, dark red roses round the crown, and a huge swaying moulting plume that almost hid her face. I didn't have a hat with me, but I reckoned Alice's would do for the two of us.

'I think I'll go home and see Auntie for a little while. I've got some money for her and when I've fixed the farm I'll come back again.' She showed me her suitcase. 'I'll catch the 10.30 rail-car tonight.'

We were a little late for church, and as we crept in, all eyes swung in our direction, and stopped. That's right, I thought, take a good look, you'll never see another like it again. The summer evening sun streamed through the clear glass window and showed up mercilessly, like strong electric light on an ageing face, all the drabness of the grey unadorned walls, the scratches on the varnished pews, the worn patches in the faded red carpets, the dust on the pulpit hangings, and the underlying greenness of the minister's old black suit.

'For all the saints, who from their labours rest,' squeaked the small huddle of people like someone locked up in a freezer. I shifted my weight from one foot to the other and leaned against the pew in front of me. Ahmmmahh, droned Alice happily above everyone else except the big-bosomed purple-gowned over-pearled organist, who pulled all her stops out and clung to the top notes like a determined lover. Alice was holding her hymn book upside down.

After the service I took Alice home for supper. She seemed a little lost and rather subdued in our sitting-room, and sat stiffly on the edge of a chair with her knees together and her hands gripping each other in her lap. I made several unsuccessful attempts to put her at ease, and then I noticed she kept glancing sideways at the piano that stood in the corner.

'Would you like to play the piano, Alice?' I suggested. She jumped up immediately with a delighted grin and walked over the music stool.

'Dadada eedeeda,' she sang on one note, and thumped up and down the keyboard. Fifteen minutes later, she turned to me. 'Pretty good, eh? I know plenty more. You like some more?' And she settled herself down for the rest of the evening before I could reply. My mother got up hastily and went out to the kitchen to make the supper. When the time came to go, Alice looked very solemn and I feared a repetition of the morning crisis. But I was wrong.

'I got something I want to show you, Jacko,' she said. 'I've never shown anyone before.' And she handed me a folded piece of old newspaper. 'That's a picture of my uncle. He went away before my Auntie got me. My Auntie says he's the best man she ever knew and one day he'll come back and look after me and Auntie and get money to pay for the house and fix the farm. He's got a good kind face, eh Jacko?' I peered at the blurred photo. A group of men were standing behind a central figure sitting in the foreground, and underneath, the caption read — 'This is the last photo to be taken of the late Lord Tweedsmuir, Governor-General of Canada, well-known throughout the English-reading world as the novelist, John Buchan.' My mother looked over my shoulder.

'But surely you've made —' I stopped her with a sharp dig in the ribs.

'Yes, Alice,' I said, 'he has got a good kind face, and I'm sure he'll come back.'

It was bright moonlight at the station. Small groups of people stood around waiting to see others off in a rail-car that looked much too small and toy-like for the long journey round the foot of the hills that lay to the north-west of the town. Alice gripped my arm till my eyes watered, and then she mistook that for something else and gripped harder still.

'Goodbye, goodbye,' she waved out of the window, the plume shedding feathers over everything near her. 'See you soon, Jacko, goodbye.'

But I never saw Alice again. I stayed on at the hospital for the rest of the summer and then went south to another job, and Alice hadn't returned before I left. Auntie must be sick, I thought, or maybe it's taking her longer to fix the farm than she expected. Several months later I received a letter from my mother. 'I've got some news for you,' she wrote. 'Alice came back not long ago, but her place in the kitchen was taken, so they found her a job in the laundry. She got on all right at first, but soon there was more of the old trouble, and when she nearly strangled one of the other women, things came to a head and they had her put away quietly. There was quite a bit about it in the paper, but of course she wouldn't know that. Poor Alice. Do you remember how she played the piano that night and showed us a photo of her "uncle"? And oh, my dear, till your dying day, will you ever forget that hat?'

The Girl From Kaeo

Noel Hilliard

T AKE this one now. Typical. When she was picked up she was wearing a man's shirt and jeans and no shoes, and she had bad teeth and crab-lice and sticking-plaster on a cut in her cheek. Look at her hair and fingernails. Note the tattoos on arms and hands and fingers and knees. There are others you can't see. She's seventeen.

this man he said to me Where you from? and I said Kaeo and he said Thats nice Im from Kaeo too, where abouts in Kaeo? but I said nothing so he said Were you right in Kaeo or round about? and when I still said nothing he said Do you mean Te Huia? and I shook my head so he said Waiare then? Opokorau? Pupuke? Omaunu? and when I said nothing he looked at me in a way to show he thought I was telling a lies about where I come from so I said to him I said All I remember about Kaeo is there was fifteen of us and we all slept on the floor and I never saw my fathers face because I was always looking at his boots

Look into her living conditions. Was she living at home, or boarding, or sleeping around? Would you say her living conditions were very high? high? average? poor? very bad?

If she was not living at home, look into her relationships with her kinsfolk in general and scale them as Very Good/Good/Average/Poor/Very Bad.

What about the people in the house? Are they active criminals? People of dubious reputation? Average types? Very good? Or have you no information?

Now apply the same criteria to her associations and relationships in general and see if the two roughly coincide.

that night I was so late at the cowshed the moon it come up when I was on my way back to the house and Mum she was sitting by herself on the old busted verandah and I sat down beside her in my beret and overcoat and leaky gumboots and Mum she put her arm around my shoulders so warm and she said Did you know the man in the moon is a Maori? and I said No and how do you know that? and Mum she said Is because he got a tattoo face cant you see? just like my great-grandfather and he was OLD when he died

Establish the extent of her possessions, savings, and property from legitimate sources. Estimate the value and classify: over $200; $1–200; none; in debt $1–100; in debt over $100.

and my mother she use to have a nice voice one time that was before she lost her teeth, lovely voice to sing my mother and my mother she use to say you cant sing properly without you got your teeth, your mouth is all funny

Examine the extent of her social involvement and community integration. Church or acceptable social-club membership are useful indicators. Find out if she is very active in one or many; moderately active; no interest; resists such activities.

Establish what her attitudes are towards authority in general and particularly towards the police, the probation service, welfare and institution officers. Classify under Very Good/Good/Reasonable/Poor/Antagonistic.

and we use to get our water from the bush, the creek in the bush, but a slip came down and spoilt the place where we use to go and so after we had to get it from the side creek where is all the wiwi and was all right too but not so good the bush water. And my mother she use to say the side creek water was not so good the bush water, that bush water it was beautiful water. Lovely water

and in the city I use to think of my mother and my eyes they would prickle when I thought of the bush water and how my mother said it was beautiful water, lovely water

and how many in the city that all think theyre so smart, how many of thems know about bush water or even there are different kinds of water and it doesnt just only come from out the tap?

and my mother she knew the taste of good water even if she lost her teeth that time my father he came home mad on the dandelion wine he call it his jungle juice even if it come off a paddock

Form an opinion on her manner and ease of communication. Would you say she was very easy to get along with? Would you describe her as moderately open? Is she suspicious and evasive? Does she lie even when she can have no doubt the truth is already known?

Examine her work record before her offence. If you find she had few changes of job, and the jobs were all of the same kind, and she was never dismissed, class her record as Very Good. If you find that her jobs were mostly but not invariably of the same kind, mark Good. If on the other hand you find she had a variety of jobs and stayed in none for long, mark Poor. At the extreme, if you find her indifferent to work, and lax about finding a job, and never attempting to keep one or advance herself in it, mark Bad.

and it was loving and it was always too hard and much too often but always good and warm and loving and it was having a lot of real and touching people close to you and yes Johnny any time Johnny please Johnny too again please yes and how often you want me Johnny how often you like Johnny you so good to me Johnny please too sleepy no not and you must and if you want yes and never stop

*and not them Johnny no just only you Johnny please just only us please
Johnny just only us this time please Johnny PLEASE*

Now look at her other attitudes. First towards her offences. Does she
show remorse? Acknowledge guilt? Is she shamed by the exposure? Is
she defiant? Is this defiance in your view related or unrelated to feelings
of guilt? (Caution needed here.)

Now her attitudes towards incarceration. Is she afraid? apprehensive?
indifferent? inured and without fear?

*and is it not a fact that to become members of this gang, girls had to
submit to intercourse with all male members?*
   yes
   eight and nine and even ten, one after the other?
   sometimes more
   and did you enjoy it?
   the question is irrelevant, mr thing
   *Im sorry your honour Now is it not a fact that girl members were
required to go out and obtain new girl members for the gang?*
   yes
   how did you go about this?
   silence
   *let me put it to you this way then, was force ever used to get other girls
to join the gang?*
   yes
   *and you yourself used force on other girls to get them to submit to the
boys?*
   yes see there was this boy Johnny see he
   *thank you And is it not a fact that you ripped a girls pants off and
when she resisted further you*
   the point is already established, mr thing

Look at her efforts at rehabilitation. Would you say she was trying
hard? Making some effort? Making no effort? Determined to keep to
crime and anti-social behaviour?

This leads to an estimate of her criminal future. On the basis of her record and known performance would you describe her as a persistent offender? Do you believe she will be in trouble for some time yet? Is she an occasional offender, depending on associations and circumstances? Could you conclude (this must be approached with caution) that she is unlikely to offend again?

and is it not a fact that when you are angry with yourself you keep hitting your teeth against the windowsill until they bleed?

Look next at her behaviour inside the institution. Has she offended against discipline? How often? More than once a week? Once a month? Is she incorrigible? What is the type of offence? Riot; escape; fighting; theft; writing illegal notes; other (give details); or minor.

Earlier in the year, on a charge of being not under proper control, she had been committed to the charge of the Child Welfare Department. Since then, stated the senior sergeant, she had been 'uncontrollable and a considerable worry' to the welfare and other authorities. She had refused to work, alleging a state of pregnancy contrary to fact.

Does she talk about crime? Is this obsessional, can she talk of nothing else? Does she refer to it only occasionally? Or does she avoid and resist such topics? Can she talk much, or well, on topics unrelated to crime? What is her influence on other inmates? Good, poor, bad, or none? Estimate the extent of her voluntary association with other inmates: more than six; four to six; two; one; solitary.

As the charges were read the accused collapsed, wailing and sobbing bitterly. Police hurried her out of the courtroom. She was still crying softly when the case resumed 20 minutes later and while the senior sergeant continued giving details of her behaviour, tears rolled down her cheeks.

Form an estimate of the interest she shows in her family. Keep a record of the number of outward letters, and after careful perusal give an opinion of their quality. Correlate this with an estimate of the interest her family shows in her, on the basis of letters and visits and inquiries about her progress.

'I cannot criticize any particular section of the police force,' said the magistrate, 'but the force at large is to be censured for keeping any person under the age of 16 in a common jail awaiting trial for seven days.'

Is she able to carry out her work assignment on her own or does she require constant supervision? How good are her relationships with staff? Classify according to Very Good/Good/Neutral/Reserved/Very Distant.

'You are not the only member of the community who is untrustworthy,' the magistrate stated. 'Nor are you the only one who is wayward and dissolute. But from my point of view you are the only one of all the sorry parade I see before me day after day who can only be described as a pest. What is to become of you? You must give some thought to trying to make something of yourself.'

Observe the extent of her involvement in education, hobbies and sparetime interests. Classify according to number and quality, and amount of time spent on them; from more than six down to none.

and this magistrate I seen him before and he got a green fountain pen and white hairs in his ears and pick his nose and he say to me you are nothing but a nuisance, do you know that? in and out of here all the time

Note the amount of care taken of her cell beyond the requirements of normal supervision. Form an estimate of the standard of cleanliness and quality of decoration. Mark her approach to unsupervised personal hygiene as Very Good/Good/Average/Poor/Very Poor.

and we use to meet these boys in Gleeson's and take them up home this place in Lincoln Street in Ponsonby and was all this beer and the old man he use to sell the bottles and was dozens and hundreds so he must get a fair bit off them and the boys they would give him beer too or wine or what he wanted but he got WILD he said to us you not to bring these boys home and we all said we said bugger you we said this is our place what we pay you this is where we LIVE and nobody took no notice and the old man he locked the door and he put boards over the windows in the daytime after a while to stop the boys getting in and the boys come they smashed the boards down yes and broke the glass and put the beer in through the window first and then they come in too yes after the beer yes all these boys gee there was LOT of them and Pauline she was trying to get this boy to give his mate some moneys so he can pay her and they was all yelling and the old man he come in yelling in his pink underpants and he told us he rang for the cops and gee the boys was WILD and gee it was funny with the cops coming in the front door and the boys all diving out the windows and there was these two on the floor and a cop he fell over them gee it was funny and Ruby she was naked and Sandra she only had her skivvy on and the old man in his pink underpants he was just standing there gee he looked funny and the broken glasses on the floor and gee they came in fast and hell they WENT fast too the boys back to the ship and we all went down after and gee was great you know this boy he borrow me his jersey I was COLD and was this old man on the ship and the boys they got him to bring out his pink underpants and one of the boys he put them on and he was making out he was this old man up at Lincoln Street the one that phone for the cops and gee it was funny the way he done it we was all laughing

One Two Three Four Five

Arapera Blank

One, two, three, four, five,
I was only half alive.

N O ONE told me when I was born. My mother was too busy. My father was too busy. We never had birthday parties. But I knew when I was ready to go to school; they told me I was five. I'd been playing a long time round the house. I played cowboys, marbles, shops, ghosts. Sometimes I just slept in the grass. Those times my mother worked in the garden, my brothers and sisters were at school. They were too busy to play with me.

Yeah, they told me I was five. I was a big boy now. I had to wear good pants, keep my nose clean, not talk Māori in school. Only dumb kids did that. Least, that's what my mother and my father and my brothers and sisters told me. They told me the teacher would strap me if I did it in my pants. Then they'd laugh and tell me it was all lies. Funny. I seen that teacher, the one for me. Always talked to my mother across the fence. Not bad really. Nice face. Nice clothes. Not smelly like my mother. She smiled at me too.

Didn't have a good sleep that night. School in the morning. I got a good bath. They scrubbed me hard. My head, my feet. Gee they were sore. Then Mum. Talk, talk, talk.

'Don't you swear in school. Don't you say "bum" or funny words like that. You say, "Please, teacher, may I go to the lav." Don't you eat crayons. Your brothers did that. Gee I was ashamed. Teacher might think your mum's too poor to feed you. Don't you put paint on your pants. Can't buy any more. No money. See this new shirt? You dirty it and you see what you get!'

Yeah I was on the bed. The other boys were snoring. I'm five. I don't feel big. My inside is banging. I'm frightened to go to school.

I must've been awake all night. I was tired. They all want to put my clothes on. I feel like I'm going to cry. My brothers said: 'Aw go on! You wait. Nice school that. And you can play real cowboys with us now.' Good idea that. My sisters said they'd look after me at school. See that no one hit me or stole my lunch. I feel good now. I like my new pants. The shirt makes me want to scratch. Nice smell though. Mum gave me a hanky for my nose. She said, 'No sniffing in school!'.

Marino, that's my big sister in standard six, she took me to school. My brothers wouldn't. They liked my new clothes though. They said some of those new kids they only had old clothes. They said they couldn't hold my hand all the way to school. Other boys might see them. Give them cheek. Only sissies hold hands. My mum she was too busy. Couldn't come. Said she took Marino and the boys too, then my other sister. Now it was their turn to take me. Too many jobs to do at home. My father he tickled my head. 'You're going to beat them all. Yeah, 'cause you're the button, the baby.'

I never seen so many children all together. Gee, noisy. Shouting, laughing, talking funny. Marino's friends they came up to the school gate. They said 'Pretty brother you got, Marino. Nice clothes. Here give him a lolly. Come with you to see the teacher.' Teacher? I don't want no teacher. What did Mum say? What did they all say? Can't remember. I'm getting frightened. Marino bumped me. 'Say "Good morning, teacher".' Couldn't say it. Never tried before. Wanted to cry.

I was standing. Marino was gone. She said she was busy. She wanted to play tennis. I stuck out my hand. 'You're a big boy now.' Oh! The teacher. That nice one my mother used to talk to. Didn't want to go with her. Don't know what to say. I want Marino. The teacher she wouldn't let me go. 'You come and play with these little children. Now there's a good boy.' Lots of them playing on the big concrete. Just in front of the school. Not schooltime yet. But they had toys and blocks.

The bell was ringing. Everybody was running. They were standing. I want Marino. I was frightened. Too many kids. I might wet my pants, might sniff, might talk Māori. Not allowed. Here's Marino. She smiled at me. She took my hand. She said, 'Don't be frightened. You show those kids you're clever. Don't talk Māori in school though. Don't want those other kids to tell me that my brother can't talk English.'

She came into my room with me. Lots of kids sitting on the floor. The teacher was standing up in the front. Kids were talking to her. Showed her their hankies. I got one too. Marino said, 'Take yours out. Hold it up.' They blew their noses. Marino said, 'Blow yours. Not too loud.' They brushed their teeth. Just pretending though. I held Marino's hand. Didn't want her to go. Funny smell this room. Like kerosene. Shiny floor. Bet it's slippery. High walls. Me. Gee I was small. Didn't want to sit down. Might get lost but that teacher she made me sit with Marino. I started to cry loud. Marino said, 'I'm still here. What you're crying for?' She said, 'Stop it. Those other kids are looking.' Don't care. She don't know I'm frightened I might wet my pants. She didn't show me the lav. Might be ghosts in it too.

She said, 'You'll be all right. I been in this room too. Nice room. You just say, "Yes please" and, "No thank you" and sit on the floor nicely and you'll be all right. Better than home. Lots of nice toys here to play with.' I could tell she just wanted to run away to her room. I held tight. She was looking at me too. She was getting wild. She didn't want to be little like me. Yeah, she was sorry for me all right but she want to go back to her own room.

The teacher was talking to the kids. She said I was a new boy. I was going to be clever too. Just like them. They got to help me. Show me things. They said, 'Yes'. They were looking at me. Gee they were big. Me, I'm too small. I crossed my legs too. Marino she dropped my hand.

'You'll be all right.' You could tell she was sick of me. 'Please, teacher, I want to go back to my own room. If Whaimata is a nuisance I'll come back again.'

'Yes. Thank you, Marino. Off you go.' I couldn't do nothing. Just sat. Long time sitting when you can't do nothing. The kids were singing. I didn't know the words. I want to cry. A little boy was talking about his mum. Just like my mum. She did the same work. A little girl poked me. She said, 'Ay baby. What you frightened for? Dopey. No one's going to eat you.' The teacher said, 'Now Awhina, we're all going to help Whaimata. It's not nice to talk like that.' You can tell she was wild with that girl.

All the kids went to do things. You know, play. 'You come with me, Whaimata.' That was the teacher. 'We'll go and find something to do. Oh, here. You come and paint a picture.'

'No. Don't want to. Not allowed. Might dirty my pants.'

'Well then, we'll go and play with the blocks over there. Make houses and trucks and tractors.'

'No. Somebody might hit me.' I want to cry. Can't help it. I know she's nice.

'Well, dear. We'll go and make a picture with crayons. Look. Lots of children at that table. They're all making pictures. Would you like to?'

Yeah, well that was all right 'slong as I don't eat the crayons like my mother said. Maybe if I had a picture they might think I'm clever. Yeah, like my father said.

'Here, Marata. You come and help him. Whaimata, hold the crayon like this.' Gee it was big. Greasy too. Too big. Funny in my hand. 'No, not like that, dear. Like this.' She's talking to me. Showing me how.

'Yeah. He's dumb. He don't know what to do.' Gee, that cheeky girl again. Wish I could give her a hiding. I know what. Tell Marino.

'Now, Awhina. Go away from this table. Go right outside and stand there you rude girl.' Good teacher that. She want to look after me, just like she said.

Pretty things all round the room. High walls though. Too big. Lots of places for drawing with chalk. Plenty things to do. That nice teacher she was talking to me again. She said not to stand. Find something to do.

Didn't say anything to those other kids. Too smart for me. They put all the things away. Those crayons and paints. I want to play now. Wish I could tell the teacher.

Gee I know some of the boys and some of the girls too. From down our road. Didn't want them to see I was dumb like that funny girl Awhina said. She don't like me. Must be jealous of my new pants and my new shirt.

They were all sitting on the floor. They were showing the things they made. I like that horse. That one that big boy is showing. He made it out of clay. Funny I used to play with that stuff. Yeah down at the river. I took some home too. You know my mum? Well, she was wild with me. She said, 'Take that muck off my steps. I got enough to do without cleaning up that mess. Do you think I'm going to wash your clothes after? Look at you. Filthy!' Yeah, I'm going to make one at school. You're allowed. You know.

Gee, here's Kauru. He live in the place next to ours. Nice house they got. Better than ours. Marino said. Must be smart. He's talking. The teacher said, 'You have a long tongue, Kauru. You talk too much.' I wish I could talk like him though. Want to hold his hand. Yeah, but my brothers say only sissy boys hold hands.

'Well, Whaimata, would you like to tell us about your brothers and sisters?' 'Course I did. But I might talk Māori. Might go wrong. They might laugh, like Marino said. Yeah, I want to tell them I got a big sister in standard six. She can give them a hiding if they get cheeky to me. Too frightened to talk. Then that teacher she felt sorry for me, picked me up. I don't like it. Funny. She's not my mummy. Yeah, I know I said she was nice. I just don't like new people to pick me up. I was wriggling about and kicking. I said, 'No.' She said, 'I want you to be happy. I want everybody to see you so they can help you. There's a good boy.' I just yelled. Couldn't help it. Those damn kids they were laughing. I was ashamed. Never been to school before.

She put me down. She growled the kids. They were quiet all right. She was nice to me. My nose was dirty. I was sniffing. She said, 'Got a hanky, Whaimata?' I know I done wrong to wipe it on my shirt. I got my hanky. I'm smart too. The teacher said, 'Now, children, when-we-clean-our-noses-we use our . . . ?' 'Hankies,' they said. They thought they were smart. Me too. I kept my hanky in my hand.

The bell was ringing. The teacher said playtime now. Don't want to go out. Want to wait for Marino. Those kids too noisy. Kauru said, 'Come on, Whaimata. Show you the slide. Show you the sandpit. We can play there.' I said, 'No. I wait for Marino.'

'Aw you're just frightened. You sissy.'

I said, 'Tell Marino. Tell her you gave me cheek.'

The teacher came. She said, 'Come, Whaimata, we'll go and find your sister, Marino.' She took my hand. She never said I was a sissy. Marino was coming to me with her mates. They took me for a walk. I saw Kauru looking at me. He could see Marino. He was frightened I might tell Marino. I'm not a tell-tale. I'm not a sissy. 'This your brother Marino? Gee, he looks like a girl. Who give him all those curls?' Yeah, some of those big boys they're funny. Must be jealous of my new clothes.

I wanted to go to the lavatory. Marino got Kauru. She said she's not allowed in our lav. Only boys. She said we got a different one from the girls. 'Kauru, you take him.' She was outside, waiting. That Kauru, he was just a show-off. He told his mates I don't know how to go to the lav. 'You want to piss? You don't take your pants right off. Here you take the buttons off. Like this.' He nearly pulled my buttons off. I nearly pissed my pants. Some funny boys they were looking at me. They gave me cheek. I finished. I went out with Kauru. They all came. They said to Marino I don't know how to piss in the lav. Kauru said ghosts in that lav too. Might bite my mimi. Marino got wild. She gave them a hiding. She said, 'Humbug. No ghosts. They just tell lies.' She said they always do that to new boys, that's why she was outside waiting.

My brothers were playing marbles. They didn't want to play with me at school. 'Spoil their game.' I know they like me though. Never give me a hiding. Only sometimes. They can give Kauru and his mates a hiding. Yeah, Marino said all the big brothers and sisters look after the little brothers and sisters at school. We were walking and the bell was ringing. All the kids were running. They got to hurry up into line and no more noise. Gee, lot of kids. Big ones too. Marino told Kauru to put me behind him. She went to her place. I don't like Kauru, he's a cheeky boy that one.

The kids were busy in school. The teacher was busy too. Just like my mother. She just told me to play with the toys. I was sitting down playing with a tractor. I was making tractor noise. One big kid he told me to shut-up. He can't write his story if I go, 'Brr, brr' all over the place. They think they're clever, those big kids. They told me they don't want to listen to baby noises. Gee, I want to paint a picture like those kids over the other table. My mother said not to dirty my clothes though. I just pushed the tractor. I got sick of it. I found some more toys. Box full. No good playing by yourself though with all these nice things. That smart girl Awhina she was reading to the teacher. She thinks she's clever. I went to see the paintings. 'Here, you paint.' Nice boy this one. 'Make a story. Show you how. Blue for the sky. No, this colour. What's the colour of your house? You don't know? Gee, you're dumb!' He gave me a big brush. He said put it on the paper. 'No, not like that. You're not allowed to paint the table. Your hands'll get dirty.'

Gee, it was hard work you know. My hands were real dirty. I rubbed them on my pants. 'Hey, you're not allowed to do that. You got to use that basin over there.'

The teacher came up. She said she didn't like the paint on my clothes. She said who told me to paint when she's not there to show me how. I said, 'That boy.' She said, 'Wash your hands in the basin.' I said, 'Yes.' She smiled. She said, 'Good boy.' I said, 'Look, I done a painting.' She said, 'You say, "I did a painting", not "I done".' I said what she said. I was clever to say what she said. Those other kids they were only jealous. They said I done no picture. Only paint. She was nice though. She said, 'Good boy, Whaimata. Good picture.'

All the kids were on the floor. She showed them my picture. She said, 'You stand here, Whaimata, you tell them all about your picture.' I said, 'Sky.' I said. 'My house.' That boy Kauru said, 'Yeah, funny house. No chimney, no nothing.' The teacher, she growled. She was wild. She don't like cheeky kids. I said, 'Finished.' She said, 'Thank you. Sit down now, Whaimata.' Yeah, those kids are only jealous. Wish I could make real stories though. Read them to the kids too. The teacher said they were clever too. She said, 'One day Whaimata will write stories too.'

I know that. Marino told me. She said all new kids are dumb. She said they get clever if they come to school all the time. Like her. She never stayed home. She used to cry if my mother said to stay home and look after me. Then my mother would get sorry and say, 'Go to school then.' Her teacher said she was clever. He said she was going far away because she was clever. The teacher said, 'Now, children, do you know it was Whaimata's birthday last Saturday? He's five years old. One, two, three, four, five. That's why he started school today. Did you have a birthday party, Whaimata?' I said, 'No. No party.' Those kids laughed. A big boy said, 'Yeah. Beer party, not birthday party.'

That Kauru, he was a tell-tale. I know. Always having parties at their place. He said we're jealous of their place.

That teacher she was nice to me. She showed us a birthday cake. Five candles on it. My cake. She said, 'This is for Whaimata. Five candles. One, two, three, four five.' Not a real cake though. Gee I'm smart. I'm not frightened. She said, 'I hold the cake. You blow out the candles.' I did. Those kids had to sing to me. A birthday song. Nice song and I was standing in the front all by myself.

It was lunch-time. We were sitting on the steps. I had plenty mates. I had a nice lunch. Marino brought my lunch. Nice lunch too. Cake and bread and jam and peanut butter. Some of those other kids they only had dry bread. They were jealous of my lunch. They said I was greedy. Not me. Kauru wanted some of my cake. I wanted him for a mate. I gave him some. He said, 'I give you a marble for some cake.' He never. Just wanted my lunch. Marino told me that. She said they hang around new boys just for their lunch. She said some of their mummies were too lazy to make nice lunches. Not like our mum. She said she don't want people to say we got no money for lunches.

Yeah, sure enough! Soon as I finished lunch, no more mates. I said to Kauru, tomorrow I have a good lunch too. He still won't give me the marble. Marino growled at me too. She said I was dopey to give those kids some. Tomorrow she is going to sit by me. She said Kauru got plenty lunch. Must be keeping it for after school. She said we wait and see. She was going to tell the teacher too.

We went to play. Some little boys were playing football with the big ones. Gee, they were tough. You know those little ones got dumped. Specially if a little one got the ball. No crying though. I saw two kids fighting for marbles. Talking Māori all the time. Gee, if the teacher catch them they're going to get it. Some kids said to me, 'Come and play.' I said, 'No.' Some big girls were singing. I know those songs. My daddy got a guitar too. Like the one that big boy got. I can dance too. Just like those big girls.

We are in school. We are sitting on the floor again. Nice. Nice floor this. The teacher said she don't like boys who eat new boys' lunches. Only greedy boys do that. Serves Kauru right. Good job, Kauru. He's showing his fists to me. He won't touch me though. Teacher's looking. Can't after school too. Marino's going to wait for me. The teacher said to me to go to sleep. I can, because I'm a new boy. She said I must be tired. Not me. I said, 'No.' She said, 'All right, good boy, Whaimata.'

The kids are singing. I know this one. 'One, two, three, four, five, once I caught a fish alive.' This one too. 'This little pig went to market.' Wish I could tell the teacher I know those. They are clapping. I can clap too. I can count too. Just like them. Right up to ten. Sometimes up to fifteen. Marino showed me.

The kids got up. They went to their chairs. No chair for me. The teacher said I can please myself. I put my hands in my pockets. I went round the room. The teacher said I was a good boy to walk round the room. Anyway, I'm not frightened of those kids. Gee, I wish I can read like some of those kids. Some of those kids said they were doing sums. But they never. Only playing shop games. Nice beads and pretty buttons and blocks. Humbug! You don't make sums with blocks. My brothers said only babies count with blocks.

The teacher told me not to stand there with my hands in my pockets. She said she's going to sew them up. She gave me some beads. My brothers said only girls play with beads. But they were nice. Pretty. I stuck the string in my mouth. I put a bead on it. Then one more. Then one more. The teacher said I was good. A little girl said, 'Put two buttons on. I give you two buttons.' Heck, she thinks I can't count. Pretty though. More beads, more buttons, more beads. I finished. The teacher said, 'Very good, Whaimata. What's that colour?' I don't know colours. She said, 'This button is red. That one is blue.' I said, 'Red, blue.' She said, 'Good boy, Whaimata.'

Yeah, they were looking at me. 'Course I'm clever. I'm getting tired. I want to make a truck with blocks. But no good. Not allowed to make too much noise. I put my hands in my pockets. I went to see some kids. Heck! They were making real sums. Pencils and books too. That's the real way to make sums. One boy there, he was nice. He showed me his work. Gee, I reckon he's clever. He told me to hold his pencil. He said, 'Do it like this.' Gee, I couldn't hold the pencil. Hard! Too big for me.

We are sitting on the floor. The teacher said, 'Nice work, children.' She said, 'Whaimata, where are your beads?' I said, 'Must be there.' I was looking at the box. She said, 'Next time you keep them. Then you can show the children what you have done.'

'He don't know how to count, miss. I put those buttons on.' Liar! She never! Yeah, funny girl that. Only two she put on.

'Who said? You never. You only put two on. I seen you.' Nice kid that one. Yeah she saw me put most of them on. The teacher said she don't like kids to tell tales. She was nice to me.

She was telling us a story. I know that story. Marino told me. About a witch. You see these two children. They got lost in the bush. Marino didn't show me those pictures. I thought a witch was a ghost. This witch had a house. Plenty of lollies on it. Real lollies. These two kids were eating them. The witch come along. She caught them. Yeah. She put them in a room to make them fat. Yeah. She's going to eat them. But those kids were cunning. They put her in the stove. Good job! They burnt her all up. They ran away home. The teacher showed us how to make a witch. You got to have no teeth. Make your nose look skinny. Like this. Gee, my granny got no teeth. Yeah. She looks like that witch.

I was making a witch on the blackboard. Gee, I know what to do if I see a witch. Chop her down with the axe. Marino said a witch is bad. My mother said humbug. She seen no witch. Only ghosts though. Her mother seen a ghost too. Kauru said to the teacher, plenty of witches down our road. Humbug! Just as well I'm going home with Marino. She's not frightened.

The teacher said, go outside and play. I want to go to the lav. Marino got Kauru. He said to me that witches come into lavs too. Specially Pākehā lavs. Gee, I nearly wet my pants. Marino said to me, 'Only fairy stories. Only humbug. They never go to lavs.' She never been in our lav though. How did she know?

We had dancing. We had to get girls. Nice girl I had. Too fast though. She said, 'Like this.' I did. She laughed. The teacher was playing the piano. She saw me. She said, 'Very nice, Whaimata.' We all sat down. Gee, I was tired. I wanted to go home.

Marino came. She said I was good not to cry for her all day. She said, 'Where's that Kauru? I want his lunch. Come here, Kauru. Where's your bag? I'll just make sure you got no lunch. You ate Whaimata's, eh?'

'Lies,' said Kauru. 'I got no lunch. I ate mine at playtime. Anyway, he gave me that cake 'cause he wanted my marbles. Good job! Whaimata was skiting with his lunch. I tell my daddy if you hit me.'

Marino didn't. She just said, 'Next time, Kauru, I give you a black eye.' 'Yeah, me too,' I said.

I was holding Marino's hand. I never saw no witches. Kauru tells lies. I told Marino, 'Sing "One, two, three, four, five".' She said. 'No, wait till we get home. I don't want to sing baby songs on the road.' She said, 'What's that you got in your hand, Whaimata?'

I had my painting. The teacher said to take it home for my mummy. She said I was clever. I said to Marino, 'I been painting.' She said, 'No wonder. You got some on your pants. Gee, Mummy will growl.'

'The teacher said she will like my picture. I got a sky and a house. Mummy won't hit me.'

Marino was laughing. Smart, yeah. Just like those other kids. She said, 'Gee, I used to make scribbles like that.' I was wild with her. I started to cry. I'm not dumb.

My mummy was at the gate. She said, 'How's my baby?' That's me she's talking about. Gee, I was glad. She picked me up. Yeah, I liked that too. She said she was sorry when I went to school. She said the house was sad. She said she was going to be lonely now I was a big boy. Aw heck! I thought she was too busy to play with me. She said, 'What's that you got in your hand?' Marino said, 'Scribble. Scribble painting. Only rubbish. He got some on his new pants too.'

My mummy said, 'Never mind. He's only a baby.' Big boy, baby, she don't know what to call me. I showed her my picture. She never said nothing. Just squeezed me and put me down.

Gee, I had a lot to tell. All about the lav and the boys and the witches and those kids hanging around my lunch. Going to tell her to make me a real big lunch for tomorrow.

My daddy and my brothers. They finished milking. They came home. My daddy said to me, 'How's the big boy?' I said, 'Good school, Daddy.' I said, 'Those kids only jealous of me. That Kauru he tells lies. He ate my lunch. He said I don't know how to piss in the lav. Daddy, you got the axe? Might be a witch in our room tonight.'

The boys they just laughed. They said, 'Aw, hell. No bloody witches in this house.' I said, 'The teacher said you not allowed to swear.' I said, 'I got a nice teacher, Daddy. She got new clothes like me. She said I'm clever.'

I went to bed. Gee, I was tired. I put my head right under the blankets. Just as well my brothers are here too. I don't want to see that witch. Might take me away. I want to go back to school tomorrow. Gee, I like that song.

> One, two, three, four, five,
> Once I caught a fish alive.

Postscript

O ngā ao e toru

People do not realise what they have done to me since I left my mother's knee for the teacher's.

My granny says to me, 'Don't talk Pākehā. You're swearing at me.'

'No I'm not, Granny. I'm speaking English.' But she's too dumb to understand.

'What's that you're singing?' I say, 'Pākehā songs.' She says, 'Hōhā!' I ask, 'What's that you're singing, Granny?' She says, 'Waiata.' She says, 'Hōhā te pātai.'

We don't get on. She won't let me sing Pākehā songs. She says I will become a snob. What's the use of sending me to school? To read and to write of course. To learn how to spend my money of course. That's why I go to school. But she doesn't want to hear about it. She says I won't visit her any more. I'm getting too smart. She'll just have to find some other mokopuna. But she's too dumb to understand that they're all like me. All speaking English. All reading and writing. We speak Māori only at home. It's not good enough for school.

Yes. I like school. I like the new games we play. I like reading about people of faraway places — Chinese, Germans, Italians. My granny never told me about them. She was always too busy making kits or talking about ghosts or cooking a meal. My grandfather liked to rub his whiskers against our faces and gave us money if we did him a favour. He was always writing. He said he had sacred books all about our ancestors. He said that's why he went to school for one year. Enough to learn how to read and to write his sacred books.

I am older now. I have finished school. And now I like everything. That's what's wrong with me. I am a three-legged creature. I can't put my three legs down at once either. The world isn't ready for such a creature. But this is what education in a European world has given me. Three legs.

Yes. When I was being educated my parents were proud of me. I liked them. I liked being at school. I was a missionary in embryo too. A kind of ambassador for my race. All the Rs (you realise there are four) were hammered into me. The teachers fashioned me and formed me. Like that man who breathed life into his statue after he had fashioned it. I was allowed to keep my Māori leg — the attractive part of it — action songs, the haka, and how to write in my own tongue. They said that's what māoritanga was. It's no wonder that my Māori leg is rather clumsy. The rest of it? Well, education is an expensive business.

> Let not ambition mock their useful toil,
> Their homely joys, and destiny obscure . . .

Now this is pleasant to think about in the long grass, but totally inadequate for my new leg — the Pākehā one. When I put this new leg down it must be strong. So I hide the other one — the one Tiki fashioned from clay. My Pākehā leg says:

> I must walk where the giant walks,
> I must put away all Māori thinking,
> Whakarērea iho te kakau o te hoe.
> I'm allowed to remember Tāwhaki's climb.
> (He must have been a Pākehā)
> He never faltered.
> Time, that's what I must remember.
> No time to sit and talk.
> No time for the tangi, the hui,
> No money for that rubbish,
> 'Uneconomical, energy-consuming'
> Better spent in reading and writing
> And getting accustomed to civilisation.
> That's my new waiata!
> Auē taukuri e!
> Whakarērea iho te kakau o te hoe.

> Get an education
> Live in a house like the next-door neighbours',
> Ming-blue. Yeah that's the rave. Brand new!
> My ancestor turn in his grave?
> So what! He knew no sophistication.
> Why he didn't bring civilisation.
> I must save for a brand-new carpet and cups and venetian blinds
>   and maybe a new car
> Yeah that's good for my new leg.
> No time to walk, no time to talk. Amen.

My third leg is what I have fashioned from looking at the other two. It's very clumsy. When I go home it gives me trouble even there, where it's not supposed to appear.

138

Yes. My father likes talking about his life. About fishing and kūmara and who's died, or who's had a big tangi. Remember that lady who used to cry beautifully? Well, she's died. Remember who used to lead the pōwhiri? She's died too. I feel sad. I stamp hard with my Māori leg. It feels good to be home.

I beg your pardon? Have you not forgiven the Pākehā? He's not an intruder! Why Dad he's made us add to our thinking. We've got to be understanding! Sensational? Who said that story about our village was sensational? Rubbish! That journalist told the truth. We do live in overcrowded houses. Get out or shut up? What are you talking about? Why, I am a Māori. I've never been anything else. Yes, of course I've got a house and a new car. Yes, of course I couldn't come to Uncle's funeral. Don't you understand? You said, grow up oh tender plant! You said, grab all the advantages of civilisation. Now you don't like the Pākehā. Why the hell did you send me to school?

Third new leg. You are too much of a nuisance. Keep out of my sight. 'One foot at a time', do you hear? When I'm using my Pākehā leg, hide yourself. I cannot walk on it if I have you coming down. No one wants to see two sides of the question. Only liars can see two things at once. No one wants to hear about māoritanga when my Pākehā leg walks. Yes, you know everything. You come down clumsily, you oaf! And now nobody wants me. All three legs are a curse. I wish I could have had only one, as I would have had if I had never turned five.

> Mamae ana e
> Taku mātenga e,
> Tino kino te taumaha,
> ki te hīkoi i ōku wae.

> Painful is my head,
> Heavy indeed it is
> to lift up my feet.

The People Before
—
Maurice Shadbolt

I

MY father took on that farm not long after he came back from the first war. It was pretty well the last farm up the river. Behind our farm, and up the river, there was all kind of wild country. Scrub and jagged black stumps on the hills, bush in gullies where fire hadn't reached; hills and more hills, deep valleys with caves and twisting rivers, and mountains white with winter in the distance. We had the last piece of really flat land up the river. It wasn't the first farm my father'd taken on — and it certainly wasn't to be the last — but it was the most remote. He always said that was why he'd got the place for a song. This puzzled me as a child. For I'd heard, of course, of having to sing for your supper. I wondered what words, to what tune, he was obliged to sing for the farm; and where, and why? Had he travelled up the river, singing a strange song, charming his way into possession of the land? It always perplexed me.

And it perplexed me because there wasn't much room for singing in my father's life. I can't remember ever having heard him sing. There was room for plodding his paddocks in all weathers, milking cows and sending cream down river to the dairy factory, and cursing the bloody government; there was room in his life for all these things and more, but not for singing.

In time, of course, I understood that he only meant he'd bought the place cheaply. Cheaply meant for a song. I couldn't, even then, quite make the connexion. It remained for a long while one of those adult

140

mysteries. And it was no use puzzling over it, no use asking my father for a more coherent explanation.

'Don't be difficult,' he'd say. 'Don't ask so many damn questions. Life's difficult enough, boy, without all your damn questions.'

He didn't mean to be unkind; it was just his way. His life was committed to winning order from wilderness. Questions were a disorderly intrusion, like gorse or weed springing up on good pasture. The best way was to hack them down, grub out the roots, before they could spread. And in the same way as he checked incipient anarchy on his land he hoped, perhaps, to check it in his son.

By that time I was old enough to understand a good many of the things that were to be understood. One of them, for example, was that we weren't the first people on that particular stretch of land. Thirty or forty years before, when white men first came into our part of the country, it was mostly forest. Those first people fired the forest, right back into the hills, and ran sheep. The sheep grazed not only the flat, but the hills which rose sharply behind our farm; the hills which, in our time, had become stubbly with manuka and ferns. The flatland had been pretty much scrub too, the day my father first saw it; and the original people had been gone twenty years — they'd given up, or been ruined by the land; we never quite knew the story. The farmhouse stood derelict among the returning wilderness.

Well, my father saw right away that the land — the flat land — was a reasonable proposition for a dairy farm. There was a new launch service down to the nearest dairy factory, in the township ten miles away; only in the event of flood, or a launch breakdown, would he have to dispose of his cream by carrying it on a sledge across country, three miles, to the nearest road.

So he moved in, cleared the scrub, sowed new grass, and brought in cows. Strictly speaking, the hills at the back of the farm were his too, but he had no use for them. They made good shelter from the westerlies. Otherwise he never gave the hills a thought, since he had all the land he could safely manage; he roamed across them after wild pig, and that was about all. There were bones up there, scattered skeletons of lost sheep, in and about the scrub and burnt stumps.

Everything went well; he had the place almost paid off by the time of the depression. 'I never looked back, those years,' he said long afterwards. It was characteristic of him not to look back. He was not interested in who had the farm before him. He had never troubled to inquire. So far as he was concerned, history only began the day he first set foot on the land. It was his, by sweat and legal title: that was all that mattered. That was all that could matter.

He had two boys; I was the elder son. 'You and Jim will take this place over one day,' he often told me. 'You'll run it when I get tired.'

But he didn't look like getting tired. He wasn't a big man, but he was wiry and thin with a lean face and cool blue eyes; he was one of those people who can't keep still. When neighbours called he couldn't even keep comfortable in a chair, just sitting and sipping tea, but had to start walking them round the farm — or at least the male neighbours — pointing out things here and there. Usually work he'd done, improvements he'd made: the new milking-shed, the new water-pump on the river. He didn't strut or boast, though; he just pointed them out quietly, these jobs well done. He wanted others to share his satisfaction. There was talk of electricity coming through to the farm, the telephone; a road up the river was scheduled. It would all put the value of the property up. The risk he'd taken on the remote and abandoned land seemed justified in every way.

He didn't ever look like getting tired. It was as if he'd been wound up years before, like something clockwork, and set going: first fighting the war, then fighting with the land; now most of the fighting was done, he sometimes found it quite an effort to keep busy. He never took a holiday. There was talk of taking a holiday, one winter when the cows dried off; talk of us all going down to the sea, and leaving a neighbour to look after the place. But I don't think he could have trusted anyone to look after his land, not even for a week or two in winter when the cows were dried off. Perhaps, when Jim and I were grown, it would be different. But not until. He always found some reason for us not to get away. Like our schooling.

'I don't want to interfere with their schooling,' he said once. 'They only get it once in their lives. And they might as well get it while they can. I didn't get much. And, by God, I regret it now. I don't know much, and I might have got along all right, but I might have got along a damn sight better if I'd had more schooling. And I'm not going to interfere with theirs by carting them off for a holiday in the middle of the year.'

Yet even then I wondered if he meant a word of it, if he really wasn't just saying that for something to say. He was wrangling at the time with my mother, who held opinions on a dwindling number of subjects. She never surrendered any of these opinions, exactly; she just kept them more and more to herself until, presumably, they lapsed quietly and died. As she herself, much later, was to lapse quietly from life, without much complaint.

For if he'd really been concerned about our schooling, he might have been more concerned about the way we fell asleep in afternoon classes. Not that we were the only ones. Others started getting pretty ragged in the afternoons too. A lot of us had been up helping our fathers since early in the morning. Jim and I were up at half-past four most mornings to help with the milking and working the separators. My father increased his herd year after year, right up to the depression. After school we rode home just in time for the evening milking. And by the time we finished it was getting dark; in winter it was dark by the time we were half-way through the herd.

I sometimes worried about Jim looking worn in the evenings, and I often chased him off inside before milking was finished. I thought Jim needed looking after; he wasn't anywhere near as big as me. I'd hear him scamper off to the house, and then I'd set about stripping the cows he had left. Father sometimes complained.

'You'll make that brother of yours a softy,' he said. 'The boy's got to learn what work means.'

'Jim's all right,' I answered. 'He's not a softy. He's just not very big. That's all.'

He detested softies, even the accomplices of softies. My mother, in a way, was such an accomplice. She'd never been keen about first me, then Jim, helping with work on the farm. But my father said he couldn't afford to hire a man to help with the herd. And he certainly couldn't manage by himself, without Jim and me.

'Besides,' he said, 'my Dad and me used to milk two hundred cows' — sometimes, when he became hated, the number rose to three hundred — 'when I was eight years old. And thin as a rake too, I was. Eight years old and thin as a rake. It didn't do me no harm. You boys don't know what work is, let me tell you.'

So there all argument finished. My mother kept one more opinion to herself.

And I suppose that, when I chased Jim off inside, I was only taking my mother's side in the argument — and was only another accomplice of softies. Anyway, it would give me a good feeling afterwards — despite anything my father would have to say — when we tramped back to the house, through the night smelling of frost or rain, to find Jim sitting up at the table beside my mother while she ladled out soup under the warm yellow lamplight. He looked as if he belonged there, beside her; and she always looked, at those times, a little triumphant. Her look seemed to say that one child of hers, at least, was going to be saved from the muck of the cowshed. And I suppose that was the beginning of how Jim became his mother's boy.

I remained my father's. I wouldn't have exchanged him for another father. I liked seeing him with people, a man among men. This happened on winter Saturdays when we rode to the township for the football. We usually left Jim behind to look after my mother. We tethered our horses near the football field and went off to join the crowd. Football was one of the few things which interested my father outside the farm. He'd been a fine rugby forward in his day and people respected what he had to say about the game. He could out-argue most people; probably out-fight them too, if it ever came to that. He often talked about the fights he'd had when young. For he'd done a bit of boxing too, only he couldn't spare the time from his father's farm to train properly. He knocked me down once, with his bare fists, in the cowshed; and I was careful never to let it happen again. I just kept my head down for days afterwards, so that he wouldn't see the bruises on my face or the swelling round my eye.

At the football he barracked with the best of them in the thick of the crowd. Sometimes he called out when the rest of the crowd was silent and tense; he could be very sarcastic about poor players, softies who were afraid to tackle properly.

After the game he often called in, on the way home, to have a few beers with friends in the township's sly-grog shop — we didn't have a proper pub in the township — while I looked after the horses outside. Usually he'd find time, while he gossiped with friends, to bring me out a glass of lemonade. At times it could be very cold out there, holding the horses while the winter wind swept round, but it would be nice to know that I was remembered. When he finished we rode home together for a late milking. He would grow talkative, as we cantered towards dark, and even give me the impression he was glad of my company. He told me about the time he was young, what the world looked like when he was my age. His father was a sharemilker, travelling from place to place; that is, he owned no land of his own and did other people's work.

'So I made up my mind, boy,' he told me as we rode along together, 'I made up my mind I'd never be like that. I'd bend my head to no man. And you know what the secret of that is, boy? Land. Land of your own. You're independent, boy. You can say no to the world. That's if you got your own little kingdom. I reckon it was what kept me alive, down there on the beach at Gallipoli, knowing I'd have some land I could call my own.' This final declaration seemed to dismay him for some reason or other, perhaps because he feared he'd given too much of himself away. So he added half-apologetically, 'I had to think of something, you know, while all that shooting was going on. They say it's best to fix your mind on something if you don't want to be afraid. That's what I fixed my mind on, anyhow. Maybe it did keep me alive.'

In late winter or spring we sometimes arrived back, on Saturdays, to see the last trembling light of sunset fade from the hills and land. We'd canter along a straight stretch, coast up a rise, rein in the horses, and there it was — his green kingdom, his tight tamed acres beneath the hills and beside the river, a thick spread of fenced grass from the dark fringe of hillscrub down to the ragged willows above the water. And at the centre was his castle, the farmhouse, with the sheds scattered round, and the pine trees.

Reining in on that rise, I knew, gave him a good feeling. It would also be the time when he remembered all the jobs he'd neglected, all the work he should have done instead of going to the football. His conscience would keep him busy all day Sunday.

At times he wondered — it was a conversation out loud with himself — why he didn't sell up and buy another place. There were, after all, more comfortable farms, in more convenient locations nearer towns or cities. 'I've built this place up from nothing,' he said, 'I've made it pay, and pay well. I've made this land worth something. I could sell out for a packet. Why don't I?'

He never really — in my presence anyway — offered himself a convincing explanation. Why didn't he? He'd hardly have said he loved the land: love, in any case, would have been an extravagance. Part of whatever it was, I suppose, was the knowledge that he'd built where someone else had failed; part was that he'd given too much of himself there, to be really free anywhere else. It wouldn't be the same, walking on to another successful farm, a going concern, everything in order. No, this place — this land from the river back up to the hills — was his. In a sense it had only ever been his. That was why he felt so secure.

If Sunday was often the day when he worked hardest, it was also the best day for Jim and me, our free day. After morning milking, and breakfast, we did more or less what we liked. In summer we swam down under the river-willows; we also had a canoe tied there and sometimes we paddled up-river, under great limestone bluffs shaggy with toi toi, into country which grew wilder and wilder. There were huge bearded caves in the bush above the water which we explored from time to time. There were also big eels to be fished from the pools of the river.

As he grew older Jim turned more into himself, and became still quieter. You could never guess exactly what he was thinking. It wasn't that he didn't enjoy life; he just had his own way of enjoying it. He didn't like being with his father, as I did; I don't even know that he always enjoyed being with me. He just tagged along with me: we were, after all, brothers. When I was old enough, my father presented me with a ·22 rifle; Jim never showed great enthusiasm for shooting. He came along with me, all right, but he never seemed interested in the rabbits or wild goat I shot, or just missed. He wandered around the hills, way behind me, entertaining himself and collecting things. He gathered leaves, and tried to identify the plants from which the leaves came. He also collected stones, those of some interesting shape or texture; he had a big collection of stones. He tramped along, in his slow, quiet way, poking into everything, adding to his collections. He wasn't too slow and quiet at school, though; he was faster than most of us with an answer. He borrowed books from the teacher, and took them home. So in time he became even smarter with his answers. I grew to accept the difference from most people. It didn't disturb me particularly: on the farm he was still quiet, small Jim. He was never too busy with his books to come along with me on Sundays.

There was a night when Jim was going through some new stones he'd gathered. Usually, in the house, my father didn't take much notice of Jim, his reading or his hobbies. He'd fought a losing battle for Jim, through the years, and now accepted his defeat. Jim still helped us with the herd, night and morning, but in the house he was ignored. But this night my father went across to the table and picked up a couple of the new stones. They were greenish, both the same triangular shape.

'Where'd you get these?' he asked.

Jim thought for a moment; he seemed pleased by the interest taken in him. 'One was back in the hills,' he said. 'The other was in a cave up the river. I just picked them up.'

'You mean you didn't find them together?'

'No,' Jim said.

'Funny,' my father said. 'They look like greenstone. I seen some greenstone once. A joker found it, picked it up in the bush. Jade, it is; same thing. This joker sold it in the city for a packet. Maori stuff. Some people'll buy anything.'

We all crossed to the table and looked down at the greenish stone. Jim's eyes were bright with excitement.

'You mean these used to belong to the Maoris?' he said. 'These stones?'

'Must have,' my father said. 'Greenstone doesn't come natural round here. You look it up in your books and you'll see. Comes from way down south, near the mountains and glaciers. Had to come up here all the way by canoe. They used to fight about greenstone once.' He paused and looked at the stones again. 'Yes,' he added. 'I reckon that's greenstone, all right. You never know, might be some money in that stuff.'

Money was a very important subject in our house at that time. It was in a lot of households, since that time was the depression. In the cities they were marching in the streets and breaking shop windows. Here on the farm it wasn't anywhere near so dramatic. The grass looked much the same as it had always looked; so did the hills and river. All that had happened, really, was that the farm had lost its value. Prices had fallen; my father sometimes wondered if it was worth while sending cream to the factory. Some of the people on poorer land, down the river, had walked off their properties. Everything was tighter. We had to do without new clothes, and there wasn't much variety in our eating. We ran a bigger garden, and my father went out more frequently shooting wild pig for meat. He had nothing but contempt for the noisy people in the city, the idlers and wasters who preferred to go shouting in the streets rather than fetch a square meal for their families, as he did with his rifle. He thought they, in some way, were to blame for the failure of things. Even so, he became gripped by the idea that he might have failed himself, somehow; he tried to talk himself out of this idea — in my presence — but without much success. Now he had the land solid beneath his feet, owned it entirely, it wasn't much help at all. If it wasn't for our garden and the wild pig we might starve. The land didn't bring him any money; he might even have to leave it. He had failed, perhaps much as the land's former owners had failed; why? He might have answered the question for himself satisfactorily, while he grubbed away at the scrub encroaching on our pasture; but I doubt it.

'Yes,' he said. 'Might be some money in that stuff.'

But Jim didn't seem to hear, or understand. His eyes were still bright. 'That means there must have been Maoris here in the old days,' he said.

'I suppose there must have,' my father agreed. He didn't seem much interested. Maoris were Maoris. There weren't many around our part of the river; they were mostly down towards the coast. (Shortly after this, Jim did some research and told me the reason why. It turned out that the land about our part of the river had been confiscated from them after the Maori wars.) 'They were most places, weren't they?' he added.

'Yes,' Jim said. 'But I mean they must have been here. On our place.'

'Well, yes. They could of been. Like I said, they were most places.'

It didn't seem to register as particularly important. He picked up the greenstone again. 'We ought to find out about this,' he continued. 'There might be a bit of money in it.'

Later Jim took the stones to school and had them identified as Maori adzes. My father said once again that perhaps there was money in them. But the thing was, where to find a buyer? It mightn't be as easy as it used to be. So somehow it was all forgotten. Jim kept the adzes.

Jim and I did try to find again that cave in which he had picked up an adze. We found a lot of caves, but none of them seemed the right one. Anyway we didn't pick up another adze. We did wander down one long dripping cave, striking matches, and in the dark I tripped on something. I struck another match and saw some brownish-looking bones. 'A sheep,' I said. 'It must have come in here and got lost.'

Jim was silent; I wondered why. Then I saw he wasn't looking at the bones, but at a human skull propped on a ledge of the cave. It just sat there sightless, shadows dancing in its sockets.

We got out of that cave quickly. We didn't even talk about it when we reached home. On the whole I preferred going out with my ·22 after rabbits.

II

IT was near the end of the depression. But we didn't know that then, of course. It might have been just the beginning, for all we knew. My father didn't have as much interest in finishing jobs as he used to have. He tired easily. He'd given his best to the land, and yet his best still wasn't good enough. There wasn't much sense in anything and his dash was done. He kept going out of habit.

I'd been pulled out of school to help with the farm. Jim still more or less went to school. I say more or less because he went irregularly. This was because of sickness. Once he was away in hospital two months. And of course it cost money; my father said we were to blame, we who allowed Jim to become soft and sickly. But the doctor thought otherwise; he thought Jim had been worked hard enough already. And when Jim returned to the farm he no longer helped with the herd. And this was why I had to leave school: if he couldn't have both of us working with him part-time, my father wanted one full-time. Jim was entirely surrendered at last, to the house and books, to school and my mother. I didn't mind working on the farm all day, with my father; it was, after all, what I'd always wanted. All the same, I would have been happier if he had been: his doubts about himself, more and more frequently expressed, disturbed me. It wasn't like my father at all. He was convinced now he'd done the wrong thing, somewhere. He went back through the years, levering each year up like a stone, to see what lay beneath; he never seemed to find anything. It was worst of all in winter, when the land looked bleak, the hills were grey with low cloud, and the rain swirled out of the sky. All life vanished from his face and I knew he detested everything: the land which had promised him independence was now only a muddy snare; he was bogged here, between hills and river, and couldn't escape. He had no pride left in him for the place. If he could have got a price for the farm he would have gone. But there was no longer any question of price. He could walk off if he liked. Only the bush would claim it back.

It was my mother who told us there were people coming. She had taken the telephone message while we were out of the house, and Jim was at the school.

'Who are they?' my father said.

'I couldn't understand very well. It was a bad connexion. I think they said they were the people who were here before.'

'The people who were here before? What the hell do they want here?' His eyes became suspicious under his frown.

'I think they said they just wanted to have a look around.'

'What the hell do they want here?' my father repeated, baffled.

'Nothing for them to see. This farm's not like it was when they were here. Everything's different. I've made a lot of changes. They wouldn't know the place. What do they want to come back for?'

'Well,' my mother sighed, 'I'm sure I don't know.'

'Perhaps they want to buy it,' he said abruptly; the words seemed simultaneous with his thought, and he stiffened with astonishment.

'By God, yes. They might want to buy the place back again. I hadn't thought of that. Wouldn't that be a joke? I'd sell, all right — for just about as much as I paid for the place. I tell you, I'd let it go for a song, for a bloody song. They're welcome.'

'But where would we go?' she said, alarmed.

'Somewhere,' he said. 'Somewhere new. Anywhere.'

'But there's nowhere,' she protested. 'Nowhere any better. You know that.'

'And there's nowhere any worse,' he answered. 'I'd start again somewhere. Make a better go of things.'

'You're too old to start again,' my mother observed softly.

There was a silence. And in the silence I knew that what my mother said was true. We all knew it was true.

'So we just stay here,' he said. 'And rot. Is that it?' But he really wished to change the subject. 'When are these people coming?'

'Tomorrow, I think. They're staying the night down in the township. Then they're coming up by launch.'

'They didn't say why they were interested in the place?'

'No. And they certainly didn't say they wanted to buy it. You might as well get that straight now. They said they just wanted a look around.'

'I don't get it. I just don't get it. If I walked off this place I wouldn't ever want to see it again.'

'Perhaps they're different,' my mother said. 'Perhaps they've got happy memories of this place.'

'Perhaps they have. God knows.'

It was early summer, with warm lengthening days. That sunny Saturday morning I loitered about the house with Jim, waiting for the people to arrive. Eventually, as the sun climbed higher in the sky, I grew impatient and went across the paddocks to help my father. We were working together when we heard the sound of the launch coming up the river.

'That's them,' he said briefly. He dropped his slasher for a moment, and spat on his hands. Then he took up the slasher again and chopped into a new patch of unruly gorse.

I was perplexed. 'Well,' I said, 'aren't you going down to meet them?'

'I'll see them soon enough. Don't worry.' He seemed to be conducting an argument with himself as he hacked into the gorse. 'I'm in no hurry. No, I'm in no hurry to see them.'

I just kept silent beside him.

'Who are they, anyway?' he went on. 'What do they want to come traipsing round my property for? They've got a bloody cheek.'

The sound of the launch grew. It was probably travelling round the last bend in the river now, past the swamp of raupo, and banks prickly with flax and toi toi. They were almost at the farm. Still chopping jerkily, my father tried to conceal his unease.

'What do they want?' he asked for the last time. 'By God, if they've come to gloat, they've got another thing coming. I've made something decent out of this place, and I don't care who knows it.'

He had tried everything in his mind and it was no use: he was empty of explanation. Now we could see the launch white on the gleaming river. It was coasting up to the bank. We could also see people clustered on board.

'Looks like a few of them,' I observed. If I could have done so without upsetting my father, I would have run down to meet the launch, eager with curiosity. But I kept my distance until he finished arguing with himself.

'Well,' he said, as if he'd never suggested otherwise, 'we'd better go down to meet them, now they're here.' He dug his slasher into the earth and began to stalk off down to the river. I followed him. His quick strides soon took him well ahead of me; I had to run to keep up.

Then we had our surprise. My father's step faltered; I blundered up alongside him. We saw the people climbing off the launch. And we saw who they were, at last. My father stopped perfectly still and silent. They were Maoris. We were still a hundred yards or more away, but there was no mistaking their clothing or colour. They were Maoris, all right.

'There's something wrong somewhere,' he said at last. 'It doesn't make sense. No Maori ever owned this place. I'd have known. Who the hell do they think they are, coming here?'

I couldn't answer him. He strode on down to the river. There were young men, and two old women with black head-scarves. And last of all there was something the young men carried. As we drew nearer we saw it was an old man in a rough litter. The whole party of them fussed over making the old man comfortable. The old women, particularly; they had tattoos on their chins and wore shark-tooth necklaces. They straightened the old man's blankets and fixed the pillow behind his head. He had a sunken, withered face and he didn't look so much sick, as tired. His eyes were only half-open as every one fussed around. He looked as if it were a great effort to keep them that much open. His hair was mostly grey, and his dry flesh sagged in thin folds about his ancient neck. I reckoned that he must have been near enough to a hundred years old. The young men talked quickly among themselves as they saw my father approaching. One came forward, apparently as spokesman. He looked about the oldest of them, perhaps thirty. He had a fat, shiny face.

'Here,' said my father. 'What's all this about?' I knew his opinion of Maoris: they were lazy, drank too much, and caused trouble. They just rode on the backs of the men on the land, like the loafers in the cities. He always said we were lucky there were so few in our district. 'What do you people think you're doing here?' he demanded.

'We rang up yesterday,' the spokesman said. 'We told your missus we might be coming today.'

'I don't know about that. She said someone else was coming. The people who were here before.'

'Well,' said the young man, smiling. 'We were the people before.'

'I don't get you. You trying to tell me you owned this place?'

'That's right. We owned all the land round this end of the river. Our tribe.'

'That must have been a hell of a long time ago.'

'Yes,' agreed the stranger. 'A long time.' He was pleasantly spoken and patient. His round face, which I could imagine looking jolly, was very solemn just then.

I looked around and saw my mother and Jim coming slowly down from the house.

'I still don't get it,' my father said. 'What do you want?'

'We just want to go across your land, if that's all right. Look, we better introduce ourselves. My name is Tom Taikaka. And this —'

My father was lost in a confusion of introductions. But he still didn't shake anyone's hand. He just stood his ground, aloof and faintly hostile. Finally there was the old man. He looked as though he had gone to sleep again.

'You see he's old,' Tom explained. 'And has not so long to live. He is the last great man of our tribe, the oldest. He wishes to see again where he was born. The land over which his father was chief. He wishes to see this before his spirit departs for Rerengawairua.'

By this time my mother and Jim had joined us. They were as confused as we were.

'You mean you've come just to —' my father began.

'We've come a long way,' Tom said. 'Nearly a hundred miles, from up the coast. That's where we live now.'

'All this way. Just so —'

'Yes,' Tom said. 'That's right.'

'Well,' said my father. 'What do you know? What do you know about that?' Baffled, he looked at me, at my mother, and even finally at Jim. None of us had anything to say.

'I hope we're not troubling you,' Tom said politely. 'We don't want to be any trouble. We just want to go across your land, if that's all right. We got our own tucker and everything.'

We saw this was true. The two old women had large flax kits of food.

'No liquor?' my father said suspiciously. 'I don't want any drinking round my place.'

'No,' Tom replied. His face was still patient. 'No liquor. We don't plan on any drinking.'

The other young men shyly agreed in the background. It was not, they seemed to say, an occasion for drinking.

'Well,' said my father stiffly, 'I suppose it's all right. Where are you going to take him?' He nodded towards the old sleeping man.

'Just across your land. And up to the old *pa*.'

'I didn't know there used to be any *pa* round here.'

'Well,' said Tom. 'It used to be up there.' He pointed out the largest hill behind our farm, one that stood well apart and above the others. We called it Craggy Hill, because of limestone outcrops. Its flanks and summit were patchy with tall scrub. We seldom went near it, except perhaps when out shooting; then we circled its steep slopes rather than climbed it. 'You'd see the terraces,' Tom said, 'if it wasn't for the scrub. It's all hidden now.'

Now my father looked strangely at Tom. 'Hey,' he said, 'you sure you aren't having me on? How come you know that hill straight off? You ever been here before?'

'No,' Tom said. His face shone as he sweated with the effort of trying to explain everything. 'I never been here before. I never been in this part of the country before.'

'Then how do you know that's the hill, eh?'

'Because,' Tom said simply, 'the old men told me. They described it so well I could find the place blindfold. All the stories of our tribe are connected with that hill. That's where we lived, up there, for hundreds of years.'

'Well, I'll be damned. What do you know about that?' My father blinked, and looked up at the hill again. 'Just up there, eh? And for hundreds of years.'

'That's right.'

'And I never knew. Well, I'll be damned.'

'There's lots of stories about that hill,' Tom said. 'And a lot of battles fought round here. Over your place.'

'Right over my land?'

'That's right. Up and down here, along the river.'

My father was so astonished he forgot to be aloof. He was trying to fit everything into his mind at once — the hill where they'd lived hundreds of years, the battles fought across his land — and it was too much.

'The war canoes would come up here,' Tom went on. 'I reckon they'd drag them up somewhere here' — he indicated the grassy bank on which we were standing — 'in the night, and go on up to attack the *pa* before sunrise. That's if we hadn't sprung a trap for them down here. There'd be a lot of blood soaked into this soil.' He kicked at the earth beneath our feet. 'We had to fight a long while to keep this land here, a lot of battles. Until there was a day when it was no use fighting any more. That was when we left.'

We knew, without him having to say it, what he meant. He meant the day when the European took the land. So we all stood quietly for a moment. Then my mother spoke.

'You'd better come up to the house,' she said. 'I'll make you all a cup of tea.'

A cup of tea was her solution to most problems.

We went up to the house slowly. The young men followed behind, carrying the litter. They put the old man in the shade of a tree, outside the house. Since it seemed the best thing to do, we all sat around him; there wouldn't have been room for everyone in our small kitchen any- way. We waited for my mother to bring out the tea.

Then the old man woke. He seemed to shiver, his eyes opened wide, and he said something in Maori. 'He wonders where he is,' Tom explained. He turned back to the old man and spoke in Maori.

He gestured, he pointed. Then the old man knew. We all saw it the moment the old man knew. It was as if we were all willing him towards that moment of knowledge. He quivered and tried to lift himself weakly; the old women rushed forward to help him. His eyes had a faint glitter as he looked up to the place we called Craggy Hill. He did not see us, the house, or anything else. Some more Maori words escaped him in a long, sighing rush. '*Te Wahiokoahoki*,' he said.

'It is the name,' Tom said, repeating it. 'The name of the place.'

The old man lay back against the women, but his eyes were still bright and trembling. They seemed to have a life independent of his wrinkled flesh. Then the lids came down, and they were gone again. We could all relax.

'*Te Wahiokoahoki*,' Tom said. 'It means the place of happy return. It

156

got the name when we returned there after our victories against other tribes.'

My father nodded. 'Well, I'll be damned,' he said. 'That place there. And I never knew.' He appeared quite affable now.

My mother brought out tea. The hot cups passed from hand to hand, steaming and sweet.

'But not so happy now, eh?' Tom said. 'Not for us.'

'No. I don't suppose so.'

Tom nodded towards the old man. 'I reckon he was just about the last child born up there. Before we had to leave. Soon there'll be nobody left who lived there. That's why they wanted young men to come back. So we'd remember too.'

Jim went into the house and soon returned. I saw he carried the greenstone adzes he'd found. He approached Tom shyly.

'I think these are really yours,' he said, the words an effort.

Tom turned the adzes over in his hand. Jim had polished them until they were a vivid green. 'Where'd you get these, eh?' he asked.

Jim explained how and where'd he found them. 'I think they're really yours,' he repeated.

There was a brief silence. Jim stood with his eyes downcast, his treasure surrendered. My father watched anxiously; he plainly thought Jim a fool.

'You see,' Jim added apologetically, 'I didn't think they really belonged to anyone. That's why I kept them.'

'Well,' Tom said, embarrassed. 'That's real nice of you. Real nice of you, son. But you better keep them, eh? They're yours now. You find, you keep. We got no claims here any more. This is your father's land now.'

Then it was my father who seemed embarrassed. 'Leave me out of this,' he said sharply. 'You two settle it between you. It's none of my business.'

'I think you better keep them all the same,' Tom said to Jim.

Jim was glad to keep the greenstone, yet a little hurt by rejection of his gift. He received the adzes back silently.

'I tell you what,' Tom went on cheerfully, 'you ever find another one, you send it to me, eh? Like a present. But you keep those two.'

'All right,' Jim answered, clutching the adzes. He seemed much happier. 'I promise if I find any more, I'll send them to you.'

'Fair enough,' Tom smiled, his face jolly. Yet I could see that he too really wanted the greenstone.

After a while they got up to leave. They made the old man comfortable again and lifted him. 'We'll see you again tomorrow,' Tom said. 'The launch will be back to pick us up.'

'Tomorrow?' my father said. It hadn't occurred to him that they might be staying overnight on his land.

'We'll make ourselves a bit of a camp up there tonight,' Tom said, pointing to Craggy Hill. 'We ought to be comfortable up there. Like home, eh?' The jest fell mildly from his lips.

'Well, I suppose that's all right,' My father didn't know quite what to say. 'Nothing you want?'

'No,' Tom said. 'We got all we want, thanks. We'll be all right. We got ourselves. That's the important thing, eh?'

We watched them move away, the women followed by the young men with the litter. Tom went last, Jim trotting along beside him. They seemed, since the business of the greenstone, to have made friends quickly. Tom appeared to be telling Jim a story.

I thought for a moment that my father might call Jim back. But he didn't. He let him go.

The old women now, I noticed, carried green foliage. They beat it about them as they walked across our paddocks and up towards Craggy Hill; they were chanting or singing, and their wailing sound came back to us. Their figures grew smaller with distance. Soon they were clear of the paddocks and beginning to climb.

My father thumbed back his hat and rubbed a handkerchief across his brow. 'Well, I'll be damned,' he said.

WE SAT together on the porch that evening, as we often did in summer after milking and our meal. Yet that evening was very different from any other. The sun had set, and in the dusk we saw faint smoke rising from their campfire on Craggy Hill, the place of happy return. Sometimes I thought I heard the wailing sound of the women again, but I couldn't quite be sure.

What were they doing up there, what did they hope to find? We both wondered and puzzled, yet didn't speak to each other.

Jim had returned long before, with stories. It seemed he had learned, one way and another, just about all there was to be learned about the tribe that had once lived on Craggy Hill. At the dinner table he told the stories breathlessly. My father affected to be not much interested; and so, my father's son, did I. Yet we listened, all the same.

'Then there was the first musket,' Jim said. 'The first musket in this part of the country. Someone bought it from a trader down south and carried it back to the *pa*. Another tribe, one of their old enemies, came seeking *utu* — *utu* means revenge — for something that had been done to them the year before. And when they started climbing up the hill they were knocked off, one by one, with the musket. They'd never seen anything like it before. So the chief of the tribe on Craggy Hill made a sign of peace and called up his enemies. It wasn't a fair fight, he said, only one tribe with a musket. So he'd let his enemies have the musket for a while. They would have turns with the musket, each tribe. He taught the other tribe how to fire and point the musket. Then they separated and started the battle again. And the next man to be killed by the musket was the chief's eldest son. That was the old man's uncle — the old man who was here today.'

'Well, I don't know', said my father. 'Sounds bloody queer to me. That's no way to fight a battle.'

'That's the way they fought,' Jim maintained.

So we left Jim, still telling stories to my mother, and went out on the porch.

The evening thickened. Soon the smoke of the campfire was lost. The hills grew dark against the pale sky. And at last my father, looking up at the largest hill of all, spoke softly.

'I suppose a man's a fool,' he said. 'I should never have let that land go. Shouldn't ever have let it go back to scrub. I could of run a few sheep up there. But I just let it go. Perhaps I'll burn it off one day, run a few sheep. Sheep might pay better too, the way things are now.'

But it wasn't somehow, quite what I expected him to say. I suppose he was trying to make sense of things in his own fashion.

III

THEY came down off Craggy Hill the next day. The launch had been waiting for them in the river some time.

When we saw the cluster of tiny figures, moving at a fair pace down the hills, we sensed there was something wrong. Then, as they drew nearer, approaching us across the paddocks, we saw what was wrong. There was no litter, no old man. They all walked freely, separately. They were no longer burdened.

Astonished, my father strode up to Tom. 'Where is he?' he demanded.

'We left him back up there,' Tom said. He smiled sadly and I had a queer feeling that I knew exactly what he would say.

'Left him up there?'

'He died last night, or this morning. When we went to wake him he was cold. So we left him up there. That's where he wanted to be.'

'You can't do that,' my father protested. 'You can't just leave a dead man like that. Leave him anywhere. And, besides, it's my land you're leaving him on.'

'Yes,' Tom said. 'Your land.'

'Don't you understand? You can't just leave dead people around. Not like that.'

'But we didn't just leave him around. We didn't just leave him anywhere. We made him all safe and comfortable. He's all right. You needn't worry.'

'Christ, man,' my father said. 'Don't you see?'

But he might have been asking a blind man to see. Tom just smiled patiently and said not to worry. Also he said they'd better be catching the launch. They had a long way to go home, a tiring journey ahead.

And as he walked off, my father still arguing beside him, the old women clashed their dry greenery, wailing, and their shark-tooth necklaces danced under their heaving throats.

In a little while the launch went noisily off down the river. My father

160

stood on the bank, still yelling after them. When he returned to the house, his voice was hoarse.

He had a police party out, a health officer too. They scoured the hills, and most of the caves they could find. They discovered no trace of a burial, nor did they find anything in the caves. At one stage someone foolishly suggested we might have imagined it all. So my father produced the launchman and people from the township as witnesses to the fact that an old Maori, dying, had actually been brought to our farm.

That convinced them. But it didn't take them anywhere near finding the body. They traced the remnants of the tribe, living up the coast, and found that indeed an old man of the tribe was missing. No one denied that there had been a visit to our farm. But they maintained that they knew nothing about a body. The old man, they said, had just wandered off into the bush; they hadn't found him again.

He might, they added, even still be alive. Just to be on the safe side, in case there was any truth in their story, the police put the old man on the missing persons register, for all the good that might have done.

But we knew. We knew every night we looked up at the hills that he was there, somewhere.

So he was still alive, in a way. Certainly it was a long time before he let us alone.

And by then my father had lost all taste for the farm. It seemed the land itself had heaped some final indignity upon him, made a fool of him. He never talked again, anyway, about running sheep on the hills.

When butter prices rose and land values improved, a year or two afterwards, he had no hesitation in selling out. We shifted into another part of the country entirely, for a year or two, and then into another. Finally we found ourselves milking a small herd for town supply, not far from the city. We're still on that farm, though there's talk of the place being purchased soon for a city sub-division. We think we might sell, but we'll face the issue when it arises.

Now and then Jim comes to see us, smart in a city suit, a lecturer at the university. My father always found it difficult to talk to Jim, and very often now he goes off to bed and leaves us to it. One thing I must say about Jim: he has no objection to helping with the milking. He insists that he enjoys it; perhaps he does. It's all flatland round our present farm, with one farm much like another, green grass and square farmhouses and pine shelter belts, and it's not exactly the place to sit out on a summer evening and watch shadows gathering on the hills. Because there aren't hills within sight; or shadows either, for that matter. It's all very tame and quiet, apart from cars speeding on the highway.

I get on reasonably well with Jim. We read much the same books, have much the same opinions on a great many subjects. The city hasn't made a great deal of difference to him. We're both married, with young families. We also have something else in common: we were both in the war, fighting in the desert. One evening after milking, when we stood smoking and yarning in the cool, I remembered something and decided I might put a question to Jim.

'You know,' I began, 'they say it's best, when you're under fire in the war, to fix your mind on something remote. So you won't be afraid. I remember Dad telling me that. I used to try. But it never seemed any good. I couldn't think of anything. I was still as scared as hell.'

'I was too. Who wasn't?'

'But, I mean, did you ever think of anything?'

'Funny thing,' he said. 'Now I come to think of it, I did. I thought of the old place — you know, the old place by the river. Where,' he added, and his face puckered into a grin, 'where they buried that old Maori. And where I found those greenstones. I've still got it at home, you know, up on the mantelpiece. I seem to remember trying to give it away once, to those Maoris. Now I'm glad I didn't. It's my only souvenir from there, the only thing that makes that place still live for me.' He paused. 'Well, anyway, that's what I thought about. That old place of ours.'

I had a sharp pain. I felt the dismay of a long distance runner who, coasting confidently to victory, imagining himself well ahead of the field, finds himself overtaken and the tape snapped at the very moment he leans forward to breast it. For one black moment it seemed I had been robbed of something which was rightfully mine.

I don't think I'll ever forgive him.

Strife in the Family
—
Rowley Habib

(S) OMETIMES the children would be left to the father's care, their mother having gone off on the booze with some friends after having had an argument with their father. The children would never hear these arguments. They always seemed to happen when they were not around, or else their parents broke off as soon as the children came into the house. But once or twice the children heard their father's voice raised and angry coming from the bedroom where he and their mother were. He never hit their mother or at least never in front of the children. But the children could tell when their parents had had a row or were angry with one another. Their mother's face would be flushed dark and set like stone. And red weals would stand out just below her eyes, as though she had had her face over the stove for some while and was very hot. And their father would be very silent and would get about with quick nervous steps, coughing all the time. A small grating cough, as though he could not quite clear his throat of some irritation. And the children could almost feel the heat coming off him, so stored up was his anger and so hard was he trying to contain it. And it made them feel as though he would blow up any minute.

The children would sense the tension between their parents almost immediately. Even if no harsh words were passed in their presence. Their parents used to try hard for the children's sake, sometimes trying to speak civilly with one another but the children sensed the strain between

163

the two, and in these times they would be a little afraid and would only talk in whispers. It was as though a wet blanket were cast over them.

Those evenings when their mother would go off on a binge with some friends or relations from down the road, the children's father would feed them on bread and cold water and the children would be resentful of their father for the bare and unsavoury meal he dished up to them. They used to chew away at the dry tasteless bread and were forced to drink their cups of water only to wash the bread down, so dry was it. And they were a little afraid their father would be angry if they did not drink it. Yet they would also feel tender towards their father in these moments and a little sorry for him, and they would be all against their mother. Motu would often wonder if she would feel this wall of antagonism against her, her husband and her children against her? But when they sat down to a good cooked nourishing meal in the morning laid out by their mother (she must have come back some time during the night, but the children never heard her) before they went off to school they were so grateful that they had to forgive her. And everything would be back to normal again. Although they tried to maintain a little of their coolness towards her, hoping she would notice it, and repent and promise never to do it again. The children would come home from school to a normally run household in the afternoons. Their mother and father would be on talking terms again and everything was back to normal. A great relief used to come over the children and they would be happy.

These occasions didn't happen often, but they *did* happen, and when they did the children couldn't understand why or how their mother could leave them. They loved her and they felt that she loved them. But in these moments they felt the bondage and the strength of her love weaken and doubt entered their minds horribly. They never questioned their mother about last night. Most times they were just too glad to have her back to care for them and they would feel their security surging back into them as they sat about in the kitchen watching their mother diligently ironing their clothes.

Then one day Mrs Joseph packed the younger children off and went and lived in an old family house (on her side) about four miles away;

away down on the fringe of some cut-out bush. The children only suspected the reason for this sudden shift and afterwards they found out for sure. Their mother had had a row with their father. They realised that it must have been much worse than the others for their mother to leave like this. But somehow they felt that this had been brewing for a long time.

The children were a bit annoyed at having to move because they had to leave their friends. They were thrown into an entirely different environment and for a while they were lonely and begrudged Luke and Arthur, their two older brothers, being able to remain behind with their father.

The children used to have to walk half a mile to the main road to catch the school bus and they did this first with mixed feelings of bewilderment and belligerence. But it was a novelty to them and after a while they got to enjoy the walk to the road. Walking the narrow roadway that was only two tracks cut into the ground the width of a car's wheels apart and that had grass growing in the middle on a raised piece of ground. And they got to quite like the place in general. For one thing it was good to be away from the dust of the roadway that their old homestead suffered from badly. And the air was so clean and fresh at their new place, they would smell the sweet odour of the bush on the hills behind the house, and for a change it was good to have no one else around you. And of course if they wanted to, they could cut across the paddocks and through a bit of cut-out bush to the Ormsby's place about two miles away or else in the other direction to their cousins the Whetus' place.

The house was cosy and big enough and it had three bedrooms in it that they could have used but the children preferred to all pile into the one room using the two beds in there. When they had first moved in they used the two separate rooms that their mother allocated for them. Aroha and Louise slept in one and Motu and Marylin in the other. They did it partly because of the strangeness of everything and partly because the idea thrilled them a bit. But afterwards they preferred each other's company and they used to lie there in bed discussing amongst themselves.

And the pepes used to come down from the bush and hit against the windows attracted by the light in their room. Big ones. The children had not seen pepes as big as them before and they used to sit up a little afraid in bed: at first exclaiming loudly because of the sizes of the things and calling for their mother and once or twice one would find its way into the room and fly about furiously, hitting against the wall and sometimes almost putting the candle out as it passed through the naked flame. There would be a great din and heads would go under the blankets and pop out again to see what had happened to the creature, only to see it crawling up the wall and there would be squeals and screams until their mother came in and knocked it down with a towel. She would pick the thing up by the back, between her fingers and go and throw it into the fire. And there would be 'Oooohs!' from the children, and 'Mum how can you do such a thing', all watching their mother with big eyes as she carried the fearsome creature between her fingers. But after a while they got used to the knockings of the pepes against their windows at night.

And the house was clean and smelt of bare wood scrubbed a thousand times with warm water and soap. And the rooms were bare but cosy.

And their mother used to make fried bread and she and the children used to sit around after tea eating great heaps of it and drinking tea. It was the one thing they really shared during their stay there. It was a highlight to their day, sitting around joyfully eating their bread and sharing the happiness with their mother.

Their mother never made this bread very often back at the old home-stead but now at the insistence of the children she made it every day. She did a lot of things that she never normally did back home and the children felt she was enjoying the liberty of it. The Maori in her came out more, living here, and she seemed to enjoy doing all the old things she used to do when she was a child. And on the weekends sometimes, she would go for a walk with the children in the bush, climbing the ridge of the hill behind the house gathering puha in a kit and resting and lighting a cigarette and looking back down over the flats below, and she used to tell them stories and old tales about the place. She had grown up there. There was another old homestead not far away. It belonged to one of their mother's older brothers. It was a much larger house that was surrounded by a picket fence. The house was in decay and unlivable in. Parts of it were beginning to fall away. There were many fruit trees growing around the house, both at the front and back; apples, peaches, plums, and greengages. The grass was growing long and wild, nearly claiming the whole of the grounds surrounding the house.

At the back against the tall fence grew some raspberries and it was these that the children enjoyed most. But they always went there with a feeling that old Pita their uncle would suddenly appear from the house and catch them in the act of stealing his raspberries, so they used to approach the raspberry canes stealthily from the side of the house, climbing through the hole in the fence and then treading light-footedly around between the house and the greengage trees, and then into the long grass that surrounded the raspberries. They were well hidden in this tall grass while they plundered the raspberries. They did this elaborate manoeuvre also partly because it was fun.

Sometimes at the weekends Arthur used to come down on his horse and stay there a while, cutting a big heap of firewood and doing odd jobs about the house. And it seemed strange Arthur leaving them later on; getting on to Goldie his horse and saying goodbye when all the time he shouldn't have to be saying that. And it was these times that the children felt nostalgia for their old home and wished for a reunion of the whole family.

And sometimes, after they had been there for about two months, their father used to come visiting their mother. He used to come down at nights, walking all the way, about four miles. The children used to know when their father was coming. They would be sitting at the tea table after the meal or sometimes even during meals (they used to have their meals quite late and it would be dark most times before they were finished) and they would see the light of a torch flickering on and off coming down the roadway. At first they wondered what it could be but even before he got to the house the children knew that it was their father. They recognised the peculiar way he held the torch. He would walk with it in his hand swinging backwards and forwards with the motion of his walking. It used to appear as though the torch was being switched on and off. But it wasn't and it was this peculiar way of his that the children recognised that first night. Their mother must have known long before then that it was her husband but she did not let on, for when the children exclaimed excitedly that it was their father, she was unmoved.

The father came in rather awkwardly that first night. The children were glad to see him and fussed about him and Motu smelled his father's peculiar man's smell and it made him a little nostalgic for the man. And at once, in that moment, he loved his father and felt sorry for him.

The man came into the room taking off his cap, an uncertain smile touching his mouth. He stood inside the door wringing his hands together nervously. 'Hullo Mary,' he said.

'Hullo Peter,' the mother said and she sat there watching him and there was no expression on her face.

'I just thought I'd — a — the come over and see how you were getting on,' their father said.

'Thank you, Peter,' the mother said. 'I'm very well. And yourself?'

'No good, Mary,' the father said. 'Why don't you come home? It's no good like this. The boys aren't getting fed properly and the place is in a bit of a mess.'

The mother did not answer. She looked away from her husband into the light of the lamp, her eyes fixed and wide as though she were hypnotised.

'I couldn't, Peter,' she said, 'not just now.'

'Why?' the man asked.

The children's mother straightened and she almost flared up then. They saw it teetering at the brim, her anger nearly overflowing, then she slumped back into the chair again.

'You know why, Peter. Do I have to go on telling you.'

'But think of the boys!' her husband implored. 'They miss you. They want you. Think of these children. It's no life for them stuck away down here in the bush. Think of the children, woman!'

'The children are happy here,' the woman said. 'They'll tell you.'

The father turned to them and said, 'Are you?'

The reply was a mixture of agreement and disagreement. Some shaking their heads and others nodding. Motu felt it was all right to stay there for a little while longer at least but apparently Louise felt it was time they were going home and now was her chance to express it.

'I thought you all said you like it here,' the mother said.

'Yes — No.'

'You see,' the father said.

The mother looked away from them tiredly yet with a certain amount of defiance on her face still. She wasn't going to give in so easily.

'I suppose you would like a cup of tea,' she said. 'Sit down.' Her husband was still standing in the middle of the room.

'Yes, if you wouldn't mind, please, Mary. I would.'

He sat himself down at the table opposite her. The children's mother got up and went to the stove and poured a cup of tea. She placed it before her husband and all the while the man was watching her. She took no notice of him.

'Thank you. Thank you very much, Mary,' he said, and he sipped gratefully at the tea. There was silence for a while in the room. No one knew what to say. Then their mother said, 'You children better go off to bed, go on and have your wash now, you must be tired after playing all afternoon.'

Once in their room they lay there listening to the muffled voices of their parents talking in the kitchen.

'I hope we go home,' Louise said. 'No,' Aroha said. 'You don't know,' Louise said, 'I hope we go home.'

'Back to that old dump,' Aroha said. 'I hope he stays the night,' Marylin said.

'Yes,' Motu chimed in. 'Me too,' Louise said. 'Yes it would be all right if he came and lived here,' Aroha agreed. 'If Luke and Arthur and dog and cat all came and stayed here. That would be different.' And they all lay there wishing that their father would stay the night. After a while they fell asleep and in the morning their father was gone and they were very disappointed.

Their father visited them often after that, every Tuesday night, about eight o'clock. They would see the torch flickering on and off, coming nearer and nearer along the narrow roadway towards the house — winding a little to the north and then curving back on to the house again

— and they would all become excited and speculate among themselves.

Their mother wasn't so hostile towards him now, and always had a hot cup of tea ready for him as soon as he came in the door. And she began to greet him with a smile now also. At first a reserved one and then gradually it became more open and unrestrained.

The children used to have to go off to bed (not until they fussed about their father for a while though and all had a turn at being nursed by him. But it was the same story, he ended up by nursing and fondling Louise in the finish while the mother bustled the rest of them off to bed.).

In the bedroom while their mother was tucking them in they would ask, 'Well Mum?' and their mother would smile and reply, 'I don't know. I don't know. But don't go asking questions like that. You just get to sleep.' And she would try to become stern and the children would say, 'Aw come on Mum, what eh!'

But she would not give anything away and would tell them to hurry up and get to sleep.

So the children would lie there and listen to the muffled voices of their parents talking in the kitchen till they fell asleep again and they never once heard their father leaving, but in the mornings he would be gone.

They began to ask their mother quite regularly after that as to what was going to happen. But their mother would not commit herself.

Then one day when the children arrived home from school their mother had some of their things packed and at their insistence she finally told them they were going home the next day.

This was met with great jubilation, and the next day Luke, Arthur and their father came down in the old Buick and the shift back to the old homestead began.

Broken Arse

—

Bruce Stewart

THE first day Henry came into the can, we could hear him cracking funnies and whistling all the way down the wing. Even while he was being stripped and even while they shore off his yellow hair, gave him a number, a well-pissed mattress, his boob blues — he still raved on. He lined up for kai, tall; you could hear him even when his mouth was full of kai.

'Hey man, she's a far-out pad. More like a hotel. It IS a hotel. When you think about it, it IS a hotel.'

And he laughed till the snot came out of his nose. He was a big man with a big laugh and made me feel good. I could see everybody's face spark up a bit. It was easy to see he was a country boy, trying to sound heavy, but you couldn't help liking him.

'She's sweet here, buddies, very sweet. Free keep, plus they pay me missus a wage. I'll tell yer she's a sweet one, buddies, a very sweet one.'

Tu and I were in the same slot. We'd come in together. He was the kingpin. Everyone liked him. He always checked the new inmates out. After we'd finished our kai we stopped by Henry's slot. He was hanging his boob gear on the nails behind the door. He was making his bed on the bottom bunk. He stopped for a bit when he saw his blankets were ripped and patched; his towel too was made up of four old towels. But he laughed again and poked his head through a ripped blanket.

'An' what's more, this patchwork stuff is a big deal outside buddies, yeer, big deal.'

He played a photo of his missus a bit like a trump card. She looked like one of those flimsy girls you see in the big cities, one of those girls with lots of smelly stuff on her sad-looking face. Didn't seem like Henry's sort of girl but he looked at the photo as if she was some kind of star or something.

Tu couldn't take his randy eyes off the photo.

'You got a spunky missus, Bud.'

'Oh . . . Tina-Marie you mean?' He tried to look surprised. 'She's not too bad — fuckin' good in the sack, yeer. Straight up and down she is, yeer, straight up and down.'

He went into a short trance, kept staring at the photo. 'She'll wait . . . yeer, she'll wait . . .'

Tu rolled a slow smoke and Henry kept on mumbling about her waiting and about seven years not being too long . . . but it was only for a moment 'cos he went outside his slot and shoved his card in its place above the door. The card said:

ATHOL HENRY BLIGH
Sentence   7 years
Date of Sentence   5.1.80
Date of Release   5.1.87

He stood back, hands on hips. 'Seven years, eh? Tha's a man's lag and I'll do it on me fuckin' head. With ease, buddies.' He punched the card and roared, 'With ease.'

His eyes were blue on white and bright. Brighter than any eyes I'd seen for a long time. Everyone started to look up to him 'cos he made you feel good. He looked so big. He was big. Tu looked at me with a knowing kind of nod. 'Too loud,' he whispered. 'A bit too loud.'

Henry got right into his lag. He played football, he played basketball. Most of his spare time was spent in the iron room. All sorts of stories went around the can about Henry's muscles. Like lifting the back of the pig truck off the ground was hard to believe, and so was the one about Henry tipping over the prison bull, Barney.

Tu and I went up to the iron room one Saturday to see Henry's muscles for ourselves. Tu could push more iron than anyone. We shoved our way through lots of little muscles, I say little muscles because they were standing around like apes. It was the same as being in church. The place smelt of iron and sweat and sort of stung my nose. There wasn't any sound except Henry's deep breathing; sweat dripped off his nose. He was shaping up to a great heap of iron.

'He's been building up to this for three hours,' someone whispered, so's we would be up on the action.

Henry moved into the heap of iron. It was more than Tu had lifted. He stood there for a long time breathing deeply and twitching his fingers. He bent down and gripped the bar like he was going to tear it apart; with a half shout, half scream hurled it up over his head.

'Chesses!'

'Fuckin' hell!' said all the little apes.

Henry ripped off his shirt in front of the mirror and struck a kind of Mr World pose and all the little apes oohed and aahed. His pumped-up body bulged out all over the place. His veins stuck out and looked something like the roots of an old pohutukawa tree. Henry struck pose after pose. He twitched his muscles, he made them shiver. They were shiny with sweat. Everybody watched him. He was the new champion. He looked like a great white giant. I looked for Tu. He was standing with his back against the wall rolling a long slow smoke.

Henry developed a kind of gorilla walk; guts pulled in and up to his chest, back muscles fully flexed so's his arms hung out from his body. Wherever he walked he managed to catch a glimpse of himself in the windows. The queens loved him, 'specially Sandra. Tu said she did a few free blow jobs on the side to get the top bunk in Henry's slot. One day Tu found them under the stage on the badminton nets. Tu was pretty sweet on Sandra. It seemed all the strong fellas got the best queens. Sandra was a Maori — somehow I knew Tu didn't like her being with Henry. Henry always showered in front of the mirror and even when he combed his hair he'd strike a pose.

Before the mail list was called Henry would be standing outside the guardroom, waiting. I saw Piggy Screw one day censoring Henry's letter. He sniffed the scent and ripped it open. I could tell by the way his fat face lit up and by the way he was chuckling he was really caught up with the secret bits.

Henry looked like a hurt little puppy waiting for a bone. Piggy Screw kept reading. Henry waited.

'Oh, Bligh, didn't see you there. I just finished censoring your letter. Here you are.'

'Th . . . thanks, mister.'

'She's quite a girl, your Tina-Marie, ay Bligh?'

'Y . . . eah, yes, mister.'

'Yes, quite a girl.'

And Henry would come swaggering up the wing offering all the boys a sniff of the scent his missus had splashed on the letter.

'Every day! Every day!'

Sandra didn't mind. The letters made Henry randy. It was Sandra who slept with Henry.

Henry went back to his slot and read and re-read the letter. He read in between the lines. By the time he had read it six times he was happy. He started doing his lag letter by letter, kept them all in a large cigar box with a yellow ribbon tied around.

Tu found out where Tina-Marie lived. He was a Trustee and drove the can's pig truck. He called in to see her every day. Everyone knew about Tu and Tina-Marie — everyone except Henry. Also Tu was working on something. I couldn't work out what it was, but he spent a fair bit of time in Piggy Screw's ear. No one else knew he was talking to Piggy Screw. No one talks to screws much. But he had a way of saying things out the side of his mouth. Piggy Screw knew how to play the game too. He'd been with crims so long he was like one himself. His best mates were crims with lots of form. He was no match for Tu, though. He was like most of the other screws, thick. Thick but cunning and dangerous. Well, that's what Tu told me.

Henry often talked about farming, about ploughing with horses. He'd been taught by his grandfather. He knew so much about the land. I liked his talk. When he talked about Tina-Marie though, he was sad. 'She taught me everything . . . I love her so much, I miss her so much . . . it hurts. Never had a girlfriend before.'

Henry got a whopping toothache, I was working with him cutting scrub in Piggy Screw's outside party. Henry was in such a bad way he could hardly speak. Plus he was too scared to see Piggy Screw 'cos Piggy Screw was starting to give him a hard time, making him do the dirty jobs. He called Henry 'Musclehead'. I said I'd go and see Piggy Screw for him.

Piggy Screw was lying down in the shade asleep. He always went to sleep in the shade while we worked in the sun. It's a wonder no one killed him while he slept. Enough fellas hated him. They always talked about it. But then he was so strong and fierce. Once he told us the best job he ever had was 'a mercenary hunting niggers in South Africa. They had spears, we had automatic rifles, hee hee.'

I got within ten yards of where he was sleeping. He jerked upright.

'Excuse me, mister. Henry Bligh has a really bad toothache: if I could get some kawakawa leaves from the bottom of this gully it would help him, mister.'

'A witchdoctor, eh,' he roared and his fat stomach shook. He got to his feet. 'Might just go down there and see Bligh the Musclehead. I'm a bit of a witchdoctor myself, a WHITE witchdoctor.' Piggy Screw looked evil.

Or maybe he was lonely too, I didn't really know. He seemed to enjoy everyone hating him. He hated kid fuckers the most, that's what Tu said. By the time he got down to where Henry was, he was puffing and sweating.

'Bit of a toothache, eh Bligh? Well, you just remember WHO you are and WHAT you're here for. Not a holiday camp is it Bligh? No. WHO ARE YOU? Go on Bligh, YOU tell me, who are you?'

He kept prodding Henry in the chest with his forefinger. 'An' watcha here for, go on, watcha here for?'

Piggy Screw kept pushing Henry down the hill. Henry mumbled back and Piggy Screw told him to speak clearly. We all knew Henry couldn't speak cause his gum was badly swollen up.

'Speak up like a man.'

I couldn't work out why he was so evil, so cruel. I couldn't stand it any longer. 'Please, mister, Henry Bligh can't speak.'

'Well what have we here. Witchdoctor speaks for the kid fucker. Bit of a kid fucker lover are y'? I thought there was sompin' queer about y'. Not as bad as a genuine kid fucker. Should cut their balls out I reckon.'

None of us believed it. Not Henry, a kid fucker! We all looked at each other and then back to Henry who was shaking his head.

'No!' he mumbled. 'No!'

Piggy Screw asked me to take Henry back to his slot.

'I'll send the nurse when I'm good and ready.'

All the way back I was trying to work out what happened . . . I knew Henry wasn't into little boys . . . he had Tina-Marie and Sandra . . . not little boys. What made Piggy Screw so awful? Maybe it was something to do with Tu . . . when he talked out of the side of his mouth to Piggy Screw.

There was a story about Piggy Screw finding a sack on the side of the road . . . it had a baby in it and it was still alive — he adopted it. The boy turned out to be a bit funny in the head, they said. Had to put him in a special home. He got a job as a screw for revenge, they said. He'd been at it twenty-five years. He was getting old for a screw but he could still swing a pick handle.

We waited in Henry's slot for the nurse. Everyone was in from the work parties, I could hear them in the showers. Henry was in a bad way. He tried lying down on his back but the hammering would make him jolt up again. He'd start pacing around his slot. I could see the pain was hammering him stupid. He was crying. He wiped away the tears and tried to make an excuse for crying in front of me, but I told him I cried too at times, and I didn't think there was anything wrong with it. He smiled a bit through his tears.

One hundred and thirty-six speakers told us it was scoff time. I left Henry in his slot; told him I'd be back after scoff.

In the dining room I could feel something was going on. Tu was the centre of it all. I could tell by the sly glances. A screw checked the muster. He whispered to one of the other screws. They both looked worried. Checked the muster again. Still one down. They checked for the third time.

'Lock the doors!'

'Who is it?'

No one knew so they called the roll.

'It's Athol Henry Bligh.'

I could see Tu had it all going well. The boys were leading the screws on great guns.

'Bligh must've gone over the wall.'

'Yeah, he had a toothache. He probably jumped over the wall.'

'Bligh's a nutter.'

'He split, man.'

Piggy Screw came in. 'Shut up, alla y'.' He asked the two screws where Bligh was. They said he'd gone over the wall.

The Super himself was called in.

'Bligh's escaped, sir,' said Piggy Screw.

'Who is Bligh?'

'The muscle man, sir,' said Piggy Screw trying to sound very polite, and he whispered something into the Super's ear.

'Oh God, no. Not him! Look, if the papers want to know what's going on, keep it quiet. Having someone escape is bad enough. Is that clear, mister?'

'Yes, sir.'

It was good fun listening to it all. They seemed to have forgotten we were there. It was good too because we knew Henry was safe in his slot. Piggy had sent him there.

But I couldn't work out what Tu was up to. True, he was liked by everyone, they'd do anything he asked. We'd been through a lot together. He was doing ten years for trapping five cops up a blind alley and beating the shit outta them with a chain. He said they were white trash. Tu made out he was a bit silly, but he wasn't. He was always working something out . . . some way to get his own back. He'd always been the kingpin; no one could match him. No screw was a match for Tu.

We were all ordered to our slots for an early lockup. Tu beat me to

Henry's slot. I got there just in time to hear Tu telling Henry to keep out of sight.

'They think you've pissed off, man. Play along. They'll find you soon. And you'll get painkillers. Sweet?'

Henry nodded. He knew he had to be staunch. I could see he was in a bad way, his teeth must've been giving him one helluva hammering. Only wish I could have got those kawakawa leaves.

An hour after lockup Piggy Screw found him. We could all hear everything he said.

'B . . . Bligh, you kid-fucking bastard. Y' set me up, y'cunt.'

'You sent me to the slot to wait, mister, f . . . for the nurse.'

'No I didn't, y'bastard, don't lay that on me or I'll cut y'balls out.'

He sounded pissed and evil. We could hear him kicking Henry in the ribs.

'That's (THUD) for saying I sent y' to your slot. Lies. That's (THUD) for pretending to escape, so by now the police are looking everywhere for you. (THUD) It's all over the radio, Bligh. (THUD) "Kid fucker at large." (THUD) "Everyone is requested to lock up their sons as Henry Bligh is loose." That's what they'll be saying.' (THUD)

We could hear a lot of scuffling, Piggy Screw was trying to shout, but it was coming out all muffled. Henry must've got him. It sounded as if Piggy Screw was being strangled. Henry could break his neck easily. Then we could hear Henry smashing Piggy Screw's head against the wall.

'Kill the bastard, Henry!' roared Tu so no one could tell where his voice came from. Everyone started chanting. Banging the heating pipes with anything they could lay their hands on. Steel against steel. Ringing, echoing, ringing, ringing. Stomping out the refrain. It was slow at first. Deliberate, heavy.

'Kill the bastard!'

'Kill the bastard!'

'Kill the bastard!'

It echoed and bounced from wall to wall. The whole place was going crazy and I was too, chanting along with the rest. It was good sticking up for Henry, he was a good guy . . . I mean, Tu reckoned all Pakehas were trash and yet here we were stomping for Henry, a Pakeha.

Suddenly I knew we were killing Henry. Because if he killed Piggy Screw he'd get life. We weren't helping Henry at all.

I looked at Tu. He was at the grill pushing everyone. Keeping it all going. He looked a bit porangi.

'Tu!' I had to yell. He swung around. I could see he was mad. He loved fights. He was in command of the whole prison.

'Tu!' I yelled again. 'Stop them, Tu, he'll get life.'

'You fuck up, boy, or I'll put y' down.'

'Y' can if y' like but you've got to stop all this.'

'Fuck up, boy, I'll . . .'

He was going to drop me — we were close friends. Screws were running down the wing. The chanting stopped. We could hear three or four screws belting into Henry.

'They're kicking the shit outta Henry,' yelled Tu.

The screws were whispering so's we couldn't hear.

'Better get the nurse.'

'No, he'll live, serve him fuckin' right. He tried to kill me.'

They locked him up. They left. It was quiet again. Tu could see Henry's slot through the grill.

'There's blood all over the place,' he screamed. 'Henry's blood. Hey you guys, Henry's nearly brown bread.'

The can started winding up, you could feel it. You could hear it murmuring. Tu was still in command, leading everyone. 'They kicked the shit outta him. The screw bastards. SCREWS FUCK SPIDERS!'

'Fuckin' screw bastards!'

'SCREWS FUCK SPIDERS! SCREWS FUCK SPIDERS!'

It was winding up again. Not only our wing but all the wings joined in. All chanting. All stomping.

'Get Bligh the nurse.'

'Get Bligh the nurse.'

'Get Bligh the nurse.'

It was building up. Nervous. Ugly. And I was right there caught in the fire of it all. Bashing steel against steel. Everybody stomping. Steel against steel ringing, echoing, ringing. Piggy Screw was running up and down the wing, yelling through the peep holes.

'Cut out y' fuckin' racket. Cut it out or I'll come and fuckin' do y'.'
But it stomped even louder.
'SCREWS FUCK SPIDERS.'
'SCREWS FUCK SPIDERS.'
'GET BLIGH THE NURSE.'
'GET BLIGH THE NURSE.'

The next thing we heard Piggy Screw on the loudspeaker. He was using his loudspeaker voice. 'Would inmates refrain from creating a disturbance. If not, we will be forced to take sterner measures. I repeat. Would inmates refrain . . .'

The more he tried to stop us the stronger we stomped. They poked a firehose into our slot. The force of the water slapped me against the back wall. The can hissed back. Everyone, steel against steel, 368 of us all shouting and stomping. Tu and I stripped naked. We danced in our madness. The prison shook. It all reached a high-pitched screaming sound.

The nurse came.

There was silence. The hate and the ugliness were still there, throbbing, but it was silent.

'Come on now, son, this will kill the pain.'

We could hear her making the screws run: she wanted hot water, clean sheets and blankets, she made them clean up the mess.

'How on earth did this happen?'

'One of the inmates got him. He'll live, won't he?' It was Piggy Screw talking in a hoarse whisper thinking we couldn't hear him.

'Liar!' Tu yelled so no one could tell where his voice came from again.

'Bloody liar!' came from a dozen slots. 'You got him bashed up.'

Piggy Screw left. We all knew he hated talking orders from a woman.

The can never settled down that night. The stomping was still there; even when it was silent. It kept turning over. Every now and again the night shattered.

'Dirty, rotten, fuckin', screw bastards!' someone screamed in their half-awake fear.

I couldn't sleep — kept turning over and over.

By morning Tu had a new plan. He was always working on ways of destroying . . . though I wasn't sure who he was destroying . . . even in his sleep I could hear him mumbling things. I knew he didn't care about Henry now, 'cos Henry was a Pakeha — of the 368 inmates, 203 were Maori. Tu ruled the prison; he was the boss. The prison had a guard placed outside Henry's slot. As soon as we were unlocked Tu called a meeting in the showers.

'We've got to tell Henry to lay a complaint outside, to a magistrate. We'll tell the newspapers and the TV. Sweet?'

'Sweet.'

'We'll riot,' said Tu. But there was a long silence and he could see some of us weren't ready for the kind of riot he meant.

'You've got to. You all know how the bastards smashed up Henry. We can't let them get away with it. Let's tear this hell-hole apart. We'll wait till the screws are standing around at morning scoff and we'll grab them.'

Tu was talking fast and I could see most of his heavies were being swayed. I couldn't agree though, not about the riot I mean, we were no match for the screws.

'No riot, Tu,' I said.

Tu glared at me. 'Let's down the bastards,' he shouted.

'No. They'd get the army in,' I said. 'Better to have a peaceful sit-out.'

'No,' Tu shouted.

'Yes we can, Tu. We'll all go into the yard after breakfast and sit down. We'll do as you say, get a letter to Henry. Henry could lay a complaint. We'll let Henry know the whole boob is sitting it out.'

Everyone agreed. Everyone except Tu.

After morning scoff Tu chased Sludge, one of the Pakeha kingpins. Chased him past the guard outside Henry's slot, to the shitter at the end of the wing.

'You fuckin', thievin', white trash bastard, I'll beans ya!' yelled Tu.

'Issat so, black? You'll be brown bread when I've finished with y'. All you Maori cunts are gutless. Y're only good in numbers!'

He shouldn't have said that, because it was only meant to be a decoy. Tu dropped him and started kicking the shit outta him.

The screw took the bait and rushed down to the shitter. 'C'mon, you two; break it up or you'll both be charged.'

I slipped a note under the door to Henry.

'Henry,' I whispered, 'chin up. Read this. We're all with you.'

After breakfast, 136 speakers ordered us to parade for work. The screws could see something was wrong, they looked a bit scared. Piggy Screw was back on duty. He must've been expecting trouble because it was his three days off. He had an unhappy face but we knew he loved trouble. We could see him reaching for the microphone.

'Would all inmates get on parade.' He waited for a while. All the young screws were standing beside him. They were looking nervous.

No one moved. No one said a word. We all sat there, 368 of us all waiting. None of the screws would come out into the yard. They were too scared. They stayed close to their microphone, close to Piggy Screw. I could see him reaching for the microphone again.

'Would inmates elect a spokesman. The spokesman should come forward and inform us of your grievance.'

Tu whispered, 'You go, boy, Henry's more your friend than any of us.'

It wasn't easy for me walking up to the guardroom and telling them we were going to stay there until we knew Henry Bligh had got a magistrate.

'What's he got a magistrate for?'

I could see he was going to play games with me so I left the guardroom and walked across the yard.

We were strong, all being together. Nothing they could do to us. It was a kind of safe feeling. Three hundred and sixty-eight of us lying there in the sun. No one talking. With my eyes closed I thought of my koroua, Tane. Must be he's thinking of me too. Wish I was with him in the bush. The birds were singing in the bush outside the prison.

Sun.

Bush.

Birds.

Tane.

And greenness,

Somewhere out there is greenness.

I was drifting. Dreaming. Floating. In my dream I could see myself . . . lying down there with the 368 . . . heaps of walruses . . . sunning . . . I looked happy with my eyes closed. The tui in the kowhai were busy. Sometimes it's hard to remember all the things of aroha Tane taught me. He said it would take a lifetime to learn its meaning. The sun heals. Tane says aroha always wins. Takes a long time, but it always does. He said it is the only way.

I woke up suddenly. For a while I didn't know where I was. Kind of lost. It was Henry. I saw him limping out of the guardroom. The Super, Piggy Screw and the four other screws were crowded into the guardroom. Smirking behind bullet-proof glass. Henry was all cleaned up, bandaged, and in some new recreation gear. Something was wrong.

Later on Henry told me what happened. He said he'd got our letter and he'd only just swallowed it when the screws came for him. He was marched before the Super himself. He was offered a roundie and a cup of coffee. Piggy Screw was there, he was being really nice.

'Sit down, Bligh.'

The Super showed Henry to a comfortable chair. 'You know, Bligh, you're in serious trouble attempting to escape.'

'But I was sent to my slot . . .'

'It's no good going over that again, Bligh. We know what you were trying to do.'

Henry tried to say something.

'Listen, Bligh, you're in big trouble so shut up and listen. Just remember WHO you are and WHERE you are!'

Henry hung his head. 'Yes, sir.'

'Another cigarette? More coffee?' Henry nodded. No inmate was allowed cigarettes or coffee.

'Well, it's like this, Bligh. You're doing seven as it is . . . and you've got a girl waiting for you outside, eh Bligh?'

'Yes, sir.'

'And she's quite a girl judging from her letters. Well, we're taking this into consideration and we are not laying charges and I know you will not take it any further, will you, Bligh?'

'No . . . no, sir.'

'No what?'

'No, I won't take it any further, sir.'

'That's talking sense, Bligh. Now you can have this packet of cigarettes. The nurse will see you and you can sit in the sun. There's no need for you to work for the next couple of weeks. I'll fix it with the nurse.'

There were 368 of us all watching Henry limping. He looked really sore. Behind the glass the screws smirked. Something was wrong. Henry stopped. He was smoking roundies!

'What . . . he's smoking roundies!'

'He's fuckin' scabbed.'

'Wassa score?'

'He's cracked up.'

The can started winding up again. This time it was against Henry. He just stood there on the spot. In the middle of the courtyard shaking his head.

'I couldn't . . . sorry, but I couldn't.'

'Scab.'

'White trash.'

'Broken arse.'

'BROKEN ARSE!'

'BROKEN ARSE!'

'BROKEN ARSE!'

The stomping started again. Henry knew he'd blown it. He looked back to the guardhouse to the Super and the screws. It was almost as if he'd wanted to take back the things he'd said. But the guardhouse was empty, the screws were gone. Henry hung his head. The stomping started building up.

'BROKEN ARSE!'

'BROKEN ARSE!'

'BROKEN ARSE!'

The more they chanted 'broken arse' the more Henry sunk to his knees, it was like a giant hand was crushing him into the ground. He wept right out there in front of everybody. He couldn't control himself.

Snot and tears running down his face. And all the time the stomping beat out the refrain, 'Broken arse, broken arse, broken arse.'

'Crying,' said someone.

'Crying like a madwoman,' said another.

'Shit, now I've seen it all, a man crying in front of everyone.'

'Fuckin' hell, makes you want to throw up.'

Some of the 368 took off. Ran to their slots. Squirming.

'Never seen anything like it before.'

I went out to see Henry. I'm not a hero at all, in fact I was really scared. But it was as if Tane was pushing me out. Helped him to his feet, put my arm over his shoulder and helped him back to his slot. It was awful . . . the brokenness was awful.

That night they demolished Henry. They stomped for two hours. The screws pretended they never heard it.

Henry spent a week lying on his bed. He couldn't eat, I managed to get him a few scraps. He was too frightened to leave his slot. Everywhere he went they called him Broken Arse.

Two weeks later when Henry went up to the iron room, they hissed at him.

'White trash.'

He pretended not to hear, but it was written all over his face. He piled a great heap of iron on the bar. It was heavier than he'd lifted before. He was going to try it cold.

He walked around the bar. The hissing stopped. He stood in front, deep breathing, fingers twitching. It was his last chance to come back. He grabbed. Lifted, pushed and pushed but it wouldn't go right up. It was lopsided, starting toppling over. He fell. Screamed. He'd ruptured something in his groin. He tried to get up.

'He's fucked himself.'

'Must've dropped a piston.'

'He's got a broken bum-bum, hee hee.'

'The original broken arse.'

When he got back to his slot someone had done a shit in his bed. They had thrown shit all over the walls. They had rubbed it over the photo.

Henry went into hospital. He came back on crutches ten days later. Wherever he limped he was called Broken Arse. He lived for his missus's letters but they weren't coming every day. Sometimes it was three days before he got one, even then it was often a scribbled page. We all knew Tu was seeing his Tina-Marie.

Henry wasn't seen much. He slid along the walls, feeling his way. His left shoulder dropped. He was always seeing the chaplain or the nurse. He didn't work. The nurse said he was too sick. He slept most of the time, didn't even read. Just slept.

I used to go to his slot as much as I could. He liked to see me, I liked to see him too. He always sparked up a bit when we talked about our old ones, about the bush, the mountains, the rivers.

He couldn't keep his slot clean. He never had a shower. His great body was withering away. On film nights Henry used to sneak in after lights out so's he'd miss the hissing. But the 368 knew. One night the film clacked on about a woman becoming tired of her man. When she finally climbed into the best friend's bed the 368 spat out . . .

'An' that is Broken Arse's missus.'

In the dark Henry picked up a chair and smashed it down on Tu's head. He downed two screws. He cut a furrow through the 368, leaving a bleeding heap. And all the time making half dog, half man noises. He rushed back to his slot and swallowed razor blades. Henry went into hospital again. When he was well enough he was committed to the nutter. Henry's head was electrocuted. Months later he was brought back.

'Broken Arse is back.'

'He's a fuckin' robot.'

I saw him starting across the yard from the guardhouse. He was swinging his legs like they were dead logs. His head was screwed to one side . . . it looked crooked. The further he walked out into the yard the slower he went. He looked back at the guardhouse — Piggy Screw and his mates were just staring. The closer he got to the spot where he went down on his knees, crying, the place where they chanted 'broken arse', the more he started to twitch. He couldn't go past it. He just stared at it like he was staring right into hell itself. His eyes were rolling. His head twisted . . . evil . . . his arms twitched. His fingers were bent . . . different ways. He froze. He looked like a statue . . . it was not Henry at all. I went out to him, so did the others, even the screws, even Piggy Screw. My guts was churning, it was mixed up with love and hate and anger, all at the same time. Only the whites of his eyes were showing. He was breathing all right, but it was as if he were dead. His face was twisted and frozen with a look of deep hurt . . . deep pain. Tears were streaming out of his white eyes. The tears were the only warm part I knew about him. It ripped at my guts. I was full of tears too. So were many of the others. Piggy Screw looked different, his bottom lip was quivering.

'Poor bastard,' someone whispered.

'Makes you feel stink all right,' said Piggy Screw. 'I gotta boy in the nutter . . . be about the same age . . . he's got yella hair too . . . makes you feel fuckin' stink all right.'

Piggy Screw was hugging Henry, the tears were streaming down his face too. 'Found him stuffed in a sack you know . . . no one wanted him . . . no one loved him . . . no one at all.'

It was sad seeing Piggy Screw crying out there in front of the others. He looked shattered, even broken, right out there where Henry went down on his knees. It seemed the same giant hand that crushed Henry was crushing Piggy Screw.

Tu was standing in the shadows, up against the back wall. So were all his Maori heavies. There were about eighty of them. They seemed to enjoy the brokenness. Henry and Piggy Screw . . . hugging.

We could all feel the stomping. It was a slow, deliberate stomp, though there wasn't a sound. They were stomping their feet, swaying their bodies from side to side like a haka. They stomped. Broken arse, broken arse. You couldn't hear a sound. They looked so black, so ugly, so strong.

Henry and Piggy Screw looked so pale, so weak, so broken.

Tu rolled a large, slow smoke.

Ngati Kangaru

Patricia Grace

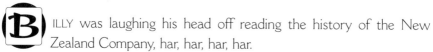

BILLY was laughing his head off reading the history of the New Zealand Company, har, har, har, har.

It was since he'd been made redundant from Mitre 10 that he'd been doing all this reading. Billy and Makere had four children, one who had recently qualified as a lawyer but was out of work, one in her final year at university, and two at secondary school. These kids ate like elephants. Makere's job as a checkout operator for New World didn't bring in much money and she thought Billy should be out looking for another job instead of sitting on his backside all day reading and laughing.

The book belonged to Rena, whose full given names were Erena Meretiana. She wanted the book back so she could work on her assignment. Billy had a grip on it.

Har, har, these Wakefields were real crooks. That's what delighted Billy. He admired them, and at the beginning of his reading had been distracted for some minutes while he reflected on that first one, E. G. Wakefield, sitting in the clink studying up on colonisation. Then by the time of his release, EG had the edge on all those lords, barons, MPs, lawyers and so forth. Knew more about colonisation than they did, haaar.

However, Billy wasn't too impressed with the reason for EG's incarceration. Abducting an heiress? Jeepers! Billy preferred more normal, more cunning crookery, something funnier — like lying, cheating and stealing.

So in that regard he wasn't disappointed as he read on, blobbed out in front of the two-bar heater that was expensive to run, Makere reminded him. Yes, initial disappointment left him the more he progressed in his reading. Out-and-out crooks, liars, cheats and thieves, these Wakefields. He felt inspired.

What he tried to explain to Makere was that he wasn't just spending his time idly while he sat there reading. He was learning a few things from EG, WW, Jerningham, Arthur and Co., that would eventually be of benefit to him as well as to the whole family. He knew it in his bones.

'Listen to this,' he'd say, as Makere walked in the door on feet that during the course of the day had grown and puffed out over the tops of her shoes. And he'd attempt to interest her with excerpts from what he'd read. ' "The Wakefields' plan was based on the assumption that vast areas — if possible, every acre — of New Zealand would be bought for a trifle, the real payment to the people of the land being their 'civilising' . . ." Hee hee, that's crafty. They called it "high and holy work".

'And here. There was this "exceptional Law" written about in one of EG's anonymous publications, where chiefs sold a heap of land for a few bob and received a section "in the midst of emigrants" in return. But har, har, the chiefs weren't allowed to live on this land until they had "learned to estimate its value". Goodby-ee, don't cry-ee. It was held in reserve waiting for the old fellas to be brainy enough to know what to do with it.

'Then there was this "adopt-a-chief scheme", a bit like the "dial-a-kaumatua" scheme that they have today where you bend some old bloke's ear for an hour or two, let him say a few wise words and get him to do the old rubber-stamp trick, hee, hee. Put him up in a flash hotel and give him a ride in an aeroplane then you've consulted with every iwi throughout Aotearoa, havintcha? Well, "adopt-a-chief" was a bit the same except the prizes were different. They gave out coats of arms, lessons in manners and how to mind your Ps and Qs, that sort of stuff. I like it. You could do anything as long as you had a "worthy cause",' and Billy would become pensive. 'A worthy cause. Orl yew need is a werthy caws.'

On the same day that Billy finished reading the book he found his worthy cause. He had switched on television to watch *Te Karere*, when the face of his first cousin Hiko, who lived in Poi Hakena, Australia, came on to the screen.

The first shots showed Hiko speaking to a large rally of Maori people in Sydney who had formed a group called Te Hokinga ki Aotearoa. This group was in the initial stages of planning for a mass return of Maori to their homeland.

In the interview that followed, Hiko explained that there was disillusionment among Maori people with life in Australia and that they now wanted to return to New Zealand. Even the young people who had been born in Australia, who may never have seen Aotearoa, were showing an interest in their ancestral home. The group included three or four millionaires, along with others who had made it big in Oz, as well as those on the bones of their arses — or that's how Billy translated into English what Hiko had said in Maori, to Hana and Gavin. These two were Hana Angeline and Gavin Rutene, the secondary schoolers, who had left their homework to come and gog at their uncle on television.

Hiko went on to describe what planning would be involved in the first stage of The Return, because this transfer of one hundred families was a first stage only. The ultimate plan was to return all Maori people living in Australia to Aotearoa, iwi by iwi. But the groups didn't want to come home to nothing, was what Hiko was careful to explain. They intended all groups to be well housed and financed on their return, and discussions and decisions on how to make it all happen were in progress. Billy's ears prickled when Hiko began to speak of the need for land, homes, employment and business ventures. ' "Possess yourselves of the soil," ' he muttered, ' "and you are secure." '

Ten minutes later he was on the phone to Hiko.

By the time the others returned — Makere from work, Tu from job-hunting and Rena from varsity — Billy and the two children had formed a company, composed a rap, cleared a performance space in front of the dead fireplace, put their caps on backwards and practised up to performance standard:

Ngati Kangaru

First you go and form a Co.
Make up lies and advertise
Buy for a trifle the land you want
For Jew's harps, nightcaps
Mirrors and beads

Sign here sign there
So we can steal
And bring home cuzzies
To their 'Parent Isle'

Draw up allotments on a map
No need to buy just occupy
Rename the places you now own
And don't let titles get you down
For blankets, fish hooks, axes and guns
Umbrellas, sealing wax, pots and clothes

Sign here, sign there
So we can steal
And bring home cuzzies
To their 'Parent Isle'

Bought for a trifle sold for a bomb
Homes for your rellies
And dollars in the bank
Bought for a trifle sold for a bomb
Homes for your rellies and
Dollars in the bank

Ksss Aue. Aue,
Hi.

Billy, Hana and Gavin bowed to Makere, Tu and Rena. 'You are looking
at a new company,' Billy said, 'which from henceforward (his vocabulary

had taken on some curiosities since he had begun reading histories) will be known as Te Kamupene o Te Hokinga Mai.'

'Tell Te Kamupene o Te Hokinga Mai to cough up for the mortgage,' said Makere, disappearing offstage with her shoes in her hand.

'So all we need,' said Billy to Makere, later in the evening, is a vast area of land "as far as the eye can see".'

'Is that all?' said Makere.

'Of "delightful climate" and "rich soil" that is "well watered and coastal". Of course it'll need houses on it too, the best sort of houses, luxury style.'

'Like at Claire Vista,' said Makere. Billy jumped out of his chair and his eyes jumped out, 'Brilliant, Ma, brilliant.' He planted a kiss on her unimpressed cheek and went scrabbling in a drawer for pen and paper so that he could write to Hiko:

' . . . the obvious place for the first settlement of Ngati Kangaru, it being "commodious and attractive". But more importantly, as you know, Claire Vista is the old stamping ground of our iwi that was confiscated at the end of last century, and is now a luxury holiday resort. Couldn't be apter. We must time the arrival of our people for late autumn when the holidaymakers have all left. I'll take a trip up there on Saturday and get a few snaps, which I'll send. Then I'll draw up a plan and we can do our purchases. Between us we should be able to see everyone home and housed by June next year. Timing your arrival will be vital. I suggest you book flights well in advance so that you all arrive at once. We will charter buses to take you to your destination and when you arrive we will hold the official welcome-home ceremony and see you all settled into your new homes.'

The next weekend he packed the company photographer with her camera and the company secretary with his notebook and biro, into the car. He, the company manager, got in behind the wheel and they set out for Claire Vista.

At the top of the last rise, before going down into Claire Vista, Billy stopped the car. While he was filling the radiator, he told Hana to take a few shots. And to Gavin he said, 'Have a good look, son, and write down what the eye can see.'

192

'On either side of where we're stopped,' wrote Gavin, 'there's hills and natral vejetation. There's this long road down on to this flat land that's all covered in houses and parks. There's this long, straight beach on the left side and the other side has lots of small beaches. There's this airport for lite planes and a red windsock showing hardly any wind. One little plane is just taking off. There's these boats coming and going on the water as far as the I can see, and there's these two islands, one like a sitting dog and one like a duck.'

Their next stop was at the Claire Vista Information Centre, where they picked up street maps and brochures, after which they did a systematic tour of the streets, stopping every now and again to take photographs and notes.

'So what do I do?' asked Tu, who had just been made legal adviser of the company. He was Tuakana Petera and this was his first employment.

'Get parchments ready for signing,' said Billy.

'Do you mean deeds of title?'

'That's it,' said Billy. Then to Rena, the company's new researcher, he said, 'Delve into the histories and see what you can come up with for new brochures. Start by interviewing Nanny.'

'I've got exams in two weeks I'll have you know.'

'After that will do.'

The next day Billy wrote to Hiko to say that deeds of title were being prepared and requested that each of the families send two thousand dollars for working capital. He told him that a further two thousand dollars would be required on settlement. 'For four thousand bucks you'll all get a posh house with boat, by the sea, where there are recreation parks, and amenities, anchorage and launching ramps, and a town, with good shopping, only twenty minutes away. Also it's a good place to set up businesses for those who don't want to fish all the time.

'Once the deeds of sale have been made up for each property I'll get the signatures of them and then they'll be ready. I'll also prepare a map of the places, each place to be numbered, and when all the first payments have been made you can hold a lottery where subscribers' tickets are put into "tin boxes". Then you can have ceremonies where the names and numbers will be drawn out by a "beautiful boy". This is a method that has been used very successfully in the past, according to my information.

'Tomorrow we're going out to buy Jew's harps, muskets, blankets (or such like) as exchange for those who sign the parchments.'

'You'll have a hundred families all living in one house, I suppose,' said Makere, 'because that's all you'll get with four thousand dollars a family.'

'Possess yourselves of the homes,' said Billy.

'What's that supposed to mean?'

'It's a "wasteland". They're waste homes. They're all unoccupied. Why have houses unoccupied when there are people wanting to occupy them?'

'Bullshit. Hana and Gav didn't say the houses were unoccupied.'

'That's because it's summertime. End of March everyone's gone and there are good homes going to waste. "Reclaiming and cultivating a moral wilderness", that's what we're doing, "serving to the highest degree", that's what we're on about, "according to a deliberate and methodical plan".'

'Doesn't mean you can just walk in and take over.'

'Not unless we get all the locks changed.'

By the end of summer the money was coming in and Billy had all the deeds of sale printed, ready for signing. Makere thought he was loopy thinking that all these rich wallahs would sign their holiday homes away.

'Not *them*,' Billy said. 'You don't get *them* to sign. You get other people. That's how it was done before. Give out pressies — tobacco, biscuits, pipes, that sort of thing, so that they, whoever they are, will mark the parchments.'

Makere was starting to get the hang of it, but she huffed all the same.

'Now I'm going out to get us a van,' Billy said. 'Then we'll buy the trifles. After that, tomorrow and the next day, we'll go and round up some derros to do the signing.'

It took a week to get the signatures, and during that time Billy and the kids handed out — to park benchers in ten different parts of the city — one hundred bottles of whisky, one hundred packets of hot pies and one hundred old overcoats.

'What do you want our signatures for?' they asked.

'Deeds of sale for a hundred properties up in Claire Vista,' Billy said.

'The only Claire Vistas we've got is where our bums hit the benches.'

'Well, look here.' Billy showed them the maps with the allotments marked out on them and they were interested and pleased. 'Waste homes,' Billy explained. 'All these fellas have got plenty of other houses all over the place, but they're simple people who know nothing about how to fully utilise their properties and they can "scarcely cultivate the earth". But who knows they might have a "peculiar aptitude for being improved". It's "high and holy work", this.'

'Too right. Go for it,' the geezers said. Billy and the kids did their rap for them and moved on, pleased with progress.

In fact everything went so well that there was nothing much left to do after that. When he wrote to Hiko, Billy recommended that settlement of Claire Vista be speeded up. 'We could start working on places for the next hundred families now and have all preparations done in two months. I think we should make an overall target of one hundred families catered for every two months over the next ten months. That means in March we get our first hundred families home, then another lot in May, July, September, November. By November we'll have five hundred Ngati Kangaru families, i.e., about four thousand people, settled before the holiday season. We'll bring in a few extra families from here (including ourselves) and that means that every property in Claire Vista will have new owners. If the Te Karere news crew comes over there again,' he wrote, 'make sure to tell them not to give our news to any other language. Hey, Bro, let's just tap the sides of our noses with the little tip of finger. Keep it all nod nod, wink wink, for a while.'

On the fifth of November there was a big welcome-home ceremony, with speeches and food and fireworks at the Claire Vista hall, which had been renamed Te Whare Ngahau o Ngati Kangaru. At the same time Claire Vista was given back its former name of Ikanui and discussions took place regarding the renaming of streets, parks, boulevards, avenues, courts, dells and glens after its reclaimers.

By the time the former occupants began arriving in mid-December, all the signs in the old Claire Vista had been changed and the new families were established in their new homes. It was a lovely, soft and green life at that time of the year. One in which you could stand barefooted on grass or sand in your shorts and shirt and roll your eyes round. You could slide your boat down the ramp, cruise about, toss the anchor over and put your feet up, fish, pull your hat down. Whatever.

On the day that the first of the holidaymakers arrived at 6 Ara Hakena, with their bags of holiday outfits, Christmas presents, CDs, six-packs, cartons of groceries, snorkels, lilos and things, the man and woman and two sub-teenagers were met by Mere and Jim Hakena, their three children, Jim's parents and a quickly gathering crowd of neighbours.

At first, Ruby and Gregory in their cotton co-ordinates, and Alister with his school friend in their stonewash jeans, apricot and applegreen tees, and noses zinked pink and orange, thought they could've come to the wrong house, especially since its address seemed to have changed and the neighbours were different.

But how could it be the wrong house? It was the same windowy place in stained weatherboard, designed to suit its tree environment and its rocky outlook. There was the new skylit extension and glazed brick barbecue. Peach tree with a few green ones. In the drive in front of the underhouse garage they could see the spanking blue boat with *Sea Urchin* in cursive along its prow. The only difference was that the boat was hitched to a green Landcruiser instead of to a red Range Rover.

'That's our boat,' said Ruby.

'I doubt it,' said Mere and Jim together, folding their arms in unison.

'He paid good money for that,' a similarly folded-armed neighbour said. 'It wasn't much but it was good.'

Ruby and Gregory didn't spend too much more time arguing. They went back to Auckland to put the matter in the pink hands of their lawyer.

It was two days later that the next holidaymakers arrived, this time at 13 Tiritiroa. After a long discussion out on the front lawn, Mai and Poto with their Dobermen and a contingent of neighbours felt a little sorry for their visitors in their singlets, baggies and jandals, and invited them in.

'You can still have your holiday, why not?' said Mai. 'There's the little flat at the back and we could let you have the dinghy. It's no trouble.'

The visitors were quick to decline the offer. They went away and came back two hours later with a policeman, who felt the heat but did the best he could, peering at the papers that Mai and Poto had produced, saying little. 'Perhaps you should come along with me and lay a formal complaint,' he suggested to the holidayers. Mai, Poto and a few of the neighbours went fishing after they'd gone.

From then on the holidaymakers kept arriving and everyone had to be alert, moving themselves from one front lawn to the next, sometimes having to break into groups so that their eye-balling skills, their skills in creative comment, could be shared around.

It was Christmas by the time the news of what was happening reached the media. The obscure local paper did a tame, muddled article on it, which was eclipsed firstly by a full page on what the mayor and councillors of the nearby town wanted for Christmas, and then by another, derived from one of the national papers, revealing New Year resolutions of fifty television personalities. After that there was the usual nationwide closedown of everything for over a month, at the end of which time no one wanted to report holiday items any more.

So it wasn't until the new residents began to be sued that there was any news. Even then the story only trickled.

It gathered some impetus, however, when the businesspeople from the nearby town heard what was happening and felt concerned. Here was this new population at Claire Vista, or whatchyou' callit now, who were *permanent residents* and who were *big spenders*, and here were these fly-by-night jerk holidaymakers trying to kick them out.

Well, ever since this new lot had arrived business had boomed. The town was flourishing. The old supermarket, now that there was beginning to be competition, had taken up larger premises, lowered its prices, extended its lines and was providing trollies, music and coffee for customers. The car sale yards had been smartened up and the office décor had become so tasteful that the salespeople had had to clean themselves up and mind their language. McDonald's had bought what was now thought of as a prime business site, where they were planning to build the biggest McDonald's in the Southern Hemisphere. A couple of empty storerooms, as well as every place that could be uncovered to show old brick, had been converted into better-than-average eating places. The town's dowdy motel, not wanting to be outdone by the several new places of accommodation being built along the main road, had become pink and upmarket, and had a new board out front offering television, video, heating swimming pool, spa, waterbeds, room service, restaurant, conference and seminar facilities.

Home appliance retailers were extending their showrooms and increasing their advertising. Home building and real estate was on an upward surge as more businesspeople began to enter town and as those already there began to want bigger, better, more suitable residences. In place of dusty, paintless shops and shoppes, there now appeared a variety of boutiques, studios, consortiums, centres, lands and worlds. When the Clip Joint opened up across the road from Lulu's Hairdressers, Lulu had her place done out in green and white and it became Upper Kut. After that hair salons grew all over town, having names such as Head Office, Headlands, Beyond the Fringe, Hairport, Hairwaves, Hedlines, Siz's, Curl Up and Dye.

So the town was growing in size, wealth and reputation. Booming. Many of the new businesspeople were from the new Ikanui, the place of abundant fish. These newcomers had brought their upmarket Aussie ideas to eating establishments, accommodation, shops, cinema, pre-loved cars, newspaper publishing, transport, imports, exports, distribution. Good on them. The businesspeople drew up a petition supporting the new residents and their fine activities, and this petition was eventually signed by everyone within a twenty-kilometre radius. This had media impact.

But that wasn't all that was going on.

Billy had found other areas suitable for purchase and settlement, and Rena had done her research into the history of these areas so that they knew which of the Ngati Kangaru had ancestral ties to those places. There were six areas in the North Island and six in the South. 'Think of what it does to the voting power,' said Hiko, who was on the rise in local politics. Easy street, since all he needed was numbers.

Makere, who had lost her reluctance and became whole-hearted, had taken Hiko's place in the company as liaison manager. This meant that she became the runner between Ozland and Aotearoa, conducting rallies, recruiting families, co-ordinating departures and arrivals. She enjoyed the work.

One day when Makere was filling in time in downtown Auckland before going to the airport, she noticed how much of the central city had closed up, gone to sleep.

'What it needs is people,' she said to the rest of the family when she arrived home.

They were lounging, steaming themselves, showering, hairdressing, plucking eyebrows, in their enormous bathroom. She let herself down into the jacuzzi.

'Five hundred families to liven up the central city again. Signatures on papers, and then we turn those unwanted, wasteland wilderness of warehouses and office spaces into town houses, penthouses and apartments.' She lay back and closed her eyes. She could see the crowds once again seething in Queen Street renamed Ara Makere, buying, selling, eating, drinking, talking, laughing, yelling, singing, going to shows. But not only in Queen Street. Not only in Auckland. Oh, it truly was high and holy work. This Kamupene o Te Hokinga Mai was 'a great and unwonted blessing'. Mind-blowing. She sat up.

'And businesses. So we'll have to line up all our architects, designers, builders, plumbers, electricians, consultants, programmers,' she said.

'"Soap boilers, tinkers and a maker of dolls' eyes,"' said Billy.

'The ones already here as well as the ones still in Oz,' Makere said. 'Set them to work and use some of this damn money getting those places done up. Open up a whole lot of shops, restaurants, agencies . . .' She lay back again with her feet elevated. They swam in the spinning water like macabre fish.

'It's brilliant, Ma,' Billy said, stripping off and walking across the floor with his toes turned up and his insteps arched — in fact, allowing only part of each heel and the ball joints of his big toes to touch the cold tile floor. With the stress of getting across the room on no more than heel and bone, his jaw, shoulders, elbows and knees became locked and he had a clench in each hand as well as in the bulge of his stomach.

'Those plumbers that you're talking about can come and run a few hot pipes under the floor here. Whoever built this place should've thought of that. But of course they were all summer people, so how would they know?' He lowered himself into the water, unlocking and letting out a slow, growling breath.

'We'll need different bits of paper for downtown business properties,' said Tu from the steam bench.

'Central Auckland was originally Ngati Whatua I suppose,' said Rena, who lost concentration on what she was doing for a moment and plucked out a complete eyebrow. 'I'll check it through then arrange a hui with them.'

'Think of it, we can influx any time of the year,' said Billy. 'We can work on getting people into the city in our off-season. January . . . And it's not only Auckland, it's every city.'

'And as well as the business places there are so many houses in the cities empty at that time of the year too,' said Makere, narrowing her eyes while Billy's eyes widened. 'So we can look at those leaving to go on holiday as well as those leaving holiday places after the season is over. We can keep on influxing from Oz of course, but there are plenty of locals without good housing. We can round them all up — the solos, the UBs, pensioners, low-income earners, street kids, derros.'

'Different papers again for suburban homes,' said Tu.

'Candidates and more candidates, votes and more votes,' said Hiko, who had come from next door wearing a towel and carrying a briefcase. 'And why stop at Oz? We've got Maori communities in Utah, in London, all over the place.'

'When do we go out snooping, Dad?' asked Hana and Gavin, who had been blow-waving each other's hair.

'Fact finding, fact finding,' said Billy. 'We might need three or four teams, I'll round up a few for training.'

'I need a video camera,' said Hana.

'Video for Hana,' said Billy.

'Motorbike,' said Gavin.

'Motorbike,' said Billy.

'Motorbike,' said Hana.

200

'Two motorbikes,' said Billy.

'Bigger offices, more staff,' said Tu and Rena.

'See to it,' said Billy.

'Settlements within the cities,' said Makere, who was still with solos, UB, check-out operators and such. 'Around churches. Churches, sitting there idle — wastelands, wildernesses of churches.'

'And "really of no value",' said Billy. 'Until they become . . .'

'Meeting houses,' Makere said. 'Wharenui.'

'Great. Redo the fronts, change the décor and we have all these new wharenui, one every block or so. Take over surrounding properties for kohanga, kura kaupapa, kaumatua housing, health and rehab centres, radio stations, TV channels . . .'

'Deeds of sale for church properties,' said Tu.

'More party candidates as well,' Hiko said. 'We'll need everything in place before the new coalition government comes in . . .'

'And by then we'll have "friends in high places".'

'Have our person at the top, our little surprise . . .'

'Who will be advised that it is better to reach a final and satisfactory conclusion than . . .'

' ". . . to reopen questions of strict right, or carry on an unprofitable controversy".'

'Then there's golf clubs,' said Makere.

'I'll find out how many people per week, per acre use golf courses,' said Rena. 'We'll find wasteland and wilderness there for sure.'

'And find out how the land was acquired and how it can be reacquired,' said Billy.

'Remember all the land given for schools? A lot of those schools have closed now.'

'Land given for the war effort and not returned.'

'Find out who gave what and how it will be returned.'

'Railways.'

'Find out how much is owed to us from sale of railways.'

'Cemeteries.'

'Find out what we've saved the taxpayer by providing and maintaining our own cemeteries, burying our own dead. Make up claims.'

'And there are some going concerns that need new ownership too, or rather where old ownership needs re-establishing . . .'

'Sport and recreation parks . . .'

'Lake and river retreats . . .'

'Mountain resorts . . .'

Billy hoisted himself. 'Twenty or thirty teams and no time to waste.' He splatted across the tiles. 'Because "if from *delay* you allow others to do it before you — they will succeed and you will fail",' and he let out a rattle and a shuffle of a laugh that sounded like someone sweeping up smashings of glass with a noisy broom.

'Get moving,' he said.

Needels and Glass

—

Fiona Kidman

GAIN she watched the women walk across the grass towards the man. They smiled and some of them laughed aloud. There were so many of them. The man's eyes were dark and watchful, his cheekbones jutted above his beard. Then Helena's father hurried her away so that she could not watch them any more. Only, that night, the wind carried the voices of the women to her. They spoke a language she did not understand.

Around her now was the night, and in the bed before her was the dying woman. Helena felt the dark around them and the wind pressed against the window pane. There were pockets of silence in the hospital and yet they were not silences if you listened with all your senses. Sounds leaned in. The sluicing room where the bedpans were cleaned was down the corridor. Spasmodic jets of water hissed on the enamel. Pans clattered together as they were picked up. Helena got up from the bedside and walked down the corridor, her feet gliding on the brown linoleum.

'Nurse Moore.'

The young woman carrying the pans stopped and did not turn.

'Yes, Sister?'

'Look at me when I speak to you.'

The young woman turned to face her. 'I'm sorry, Sister,' she said, before Helena had spoken again. 'Mrs Carrington's flooding.'

Her hands shook slightly as she clasped the pans. A wedding ring glinted on the left hand. Her face was fair and pretty, but tired, her hair greasier than it should have been and straggling from under her cap.

'More quietly, how many times must I tell you . . . Well go then, if you're needed.'

Nurse Moore began her journey down the corridor again. 'And see me in the morning before you go off duty,' said Helena.

The nurse cast a quick agonised glance over her shoulder, her eyes beseeching, and walked on.

And why did I do that, Helena wondered. Who's to gain, when an exhausted woman waits back for a reprimand which I have not even composed, while her children wait for their breakfast and their father is about to leave in search of work again?

Ah, the unemployed. Like beggars at the door. They had fed ten of them that night and God knows where they were sleeping now. At least Moore and his wife had a roof over their heads, and some thanks to her for that too, keeping Moore on, for she was a nurse of only average capability. No, standards must not slip, she had no reason to reproach herself.

Back at her vigil, she thought to lean her face against the window, but stopped herself. She expected better discipline than that from her staff. Was she not Helena McDonald McGlone, with a standard to set? We are the best, her father had told her, we are from a proud line, we own castles, we are lairds among our own, we must not forget it here.

The hospital was on a high hill and the sea was below. There were no stars and she thought she heard a storm rising out beyond the harbour reef. A light jerked far below her and it seemed to be on the water. The ships, like the poor, were restless. How the hungry wandered, not just now, but always. They would stop at the farmhouse door, and the servants would give pitchers of water to the swaggers, and sometimes her mother would come out to buy soap, or pins, or some herbal remedy from the passers-by. Why did she buy things she would never use, Helena would ask her, and her mother, delicate as the silk roses she sewed on her cushions, would sigh and say that they must help the poor. Won't we be poor too, if we help too many of them, Helena had asked

then, but her mother had shaken her head at such cosmic incompre-
hensibility, and told her that they must do what they could to relieve the
sufferings of others.

Which was more or less why she was here, Helena supposed. Only
lately the poor seemed to have increased. It occurred to her that Nurse
Moore was pregnant. She couldn't understand how she had failed to
notice this before, or why she had happened to notice on this particular
evening, for that matter.

Something to do with the way she had straightened her back and
turned carefully when Helena had spoken, perhaps. Helena sighed,
thinking about it. There would be nothing else for it. It was so difficult,
the way things were going, and the riots and the looting in the towns.
She hoped Moore's husband would keep his head. Oh but if the fool had
kept other things under control.

She wrapped her arms around her. It had become colder in the room.

And the dark women moved over the grass again and the land was
covered with light. The sun beat fiercely and the beads they wore
twinkled and shone. The man was impassive as they came to him, but
his eyes seemed to single out one of them.

Which one had it been, which one?

Some of them sang that night in the woolshed where her father let
them stay, before their journey north began again next day. The man
helped her father to dig a ditch in return for their food and shelter. It was
hard work in heavy clay and it had tired her father a great deal. Was the
man tired too, and did he, that night, lie down to rest as her father had
done, quietly, and in a separate room from her mother, who lay in the
double bed with her fine hair spread upon the lace-edged pillowslip? She
knew that he did not. There were no separate rooms in the woolshed,
only bare boards and the deep and greasy smell of sheep fleece.

Which one? Why did the others sing?

The crumpled body in the bed before her now was stirring. Helena
reached to pull up the covers, thinking that the cold must have woken
her patient. But by the light from the corridor, Helena could see that the
eyes were wide and unnaturally bright. She switched on a night-light.
There was a syringe of morphine on the table beside the bed. The table

was lustrous and bare except for the small tray holding the syringe. Helena expected she would have to use it before the dawn. It was only two o'clock now, and it was too soon.

But when the pain came, it bit hard and with only the briefest warning, and though the woman would fight against it, once it began she would scream, and the hospital ring with the sound of agony.

'Is the pain coming, Mrs Hardcastle?'

'I'm not sure.'

'Tell me if you need an injection.'

'You'd let me have it?'

'If you need it.'

'If I need it?' For a moment the voice was waspish. 'Since when did I decide when I needed it?'

When Helena didn't answer, she said, 'Then it's as I thought.'

'What did you think?' said Helena.

'Oh, you know, that it'll happen soon.' Her fingers plucked the sheet. 'I'll be glad, you know.'

'I expect so.'

'You expect so, eh? That's a strange thing to say. As if you'd like me to. Well, why not, I can't say I blame you, you've put up with me long enough.'

'No, it's not that. I expect you're tired of this, that's all.'

'Yes, that's true, I'm tired all right.'

Mrs Hardcastle was silent awhile, frowning to herself. Far away, in another part of the hospital someone began to shriek. Both women cocked their heads.

'Shouldn't you be there?' the patient asked.

'The doctor's with her.'

'Such a fuss some of them make. Oh I'm not one to talk, I suppose you'd say, look at all the noise I've made. But babies, that's a different matter . . . no dignity some of them.'

'No two are the same.'

'You'd know I suppose.'

Helena caught sight of her reflection in the glass, illuminated by the night-light, and it occurred to her that she knew nothing at all. Her face was pale but then that was always so, her eyes nearly as black as her hair: a McGlone, her father had said, with approval. Yet in this strange night her image on the glass might have belonged to anyone, even one of the women who walked across the grass.

Outside the wind was dropping and a prickle of stars emerged from behind the clouds. If the night could have penetrated the room it would be full of frost now, and not a storm at all. By this new light a shadow moved. It would be the beggars, searching for food. Helena remembered her mother's dying and the moustache which grew on her finely moulded upper lip before the end, where food and saliva would gather, and it had become so hard to kiss her once-beautiful face.

'Will I get someone for you?' Helena asked.

'Is it as close as that, d'you think?'

Helena took the woman's pulse, so that it was some time before she answered. 'It's difficult to tell,' she said at last. 'Have you still no pain?'

'No,' said her patient. 'It seems to be taking a rest.' She touched the spread covering her distended stomach, speaking of the tumour as if it were a live creature, apart from her.

'You can have the morphine if you want.'

'Thank you. But let's wait and see what it thinks.' She touched the coverlet again.

'And you don't want anyone?'

Mrs Hardcastle was not very old, or certainly not old enough for it to be said that her time had come. Helena had forgotten exactly how old, although she had seen it on the records, but she knew she was closer to sixty than seventy. Her hands were thick and even after months in hospital there was still a roughness about them from scrubbing with cold water, and helping out on the farm when her son's wife was in having babies. She and the man she called Dad, or Jack, depending on how she was feeling about him after a visit, still took their turn on the farm. Helena supposed that in a sense she must still have a role to play there, to help out like that while the next generation were being born and raised. There was a useful place in the world that she would leave empty with her death. Helena wondered if that could be possible in her own life. It seemed unlikely. There would be other nursing sisters to run small country hospitals, the world was full of unmarried women who did their work well.

'He's got to do the milking this morning, it wouldn't be fair,' said the patient, coming to a decision.

'But . . .' Helena checked herself, it felt like giving special leave to one of the staff to attend a wedding or a ball.

Mrs Hardcastle was almost apologetic. 'Young Rob had to go to town overnight, see. The separator broke down. You can't be without the separator.'

'No, of course not.'

'It'll be all right. You'll stay, won't you?'

'Oh yes.'

'Besides, it mightn't be till after the milking.'

'Shall I put the light off?'

'It doesn't make much difference. No, leave it on.'

For a long time then, they sat in silence. Mrs Hardcastle appeared to doze and didn't move when Nurse Moore came to tell Helena that Mrs Carrington had given birth to a daughter and was safe. The doctor put his head in the door a little later, and took Mrs Hardcastle's pulse and temperature, and still she drowsed on without seeming to notice. Out in the corridor Helena told him what had taken place, and he said the patient might last until the morning or longer, who knew, she was closer to death than either of them and might know more about it. He said he would sleep at the hospital if Helena wished, but he was white with exhaustion, and besides she had the needle on the shining table, and she sent him away. Somewhere out on the rim of the world the light would be weaving its way towards them, but still it was not dawn. Now Helena knew that there was indeed a frost outside, and she thought how hard it would be for Jack Hardcastle as he faced the milking alone in another hour or so. Now that the wind had dropped she knew it could not be the trees that moved outside but surely there were not so many of the poor out there roaming the night either. There were too many shapes. She rubbed her eyes. The women were moving again, only this time they were moving towards her. Their hands were empty but there seemed to be something bounteous about them, as if they carried fruit and flowering branches. One of them held her hands in front of her as if she was holding melons but then Helena saw that it was her breasts she was holding high.

'What time is it?' asked Mrs Hardcastle.

Helena jumped, trembled. 'Nearly five o'clock,' she said.

The palest sliver of light was slitting the sky.

'Could I have half the needle now?' said Mrs Hardcastle. Her breath was panting quietly.

'You can have it all.'

'No . . . I want to be awake when it comes . . . aah, yes, yes. Thank you, Sister, you're a good girl, yes.'

'Lie back now; it's all right, I'm here with you.'

But Mrs Hardcastle's hand had floundered towards the table where Helena had replaced the now half-empty syringe.

'What is it?' Helena asked.

'My spectacles. Will you put them on me, please?'

'Why yes, if you want.'

She hooked the steel frames around Mrs Hardcastle's ears and propped the bridge as comfortably as she could on her thin nose.

'What do you see?' she asked, for Mrs Hardcastle was peering around her in a distracted way.

'I don't know. Everything and nothing. You can see so much and still do nothing about it, can't you?'

'I suppose so. Yes, I'm sure you're right.'

'I've seen a lot of things in my time. Too late to tell you now. Should have. Would you have been interested? Would you have listened?'

'Of course.'

'Ah, would you though? Tell me, Sister, what have you seen?'

'Oh . . . I don't know. Not much. The things that have happened in hospitals, sick people, things like that you know.'

'Oh that, yes I can see that. But I mean, what have you seen? Really seen?'

Helena walked to the window again and thought, I should not be having this conversation, I am a nurse, it is not for me to tell people about myself, my private self. And yet, what did it matter, in a few hours this would all be over, there was nothing to lose. Her face closer to the glass, the reflection full of fine lines. No girl this, a woman growing older; soon she would be middle-aged, and then before you could turn around, an old woman like the one in the bed beside her, if she made it that far. She reached back into her memory for something she might have seen that this woman had not. The McGlones and the McDonalds, perhaps, but they were only her parents and, if it came to that, maybe not quite so different as they would have had her believe.

'I saw the women,' she heard herself say.

'The women, what women?' mumbled the figure on the bed.

'Rua's women, I saw Rua Kenana.'

'Rua, the one they called the prophet? He was a bit of a madman, wasn't he?'

'Oh, who knows. They called him a mystic man too, a messiah. You do know who I mean?'

'Oh yes.'

'He'd travel the land with his band of many wives, looking for work on the farms. Well, he stayed a night at my father's farm and his wives were with him. He worked alongside my father, and at night they slept in the woolshed. All together, you understand?'

'Yes, I understand,' said Mrs Hardcastle.

'They wore beautiful hats and finery. Later, I heard that he built them a house with many rooms . . . for all the wives . . . and the children . . . Afterwards, they captured Rua, took him away. You can understand that he would make people angry, I suppose. So many wives.'

Mrs Hardcastle's breath came out in a long sigh from the bed. Helena glanced at her, suddenly afraid that her companion would leave her too soon, before they were done.

But, 'What were the wives really like?' Mrs Hardcastle asked.

'I can't tell you. I wasn't allowed to go near them. Or not near enough to be sure of anything,' Helena said.

'You must have seen something.'

'Well, I don't know for sure . . . but I think they were happy.'

Helena saw that the sky was now full of delicate pale light. Mrs Hardcastle mumbled something she could not understand.

'What did you say?' Helena gasped, bending close to her, for now it was imperative to know what the other woman thought about all of this. She had never told anyone before, never shared such confidences. Mrs Hardcastle mumbled again. Helena leaned nearer.

'I expect Jack'll come after the milking.' The words were deathly quiet.

The new day took over and possessed the room, and Helena began the last work on her shift, methodical, tidying up as she went. When she had done all there was to do, and spoken to everyone, and given comfort to the bereaved, then remembered to give Nurse Moore a month's notice, she let herself into her room in the adjacent nurses' home. She turned the key in her lock and sank down on the narrow bed, easing off her shoes as she did so. She was thoughtful as she pulled out the trunk beneath the bed and opened it. Inside the trunk, among her summer clothes stored away for the next season, there lay an assortment of items. They included several syringes and twenty or thirty pairs of spectacles. From her pocket she took the pair of spectacles which Mrs Hardcastle had worn, folded now in a narrow red case, and the half-empty syringe. For a moment she thought of throwing the syringe away, for what use was half a needleful to anyone? But there was so much waste around, and one never knew when any of it might come in handy. She tossed the spectacle case and the syringe in with the others, and when she had closed the trunk, lay down at last, to sleep.

The Affectionate
Kidnappers
—
Witi Ihimaera

T HE two kuia began to weep when their rangatira came in. They wept not because they were frightened but because they were ashamed that their big chief should see them like this, in the whareherehere. For a long time they sat there, not looking at him, faces downcast, grieving with one another, and the tears were like wet stones splashing in the dust at their feet.

— Hei aha, the chief said after a while. Then he turned to the sergeant standing behind him and said, Can I speak to my women alone, boss?

The sergeant knew that Hasbrick, the Maori guide, was a good and trustworthy fellow, but the law was the law and the two women might still be capable of some treachery — still waters ran deep among the Maoris. Nevertheless, while putting on a stern appearance, for at Police School he was always told that 'appearances must be maintained,' he responded:

— Well, just this once, Hasbrick. But no funny business, mind.

As he left he closed the door to the cell and with an obvious gesture, all the more melodramatic because it was so ludicrously lofty, turned the key in the lock.

The rangatira sighed as he sat down beside the two women.

212

— You two are old enough to have more sense, he said.

At that rebuke the kuia redoubled their tangi, turned away and tried to press themselves into the corner.

— Well, the chief said insistently, it's your own fault, ne?

The kuia were silent, their lips quivering.

— Kati, the chief relented. Enough. You two are just like the two birds making your roimata toroa on the ground.

The women smiled at their chief's remarks. He proffered a handkerchief but, shaking their heads, the women used their own scarves to dab at their eyes. Then, hesitantly, they reached out for their chief to hold his hand tightly.

— Kei te pai, he said.

— You should leave us in the jailhouse, they answered. You should tell them to shut us away forever.

— Kei te pai, Kuini, the chief soothed the kuia in the red dress. Kei te pai, Puti, he said to the old lady in the yellow and green. I know you two didn't mean to do wrong.

— She was such a pretty little blonde girl, Kuini said. She was swinging on a gate, all by herself, you know, down there by the hotera. As soon as I saw her I knew she was the Buttons' little girl. You know, they come every summer and me and Puti, we did some work for Mrs Button last summer, cleaning and that. Ay, Puti?

— Ae, Puti agreed. Kua mahi maua mo te wahine Pakeha. A strict lady that lady.

— Oh, and Pearl had grown, Kuini said. The year before she only came up to here and this year . . .

Kuini's eyes softened with tenderness.

— And her teeth were so white. But it made us sad to see her all alone. A tamariki all alone — no good. Especially near a hotel with all those boozers around. So I said to her, 'You want to come with us, Pearl Button? Haere mai koe ki te marae?' And she nodded. And I saw Mrs Button in the window . . .

— Ae. We waved and waved at her, Puti said.

— And when she saw us she waved back, Kuini continued. So we made signs that we would take Pearl with us for our mate. We pointed

213

to the marae. And Mrs Button waved her apron at us as if to say, 'Go right ahead!' So we did.

— We told the pirihimana this, Puti said. We told him loud but he didn't want to hear us, I reckon. What did we do wrong?

Her face screwed up as if she had tasted a lemon and she started to quiver. The tears started again, as if she was a bottle of aerated water that had been shaken too hard.

The rangatira kept a calm face. This was a no-good business this.

— Didn't you stop to think that this was a Pakeha little girl? he asked gently. A white girl?

Kuini was offended. Her eyes opened wide.

— Kaore, she said. This was a tamariki. Pearl.

Hasbrick's eyes flickered, betraying his incredulity. Not only was this a white girl but this was also a pretty-as-a-picture blonde girl. Pakehas didn't like their girls being messed around by Maoris. The idea of a pretty curly-haired white girl being taken away by Maoris brought all sorts of pictures to their minds — of sacrifices to idols, cannibalism, white girls being captured and scalped by Red Indians. He knew because these were the sorts of questions tourists asked him: Do you worship these wooden gods? Are there still headhunters in New Zealand? Do you have tomahawks? No wonder the pirihimana had raised such a big posse.

— This was Pearl, Kuini said again, emphatically. What's the fuss? Maori tamariki wouldn't have such a fuss made for them.

At this, Puti smiled.

— Maybe because a Maori mother would be glad to get rid of her kids for the day, she joked.

— So we took Pearl down to the marae, Kuini continued, and she was as happy as anything. Everybody was helping to get kai ready for our hui today. Lots of people. They all made a fuss of Pearl. Old Joe, he said to me, 'You're too ugly to be this kid's mother!' Then he made a pukana at her and gave her a peach to eat. 'Kei te matekai koe?' he asked her. And, boy, she was hungry all right. She started to hoe in and the juice ran down her front. It made us feel very happy, ay, Puti, to see that kid eat so much. Too skinny, the Pakeha children. But, she sighed, that's the Pakeha way.

— Didn't it ever pass through your minds, Hasbrick asked, how her mother would feel about her daughter eating the Maori kai?

Kuini looked startled.

— What's wrong with the Maori kai?

And Hasbrick knew they wouldn't understand the violence of the reaction of Pearl's mother. *Oh, Pearl, did you eat something from the floor? John, darling, did you hear what the Maoris did? They forced food on her. There's no telling what sort of diseases she got down there. All those dogs they have. And no hygiene. The place should be burned down. Harbouring diseases and diseased people. Oh, darling, she drank some water too. Some filthy Maori water. Oh. Oh.*

— Then all of a sudden, Puti said, the koroua, Rangiora, came in, cracking his whip. 'Haere mai koutou ki te ruku moana,' he shouted. 'Kia tere, kia tere.' And before we knew it, Old Joe had snatched Pearl up and put her in his green cart. He said, 'You can drive the trap, tamariki,' and Pearl just loved it. Kuini put her on her lap, and Old Joe gave Pearl the reins, and we were off. You should have seen those ponies of Joe's. They knew they had a little Pakeha on board. The red pony trotted along with a high proud step and the black pony tossed its mane as if to say, 'Anei! Titiro koutou ki ahau!' And Pearl also played with Auntie's pounamu. She was very happy, and that made us happy.

Puti fingered her kete nervously.

— I suppose that is where the wrong lies, she said in a small voice. Making her happy. And we shouldn't have taken her to the sea.

— What's done is done, the rangatira said. But in his ears he could still hear the burning words of Pearl's mother. *How dare they. How dare they take her to the sea. She could have drowned. Haven't they got any sense? Not only that, but they were all naked down there. And they unbuttoned Pearl's drawers. My little daughter, defenceless, in the midst of savages. It is too horrible for me to contemplate. Touching her rosy skin with their dirty hands.*

— She'd never seen the sea before, Kuini said. Fancy a kid never seeing the sea! She was frightened at first. But we showed her that it wouldn't hurt her — not the kingdom of Tangaroa. We took her over to Maggie's place first and then across the paddock to the beach. There we started digging for the toheroa. And soon Pearl started to dig too. Ka nui tana mahi! Oh it was such fun to have a Pakeha tamariki. A Pakeha moko. And *then*, when she felt how warm and tickly the sea was, she started to scream with delight. 'Oo, oo! Lovely! Lovely!' She was so excited that she threw herself into my arms, kicking and screaming. Oh, the joy of it! Feeling that little body having such fun!

But that's not what the policemen saw, Hasbrick thought. He conjured up the event in his mind — a little naked girl, kicking and screaming, beating her fists against two black women, a Pakeha blonde girl, looking for all the world as if she was going to be drowned by two black women . . .

The sergeant reappeared, rattling his keys in the lock. The two women shrank into the shadows. Their eyes were like glowing paua. Then Kuini said, with dignity, to her rangatira:

— E koro, kei te pirangi maua ko Puti ki a hoki atu maua kia maua whare. Puti and I wish to return to our homes.

The rangatira felt anguish in his heart.

— Kei te pirangi maua ko Puti ki a maua wharemoe, Kuini said. We also wish to sleep in our own beds. Not here, in this place of shame.

Her voice trembled with the words.

— Aue, kui, Hasbrick answered. And the two women realised by the tone of his voice that they would be lost — gone into the darkness, gone into the stomach of the Pakeha, gone into the realm of the night, eaten up by the white man.

— You are facing a serious charge, Hasbrick continued. The Pakeha think you kidnapped the little girl.

Puti cried out, and Kuini began to grieve, not because of the charge but because she had never slept anywhere else but in her own bed in her own house. And here, for the first time, she would have to lie down on a foreign mattress in a strange room which was noa and could not give her any protection. At that moment, something died inside her, something that had given her strength all her life. She felt it ebbing away, slipping away, leaving her a mere husk. Dimly, she heard Puti say:

— But Mrs Button knows. She knows us.

And she heard her chief reply:

— No, Mrs Button doesn't remember either of you.

And it came to Kuini, with blinding clarity, that Mrs Button was to be felt sorry for — it was not Mrs Button's fault that she couldn't tell one Maori apart from another. And Kuini reached for Puti's hands and face and pressed her face against Puti's saying:

— Never mind, kui. You and I will be mates for each other, just like the two birds.

— I will be back in the morning, the rangatira said. But you will not be alone. Some of the people have already gathered outside and will stay there to keep you company through the night.

And sure enough, as he was speaking, the two women heard soft singing drifting through the window.

— After all, you two are our kuia.

Then the rangatira was gone. The two women sat in a gathering dark.

Puti thought, *I will never forget. All those little men in blue coats. Little blue men. With their whistles. Running, running towards us. With their police batons raised. It was . . .*

Suddenly, Puti felt Kuini nudging her and pointing down to the floor. Kuini's voice was still and drained of life.

— Anei, she whispered.

Although the light was waning, the pattern in the dust could still be seen.

— Anei, te roimata toroa.

The soft sounds of waiata swelled in the darkness like currents of the wind holding up Kuini's words.

— E noho ra, Pearl Button, Kuini said, taku moko Pakeha.

The syllables drifted like two birds beating heavily eastward into the night. Then the light went, everything went, life went.

He Tauware Kawa, He Kawa Tauware

Keri Hulme

HERE was no-one outside waiting for us.

So we stood in the dark and waited.

A child came to the half-open door and banged it shut. Open. Shut.

Waina whispers, 'They must be getting ready inside.'

I shrug. I feel excited and tense and the shrug takes an effort. I say, 'We've got a minute I think. Let's have a quick practice. Voices low.'

I struggle with the guitar strap. My fingers are numb. It's June in St Mungo's and there's frost on the ground.

Even singing quietly our voices sound clear and resonant and much sweeter than in the old hall at home. Does the dark make them sound sweet, the resonance come from the empty spaces of the night?

The child peeks out again, but shuts the door quickly.

Old Mrs Parker tugs my sleeve, 'Morrie, what about the dark? D'ye think they might have a thing about the dark?'

Me, in my best lecturing manner: In the old days it was dangerous. You didn't know whether the other people were going to welcome or murder you, and they didn't know whether you were paying a friendly visit or coming club in hand. You time it so you get there in daylight, or go hide somewhere until morning. They were polite interest, shuffling feet, smoking, looking at each other and round the old hall.

'Na I don't think so,' I say to the old lady. 'This is an urban set-up, for everyone no one people in particular. Anyway they know we had to start late.'

'And travel three hundred miles.'

James is stamping his feet, swinging his arms hard against himself, muttering 'jeez 'kin cold, 'kin cold.'

'Just as well I didn't make you fellas get into maro and piupiu,' I joke.

'Yeah, some things'd be getting pretty crisp by now.'

I didn't like James before the group started. Greasy-haired Pakeha, forestry worker, big bike, drinker, trouble. Give him his due, he's come along every practice night full of noisy energy. He puts his heart into the haka, tolerates the singing, keeps his swearing to a minimum, and has grown a surprising affection for Mrs Parker. He leans over and whispers in her ear now, and the old girl giggles and switches her hips. Give her another moment like that and she'll break into a hula from her girlhood.

No-one comes out yet.

'They're taking their time,' grumbles Allison. Her spotty face looks sour in the electric light.

'Probably as nervous as we are. They're a new place, wouldn't have done this often.'

I hope she won't get on her high horse. It was her greatgreatgreat grandmother that was the Maori princess I think. Might have been the greatgreatgreatgreat. Can't remember though I vividly recall the thirty-foot scroll of whakapapa she brought along to prove it. All of us down on the floor following through the branching lines of dead people to Allison, a twig on the bottom line. She's proud of that whakapapa. As she's one of the blue-eyed white-blond kind of Maori, she probably feels she needs it, nei?

I shiver. My teeth are knocking. I try a quick chilled chord.

The child has the door open again.

'Hey boy, cm're.'

He does. He's got bare feet. He scuttles over the icy gravel like it's shagpile though.

'Are they nearly ready inside?'

He looks blank.

I look blank back at him. Then I think, They don't know we're here. The cars can't have made much noise, pulling up on a busy street. Maybe they didn't have anyone watching out for the arriving parties.

'Go tell someone we're here — look, you know Bessie Rongomai? The big lady with one eye? Yes? Tell her Ohaupai's arrived.'

He scampers inside. The door bangs shut again. Could hate that door.

> On the second night, we made up our song. Ohaupai? asks James, I thought we were Bismarck Break. Not for this, I'm firm about that. In a Maori world you do things in the Maori way, and there's nothing more Maori than the marae. What do we need a song for anyway? he's genuinely puzzled, I thought it was all hakas and that. It's for after the speaking, the oratory, I say. The old people call it the kinaki, the relish for the food of speech. O, they all say, O.

'Everyone feel OK?'

Nods and shudders. Waina and Allison and Mrs Parker and Connie are the lucky ones. They've got their fancy cardigans on, natural wool with kowhaiwhai patterns across the chest. They come from our part of the world, I said, good as a piupiu for those people over the hill eh? We better wear bush-shirts then, says Steve, grinning like a fiend. You can always scrawl some of those fancy spiral things on them. Steve, the quiet Pakeha with the Maori sense of humour. He's shaking now in the thin red shirt I thought would make a good background for the women.

> Connie had asked, Do we have to all wear the same? It looks good and shows respect, I said. We're a visiting party, part of the cere-mony, the show if you like. She was worried. I've got this nice brown cardie, she said. We all knew she meant Tommo wouldn't give her any money for a new cardigan. Bastard, I'd thought. He's

the one who should be leading this, not me. Big man's son from Gisborne, brought up by his grannies in the old way, Pomare Cup winner when he was at school, speaking the lingo like a native as my Dad used to say (because he was a native and couldn't) — bloody Tommo. The group must have felt my tangled angry thoughts. Steve spoke to Tommo at the pub and got, 'I'm not having anything to do with your stupid mongrel group. Waste of time playing round with things you don't know about.' Then the offer of a fight. The women, however, got together and bought Connie her cardigan and black slacks, and somehow leaned on Tommo so he didn't interfere with her taking part. Five weeks, I'd thought then, just five weeks and already the aroha grows.

God, I wish I could warm my hands. Our breaths come in quick clouds. In the heartless electric light, we look as though we're steaming. Waina is trembling beside me. Is it just the cold? Or is she thinking her impetuous husband has got himself up the creek again? Don't worry about it all, I love you as you are, she'd said coming over. Reassuring Waina. But I do worry. For one thing, it's my first sole-charge job. Big deal eh. Bismarck Break: two hundred people spread over about two hundred square miles. One sawmill, one pub, one hall, and one sole-charge school. A dozen farms and half a league team and now ta-daaa! one cultural group. For the first time ever in Bismarck Break. That bigheaded new teacher's idea.

The door opens. Half a dozen kids straggle out.

'Quick, into line! I'll just go "toru wha — hope!" when we're ready, one chord OK?'

A big woman pushes through the kids, stands on the single concrete step.

'Hey you fellas, Bismarck Break, kia ora you fellas! It's just me and my black self to be your welcome. Haere mai, haere mai, haere mai!'

Waina shivers. Her voice rises in a beautiful quaver, controlled keening, as she karangas in return. But properly.

'Tena koutou, tena koutou' I can feel her wince, 'tena koutou e nga iwi o tenei marae, tena koutou katoa e . . . ee . . .'

Her voice trails away into the night.

'Ka pai, you did that nice,' says Bessie. She fidgets by the door.

Hey Dad, give us a hand. You must be able to remember something. I'm going to be the main speaker, and I'll have to teach Steve and James something in case they put up two or three.

He'd made a special trip coming up from the North, and we'd welcomed him with our song. Big hit, the old man. Showed us the right gestures, how to pace and turn — o, he remembered a lot more than he'd told me he'd remembered. Or he'd been taking a lot of lessons since.

You'll be all right, he'd said seriously, nodding to each of us. You all do your best and the old people will do the rest. You'll have them on your shoulders when you go on, all of you remember that! Be proud, you are carrying your dead onto a strange place as well as yourselves. It is a time to be strong and very careful, but also a time to be very proud. Kia kaha, kia manawanui, kia u!

The gravel glints. The light blurs. I am furious to the point of tears.

They can't do this to us!

I thought of Waina, practising her karanga for hours out in the back paddock where she thought no-one could hear; I thought of James, giving up his lucrative Saturday night shift at the mill; Steve travelling thirty miles into town each practice night; Mrs Parker with her arthritis, stiff and hurt after a five-hour journey by car, but the old lady is here with us, standing there shivering in the dark.

I yell out, boom out, my voice fierce and rough,

'TORU! WHA! HOPE!'

and chord down hard.

The little group of kids claps uncertainly. I hope I'm strumming properly. My face is hot, my heart is burning, but I can't tell where my fingers are any more.

In our shock, we sound ragged, gestures ragged, we are all ragged beggars in the night.

Ten weeks in the old hall. Ten weeks of learning, not just the things I tried to teach, but learning each other, helping each other, being fired by an idea that said

In this Maori context you will be important and welcomed and accorded respect because anciently this is the way things have been done. You are no longer lonely individuals: you have become part of something great and deep-rooted and vital. Welcome!

'Ka pai,' says Bessie again. She slips into the shadow of the door. 'Come in quick, it's cold out there eh? We got some important people from Maori Affairs, surprised us eh, they're in there talking now but we can slip down the back and have a kaputi, get warm eh?'

And then you will hongi with each person in the welcoming line, manuhiri turning into tangata whenua, and some person will call out Ae! Kua puare te tari o te ora! Haere mai koutou! and we will all walk in together to taste the special foods the local people have readied for us. Neat! said Connie, her thin face glowing, and James and Steve had grinned, and Allison said Ahhh! and Mrs Parker gave Waina a hug and my wife smiled her secret touching smile to me.

Someone shuts the door again. One of the kids, after Bessie.

We can't see each other's tears in the dark. We can only feel them, swelling out of our hearts.

The Basketball Girls

—

Ngahuia Te Awekotuku

TIHI looked at herself in the mirror. Closely, critically. Decided she was ready to go out into the kitchen and show herself off to the family — Koro and the kids, maybe an auntie or two or three, having a cup of tea and warming their feet by the coal range.

Everyone — everything — stopped as she came through the door. Tall, fair, and slim. She let them all inspect her; she was proud of her long shapely legs in the sheer black stocking (two and eleven from Matthias, what a bargain eh), her firm supple knees (she was too quick to fall, and much too vain to graze them on the knotty asphalt court); and her flexibly fine ankles cased in the black canvas boots. Tihi was a Basketball Girl. And she was one of the best.

And oh, how I loved to look at her. Saturday afternoons that winter, off I'd rush next door, straight after breakfast, quick as whitebait, into Koro's kitchen to ogle and admire. Staring at Tihi was a treat. And following her from a safe distance was even more of a treat, as long as we didn't 'cramp my style, you kids'.

She'd meet her mates at the Hindu shop. Two of them, Cindy and Pera. And they'd buy soft drinks in slender glass bottles, with long wax pink straws. Green River, they'd say. Matching the colour of our girdles and ties. Green River — for luck.

Meanwhile, we'd all be hanging back — if there was a gang of us — and we'd wait for the bottles, which were dropped more or less in the same place every time. One with a chewed straw (Pera), one with the straw rammed and buckled in the bottle (Cindy), and one still neat and whole (Tihi). Each bottle was worth fourpence. Three made a shilling. Wow, that was a fortune!

Which I never made, for I was too busy watching Tihi. She walked like a princess. Very straight, yet there was a ripple in there too. Maybe like a panther, with her long black legs. Her gym was always pressed and almost sharp at the edges of every one of her six box pleats — three in front, and three at the back, that made twelve edges. Done early every Saturday morning, with the iron hot from the range, and a well-scrubbed, damp, worn-out flour bag with the edges picked out. Every pleat was just right; so that the gym hung from her shoulders like a straight black box, with big sections in it, like panels. Over a snowy white long-sleeved blouse, with a specially stiffened collar. And a carefully knotted emerald green tie. Koro himself taught Tihi how to do the tie up 'tika' — properly; and he was truly pleased with himself that day, folding the green silk fabric in his barky old fingers, chuckling at his attentive mokopuna. Tihi. Te Tihi Teitei o Kahukura. The highest arch of Kahu-kura; Rainbow's End. She was well named. And she showed how well she'd learned to do the tie, by skilfully knotting the girdle as well. The colour of new spring grass, woven into a length of narrow wool, two yards long, cutting the box pleats in half, nipping into her waist, lifting the hem even shorter! This always interested me — the gym no longer looked like a big black box; it pulled out very slightly over Tihi's chest, while still going straight down the back, though all the pleats gathered and crimped, just a little way over the girdle, and fell in a skirt to the middle of her thighs.

Underneath the hem were other things too; they popped and snapped and kept the black stockings up, pulling taut an inky black line that ran from her heel all the way up the back of her leg. Cindy, Pera, and Tihi spent a lot of time worrying about these lines — those damn seams they were called, as the three twirled and danced and twisted, craning their necks over their shoulders, peering down at the back of their knees. Pera had the most trouble; she was the shorter, but somehow much fuller, and though she ironed her gym just like Tihi, it just flared and flounced, swelling out in the front at the top, and jutting like a shelf from the back of her bum. So her hem was sort of even.

Tihi always made sure her damn seams were straight. 'Cos that's a *rule*', Pera would roll the words out, husky and rich, and they'd laugh and laugh. Even Cindy, who seemed a bit sour, she'd laugh in a gravelly, raw-voiced way. Her knees were always grazed, her eyes were always there, on Tihi. They would shine like dark embers from her strong face; though not the prettiest, she was the tallest in their trio. And she starred on the basketball court, shot after shot after shot.

Off down the street they'd stride, arms linked. Tihi in the middle, Pera on the right, Cindy on the left, all in rhythm. The Basketball Girls. Pleased with the world, and with each other. Going to meet their mates. Going to play the game. Going to win.

Saturday after Saturday, I followed them, and I wondered at their pride, and their grace, and their beauty. Even on wet days, when the rain lashed the asphalt like acid, and their boots would slide and slip, their pony tails flop and straggle. Even on days when they got 'cleaned up', usually by a visiting team from a bigger town — because at home, they knew they were the best. They had the trophies to prove it. And Auntie Lily, with her green lapels lined with a brazen glitter of badges, she said so. She was the coach, and a ref, and the selector, and she knew. That was that.

So spring came, and all the skinny willow trees turned the colour of the river, and the season was over. No more basketball till next year. No more following Tihi and her mates down the street on a Saturday afternoon. No more till next year.

And eventually, next year, winter arrived. After a summer of blinding white softball pants and Tihi with a sunburned nose and cracked mouth and peroxide streak in her hair. Which was still in a ponytail, with the same green ribbon.

Winter arrived. And with it came Ahi. In a gleaming two-toned Zephyr Six, with bright red stars that flashed like rubies on the fenders.

The Basketball Girls

Ahi turned up to take Tihi to basketball, every Saturday. Just Tihi, because Pera had moved to the coast to look after her Kuia, and Cindy — well, she had just sort of vanished. Dropped out of sight. Who knew where.

Still young, still nosey, I'd hang around next door while Tihi got ready for the game. She still had that magic for me, even though she didn't meet her two mates any more at the Hindu shop; and with no Green River bottles to fight over, the other kids weren't interested in staying around. Tihi would meet Ahi instead; Ahi, who pulled up in the gateway in that amazing car. Ahi, with thick, jet-black hair cut like Elvis but a little longer at the back, like a fat duckbum. And dark glasses, green green glass in thick plastic frames. Ahi, who never smiled . . . and never got out of the car to go in and meet Koro either. Just waited, quietly, then revved the motor as Tihi gaily pranced out, flipped open the passenger door, kissed Ahi on the cheek, and then with a filmstar wave at her greatest fan (me) was off. Down the road with Ahi, who somehow felt familiar to me. Somehow.

Then it happened. Koro had a turn one Saturday morning, just as Tihi was ironing the sleeves of her blouse. She rushed out the door and was back in five minutes with Auntie Nel who had a car and worked at the hospital. They took Koro up there, where he was to stay and get fussed over for a couple of weeks.

And I was told to wait, and tell Ahi.

Oh, I thought, my eleven-year-old brain buzzing with the responsibility, my face a smear of tears. What was I going to say?

The car pulled up, all polished and shining. Ahi was checking the dark glasses in the rear-vision mirror. Slowly, I walked over, carefully arranging my story. It still came out all garbled though, but Ahi got the message, while I blubbered on pitifully.

The car door opened, and Ahi got out, kneeled down, still not saying a word. One strong arm went around me. I stopped snivelling, leaned into the black satin shirt of Tihi's hero, Ahi. Who took off the dark glasses, and looked at me. Smiling, talking softly in a voice I *knew*!

'Don't worry, Huri girl, Koro will be fine, you'll see.'

227

It was Cindy. Ahi had Cindy's eyes, and Cindy's voice. Cindy had come back as Ahi. Wow! It felt like a secret — it felt neat, though! I was dying to run away and tell someone.

But I didn't. I just went to church and to youth club and to school and waited for Saturday mornings. And the magic of Tihi, getting ready for the game, getting ready for Ahi.

Getting ready for us.

For Crying Out Loud

Bill Payne

S money machines all over town reply to cash requests with 'Sorry — Insufficient Funds', the Thursday morning crowd at Social Welfare grows. They pack the third-floor foyer, more righteous with each passing minute, convincing themselves that any mistake in their benefit payments can't possibly be their fault. But the lift doors keep opening, spewing forth new loads, and by 9 a.m. the air is blue: with tobacco smoke and curses, and with body sweat and baby shit and battered attitudes.

As opening time nears, some rough heads at the front become impatient and start banging on the doors. They squash up, mouthing at the window, obscene pink lips leaving smear-trails down the glass. They eyeball the receptionists inside but the two women seem more interested in drinking coffee and moaning about 'that new acting supervisor who thinks she's bloody God . . .'

'You see that bitch on telly last night?' says a tattooed man in the crowd. 'Our millionaire Minister of Anti-Social Warfare?'

'I saw her,' replies his offsider, 'sitting up there like Lady Muck. How long you reckon since her kids went without?'

'Never, mate, never. They come in on a pig's back, didn't they?'

Sly snickers grow into chuckles and guffaws as the joke is repeated and explained. The lift doors open on another full load and an older, female voice pipes up. 'She's not so bad,' protests the woman, a pear-shaped fortysomething. 'Not as bad as that last bastard, anyway.' She fiddles with a button on her cardigan, blushing under the stares of some Maori kids nearby. 'Isn't that right, Monique?' she adds, looking at her mate for support.

'Of course it is,' agrees Monique. 'All this pick-pick-pick is just 'cause she's a woman. The last one got away with blue bloody murder but you never heard boo about him!' She glares at the children until they look away and slides an arm around her partner's waist. 'I read the other day where *Broadsheet* voted her the woman most likely.'

'The woman most likely to what?' barks the guy with facial tatts. 'Marry outside the species?' He and his friends laugh in short, humourless bursts.

The Otis elevator — maximum load nine persons — opens on a wall of stale, complaining flesh, with no apparent space for Tossy to go forward or back. The lift empties around her before she can get the pushchair out and she's not even halfway through when the doors begin closing, bump-bump-bumping against her. She forces them open, jammed there in the middle, collapsing the pram with one arm and trying to hold Zac with the other. She appeals for help but everyone discovers subjects of interest in other directions. The only advice comes in the form of muffled abuse, echoing up the lift-shaft from the ground three floors below. 'Shut the fuckin' door, ya dropkick. There's other people in the world, eh?'

After an eternity, imagining herself the focus of an entire building's scorn, Tossy wrestles clear. She wedges herself into an unavailable space and gets a hefty shove for her troubles. 'Hey!' someone calls, 'get to the back of the queue, eh?' She's about to let rip when the office doors open and the crowd starts surging forward.

The human tide moves into Social Welfare, Tossy and Zac in its backwash. Impatient beneficiaries stand three-deep at the desk, swamping the receptionists with interview requests. Conferences are beginning in booths along one side of the room — for those who missed out the day before and those who were cunning or aimless enough to have been there since the building first opened. It's not yet 9.40 but already some voices are raised. One old soldier is waving his arms around and shouting at a Polynesian interview clerk. 'Not approved?' he yells, 'whaddya mean, not approved? I put my balls on the line in Italy, I get a hunk of bloody steel as big as bloody Tawa up my arse and what the hell for? So some brylcreemed spearchucker can put the kibosh on my sickness benefit? Go and get your supervisor, feller-me-lad. I've no time for you.'

The Samoan clerk, barely out of school but already the holder of two anger management certificates, just shrugs and ambles off. But before he can make cover the old soldier aims and shoots him in the back. He blows smoke from his imaginary gun-barrel, reholsters the weapon, and gives an elaborate bow. He straightens then and smiles, his few remaining teeth showing cracked and discoloured.

It's 10.15 when Tossy makes the front of the queue. She gives her name to an indifferent receptionist and scans the room for a seat. There are dozens of colour co-ordinated chairs but every one is taken, slouched and sprawled upon by depressed-looking individuals. They pass the time nodding off or making desultory small talk with anyone careless enough to sit beside them. They bitch about the weather and their desperate financial straits, they criticise Social Welfare and those 'rich bloody wankers' at parliament.

'A job 'til I retired, they reckoned. A respected and valued team member, they said. Twenty years down the gurgler for a change in company policy . . .'

'Learn new skills? I said. With three kids? Who's got the time, luv? Who's got the bloody time?'

Now and then they halt their pronouncements, turning in unison each time an interview clerk appears, but when the requested name isn't theirs they resume their perpetual whine.

Pre-school children run amok, tearing unchecked around the room while their parents look intently away. Dozens of toddlers swarm over a large playing-block pyramid in the furthest corner, fighting and arguing over the top block, pushing each other to the ground and making a deafening noise. Tossy declines the offer of a seat from two Mongrel Mobsters and takes a possie on the floor, leaning against a column underneath the clock. She unzips Zac's jacket and stuffs it in her bag, then sniffs at his backside and turns him loose. He heads for the blocks in a stumbling, tottering run. He falls once or twice but quickly gets up, his face still shining and full of adventure.

Toss watches until two little girls start organising his life, and that's when she allows herself to think about Dion. She wonders if he's still allowed visits after last weekend. She yawns and checks the clock, nearly half-past ten, then yawns again and starts to nod. Her eyes close for a minute.

'Mrs Hope! Last call for Mrs Hope!'

Tossy wakes up in confusion. She blinks and rubs her eyes, fights to keep them open. She checks the clock and is shocked to discover it's nearly 12.30. A middle-aged woman with a manila file is calling her name from an interview booth. 'Over here!' says Toss, waving her arms to attract the woman's attention. 'I'll just be a sec.'

She looks around the room and has a momentary flash of panic when she can't locate Zac. She paces up and down, picking a path through curled-up beneficiaries and searching for clues among large hollow blocks. Her unease develops to gut-churning fear before she spots her little boy, chewing on a taro and colouring in picture books with his two new girlfriends.

Several Pacific Islanders — all women, all brightly dressed and all, it seems, from the same extended family — sit together, murmuring over the part-Palagi child and watching their daughters play. They seem to possess knowledge from some idle and exotic place, although each carries some form of injury. One woman has scratches, gouges almost, across her nose and cheek, another has a neck-brace and a heavily bandaged wrist, a third has facial bruising and a blackened eye, poorly concealed by dark glasses and a headscarf. The women sit in crowded isolation, their disfigurements diminished by their almost royal air, waiting for their names to be called and smiling together at Tossy when she comes and picks up Zac.

'That one's going to break a few hearts,' says the one in shades. 'They'll follow that smile into a burning house.'

'You're not far wrong there,' Tossy tells her. 'He's broken mine a few times already.'

'Mrs Hope! Will you hurry along please?'

Tossy takes a seat opposite Kuini Olsen. She plonks Zac on the desk but he immediately makes a beeline for the sole fun possibility in the child-proof and characterless booth: he bangs his fists on the computer keyboard and snatches out leads from the back. Tossy attempts to amuse him by bouncing him on her knee but he twists and squirms and nearly throws himself off. She catches him before he hits the ground but then he goes limp and starts whining, refusing to stop until she hisses in his ear. He yells and kicks and tries to scratch her face but stops when he notices, behind her back, his two waving, smiling friends. Toss puts him down and lets him go for it.

She closes her eyes. She swallows something back and massages her temples. She breathes deeply until she's relatively calm and then looks across at Kuini, who's flicking through her file and frowning, now and then giving an almost imperceptible shake of her permanently black-lacquered hair. Tossy's on the verge of hurrying the woman along when there's a heated exchange from the booth next door.

'How'm I supposed to feed my kids with no power?' says a voice through the wall. 'How'm I supposed to give them baths?'

'You wouldn't have this problem if you'd stuck to your budget, Mrs Duke,' replies another, more reasonable voice. 'You were supposed to set aside money for . . .'

'Look!' interrupts Mrs Duke, 'piss on your stupid budget, okay? Don't tell me what I'm supposed to do, I only care about my kids. *Jason! Cut that out right now or you'll get a clip round the bloody ear!*'

'Kindly watch your mouth. Smoking and abusive language are prohibited in this office. Now then, let's just check your budget and see if we can't make some adjustments.'

'Okay, if you insist. But it'll need to be one mother of an adjustment to make way for a $350 electricity bill.'

A flickering fluorescent light makes Tossy look up. She looks back down at Kuini Olsen. 'If you're quite ready, Mrs Hope,' says Kuini, drumming her fingers on the desk, 'I'd like to get on with it. There's no shortage of people waiting, you know.'

'Oh!' says Tossy, suddenly irritated at the woman's officiousness, 'excuse me for not feeling humble. Excuse me for not feeling grateful at being allowed to hang around here for the last three-and-a-half hours.'

'Now come on, Mrs Hope,' counters Kuini, 'there's no need for all that. We do the best we can with the resources we've got and, besides, Thursdays are a nightmare for everyone.'

'Well if the best you can do is waste time, energy and money hassling me about a couple of days' cleaning work,' says Toss, taking a letter from her bag and throwing it on the desk, 'then it's just not bloody good enough, is it? It's all I can do to keep our heads above water anyway, without you lot standing over me.'

'Rules are rules and we're obliged to stick to them, I'm afraid,' says Kuini, taking a report from her file and reading it over the top of her glasses. She studies it for a moment, resurrecting the frowning and hair-shaking, and then looks across at Tossy. 'Our information is that the two days' alleged "cleaning work" referred to in this letter was only what your employer — a Mr Ron Cocker, I believe — chose to declare for tax purposes.'

'Information?'

'Put simply: our sources have revealed that rather than doing temporary cleaning work you are actually working as a part-time masseuse at the Blue Lady Fun Emporium.'

'Sources? You're bluffing. I don't believe you.'

Kuini closes the file and looks directly at Tossy. 'We don't reveal our sources at Social Welfare, but acting on information received via a telephone call, one of our benefit investigation units observed your movements for the period May 30th through June 28th this year. The findings were — and I have a signed and sworn report right here in front of me — that on eleven different occasions you were seen entering the Blue Lady at approximately 6 p.m. and did not leave again until the early hours of the next morning.'

'A telephone call, eh? I bet it was that hard-faced old bitch next door.'

'That's classified information, I'm afraid. But since you did not list payments for cleaning or any other kind of work on the relevant Declaration of Income statement, the department has concluded that you've knowingly abused the system — not to mention broken the law

— and has decided to cancel your benefit forthwith. You're legally entitled to appeal this decision but you should be aware that the department is considering further action through the courts.'

Tossy chews her lip. She tries to stare Kuini down but her eyes film over and she ends up hiding behind her hands. 'You mean they're cutting my benefit *and* taking me to court?' she says, taking a tissue from her bag and blowing her nose. She balls it into a wad and looks around for a bin, but then figures what the hell and just drops it on the floor. When she faces Kuini again, there's no colour in her face. 'Look,' she says, 'you've got the wrong idea. Sure, I work the Blue Lady sometimes, but only as a favour to Ron. I fill in for his receptionist when her boyfriend's in port — that's all. I don't crack it, I'm no whore.'

'You're missing the point, Mrs Hope. Whether you worked as a receptionist, a cleaner, a masseuse or even a green jelly wrestler you've still broken your legal agreement with the department by signing a Declaration of Income statement on which it is printed — quite clearly — that *any* extra income must be declared.'

'But you don't understand. If my benefit's cut or I end up in court, Dion'll find out.'

'Shouldn't you tell him anyway?'

'Are you kidding? If he finds out I've been working in a parlour — even just answering the phones — the shit will really hit the fan.'

'I think it might've done that already.'

Tossy shakes her head. 'I bet it was her next door,' she says, searching Kuini's eyes for confirmation. 'The fat bitch just can't keep her nose out of other people's business.'

'That's beside the point,' says Kuini. 'You people don't seem to realise that if you're going to break the law you will eventually be found out and then you will be punished. The department has a legal obligation to prosecute — they've got a mandate from the taxpayers.'

'Bullshit. It's only the government and the media who jump up and down about this sort of thing. No one else'd give two stuffs if those wankers weren't going on about it all the time.' She blows her nose again. She wipes her eyes with the back of her sleeve. 'What's happening to this country? eh? People dob each other in for the slightest bloody thing.

They've forgotten how to mind their own business because they're encouraged not to all the time. *Crimewatch?* Undercover policemen? Benefit Investigation Units? We're a nation of bloody narks.'

Kuini Olsen pushes back her chair and stands. 'Really, Mrs Hope,' she says, picking up the file. 'This is getting us nowhere. I'm not surprised you're in this mess with an attitude like that.'

'For someone who's supposed to be a social worker,' says Toss, glaring back, 'your attitude isn't so great, either.'

Kuini bends forward, knuckles on the desk. 'Well you try sitting here every day, listening to people tell you their fridge is empty, their kids haven't got any shoes or their power's been cut or they can't afford the doctor's bills. And then you go out for lunch and see them coming out of the TAB, you see them coming out of the Lotto shop and smoking cigarettes, or spending $30 to $40 on takeaways and shovelling it into their kids in some old heap in the hotel carpark. And if you have to work overtime — because there's not enough hours in the day, because the genuine cases get lost in the stampede of others trying to get what they're not entitled to — then you can see them after the pub shuts, staggering around like zombies, fighting and throwing up and falling asleep on the pavement. So don't talk to me about attitude, I don't have to justify my attitude to you. It's not in my job description.'

'For crying out loud!' says Tossy, forcing a word in edgeways. 'Calm down, okay? I know how this place makes me feel just visiting. I can't imagine what it must be like to be here every day.'

Kuini relaxes slightly but remains cool and distant. 'I should also advise you that any further claims before this is settled are almost certain to be declined.' She straightens away from the desk and takes a half-step backwards. 'I've explained the department's position, I've outlined the reasons for their decision, and I've informed you of your rights regarding an appeal, all of which will be confirmed by letter within the next few days.' She takes another step backwards and looks at her inlaid paua shell watch.

'So that's it?' says Toss. 'I'm out of here? There's nothing else I can do?'

'If you want to take it further then you'll have to see my supervisor.'

'What's the point? Your minds are made up already.'

'For God's sake, girl!' Kuini snaps. 'Don't be so bloody self-pitying.' She waves a bangled arm around the room. 'There's plenty here far worse off than you are, girl, believe me. So your husband's in jail, so what? There's families here who'd be a darn sight better off if their old men were in jail, too. Haven't you got any other family you can turn to? What about your parents?'

'What about them?'

'Well, can't they help you out? What's their situation?'

'What business is that of yours?'

'If it's none of my business, what are you doing here in the first place?' Kuini replies, tucking the file firmly under her arm. 'Look, Mrs Hope, I'm sorry but we're wasting each other's time. I've done all I can, all I'm obliged to do, so if you just hold on here I'll go and get my supervisor.' She turns and moves quickly behind the office partition. Her neck appears rigid and she doesn't look back.

But Tossy does — she looks back and remembers how her mother would leave rooms in the middle of an argument, nose in the air and refusing to give an inch. Toss remembers how she'd argue black was blue if it suited her purposes but how she'd always stick up for Dion when the old man grumbled and whined, complaining from behind his newspaper about how everything the 'young tearaway' did just wasn't bloody good enough, and how did Tossy expect to get on in life if she wasted her time with a no-hoper like that? She remembers one conversation in particular when her father, a carthorse all his life who never had a day sick and was never on the dole and — right up until the day he was laid off and stopped having strong opinions about anything — never really took to Dion, had been taking shots all through Sunday dinner.

'Leave the boy alone,' her mother had said, 'he's got more go than you had at his age.' She gave him the evils from behind Dion's back. 'How's that car of yours been running lately, Dion?'

'Not too bad, thanks, Mrs A. Been having some trouble with the. . . .'

'Car?' the old man interrupted. 'Bloody Christmas tree, more like. Looks like a mobile whorehouse.'

'Just get back behind that paper, you! You were no different at his age,

hanging round the dairies and youth clubs with your sideburns and Mark Ones.'

'They were a bloody good car,' said her father, 'good enough for you and me to do our courting in, anyway.'

Her mother blushed. 'Come on, Dee,' she said, handing Dion a stack of dishes and sticking her nose in the air, 'let's leave him to his misery. You can tell me all about it in the kitchen . . .'

Once they'd gone Tossy tackled her father. 'What's your problem, Dad? You never give him a chance.'

'Huh!' he said, snapping his newspaper. 'A chance you reckon? In my day you didn't get given chances, you grabbed them. The only thing he ever grabs is his dole every week.'

'I wouldn't be so sure about that. . . .'

'. . . and then he goes and blows it all on that poncey car of his, anyway.'

'He does not! He's paying it off. And besides, it gives him something to do while I'm at polytech.'

'If he wants something to do, why doesn't he get a steady job?'

'What jobs? There are no jobs. He prefers working for himself, anyway. He can't seem to get along with people.'

'Right. Like bosses, foremen, charge hands . . .'

'That's right. They don't understand him.'

'What's to understand? What's he supposed to be, a poet or something? Christ a'bloody mighty — Vincent Van builder's labourer.'

Tossy had laughed despite herself. 'He was a painter, you silly old sod.'

'Now there's a good trade for you,' quipped her dad, before she crumpled up his paper and the fun fight began, tickling each other and giggling on the floor. But when Dion came back for more dishes he brought an uneasy silence with him, and they were suddenly embarrassed by their tomfoolery. The old man had straightened his newspaper and, plainly irritated, got back into his seat, unable to look his daughter in the eye until Dion left the room again.

'Now then, Mrs Hope,' says a woman with a passing resemblance to Dame Cath Tizard, sliding into the seat opposite Tossy. 'What seems to be the problem? I understand you're having some difficulties with the situation?'

Tossy takes her in with a glance, from the supervisor's badge on her immaculate powder-blue suit and the turquoise brooch at the throat of her cream silk blouse, through the mannish, subtly made-up face and confident yet obliging gaze. 'Difficulties?' says Toss, remembering Zac and spinning around. She locates her boy and stands, snaps her bag closed and tucks the folded-up pram under her arm. 'Nothing a bit of creative thinking won't fix,' she says, turning to leave. 'Nothing a food bank and a knockshop can't take care of between them.'

'But Mrs Hope,' says the supervisor, her jumpy smile revealing cracks in her composure, 'won't you sit down? We really should discuss your options further.'

But Tossy's already gone, scooping up Zac on the way, gone with a nod to the Pacific Islanders and the two tattooed Mobsters, past the screaming kids and complaining beneficiaries, quickly through the smoke-filled foyer and down inside the lift and, feeling as though she's broken through a wall, out into the fresh free air.

Freedom Hill

—

Apirana Taylor

I am a blom di blom di blom. I live in bum di bum land. My wife is a blim di blim. Our children are blim di bloms or blom di blims.

The problem with being a blom di blom in bum di bum land is that the bum di bums always try to bum us out. All I can say is bum di bum di bum. Bum di bum di bum . . .

Lord, let me open my mind. Let me clear it.

When I was a kid we lived in the bush. We used to go out pig-hunting in the weekends. Then we moved to Wellington and jeez, did I get a fright. I never thought there were any pigs in Wellington. But hell, there's heaps of them. And you know what? The pigs in Wellington come hunting you on weekends.

In the bush you never let yourself get caught downhill of a pig, 'cause they're the fastest critters in the world when they charge downhill straight at you. They are mean, fast and cunning.

The pigs in Wellington snort and grunt a lot, but you don't have to worry about staying downhill from them, 'cause they're always trying to send you up the hill.

They want to put you in the pen. It's a big pen built by them for us. You know, I can smell a pig and it's good to try and stay upwind of them. Pigs are pigs as pigs go, I suppose, and you know maybe they're humans just being pigs.

I do feel aroha for the pigs. I knew one. His name was PC Pig. He was okay as pigs go. But I tried to have as little to do with him as I could. It was PC Pig who was always trying to get hold of me.

For that reason I took off to the hills and bush of my childhood and waited for the pigs to come. So now PC Pig and his mates are after me. Unlike when I was a hunter with pig-dogs, they now have pigs and are after me.

It'll be sunrise soon. Early morning light, that's when the pigs will come out of the bush and into the clearing below. I've been out in the bush about a week now and I've had time to think. PC Pig and his mates have all been badly brought up. Bad upbringing. That's how come they turned into pigs. And maybe something went wrong in their life. So I suppose I'm a bit like them in a way. I mean I never had a mother and was always shunted around.

Why are the pigs after me? They are after me 'cause I stuck one of them with my knife. One prick in the heart hit the spot straight off. I stabbed him in a brawl outside the pub. He died before he knew he was dying.

Here I am now sitting on my own hill of freedom and I'm waiting for the pigs to come. They're gonna get me, I know. Maybe they're gonna try and put me in the pens they built, but I'm not gonna go. I've got a rifle, and what's ahead of me if I throw it down and walk out with my hands up? I'm not going away again. That's for sure.

I love the bush. Wish I'd lived here all my life. It's a fine place to live and a fine place to die.

The last thing I want to say, friend, is don't mess with the pigs, friend, and don't let the pigs mess with you. Otherwise it could end like this.

They'll be here soon. Flying in on helicopters. Pigs with wings. Snorting in the valleys below. It's easy to kill someone if you think of them as not being human, when they are pigs. They don't think of me as being human either.

This is what happens when two negative forces meet head on. You get such things as world wars. I've been violent. Live by the sword and die by it. This is a violent story, but more than that, I understand it now and see that in truth it's a sad one. I have one bullet in the breech and there is no way I can win.

Auntie Netta

—

Marewa Glover

THEY had to hold the funeral on the weekend so everyone from work could be there. The factory didn't stop for anyone. They never even had a minute's silence in respect of Auntie Netta's work.

Auntie Netta had worked in the condom factory for over 40 years. She started there when she was 16 and worked every day since. She never took a day off sick and she never took a holiday, till a couple of months ago.

A telegram had come telling her that her brother had died. He was to be buried in Tahiti. So Auntie Netta took leave to attend the funeral. She was only gone two weeks, then she was back at work. It certainly wasn't the same at work with her gone. Now we'd have to get used to it. Anyway she was different when she came back. There was something about her. A silent invisible sickness had taken over and it killed her. Chemical annihilation. That's what Betty was saying. Chemical annihilation!

A karanga rang out, drawing us forward. Some of the old kuia who worked with Auntie Netta began their waiata. Only the senior women worked in the lab mixing chemicals. Everyone started on the floor, stripping the fat from the lambs' intestines. After years of that you might get promoted to the lab.

The chemicals helped dissolve the fat. But, from what they were saying now, the chemicals also helped dissolve your health. All the

242

women were concerned now that Auntie Netta had died that it was going to happen to them, too.

It's hard to know whether it was the mixing job that did it or the fact that she'd been around it all for so long. We all worked in chemical baths. A lot of women got sick. Rheumatoid arthritis the doctors said. It's shift work, though. Bound to wear you down every now and then.

We just had a go at trying to get the heating system improved. It's broken they said. Get it fixed we said. It's going to cost too much they said. Get it fixed we said and they said they would. We're still waiting.

Cass reckons Auntie Netta had a heart attack because she was all grown out of proportion. Her right arm, her stripping arm, was built like a weightlifter's, while her left side was all wasted away. Personally I can't see how that would kill her.

Some of Auntie Netta's family up front were crying loudly. She had a big family. Only two daughters of her own, but lots of children she had looked after for other people, family or not. She was a mother to everyone, that's why she was called Auntie Netta. She was the woman all the young girls went to for advice. Her house had been a refuge for many a girl running from a violent home.

Her real name was Antoinette. Such a flash name. A soft, pretty name that just didn't suit Auntie Netta, who was a large woman with wart-like growths all over her hands.

Janet reckoned she'd died from shock. Auntie Netta had never been out of New Plymouth, she'd never been on a plane. Just having two weeks off work must have been a shock to her system, let alone the reunion with her family in Tahiti. Angela thinks Auntie Netta died from regret. Seeing there was more to life than making bloody condoms. All that time wasted for whose benefit?

I must say I had to laugh when Trish said we were saving people from getting AIDS and VD, and we were saving women from pregnancy. Not that pregnancy is a sickness or anything. It's just that it can be a curse if you're not ready for it. We've had a number of women had to quit their jobs because they got pregnant. And once you've got no job, you're shot these days. You have to depend on some bloke or welfare. Yeah, getting pregnant before you're ready is like being sentenced to a life of poverty.

Most of the condoms get exported to Asia. Millions and millions of them. They don't like using latex. They prefer natural products, like New Zealand Naturalambs. I could tell you the jokes we have about condoms, but we're at Auntie Netta's funeral and it wouldn't be right. I don't think Auntie Netta ever thought about the final product. It's easier concentrating on your part in the production process rather than on the use of condoms.

A lot of women get jobs with us, but they don't last long. Either they can't hack the work, because it is hard on your back, standing in gumboots on concrete floors all day, or the whole thing just makes them sick. That's where the jokes come in handy.

Honestly, just between me and you, I could never do it using a condom again. It would put me off well and truly. Don't get me wrong, I think it's really important to be safe and all, but I just couldn't stay turned on if I knew my boyfriend was wearing a lamb intestine. I'd be able to see the intestine before it had been stripped. Now that is a turn-off.

People began to wander away from the grave. Single flowers lay strewn on top of the coffin. It would make us all think about our own lives, this death. Some of the women were already talking about getting out. But jobs were scarce.

Betty said she didn't need the money since her husband worked, and though it would be harder living on one income, she said her health was worth the sacrifice. Cass was proud of her figure. She wanted to be an aerobics instructor. She didn't want to grow all out of proportion, so she said she was going to leave, too.

Janet wanted to travel overseas. She was only staying long enough to save the fare. Angela was determined she wasn't going to waste away in a condom factory. She'd applied for a job at Tegel and knowing her she'd probably get it, but it wouldn't be long before she moved on from there. She was never satisfied to stick around in one place long. Trish didn't think the work was that bad. She looked forward to working her way up to the lab.

Me? Well I'm concerned about this chemical annihilation business. I'm going to talk to the union about it. The others have warned me not to. I'll get the sack, they said. 'But what about Auntie Netta?' I asked them. 'What about the other women who work here? What about us? We don't know what it's doing to our bodies.'

So I'm going to the union. Someone's got to. If I get the sack, well I'll deal with that then. At least I'll be able to live with myself. At least I'll be alive.

'For you, Auntie Netta!' I said and tossed my white carnation into the grave.

Redemption

—

Phil Kawana

WE only had the one capsule left, and so we broke it open and carefully tipped its contents out on to a saucer. Jaffa grabbed a drinking straw from one of the drawers, and we carefully divided the tiny granules up into two even piles before snorting them. I had a bit of a cold, and so it took two or three snorts to clean up my share. Then, while we waited for it to take effect, I rolled us a five-paper joint which we smoked out on the back step, seeing as Jaffa's brother didn't like us smoking inside.

'What did ya say that stuff was?' Jaffa asked between tokes.

'Can't remember,' I said. 'Dog did tell me, but I was off my face at the time. He said he had a whole box of the stuff, and we could score a couple of bags anytime.'

'Cool.'

The joint was half gone, which meant there would be a good build-up of resin in the roach, so I flipped it around and held it, burning end towards me.

'Shotgun time,' I said, closing my lips around the joint, being careful not to burn my tongue the way Jaffa had the first time she had tried it. She leaned forward until her lips were half an inch from the end of the roach, and then I exhaled, blowing a stream of smoke into her eagerly sucking mouth. We swapped roles two or three times until the roach was too small, then I pulled out my bag to see how much grass I was still

246

holding. There was maybe enough for a real small doobie. I couldn't be bothered with something that little.

'Come down here,' Jaffa said, and led me down towards the back gate. Beyond it were the garages and sheds for her brother's house and the place next door. They used to be power board houses, and had heaps of outbuildings for all the linemen's gear. Jaffa had turned one of the garages into a crash pad. Sometimes I would sleep out here when it wasn't safe to go home. Jaffa's unfinished tukutuku panel stood off to one side, and I had painted a giant koru design on the opposing wall. Jaffa's niece had been in too, and pinned her Jonah Lomu posters to the wall by the old mattress that we used as a bed. Jaffa pulled them down carefully, folded them and placed them on the bench. She started pulling bits and pieces out of a cupboard while I stretched out on the bed.

'Here we go,' she said, and pulled out a large plastic bag. I could smell the glue before she got within reach of me. 'This'll really fuck you,' she giggled. She took a few deep chugs then held out the bag towards me.

'Nah, bugger that,' I said. 'I'd rather get fucked by you.'

'Just be patient,' she said, before taking a few more deep chugs. Jaffa dropped the bag on the old grey blanket at the foot of the mattress and then lay down on top of me. 'What you gotta do this week?'

'The old man wants me to go down to Porirua and work for Uncle Roto. Fuck! He reckons I either get a job or he's gonna kick me out.'

'Sleep here.'

'When I'm here, who wants to sleep?' I slipped one hand down the back of Jaffa's jeans. She squirmed a little to let me get in a bit further. She kissed me, but the taste of glue in her mouth was so strong I nudged her head away and started to nip and bite her neck. After a little while she sat up, shuffled down until she was sitting across my thighs, and then slowly, teasingly, stripped off her shirt and bra. 'Time for Redemption,' she said.

Redemption was our own private game. Jaffa went first. She turned around so that I could see the five long, thin welts across her back, three of them ending in deeper cuts.

'Dad saw that picture that Huia took of us doing it,' she said softly. I reached out and touched the marks gently with the tips of my fingers.

'It's got nothing to do with the bastard,' I said. 'You don't live there any more.'

Jaffa looked at me over her shoulder. 'Makes no difference to him. He came around and brought the whip with him.'

The whip was a length of electrical cord her father had pinched from a building site years ago. He had seen some film where Jesus got whipped with a cat-o'-nine-tails and he had made his own version. He had stripped back the last foot or so of the cord to free the three insulated wires within. At the end of these wires he had taken off the plastic coating and tied the copper wire into knots. When he hit the kids with it, the copper wire would slash into the softer skin at the side of the back.

I guided Jaffa off me and on to her stomach. The red marks seemed to glow in the harsh light. I leaned over her and started to kiss her back, running my tongue along the raised ridges left by her father's whip. There were older scars there too, pale tracks across the toffee-coloured skin. I ran my fingers along them, tracing out a fan-shaped pattern that broadened on her right side. Once I had kissed all five of the fresh marks, I lifted her hair off her shoulders and kissed the back of her neck.

'My turn,' I said, and pulled off my jeans. My thighs were latticed with deep, black-brown bruises. 'Mum and Tony again.' Tony, my older brother, would hold me down while Mum laid in with the jug cord.

'What for this time?'

'I forgot to put some salt in with the poroporo.' When Mum hit the Jim Beam, it didn't take much to set her off.

Jaffa touched her lips gently to the bruises. With the faintest of suckings, she drew out the pain we felt. By kissing each other's wounds, we told each other that there were other ways of living.

'Fuck them,' I said, biting back the urge to cry. Jaffa could see the bruises, but I would never let her see me cry.

The stuff we had snorted earlier was starting to kick in. Colours started to separate, and each sound became an object that we could see moving through the air. We took off the rest of our clothes and lay down together, running our hands slowly over each other. I could feel Jaffa's breath enshrouding me.

We had it off for what seemed like hours. Afterwards, as the pill started to wear off, Jaffa looked a little green.

'You okay?' I asked.

'I'll be right,' she said. 'I'm just a little late, y'know?' She sat up, hunched over on the side of the mattress, holding her stomach. 'Maybe I should have skipped the glue.'

I didn't answer. I was wondering about sneaking home and grabbing my stash, then coming back for another screw. Jaffa went outside for a while, and I could hear her throwing up in the weeds. I decided against going home. I felt like sleeping.

Jaffa came back in, turned off the light and then lay down next to me. I grabbed the grey blanket and pulled it over us. We both fell asleep quickly.

When I woke up, the sky was just starting to lighten. Jaffa was still sound asleep on her stomach, so I went inside and made us a cup of tea. When I got back to the garage, she hadn't moved.

'Hey, wake up lazy. Tea. C'mon.' I leaned over her to shake her shoulder. It was then that I noticed all the vomit. I dropped her tea on the concrete floor, the cup shattered and sprayed its contents over my feet. I yanked off the blanket and pulled her face out of the spew. She felt cold.

I cleaned her up as much as I could, wiping her up with the blanket. I held her close to me, tried to warm her with my own body heat. She just flopped against me limply. I kissed her eyes, her cheek, her lips, her breasts, tried to buy her back with my kisses. She could not wake up. It was simply too late.

I gave up just after dawn. I dressed Jaffa carefully, lay her on the mattress with her head away from the pool of vomit, and then kissed her goodbye. Taking one of the broken pieces of cup off the floor, I gouged a deep cut across my chest, dabbed some of the blood with a finger and anointed her lips with it. Then I turned away and went to tell her brother.

Rongomai Does Dallas

Briar Grace-Smith

ALLAS was late. Ten minutes late, and Rongomai had something to tell him. Something that would change their relationship forever and leave him wide-eyed, trembling and gasping for breath at the very thought of what might happen next.

Oh yeah. Tonight was gonna be a night the pair of them would never forget.

Rongomai took a Dunhill from the packet that lay open on the kitchen table and lit it. She took a long drag and exhaled slowly. With eyes cast downwards she watched the smoke escape over the curve of her top lip. Then with expert timing she drew it back in.

Recycling it with flared nostrils. Rongomai and Dallas. They'd been mates for an entire year now. Close as. Like skin and sticking plaster, carrot cake and cream cheese icing, pork bones and puha — they were created to be together. One without the other left appetites unsated and made the world a sorrier place. Together they were a force equal to the combined powers of cyclones Bola, Dena and Harry.

Dallas was her brother, her friend, her warrior, her . . . well maybe not yet but soon. Very soon. It hadn't been love at first sight, though. Rongomai had met Dallas at a nightclub in Wellington. A pair of clean-shaven young men had slithered their way into the conversation she'd been having. Cleverly, they'd sabotaged the Treaty talk and replaced it with rugby, and her mates, rugby groupies from way back, were easy prey for such sporty sweet-talkers. They sighed about Jonah's kidneys, made bets on the upcoming Hurricanes match, and listened intently to game plans.

Soon collars were being loosened and Charlie and what's-his-face were leaning back in chairs and blending right in. The air was thick with the smell of aftershave and locker-room type laughter, and while the girls drank beer Rongomai noticed the two studs sipped sedately on OJ. These guys wanted to score all right but it wasn't tries they were after and Rongomai at least was in no mood for game-playing . . . in fact if they dared venture into her space she'd give them one hell of a head-high tackle. She skulled the last of her rum and Coke, slammed down her glass with a force that shook the table and made her way to the bar.

Striding through a dense forest of pulsating reggae divas, cigarette smoke and beer-drenched tables, she saw him.

He stood leaning sideways against the bar sucking lazily on a DB Export. He wore a moko . . . if you could call it that. The lines were blurred and careless, and she was sure there would've been no aroha exchanged in the giving or receiving of its angry stamp. Rongomai imagined this stranger held down while a carver hacked relentlessly into his bleeding face with a piece of glass. Another stood over him, calmly filling the gaping valleys of flesh with ink from a green ballpoint pen. Here was a bad brother from way back and if Rongomai didn't divert from the main track she was looking at a head on collision with the arsehole.

But before she could turn, Dallas had snared her. Caught her with eyes dulled and yellowed where they should've been white. Eyes infected by too many drugs, too much pain. The spirals carved into his face pulled her into places that had no beginning. She felt unbalanced and suddenly overwhelmed by sadness. To hell with this, she hadn't expected it.

'I am,' she began silently, '. . . I am a beautiful positive intelligent wahine toa and I don't need this shit . . . I am a beautiful positive intelligent . . .'

'Sorry sister,' he was speaking. 'I didn't realise I was in your way, you . . . you are a . . . you don't need this shit.'

Rongomai's jaw dropped and her thoughts stopped mid-mantra. He had read her mind. Well, this leather-clad tekoteko surely was the master of the unexpected. Dallas reached out to her. A neatly rolled cigarette nestled between his thumb and forefinger. A peace offering. Rongomai considered the cigarette for a minute but she hated rollies.

'You could at least shout me a drink,' she said. Two hours later the bar was on fire and he was too spellbound to put it out. She talked of passion. Food. Love. Language. Land. Culture. Reclamation. Maori women. Goddesses. Herself. Beauty. 'I am!' she screamed, spilling her rum and Coke. 'We will!' She was positively powerful, positively passionate, positively fuckin' amazing.

Dallas talked too, and the woman who was used to being heard took a deep breath and surprised herself by listening. His words were air slowly leaking from a tyre, over the days and months they came. Ever so slowly.

At first he spoke about loss. The loss began when he was born with two inches of bone missing from his right leg. This was followed closely by a missing mother. She'd left because, 'Dallas was an ugly little sucker who carried the curse of the short leg.' That's what his dad had told him, but this wasn't a sufficient explanation for Dallas. He would not believe his mother didn't care so he'd made up a memory of being left on a doorstep. He called it 'Life before Dad and Maddie'.

When he was a kid he'd crawl into the big pipe that lay outside their house. Inside the pipe he felt safe, embraced by the curve of the concrete. There, he could relax and let the fuzzy yellowness of the made-up memory cover him like a blanket.

His mother had been a poor girl who couldn't afford to keep Dallas. So, she'd left him on the doorstep of a millionaire who gave lots of money to charity. There he was, Dallas, in a white wicker basket cooing and giggling and heartily draining the last of his bottle of warm milk. He was so happy in his dry nappies, so warm in his blue blanket and so cute in the woollen beret. There was a blue bow tied to the bassinet with a card that read. 'Please kind sir look after my beautiful baby, his real father is a famous black basketball player from Dallas, USA.' Trouble was, Dallas's Mum was dyslexic and she'd left him at number 64 Ruby Road instead of number 46 (the millionaire's house). Big difference.

This is where the made-up memory ended and reality began, and the concrete pipe would fill with darkness and sharp edges. Dallas's father was an evil man who kept a red leather strap called Maddie. Dad and Maddie had been great mates, Dad asked Maddie's opinion on just about everything Dallas did.

'We'll see what Maddie thinks about that, eh boy?' Dad would say, and the red strap hanging limply from its nail on the wall would start to tremble.

'Do it,' Maddie would whisper. 'I'm hungry.' Maddie and Dad were like a ventriloquist act gone wrong. Dallas reckoned Maddie had possession of Dad's soul, the way he laughed and sweated at everything Maddie did. Dallas was so scared of Maddie that at night he would stuff the gap under his bedroom door with underwear and socks so she couldn't slither her way in and strangle him in his sleep.

On the day Dallas turned thirteen Dad came home and found Maddie dead, drowned in the toilet, her shiny bronze buckle decapitated and buried in a shallow grave next to the compost heap. The murderer had fled the scene, never to return. With the smell of damp leather still on his hands Dallas had joined a gang.

There he had stayed for eight years, slowly but surely kicking arse all the way to the top. No one fucked with Dallas. But one day as he put the boot into the head of a young prospect Dallas realised he was experiencing a not unpleasant numbness. The more the kid cried the more the numbness tingled and spread, making him feel warm and alive all over. He knew then he was sick inside and because he didn't wanna turn out like Dad, he split. He'd hurt a lot of people in his time, done a lot of bad shit, but it was over now.

'And . . .' he said quickly, knowing the question that was about to high-dive off the tip of Rongomai's tongue, 'I have never violated or disrespected a woman. Neither have I knowingly let incidences of the like occur.'

Then realising he sounded like he was in court with Judge Rongomai presiding, Dallas added, hands in pockets, 'I ain't no fuckin' rapist. That's not me, that's just not me man.'

Ever so slowly the worst of it leaked out until there was nothing left but a trickle of good memories. Real ones. When Dallas was a kid Dad would send him to his grandmother. There . . . there was red clay at that place and black eels, a twisting river, green hills and her. Kuia.

The memory of her was an oasis in a desert of parched earth, cans and car bodies, and he was so surprised to find it that the beginnings of tears came. They started in the corners of his eyes and filled them up, but there they stayed, trapped between blinking lids. Wobbling like transparent jelly but refusing to roll down his face. Rongomai wished he could cry. It wasn't right that he had to stay all fishy-eyed like that. Tears that don't come out end up as water on the brain, lungs and heart. Your thinking, breathing and emotions are all clogged up.

Dallas moved Rongomai. He'd planted a tiny seed into the pit of her stomach. It had stirred, dug soft new roots into her flesh, taken hold and now it was outta control.

Rongomai was sprouting branches and leaves everywhere. She was sure that by now he must've noticed how closely she resembled the South American rain forest but, like a child, Dallas had absolutely no idea how he affected her. Rongomai would like to stretch herself over his body and with her fingers unravel the markings on his face. Then she would recurl them, as neatly as fern fronds. She would massage his leg until it grew another two inches just to please her, and undo his hair. Let it spread, wild across a satin pillow (embossed with the letter R), pin him down and kiss him for ten hours. Prove to him that he could feel safe, even tied to the bed and without a leather jacket on. Hair on hair, skin on skin. They would mix themselves together and become the richest chocolate cake imaginable.

Without words Rongomai would show him it was meant to be. Afterwards, she would either give up smoking because it would take away the potency of the moment or smoke a whole packet to stop the earth from shaking.

'Yes,' she hissed. 'It's time I told Dallas that deep down inside I think he's a spunk. Time to stop pretending. I want him and I know he must want me too . . . I mean, why wouldn't he? He's just shy, that's all.'

Of course he wanted her. Like a smiling cobra Rongomai sat curled on the kitchen chair. Waiting, anticipating his purple Holden coming charging up the driveway.

Roaring and spitting carbon monoxide.

Dallas sat inside his car watching the minute hand of the clock slide down one side of the face then climb steadily up the other before getting stuck for eight beats on number nine, as usual. He was late, and Rongomai would be just about ready to explode.

He moved by shades of light, weather and mood. Rongomai wasn't into Maori time, it fucked her right off, she reckoned. In fact she wasn't into time at all. She wished life was an instant pudding.

The morning after he'd first met her, Dallas had gone to the library and looked up her name in the Maori-English dictionary. 'Rongomai' — it was the name of some flame-throwing comet, and that's how she had appeared to him that night. Her skin was dark and her eyes flashed. She'd stepped out of the darkness and lit up the whole fuckin' nightclub. Her hair was big, beautiful. Instead of draping sedately around her shoulders it flew out and up. She had looked at him with a scowl that knocked him like a right hook and feeling like fresh roadkill, Dallas had taken a long swig on his beer and as coolly as possible stared at this comet in baggy jeans and boots.

Dallas imagined that if Rongomai had been alive during the Land Wars, she would've been out there fighting with the best of them. A baby strapped to her back, a gun at the ready, she would've crouched in the trenches up to her waist in mud. Ready to strike.

She definitely would've been mates with da man, Hone Heke. If Dallas had known her twenty-five years ago, she would've saved his life. With Rongomai there was no halfway because she didn't understand it, she'd given their friendship all she had right from the start.

Oh Rongomai. Her eyes burnt inside him and there she had found stories that had never been spoken, she had plucked them out, listened to them and locked them carefully away in her heart. He trusted her. He loved her. It was strange because previously he'd believed love came immediately after or during sex, then hung around for a minute or two before vaporising into the steamy night air. But he'd never touched Rongomai and for a year now he'd loved her. Intensely. He'd tried not to let it in, but it was always there waiting around the edges, tickling his thoughts, and now he was weakening it was starting to drip in through holes. In sleep where he was the most vulnerable it seeped into his dreams and took control of his mind, soul and bodily functions. He'd wake up saturated in sweat, hyperventilating and feeling like a complete fuckwit. So he fought it. He fought it with crosswords, tea drinking, toenail cutting, walking . . . anything to stop . . . well . . . stop thinking about her and . . . and what it would be like . . . with her . . . if . . . shit my god! And what if . . . she didn't feel the same way, and why should she?

What the hell did he have to offer her? A rented room up the East and a lifetime of periodic detention? What if she laughed in his face?

Nah, she wouldn't, not Rongomai, but then again he was a loser and she . . . she was special, out of this world. Oh god! If he left it he was gonna turn into a nutcase and if he told her he could be looking at rejection, and he didn't wanna go there. Lay it all on the line and then be laughed at? Nah man, fuck that. So what would it be?

With grim determination Dallas swallowed his fear and slid his keys into the ignition. The Holden purred. Rongomai waited. Four hours passed before it occurred to her that Dallas might not show. She rang his flat once more and this time the landlady answered.

'He's left,' she said. 'Done a runner on the rent and stolen the toaster and my pink duvet.'

Rongomai put down the phone. Tiny needles began twisting their way into her skin. Left? What did she mean by left? Gone? Dallas gone? Just like that? He'd left her and was gone forever? She was a fool she should never never have trusted him he was just another user another idiot dickhead he never loved her never loved her never loved her never loved her . . . never loved. She expected far too much from the master of the unexpected.

The hurt was unrelenting. At first it came in the form of a fist twisting round and round in her stomach. She wanted to vomit. Then it picked her up and threw her tumbling into blackness. As she fell splashes of light danced around her, teasing her with promise. She tried to grasp hold of them but they leapt out of reach and made her angry. So angry. But when she finally hit the bottom, she didn't scream or punch her fist through the wall in rage. Just stayed little and still, refusing to explode. Sometimes, she thought, you just gotta handle things. Sometimes you just gotta. Rongomai pulled the quietness of the house around her shoulders and wondered how long it would take before she stopped feeling like shit.

There are things in life so beautiful that you block out their colours. Seeing them will only make you want to soak in their beauty, and that surely is asking too much. Dallas did not look at the sunset-drenched hills and houses as he drove out of Porirua. As he travelled north, he kept his eyes focused steadily on the motorway, disregarding the sea glowing gold and green. But as he flew through Taihape he could not ignore the thousands of stars sparking hotly in the blue-black sky. 'Rongomai, Rongomai,' they spat. Hearing her name caused a fire to burn at his insides and his skin to redden. He needed water. He stopped at the river and drank deeply. The water travelled along arteries leading from his lungs, brain and heart. It poured warm salty rivers from his eyes. Changing them from yellow to white.

For the first time in his life Dallas cried.

Biographical notes

ALFRED A. GRACE (1867–1942) was a son of missionary T.S. Grace, who ministered among the Tuwharetoa. His first book of stories was *Maoriland Stories* (1895); the title of his second, *Tales of a Dying Race* (1901) perhaps says it all about his approach. He also wrote the *Hone Tiki Dialogues* (1910), and his novels include *The Tale of a Timber Town* (1914).

HENRY LAWSON (1867–1922) is regarded as Australia's greatest short story writer. He spent two sojourns in New Zealand and wrote stories of 'Maoriland', as New Zealand was then referred to in literary parlance. 'A Daughter of Maoriland' comes from his second stay, in 1897, when, as a recently married man, he taught at a Native School at Mangamaunu, near Kaikoura. W.H. Pearson analyses 'A Daughter of Maoriland' in his book, *Henry Lawson Among Maoris* (1968).

BLANCHE BAUGHAN (1870–1958) lived the early part of her extraordinary life in England. When she was ten her enraged mother killed her father, and Baughan and her four sisters ended up looking after her mother who was judged to be criminally insane. Despite this background she was one of the earliest female university graduates in England. She published her first book of poetry, *Verses* in 1898, settled in New Zealand in 1902, and subsequently published three volumes of poetry and one book of fiction, *Brown Bread from a Colonial Oven* (1912). In later life she converted to Hinduism, campaigned tirelessly for prison reform and, in 1930, became a town councillor for Akaroa on Banks Peninsula.

WILL LAWSON (1876–1957) was born in England, moved to New Zealand in 1880, and thereafter spent his life between New Zealand, Australia, the United States and Asia. His first book was *The Laughing*

Buccaneer (1935) and his second was the popular *When Cobb & Co. Was King* (1936). He was a hardworking writer with fifteen further novels, seven poetry collections, and works of non-fiction to his credit and he was still writing in the 1950s.

KATHERINE MANSFIELD (1888–1923) was born in Wellington. She was the first New Zealand writer of world stature, and her work and life have turned her into the *monstre sacré* of New Zealand literature. Her volumes include *In a German Pension* (1911), *Bliss and Other Stories* (1920), *The Garden Party and Other Stories* (1923), and other works published posthumously by her husband and editor, John Middleton Murry. Most of her work was written and published overseas. Mansfield's most famous stories include 'The Woman at the Store', 'At the Bay', 'Her First Ball', 'The Garden Party', 'The Doll's House' and 'The Daughters of the Late Colonel'.

FRANK SARGESON (1903–82) is an icon of New Zealand literature. His publishing career began with *Conversations with My Uncle and Other Sketches* (1936) and went on until the 1980s spanning short stories, novels, plays and autobiography. Some of his books include *A Man and His Wife* (1940), *That Summer and Other Stories* (1946), his first novel *I Saw in My Dream* (1949), *Memoirs of a Peon* (1965), *The Hangover* (1967), *Joy of the Worm* (1969) and an autobiographical trilogy *Once is Enough* (1973), *More than Enough* (1975) and *Never Enough* (1977).

RODERICK FINLAYSON (1904–92) was the first short story writer in New Zealand to create a substantial body of fiction in which the Maori, and Maori-Pakeha relations, were the primary locus. His books include *Brown Man's Burden* (1938), *Sweet Beulah Land* (1942); the novels *Tidal Creek* (1948), *The Schooner Came to Atia* (1952) and *The Springing Fern* (1965); *Other Lovers* (1976) and *In Georgina's Shady Garden and Other Stories* (1988). Finlayson's range is often underestimated by readers who know him only from early work like 'The Totara Tree'. His later work saw him extending his characters and settings from the rural north to urban Auckland.

ROBIN HYDE (1906–39) was a contemporary of Sargeson and Finlayson. In her short career she traversed poetry, fiction and journalism, and her brilliance is only just beginning to be recognised. Hyde was the author of the poetry collections *The Desolate Star and Other Poems* (1929), *The Conquerors and Other Poems* (1935) and *Persephone in Winter: Poems* (1937); and the novels *Check to Your King* (1936), *Passport to Hell* (1936), *The Godwits Fly* (1938) and *Wednesday's Children* (1937). *Dragon Rampant*, a collection of her best articles, came out in 1939, and an autobiography written in 1937, *At Home in This World* was posthumously published in 1984. She committed suicide by Benzedrine poisoning.

DOUGLAS STEWART (1913–85) is best known for his play, *The Golden Lover* (1944), the plot of which has affinities to Richard Strauss' *Die Frau Ohne Schatten*. It tells of a Maori woman who is torn between her mortal husband and fairy lover. Born in Eltham, Taranaki, Stewart had a distinguished career as a journalist working on the *Bulletin* and as publishing editor for Angus & Robertson, Australia. He published volumes of poetry, plays and critical essays, all with subjects ranging through the histories of New Zealand and Australia. His one book of short stories is *A Girl with Red Hair* (1944).

ANNIE WRIGHT (??–??) is the author of a collection of short stories and poems entitled *Romance of Old New Zealand*. I have no other information about her and would welcome any correspondence. The inclusion of her story 'Hinemoa' is the only indulgence I have permitted myself in selecting for this anthology, yielding to my love of opera and the voice of Kiri Te Kanawa.

MAURICE DUGGAN (1922–74) is regarded as one of the pantheon of New Zealand short story writers. Born in Auckland, he produced a small but influential body of short fiction, including the collections *Immanuel's Land* (1956), *Summer in the Gravel Pit* (1965) and *O'Leary's Orchard* (1970). He also published a children's book called *Falter Tom and the Water Boy* (1957). In his 1966 OUP anthology, C.K. Stead said of him: 'Maurice Duggan is perhaps better equipped to turn a sentence than any other New Zealand writer.'

JANET FRAME (1924–   ) is described by *The Oxford Companion to New Zealand Literature* (OUP, 1998) as 'New Zealand's most distinguished writer'. Born in Dunedin, Frame has led a life beset by trauma, including a period of voluntary commitment in mental institutions. While in hospital she wrote the stories collected in her first book, *The Lagoon* (1951). Among her works of fiction and poetry are *Owls Do Cry* (1957), *Faces in the Water* (1961), *The Reservoir: Stories and Sketches* (1963), *Intensive Care* (1970), and *You Are Now Entering the Human Heart* (1983). Her award-winning autobiographical trilogy became the basis for the film *An Angel at My Table*, directed by Jane Campion.

J.C. STURM (1927–   ) is the author of a collection of short stories, *The House of the Talking Cat* (1983), which was written several decades before its eventual publication. She has also produced a poetry collection, *Dedications* (1997). Born in Opunake, she was married to the poet James K. Baxter. She was the first Maori woman to obtain a university degree and the first writer of Maori descent to be anthologised, 'For All the Saints' appearing in C.K. Stead's *New Zealand Short Stories: Second Series* (OUP, 1966).

NOEL HILLIARD (1929–97) was born in Napier. He had a successful career in journalism and, throughout his career, maintained an active role in left-wing politics. His first novel, *Maori Girl* (1960), was serialised in the *New Zealand Free Lance* and had enormous impact on a Maori reading public. His subsequent books included *A Piece of Land: Stories and Sketches* (1963), *Maori Woman* (1974), *Send Somebody Nice* (1976) and *The Glory and the Dream* (1978). Noel Hilliard was one of my mentors when I began writing. He was a sub-editor at the *New Zealand Listener* when it received my short story, 'The Liar', and it was on his recommendation that the story, the first of mine ever to see print (apart from 'The Prodigal Daughter' in the Gisborne Boys' High School magazine), was published.

ARAPERA BLANK (1932–   ) has spent most of her life as a teacher. Education's gain has been literature's loss, however, and when I asked Blank why it was that Maori writing didn't begin during her time in the 1950s, she fixed me with a beady eye and said, 'Witi, dear, literature was not a priority for Maori; survival was.' Nevertheless, Blank managed to find time to be a prize-winner in the Katherine Mansfield Memorial Competition, 1959, support Maori writing via the Maori Writers and Artists Society, publish a collection of poetry, *Nga Kokako Huataratara: The Notched Plumes of the Kokako* (1986), and write one of New Zealand's best short stories — 'One, Two, Three, Four, Five'.

MAURICE SHADBOLT (1932–   ) is one of New Zealand's foremost chroniclers, articulating our history and evolving national ethos with a magisterial approach. Born in Auckland, he has had a number of brilliant careers. His first book was *The New Zealanders* (1959), and it has been followed by an award-winning oeuvre of novels, short stories, plays, autobiography and non-fiction. The majority of his books tackle big, exuberant themes. Among his works are *Summer Fires and Winter Country* (1963), *Among the Cinders* (1965), *The Presence of Music* (1967), *Strangers and Journeys* (1972) and *The Lovelock Version* (1980). More recently he has achieved plaudits for the historical trilogy of *Season of the Jew* (1986), *Monday's Warriors* (1990) and *The House of Strife* (1993).

ROWLEY HABIB (1935–   ) is of Ngati Tuwharetoa descent, and lives in Taupo. A playwright, poet and fiction writer, he had his first work published in New Zealand and overseas in the 1950s. He was a founding member of Te Ika a Māui Players in 1966, was a prominent member of major land protests in the 1970s, and was the Katherine Mansfield Fellow in Menton, France, in 1984. He has been a keen support of younger Maori writers including Witi Ihimaera, Keri Hulme and Apirana Taylor.

BRUCE STEWART (1936–   ) has had such a hard life that it's amazing he hasn't been beaten down into the dust by it. Much of the early substance of this life can be read in his brilliant collection of stories, *Tama and Other Stories* (1989). Stewart came to writing late and, as with

Apirana Taylor, the raw power and anger in his work can be seen as a precursor to Alan Duff's adoption of similar strategies in his fiction in the 1990s.

PATRICIA GRACE (1937–   ) published her first book, *Waiariki* (1975), at the age of 38 and, ever since, her writing has taken us through the centrality of Maori experience. Further works include *Mutuwhenua: The Moon Sleeps* (1978), *Wahine Toa* (with Robyn Kahukiwa, 1984), the acclaimed novel *Potiki* (1986), *Electric City and Other Stories* (1987), *Cousins* (1992) and *Baby No-Eyes* (1998). She has also written nine books for children. Grace has won awards both nationally and internationally, among them the Liberaturpreis, Germany, 1994. Through her work with the Maori Writers and Artists Society and, latterly, Te Haa Maori Writers Committee, she has maintained her role as a mentor and supporter of young Maori writers.

FIONA KIDMAN (1940–   ) is the author of *A Breed of Women* (1979), a book that really did change the lives of many New Zealand women. Her other works of fiction include *Mandarin Summer* (1981), *Mrs Dixon and Friends* (1982), *Paddy's Puzzle* (1983), *The Book of Secrets* (1987), *Unsuitable Friends* (1988), *True Stars* (1990), *The Foreign Woman* (1993) and *Ricochet Baby* (1996). Apart from novels and short story collections she has also produced four volumes of poetry, plays, non-fiction and an autobiography. She was knighted Dame of the Order of New Zealand in 1998.

WITI IHIMAERA (1944–   ) is the author of *Pounamu Pounamu* (1972), *Tangi* (1973), *Whanau* (1974) and *The New Net Goes Fishing* (1976). He placed a ten-year embargo on his fiction and returned with *The Matriarch* (1986), *The Whale Rider* (1987), *Dear Miss Mansfield* (1989), *Bulibasha* (1994), *Nights in the Gardens of Spain* (1996), *Kingfisher Come Home* (1995) and *The Dream Swimmer* (1997). In between times he has edited anthologies and other works, and written for theatre and opera. He teaches English and creative writing at the University of Auckland.

KERI HULME (1947–   ) won the Booker-McConnell Prize for her first novel, *the bone people* (1983). She is also the author of two poetry collections, *The Silences Between: Moeraki Conversations* (1982) and *Strands* (1992), a small poetic/prose work *Lost Possessions* (1985), *Te Kaihau/The Windeater* (1986) and a homage to her roots in the South Island called *Homeplaces* (1989). Hulme lives in Okarito, on the West Coast of the South Island.

NGAHUIA TE AWEKOTUKU (1949–   ) is professor of Maori Studies at Victoria University of Wellington. A radical lesbian feminist, she is credited as being one of the architects of gay liberation in New Zealand, and has also been closely associated with Maori rights. She is a charismatic speaker; I had the honour of sharing the spotlight with her speaking out for gay indigenous peoples at the 'Beyond Survival' Conference, Ottawa, Canada, 1992. Within a busy life, Te Awekotuku has also managed to write poetry, short stories and non-fiction. Her short story collection, *Tahuri*, was published in 1989.

BILL PAYNE (1951–   ) is the author of *Staunch: Inside the Gangs* (1991), an out-of-print book about gang life in New Zealand, which has consequently become one of the most popular books stolen from public libraries. He followed this up with a collection of stories, *Poor Behaviour* (1994), which should be better known. He lives in Auckland and continues to write short fiction.

APIRANA TAYLOR (1955–   ) published his first collection of poetry, *Eyes of the Ruru*, in 1972, when he was only 17. He followed up by appearing in *3 Shades* (1981) and *Soft Leaf Falls of the Moon* (1997). Interspersed with his poetry collections he has produced two short story collections, *He Rau Aroha: A Hundred Years of Love* (1986), and *Ki Te Ao* (1990). Taylor has also produced a novel, *He Tangi Aroha* (1993), and a volume of two plays *Kohanga and Whaea Kairau* (1999).

MAREWA GLOVER (1961–   ) has published *Mooncall* (1990) and numerous short stories. She was anthologised in *Te Ao Marama* vol. 3

(Reed, 1993) with two stories — 'Auntie Netta' and 'Putting Out Her Fire'. She started performing and publishing her poetry and short stories in 1986. Hers was considered 'a strong unflinching voice, one of the finest new voices of the 1990s', and she has yet to produce her finest work. She has just completed a doctoral degree in behavioural science at the Auckland School of Medicine.

PHIL KAWANA (1965–   ) is the author of two collections of short stories, *Dead Jazz Guys* (1996) and *Attack of the Skunk People* (1999). He was the winner of the inaugural Huia Short Story Awards, 1995, and won the award again in 1997. His arrival was heralded by Graham Beattie as the most exciting debut by a Maori author since Alan Duff.

BRIAR GRACE-SMITH (1966–   ) is best known as a playwright. In 1995 her play *Nga Pou Wahine* won the Peter Harcourt Award for best short play, and she herself received the Bruce Mason Playwrights Award that same year. Her second play, *Purapurawhetu* was performed to sellout houses and critical acclaim in Wellington in 1998 and Auckland in 1999. The *Listener* called it 'a new classic.'

Acknowledgements

The editor would like to thank the publishers of the following books and periodicals in which the works listed first appeared or were reprinted.

Every effort has been made to locate copyright holders or their agents, but in a few cases this has not proved possible. The publisher would be interested to hear from any copyright holders who have not already been acknowledged.

Alfred A. Grace, 'Te Wiria's Potatoes': *Tales of a Dying Race*, Chatto & Windus, 1901.

Henry Lawson, 'A Daughter of Maoriland': *On the Track and Over the Sliprails*, Angus & Robertson, 1913.

Blanche Baughan, 'Pipi on the Prowl': *Happy Endings*, Allen & Unwin/Port Nicholson Press, 1987.

Will Lawson, 'The Slave's Reward': *Tales by New Zealanders*, British Authors Press, 1938.

Katherine Mansfield, 'How Pearl Button Was Kidnapped': *The Stories of Katherine Mansfield*, Oxford University Press, 1984.

Frank Sargeson, 'White Man's Burden': *Collected Stories, Frank Sargeson*, Blackwood & Janet Paul, 1964.

Roderick Finlayson, 'The Totara Tree': *Brown Man's Burden*, Auckland University Press, 1973.

Robin Hyde, 'The Little Bridge': *Tales by New Zealanders*, British Authors Press, 1938.

Douglas Stewart, 'The Whare': *A Girl with Red Hair*, Angus & Robertson/HarperCollins Publishers, 1944.

Annie Wright, 'Hinemoa': *Pataka, Selected Stories by New Zealand Authors*, K System Publishing, 1936.

Acknowledgements

Maurice Duggan, 'Along Rideout Road That Summer': *Collected Stories*, Auckland University Press, 1981.

Janet Frame, 'The Lagoon': *The Lagoon and Other Stories*, Caxton Press, 1951.

J.C. Sturm, 'For All the Saints': *Te Ao Hou*, December 1965.

Noel Hilliard, 'The Girl From Kaeo': *Send Somebody Nice*, Robert Hale/Whitcoulls, 1976.

Arapera Blank, 'One Two Three Four Five': *The Maori in the 1960s*, Blackwood & Janet Paul, 1968.

Maurice Shadbolt, 'The People Before': *Summer Fires and Winter Country*, Eyre and Spottiswoode, 1963.

Rowley Habib, 'Strife in the Family': *Te Maori*, December 1969.

Bruce Stewart, 'Broken Arse': *Tama and Other Stories*, Penguin Books, 1989.

Patricia Grace, 'Ngati Kangaru': *The Sky People and Other Stories*, Penguin Books, 1994.

Fiona Kidman, 'Needles and Glass': *Unsuitable Friends*, Century Hutchinson, 1988.

Witi Ihimaera, 'The Affectionate Kidnappers': *Dear Miss Mansfield*, Viking, 1989.

Keri Hulme, 'He Tauware Kawa, He Kawa Tauware': *Te Kaihau/The Windeater*, Victoria University Press, 1986.

Ngahuia Te Awekotuku, 'The Basketball Girls': *Tahuri*, New Women's Press, 1989.

Bill Payne, 'For Crying Out Loud': *Poor Behaviour*, Secker & Warburg/Reed Publishing, 1994.

Apirana Taylor, 'Freedom Hill': *Ki Te Ao*, Penguin Books, 1990.

Marewa Glover, 'Auntie Netta': *Te Ao Marama* vol. 3, Reed Publishing, 1993.

Phil Kawana, 'Redemption': *Dead Jazz Guys*, Huia Publishers, 1996.

Briar Grace-Smith, 'Rongomai Does Dallas': *Penguin 25 — New Fiction*, Penguin Books, 1998.

Afterword

Thanks to Jessica and Olivia Ihimaera Smiler for being my constant inspiration and support. Also thanks to Donald Kerr (Auckland City Library), Rowan Gibbs (Smith's Bookshop, Wellington), Terry Sturm and the University of Auckland English Department and Library.

E nga rangatira kaituhituhi, the future lies with you.
Be strong. Be vigilant.
Write your truth.
Bend your head to no other person.
Put your ancestors before you.
Put your dreams before you.
Seek your sovereignty.